My ...rest Sophia,
...hope you can come to visit me soon. I miss you terribly
a... ...really is rather lonely here in the hospital. I see your
... ..., of course – Tuesdays and Fridays like clockwork! –
... ...r company is not nearly as amusing as yours. Have you
... ...ceiving my letters? I do understand that you youngsters
... ...y busy lives. I hope the address your mother has given
... ...orrect. I have never been to Hackney. Is it nice?
... ...u know, I am a very sick old lady, and it would please
m... ...ink that, with my diaries, somebody, somewhere, has
... ...of my life the way it really happened. I want someone
... ...more than the cameras caught, more than what the
... ...s said. I have little to do here other than to daydream
... ...y past and write down those things that otherwise will
... ... me. There's so much from before I ever stepped into
... ...elight. And so much unsaid from after. When you were
... ...girl, you were always happy to listen to my tales, so it
... ...u that I choose to send my scribblings. Do with them
... ...ou will, but please know that these words are all I have
lef... ...f what has been, on balance, a truly wonderful life.
... I hope you are well and happy, my darling girl.
With all my love, always,
Granny
xxx

Katie Agnew was born in Edinburgh in 1972 and spent her childhood in Lasswade. She studied English at Aberdeen University and then journalism at City University in London.

She's written articles, celebrity interviews and columns for many newspapers and magazines including the Evening Standard, Cosmopolitan, and the Daily Mail, before becoming the Features Editor at Marie Claire.

Katie lives in Bath with her family.

Also by Katie Agnew

Wives v. Girlfriends
Saints v. Sinners
Drop Dead Gorgeous
Too Hot to Handle

The INHERITANCE

KATIE AGNEW

An Orion paperback

First published in Great Britain in 2016
by Orion Books
This paperback edition published in 2017
by Orion Books,
an imprint of The Orion Publishing Group Ltd
Carmelite House, 50 Victoria Embankment,
London EC4Y ODZ

An Hachette UK company

1 3 5 7 9 10 8 6 4 2

A CIP catalogue record for this book
is available from the British Library.

ISBN 978 1 4091 3513 5

Typeset by Deltatype Ltd, Birkenhead, Merseyside

Printed in Great Britain by Clays Ltd, St Ives plc

www.orionbooks.co.uk

For Matt

Part One

The Descent

I must be a mermaid ... I have no fear of depths and a great fear of shallow living.

Anaïs Nin

Chapter One

My dearest Sophia,

I do hope you can come to visit me soon. I miss you terribly and it really is rather lonely here in the hospital. I see your parents, of course – Tuesdays and Fridays like clockwork! – but their company is not nearly as amusing as yours. Have you been receiving my letters? I do understand that you youngsters lead very busy lives. I hope the address your mother has given me is correct. I have never been to Hackney. Is it nice?

As you know, I am a very sick old lady, and it would please me to think that, with my diaries, somebody, somewhere, has a record of my life the way it really happened. I want someone to know more than the cameras caught, more than what the reporters said. I have little to do here other than to daydream about my past and write down those things that otherwise will die with me. There's so much from before I ever stepped into the limelight. And so much unsaid from after. When you were a little girl, you were always happy to listen to my tales, so it is to you that I choose to send my scribblings. Do with them what you will, but please know that these words are all I have left of what has been, on balance, a truly wonderful life.

I hope you are well and happy, my darling girl.
With all my love, always,
Granny
xxx

'So, are you going to put the old dear out of her misery and actually go and see her now?' asked Hugo, reclining grandly on the rumpled, coffee-stained bed as if it was a four-poster in a suite at the Savoy.

He had the letter from Sophia's grandmother in one hand and a French cigarette in the other. Actually, the correspondence – the third letter to arrive over the past two weeks – was more of a novella than a letter. In his elegant hand, Hugo was clutching pages and pages of handwritten notes. He was the very definition of louche, although the look was not exactly natural and had been carefully studied and practised over the years. He flicked his cigarette ash onto a makeshift ashtray that lay amid the debris, and checked his appearance briefly in the mirror. If Hugo had had an ounce of drive, he would have made a very good actor.

'She is your grandmother,' he declared dramatically. 'She is going to die imminently and, may I remind you, she is also worth an absolute bloody fortune. How can you ignore her?'

He sniffed, a little judgmentally for a man with no job, no work ethic, no qualifications and no prospects.

Sophia more or less ignored him and continued to root around on the floor for her black bra. Or at least she pretended to ignore him. It wasn't that she didn't care about her grandmother. She had been incredibly close to her when she was younger but what was she supposed to do? If she visited the hospital, she would open Pandora's box.

'Hugo,' she eventually said, 'my granny was an actress. She won an Oscar for being good at it. You know, pretending? She still *is* an actress. She just hasn't worked for years. But this is what she does. This is what she's good at. She's playing the role of the adoring grandmother to get me to her bedside so that she can persuade me to make up with my parents.'

Perhaps her mum had asked her grandmother to write to her? Sophia wouldn't – and couldn't – allow herself to get drawn in by her grandmother's ruse. And so she stubbornly stayed in the moment and kept foraging for clothes. 'I can't think about all that right now,' she replied, waving her hand dismissively at her best friend, hoping she looked more disinterested than she felt. 'I can't find my bloody bra!'

'Is it this one?' asked Hugo, gingerly picking up a black lace garment from the bed with the very tips of his fingers and flicking it onto the floor at Sophia's feet as if it was a venomous snake that might bite him at any moment.

'That's it,' grinned Sophia, picking up the bra and securing it round her. 'Thanks.'

'So anyway,' Hugo went on, averting his eyes from Sophia's naked body with a pained look on his face, 'your grandmother. She's only in St John's Wood. Here, she included a card this time with her ward, room number and direct phone number.'

He threw the business card in Sophia's direction. She ignored it.

'One little trip to north London and you could secure yourself a nice little fortune and then you and I can bugger off on holiday. East London is so over. We need a new project. Let's visit your granny tomorrow. Let's find out all the family scandals and nab ourselves an obscenely large inheritance in the process. Come on, Soph, what have you got to lose?'

The truth was, Sophia was scared: scared of her grandmother's terminal illness, scared of facing her parents, scared of the past and scared of the future. Her grandmother knew this. Why else would she be trying to entice Sophia to her hospital bedside with mysterious hints about family secrets?

'All I want to do right now is get ready to go out and have a bit of fun.'

It wasn't exactly the whole truth. Sophia was completely torn between wanting to hear Granny's stories, and wanting to pretend her entire family didn't exist. She had put aside all three letters at first, unopened; a glance at the elegant handwriting and postmark convinced her that reading them would only lead to heartache. It wasn't hard to ignore post in a place like this, where all the letters were junk mail, or final reminders, or correspondence for previous tenants who'd long since done a bunk.

It was Hugo who had opened them in the end. Curiosity had finally got the better of him the day before yesterday when the third letter arrived and Sophia had found him curled on his bed devouring the pages hungrily. He'd jumped, like a cat caught lapping from the saucepan, when she'd walked in.

'Are those letters supposed to be for me?' she'd asked, already knowing the answer.

Hugo had nodded, his cheeks flushed with the shame of being caught. He'd immediately gone on the defensive: 'But you clearly weren't interested in opening them and it seemed rude to ignore them so—'

'So you thought you'd open someone else's post and read the contents in secret? And you didn't think that was rude?' she'd continued, more hurt than angry.

'They're from your grandmother,' he'd said, finally handing the wad of pages to her. 'I think you should read them. They're important. She's not very well.'

A lump had formed in Sophia's throat as she took the letters from Hugo. Of course her grandmother was ill. Why else would she get in touch now? After everything that had happened?

'Aren't you going to read them?' Hugo had asked, finally catching her eye. She could see from his unusually grave expression that the news was serious.

'Later,' she'd replied, curtly.

Sophia had read the first letter and the first instalment of her grandmother's memoirs in bed that night. It had made her cry so she'd shoved it in a drawer by her bed. Last night, she hadn't been able to sleep and the letters had called to her from inside the drawer. She'd read the second one, every word, until she'd felt herself being drawn down a tunnel like Alice in Wonderland, down into a parallel world where everything was different and yet all the people familiar. And now Hugo was insisting on reading the third letter to her and she was desperately trying not to care and yet, as Hugo started to read, nothing else seemed to matter any more.

'I do like the sound of your great-grandfather ...' he snorted in amusement from behind the letter. 'I wonder if he swung both ways?'

'Quite possibly. He did go to Eton,' Sophia replied, seeing a way to steer the conversation away from her family and back onto Hugo's favourite subject: himself. 'I thought all you Old Etonians were sexually ambiguous,' she added, nodding at him knowingly.

'I am not sexually ambiguous!' Hugo took her bait immediately. 'I am one hundred per cent homosexual. That girl was a mistake. A stupid, drunken mistake. And she was very gamine, if you remember. She looked like a boy. I swear!'

Sophia grinned. Bingo! Subject changed. Plus, she loved winding Hugo up. It had been one of her favourite pastimes ever since she was a small child. Hugo was the son of her mother's ex-best friend and he'd been around for ever. He'd irritated her at first: this little blond boy, two years her junior, who'd insisted on following her like a stray puppy. He'd tag along behind her, all around the garden, saying he was helping her look for fairies, when all Sophia wanted to do was escape from her angry father, or her melancholic mother, and hide up a tree. Or he'd sneak into her bedroom and dress up her dolls immaculately and brush their hair and wash their faces. Didn't he realise Sophia preferred her Tiny Tears naked and kind of wild-looking?

She remembered being quite mean to him back then. But, no matter how many times she taunted him, Hugo remained loyal to Sophia. If her dad told her off (and her dad was *always* telling her off) he'd smile at her reassuringly from under his long fringe. If her mum sent her to her room he'd tiptoe up the stairs and keep her company. And if she got into a fight with one of the local kids, he would always take her side – even though he was skinny and posh and had no idea how to talk back to the cool kids.

Over the years, with his dogged devotion, Hugo gradually won Sophia over. And at some point during their childhood, irritation turned into tolerance, and then tolerance turned into genuine fondness, and by the time they were teenagers they'd become known, by their families, as the Terrible Twins. And now? Well, now Sophia adored Hugo. She couldn't imagine life without him by her side. Sophia was an only child and Hugo was the nearest thing she would ever have to a little brother.

Sophia's and Hugo's mothers had fallen out years ago, over some disagreement about whose turn it was to have the Wimbledon Final tickets that year, but Hugo and Sophia remained as thick as thieves. Which, very occasionally, was exactly what they were when they both had their allowances cut off at the same time. Fortunately, it was only Sophia who had been disowned at the moment so they were both living off Hugo's family. Neither of them considered the arrangement a problem. But then neither of them had ever had to work for a living. Not at a proper job, at least.

'Aha! Gotcha!' shouted Sophia triumphantly, fishing out a stray black shoe from inside a pair of jeans. 'That calls for a drink. What have we got?'

Hugo passed her an open bottle of warm Prosecco.

'So?' he demanded, suddenly, unravelling his tangle of long, skinny limbs and kneeling up on the bed.

'So, what?' asked Sophia, pulling on her second stocking.

'So, are we going to visit your grandmother tomorrow?' he demanded.

Oh God, she'd thought she'd distracted him.

'Of course not,' she scoffed. 'Don't be ridiculous. We're going out to party in a minute. We both know it's going to get very messy indeed and there is absolutely no way we'll be getting any sleep tonight. Tomorrow is not going to exist, Hugo. So what's the point in making plans?'

She wriggled into her tightest little black dress, added an enormous ruby cocktail ring and her killer stilettos. She piled her tangled mane high up onto her head and pinned it into a sort of beehive-bun concoction thing. Sophia sprayed the finished confection generously with hairspray. She added some extra-black eyeliner for good measure.

'There,' she said. 'All done.'

'How the hell do you do that, Soph?' asked Hugo in amazement.

'Do what?' she asked, innocently.

'Create such perfection from such absolute chaos!' he declared.

Sophia smiled at him – beneath the banter he was still her one-man cheerleading squad – and then she helped herself to one of his cigarettes.

'Are the others coming?' she asked, nodding her head towards the door to indicate their housemates, Ben and his girlfriend Amelia.

Hugo shook his head. 'They said they don't want to. They're having a curry and watching *Strictly*. Apparently we're all getting a bit too old to go clubbing.'

Sophia laughed, but there was a part of her that agreed with them. If she had anything better to do, and a boyfriend to do it with, perhaps she would avoid the party circuit too.

'I think, when you get your grandmother's money, we should think about moving back west,' announced Hugo suddenly. 'Notting Hill, maybe. I mean I know that everybody says that the East End is where all the hipsters are but I've never really felt at home here. Don't get me wrong, I loved it in the East End during the Olympics. All those lithe young athletes wandering around in Lycra – whats not to love? But now that's over, and everyone's gone home, it feels a bit dull round here; tarnished even. I think this party's over, Sophes. I don't like it anymore. I want to go home. Back up West. Please? Say we can. To be honest, I feel a bit like a tourist who's accidentally wandered onto the frontline of a civil war. It's like Mexico – if you stray out of the luxury resorts you're likely to be shot.'

Sophia pulled back the moth-eaten velvet curtains and surveyed leafy Victoria Park, twinkling in the streetlights below. The view from this second floor window of the Georgian townhouse was beautiful. This was posh Hackney. Sophia knew that. Hugo, however, seemed to be under the impression that he was properly roughing it in E9.

'I'm not going to get any money from my grandmother, Hugo,' she told him, as a gentle wake-up call. 'We can't afford to move. When was the last time Ben remembered to ask for any rent? We're not going to find an entire Georgian townhouse free of charge anywhere else in London. We're lucky to be here. I'm amazed Hugo's parents didn't kick us out for the Olympics. Think of the rent they could have got for this place! We should be grateful, Hugo. It might not be perfect but it's a roof over our heads at least.'

The house belonged to Hugo's schoolfriend Ben – a loveable stoner with a heart of gold and the ambition of a sloth – or at least it belonged to Ben's family. It had been left to them by an eccentric great-aunt who had rebelled against their Belgravia lifestyle and lived with her female lover, writing poetry that was never published and collecting a menagerie of dogs and cats. When she died the family didn't know what to do with it – who in their set wanted to live in Hackney? But, not being short of a bob or two, they had no urgency to sell it. So, several years later, when Ben showed a mild interest in moving there, they'd been happy to let him have it. Not only did it mean they could stop paying the rent on his penthouse apartment in Kensington, but it also meant he was safely hidden away on the other side of the city where they wouldn't be reminded of his failings on a daily basis. Ben had promised his family that he and his friends would start to refurbish the old house while they were there but, so far, after numerous housemates and transient sofa surfers had come and gone, nobody had got round to cleaning the windows, let alone painting the walls.

The three-storey house was one of the few in the street that had not been converted into flats. It was almost certainly the only house on the street that had no central heating and only one bathroom to share between its residents. The shabby, peeling exterior was an embarrassment to the rest of the road. The interior walls had not been painted in fifty years and still boasted 1960s psychedelic wallpaper. The decrepit kitchen had no cupboard doors and the vile bathroom had no shower (but both had a great deal of damp and mould). Sophia, Hugo, Ben and Amelia shared their home with infestations of mice, ants and even the odd rat.

None of them had ambitions. All of them had once had what their teachers called 'promise'. But that was a long time ago. Now they didn't even have purpose. Luckily, all of them had – or had had in Sophia's case – trust funds. Their sorely disappointed families threw them enough scraps off the family dining table for them to scrape by without having to work. But that was just a ruse to keep them from turning up and begging on their parents' doorsteps and embarrassing them in front of their well-to-do neighbours. Sometimes it felt as if this house on Victoria Park Road was the place where potential came to die.

The housemates had little in common other than memories of childhoods filled with expensive schools, ponies, holidays, houses and cars. They had met when they were much younger, and still full of dreams, but had somehow ended up here, washed up in their upper-class slum.

Sophia was the linchpin of the group. Or at least she had been. She was the link that bound them all together. Amelia had been at Westonbirt with Sophia. Sophia had grown up with Hugo. Hugo had met Ben at Eton. And at some festival or other Sophia had introduced Ben to Amelia. That night Amelia abandoned Sophia and crawled into Ben's tent instead – and the rest, as they say, is history. They were a sweet couple, very much in love, and well suited in every way, right down to their matching piercings, but there was something sad about them. 'Wasted' was the word that often came to Sophia's mind. And not just because of the skunk the couple smoked. In another world Ben and Amelia would have met at university, fallen in love, had fabulous careers in the City, and now they would be married, living in a nice house in Surrey with their first child on the way. That's what Sophia would have wanted for them. Perhaps there was a bit of Sophia who still wanted that for herself.

She swallowed the lump that had formed in her throat. It had taken her by surprise. She tried very hard not to think about what might have been if she'd made different choices in life. She'd used a lot of energy building up her 'happy front' and she hated it when the cracks began to show. Normally she saved her breakdowns for the dead of night when nobody could witness them.

She forced a bright smile and said, 'Do I look OK?'

'You look fabulous,' Hugo replied loyally. 'I'm thinking Holly Golightly meets Amy Winehouse at a *Playboy* convention.'

'I can go with that,' grinned Sophia. 'But maybe I need a necklace if I'm channelling *Breakfast at Tiffany's*?'

She rummaged around in the shoebox that doubled as a jewellery box. She had an eclectic mix of stolen family heirlooms, charity-shop finds, Camden Market tat and high-street copies of more expensive designs. She chose a pearl choker that looked a little like Audrey Hepburn's.

'Wow! Is that real?' asked Hugo. 'It's gorgeous.'

'Don't be daft,' scoffed Sophia. 'It's plastic from Topshop circa 2003. If this was real we'd be driving to the West End in my Ferrari, not getting the bloody Central Line. Right, ready when you are.'

Hugo looked at his reflection one more time and frowned. 'I'm not happy with this shirt,' he announced suddenly. 'It only works with a tan.'

'Hugo!' Sophia scolded, slumping back down on the bed. 'You'll be ages if you have to choose a different shirt.'

'Two minutes, I promise,' he said. 'How long can it take to make a decision?'

'It's taken you twenty-eight years to decide what you want to be when you grow up,' Sophia reminded him, but Hugo was already out of the door.

Chapter Two

Lower East Side, New York, 2012

Dominic rested his forehead against the cool glass of the window as the cab crawled through Brooklyn at a snail's pace. He could probably have walked home from JFK quicker had he not had a trunk full of heavy luggage and equipment with him. He'd left the airport almost an hour ago. The journey should have taken about half an hour but it was evening rush hour in New York City and the streets were gridlocked. As the cab inched across Williamsburg Bridge and over the East River, Dom's stomach twisted with an uncomfortable mix of anticipation and dread. Finally he was home in Manhattan. And God, how he'd missed the place! But how could he feel so pleased to be home and yet so terrified of what would be waiting for him when he got there?

The radio was playing a catchy R&B song that Dominic had never heard before. It had probably been number one all summer. Dom wouldn't know about that though. He wondered what else he'd missed since he'd been away. It all looked the same as it had when he left – except that the bright blue July sky had been replaced by a leaden October haze. It was a strange, bittersweet feeling to be back in his native city after such a long time away, particularly when his departure had been so traumatic.

Dom had missed the noise, the familiar smells, the proud brownstones, the soaring skyscrapers, the bustling sidewalks, the colourful characters and the constant adrenalin rush. He had missed his dog, his buddies, his widescreen TV, his favourite diner, his cold beers and his own bed. But had he missed his married way of life – or his wife, Calgary? He had thought of little else during the past three months. And finally, in the faraway depths of the Amazon rainforest, he had convinced himself he'd made his peace with the situation. He had thought he'd got his head around the whole, messy business and he'd even tasted fleeting feelings of relief and release. Yes, he had lost all the good bits but he was free of the bad bits too, right? And from a comfortable distance, he had finally realised that his friends had been right: there had been a hell of a lot of bad stuff to deal with when it came to Calgary. The scales had finally fallen from his eyes and he had seen clearly that his marriage had been far from perfect.

But that was then, and three thousand miles from the Lower East Side and the apartment he'd shared with Calgary for the past three years. Now, as the yellow taxi edged along Delancey Street getting ever closer to their – *his* – Orchard Street home, the gentle butterflies in his stomach had turned into angry birds of prey, thrashing their wings against the pit of his stomach.

'You far along Orchard?' asked the cab driver jovially.

'Just above Rivington,' answered Dominic.

'Figures,' replied the driver, who was grinning at Dom in the rear-view mirror. 'I had a feeling you'd say that. One of those new luxury condominiums, I'm guessing?'

Dom wriggled uncomfortably in his seat.

'Why d'you say that?' he asked.

The driver laughed. 'Well those army boots and that stubble ain't fooling no one. You live in the Lower East Side and you try to be so cool and so different from those snooty Upper East Siders, so you dress all hobo and you talk all street, but you give yourself away, man. Your shades are Raybans and your watch is a Tag, and your backpack is some flashy European brand, and you don't go hauling cameras like that around the globe for nothing, so I'm guessing your apartment is squeezed between a boutique hotel and a designer store and it's in one of them crazy new buildings that look like a game of Jenga, and you don't get no change outta five thousand dollars' rent per month, right?'

'You got me all figured out, dude,' replied Dom, cringing inside. 'One more block. Just past that hotel on the right there.'

The driver nodded knowingly and tapped his head as if to say, 'I see it all from my cab. I understand New York City like no one else. I know everybody's story, man.' And maybe he did. But Dom wanted to explain he'd got *this* man all wrong. He wanted to say, 'Look buddy, I'm from Southeast Yonkers. I'm half Irish American, half Italian American and not one member of my family has had a spare dime to their name since they stepped off their frigging ship. We're blue collar all the way back to Cork on one side, and Naples on the other. My old man was a mechanic and my mom's worked her fingers to the bone as a seamstress for forty years. I went to public school and worked my ass off to get to college, where, incidentally, I paid my own way through by working three jobs at a time. What's more, I'm proud of my roots. But I met a girl one day who was classier than me, cooler than me and more beautiful than any girl I'd ever seen before. She was smart and successful and, guess what? I fell in love. When we got married she wanted to live here. And I wanted to make her happy. So this is where we lived. And now she's gone and I'm still here. So deal with it because I sure as hell have to!' But Dominic had been brought up to have better manners than that, so of course he kept his mouth shut, smiled warmly and gave the driver a big tip.

Once the cab had driven away, Dom stood on the pavement outside his building with his luggage and equipment at his feet. It was a cold autumn evening in New York. After the long flight, the lack of sleep and the change in temperature, he was freezing cold but he couldn't face going inside. Not yet. The minute he stepped into the building the whole nightmare, that had seemed so distant in Ecuador, would suddenly become very, very real. He stamped his boots on the sidewalk trying to get some feeling back into his toes, pulled his woolly hat further over his ears, zipped his puffa jacket right up to his stubbly chin and lit a cigarette. It was an old bad habit he'd recently reacquired. No, that wasn't quite right. It was more an old bad habit that he'd recently admitted to still having from time to time. The truth was he'd been secretly stealing his friends' smokes for years, when Calgary wasn't around, and then manically chewing gum to mask the smell when he got home.

He was halfway through smoking his Marlboro when he realised he could have smoked it on the roof terrace, or even, shock horror, inside the apartment itself. And he wouldn't even have had to open the windows. With Calgary gone there would be no one to nag him about any of his bad habits. He could do whatever the hell he pleased. He could read in bed with the light on until way past midnight. He could let the dog up onto the couch. He could cook fish without having to fumigate the entire apartment before Calgary got home from work. He didn't have to shave every day (hence the not-so-designer stubble he was sporting). He no longer had to apologise for the tattoo on his right arm every time he got undressed. Dominic McGuire was king of his own castle now. So why was he dreading going in there so much? Dom took a deep breath, collected together his belongings and, with tired legs and a heavy heart, he made his way into the building.

'Dominic! Dominic!' cried the porter, Guido, rushing out from behind his desk and hugging Dom warmly. 'I have missed you. I am so glad you are home. You look a little thin. And very tired. You have been working too hard. Here, here, let me take some of those bags.'

Dominic allowed Guido to carry the lightest camera bag. It was more a gesture of kindness towards the porter – who liked to feel useful – rather than through any need of his own. Guido was twice Dom's age and half his size and, besides, Dominic had got all this stuff back from the depths of the Ecuadorian rainforest single-handedly. He was pretty certain he could make it a few feet towards the elevator. Still, it felt good to see Guido's familiar, friendly face. The porter always reminded Dom of his Italian uncles back in Yonkers.

'So how was Peru?' asked Guido enthusiastically.

'Great, great, very interesting,' said Dom. He didn't have the heart to put the old guy straight. 'A lot quieter than Bowery though!'

'Sure, sure,' said Guido, struggling into the lift with his one light bag. 'Well, it is good to have you back.'

He smiled at Dominic sympathetically. The 'Big Subject' loomed over both their heads but neither of them wanted to be the first to broach it.

'So, um, have you, eh, seen Calgary much?' asked Dom finally, staring at his feet. 'Has she been back while I was away?'

'Not so much,' said Guido apologetically. 'I think she won't be back. She has gone now. She come over once, maybe twice more, after you leave for your trip. But since then, nothing. I forward her post to an address she gave me uptown if you wanna know where she is?'

Dom shook his head and then shrugged as if to say, no big deal, but he wasn't fooling anyone. So she'd gone back to her old stomping ground. No surprise there. The two men stood in awkward silence as the elevator reached the penthouse.

'I am so sorry, Dominic,' said Guido, gently. 'I know it is your personal business and I no want to intrude but, you are always such a nice man and I do not understand why your wife would do this to you. You seemed the perfect young couple. What happened?'

'Pretty simple really,' explained Dominic sadly. 'I wanted a family, she didn't want kids. My mistake, I guess. She was a career girl when I met her, I was stupid to think that would change.'

Guido shook his head forlornly.

'Is such a tragedy,' he lamented. 'My oldest daughter, Isabella, she is a lawyer, you know?'

Dominic did know. Guido never tired of boasting about his brilliant children – or showing the residents of the building photographs of his offspring. It was one of the things Dom admired about Guido the most – his immense pride in his family.

'But she has three kids now! She never sleeps, the poor girl is exhausted, but she has three bambinos *and* a good job. And she is happy. Why no Calgary do the same?'

Again, Dominic didn't have an answer. He wasn't quite sure he understood Calgary's reasons himself. How could he explain that to anybody else without sounding like the bitter jilted ex? And bitter was not Dom's style.

'Anyway, I am sorry,' said Guido. 'That is all I wanted to say.'

'Thank you, Guido,' said Dominic, as the doors opened on the top floor. And he meant it.

Guido trotted along the corridor behind Dom until they reached the door to the apartment. As Dominic searched for his keys in his pocket, Guido cleared his throat.

'Um, there is one more thing,' he said, bashfully. 'When Calgary come back, she, erm, she take quite a lot with her. She had a van and some men. They took furniture, TVs, the fridge … I think, maybe, the apartment is …'

Dominic found his key and turned it in the lock.

'Completely empty?' Dom finished Guido's sentence for him.

The door stood open and revealed the gaping, cavernous space of what had once been their tastefully furnished home. All that remained were feet of solid oak flooring, bare white walls and one, very lonely, battered leather armchair. It had been a flea market find, left over from Dominic's college days. Calgary had always hated it. She said it offended her and that it jarred with the Wenger, Jacobsen and Panton pieces 'they'd' collected – although Dominic had no recollection of ever having had any say in the choice of furniture in the apartment. Dom had teased her, saying it was the height of cool to have unique 'distressed' vintage pieces in their home. Calgary had retorted that she was the one who was distressed every time her friends came to the apartment with *that* heap of junk cluttering up the place. Now he was even more pleased that he'd insisted on keeping his beloved leather chair. At least he had something to sit on tonight.

And, as he wandered tentatively into his home, with the noise echoing around the bare walls, he saw that he still had his books too. They were no longer neatly ordered by spine colour on a designer Scandi-chic bookcase but they were all there – the photography and art books, the natural history ones, the Swedish thrillers, his Hemingway, Fitzgerald and Capote collections – piled on the floor in a dozen tall, drunken towers. Well, Calgary never was one to read: unless it was something she'd written, or a copy of *Wallpaper* or *Vogue*, of course. Mainly Calgary liked to look at the pictures in magazines, particularly ones of herself. She liked how her husband's books made her look intellectual when her friends came round for dinner, but none of them had belonged to her and Dom had never seen her read any of them. In fact she used to tut when Dom took any of them down to read. She said it ruined the aesthetics. But what's the point of a book you can't read?

Dominic dumped his bags on the floor beside the book towers. Guido had followed him inside uninvited. It was probably unprofessional of the porter, but Dom didn't mind. The little Italian put down the bag he had carried and stood open-mouthed but utterly silent while Dominic checked the kitchen (no fridge, no washing machine, no dishwasher), the office (no desk, no chair, no computer) and finally, the bedroom. The bed had gone, which didn't surprise Dominic, seeing as it had cost an absolute fortune and had been shipped in from Germany, but Calgary had had the generosity to leave him the mattress, if not a duvet or any sheets. The wardrobes had also disappeared, and Dom's clothes and shoes were now lying in heaps on the floor. He bent down and picked up a stray tennis ball and wandered back into the living room.

Guido glanced at the ball and for a second Dom thought the old man was going to cry.

'No ...' he mumbled. 'No, no, no. She could not be so cruel ...'

Dominic looked at the dirty, chewed ball in his hand and laughed.

'No, Guido,' he said, patting him on the back fondly. 'She hasn't taken Blondie. She wouldn't dare! Calgary knows I can live without a couch, a bed or a plasma TV but she would never be so cruel as to take my baby from me. Besides, Calgary is not Blondie's biggest fan. I doubt she'd pack Blondie even if the apartment was on fire!'

'So where is she?' asked Guido, looking around the apartment as if Blondie might be hiding in a corner somewhere. As if Blondie was small enough to hide anywhere!

'She's been staying at my buddy Dave's place. You remember Dave? Tall guy, reddish-brown hair, always wise-cracking.'

Guido nodded. 'I remember,' he said. 'Always smiling, always telling the jokes. Very dirty jokes!'

'Yeah, that's the guy,' said Dom. 'Best buddies since elementary school. Blondie's been staying across in Brooklyn with Dave, his wife and their two kids. Great family. Their house is very noisy, a little chaotic, but Blondie's had a ball there. She's looking a little fat maybe – they sent me pictures – Ellen's a good cook and those kids spoil Blondie rotten – but she's just fine. I'll go fetch her in the morning. I can't wait!'

'So, you will be all right?' asked Guido. 'Here on your own tonight?'

Dom nodded. 'Sure, sure. I have somewhere to sit, somewhere to sleep. I can watch TV on my laptop and I can order in pizza. I haven't had pizza in three months. I could kill a pepperoni. Maybe I'll grab a couple of Buds from the store. What more could a single man want, huh?'

'A woman,' said Guido firmly. 'My Alessia is still free. You want that I call her?'

Dominic grinned but shook his head. Alessia was the youngest of Guido's four children. And, although she was undeniably pretty, she was also still at college and barely out of her teens. Dominic had recently turned the wrong side of thirty-five and he wasn't interested in jailbait. To be honest, he wasn't interested in women at all these days – Calgary had cured him of that!

'Your daughter is beautiful,' he told Guido, 'but she's far too young and innocent for a cynical old guy like me. Let's leave her to the college boys, eh?'

Guido sighed, obviously disappointed. 'But you are such a nice man, Dominic. You should be happy. A man needs more than a dog.'

But Dom just smiled and shook his head. He really wasn't sure he agreed any more.

Guido left the empty apartment to go back to his position in the lobby. Once the door was closed, the apartment felt eerily quiet and empty. Dominic hadn't remembered it being this enormous. It had felt much cosier with furniture, a wife and a dog in it. It was probably too big for him now. He'd thought it was too big (not to mention too expensive) the first time Calgary had taken him to the building to show him the newly built penthouse. He'd thought they didn't need so many square feet just for the two of them. But, at the back of his mind, he'd reckoned that it wouldn't be 'just the two of them' for much longer, so what was the problem? They were newly-weds, they'd grow into the space soon enough. He'd made the mistake of assuming that Calgary was thinking the same thing, so he'd happily signed the lease.

Maybe he should hand in his notice on the apartment now. He liked it here in Bowery, and he'd been living in Manhattan for so long that he'd come to consider it home, but he liked the rest of New York City too. He could move to Brooklyn to be near all his friends, or maybe even back to Yonkers to be close to his family. Hell, out of Manhattan he could afford a house with a garden. Wouldn't Blondie just love that? But could Dom handle living in Brooklyn alongside all those smug married couples? Or back in Yonkers with his mom breathing down his neck, trying to matchmake him with all her friends' daughters, just like she used to do when he was in high school? He loved his friends and he worshipped his mom but perhaps it would be better, as a single guy, to stay in Manhattan. The future stretched out before Dominic like a highway in the desert. There were no signposts, no exits, just a long, lonely road to who knows where.

Chapter Three

Sophia took another gulp of cheap bubbly, lit a cigarette and tried not to stare at the splayed pages of the long, long letter that lay, face-up, on the pillow beside her. Tentatively, almost in spite of herself, she picked up the pages and finally allowed her eyes to devour the words she'd been trying so hard to ignore.

Mayfair, London, 1938

I will never forget the day my father took me to Bond Street. It must have been 1938. It was autumn. I remember how the leaves covered the paths in Hyde Park and Nanny scolded me on the hurried walk from the underground station to Papa's hotel for kicking the muddy mounds with my brand new patent leather shoes. She said I would ruin them and that that would be a great shame seeing as she'd gone to such a lot of effort to make me look presentable for my father. They were red with silver buckles. I was eight years old.

It was a day quite unlike any other: not least because it was the first and last time I ever went shopping with Papa. The world was on the cusp of great change but, of course, I was blissfully unaware of what was about to take place. Perhaps, had I realised what a rare and delicious treat that one little day would be, I would have relished it all the more at the time. And yet, somehow, I must have understood its significance. Why else would I have sugar-coated the memory and wrapped it in gold foil for all these years? Of all my memories, it is amongst the sweetest.

I didn't see much of Papa in those days. He was a peripheral figure, although terribly dashing and romantic, in my childhood. Mama was distant from me too, although not in the same way. When I wasn't at boarding school at Westonbirt we shared the same home – Beaumont

House, a sprawling mansion built in Wiltshire in 1705 and inhabited by Papa's family ever since (I believe it's a hotel these days) – but Mama was always busy. Mama – or Lady Charlotte Beaumont as she was known to the rest of the world – ran the house, went to the theatre in Bath, had luncheon with friends, and played tennis rather a lot. She was patron of the local cottage hospital and did lots of 'good work'. Or so the staff told me when I asked where she was. I had a full-time nanny, even though I boarded at my prep school during the week in term-time and there were no other children in the house. It wasn't until I became a mother myself that I realised quite how thoroughly Mama had washed her hands of me. But by then I also understood that she had her reasons for doing so.

At the weekends, during the season, Mama would hunt. And when it wasn't the season she would ride with friends. I have a clear image of her in my head; she's leaning against the stable wall, cigarette in hand with some adoring chap or other hanging off her every acerbic word. She was a truly striking woman, always graceful and poised and groomed to within an inch of her charmed life. Yes, I can see her now, black hair gleaming under her riding hat, long legs clad in pristine white jodhpurs, black riding boots so polished that she could admire her reflection in them. She had a half smirk, half smile playing on her crimson lips. Perhaps I was spying on her. I did that sometimes. I was always trying to close the gap between us. I once saw her kiss Papa's second cousin, Aubrey, in the summer house. In hindsight she had rather a lot of gentlemen friends. But then Papa was away a lot.

I was a lonely child. An only child. With an emotionally distant mother and a geographically distant father. I can see now that their marriage was more of a business arrangement than a romantic relationship, but that was another time and another world and I'm not one to judge. And they did look awfully glamorous together on the rare occasions they met. I think their marriage probably worked for them far better than it ever worked for me. I turned into a terrible show-off – forever putting on plays and singing songs in a vain attempt to capture my parents' attention. It didn't seem to work at the time although it did stand me in good stead later in life where I often found myself the centre of attention.

I had much closer relationships with my nanny, my dogs and my ponies than I ever had with either of my parents but, as a young girl, I admired them both a great deal from afar: particularly Papa. I was completely in love with the idea of him, although I'm not sure I ever knew him well enough to love him for the man he actually was. I wish I had known him better. I think that day in London was probably the closest we ever came to being friends.

Papa had been overseas for some time. He was usually away 'on business'. Our family owned things – rubber companies in India, tea plantations in Ceylon, a cattle ranch in Argentina, a distillery in Scotland. I don't know how or why we owned these companies. We just did. Families like ours owned vast swathes of the Commonwealth for centuries. And then we lost them very swiftly. But that's another story. Papa had been overseas for some time but he was back in London, briefly, and had summoned me to visit him there. When Papa summoned someone they did what they were told. He was a marquess, you see, and lords do tend to get their own way. My smart private school must have understood this because it was in the middle of morning lessons, in the middle of the week, in the middle of term, when Nanny collected me from school and bundled me into the chauffeur-driven car.

It was always lovely to see Nanny unexpectedly. I suppose what I felt for her was what most little girls feel for their mother. She was younger than Mama, and although she was nowhere near as sophisticated, glamorous or as polished as my mother, I found her equally beautiful. Nanny Miller was petite and curvy with a hand-span waist and a head of blonde bubble curls. Her cheeks were always a little flushed, as if she were on the verge of blushing, and the buttons of her blouse always seemed to be fighting a losing battle against the strain of her bosom. I once heard Mama describe Nanny as a cheap 'Cheesecake' (which, as Tony the gardener's son explained to me, meant she looked like a saucy pin-up girl) but I thought she was the spitting image of Betty Grable.

I admit that sometimes I fantasised that Nanny was my real mother. When she was around I felt safe and loved and special. She scolded me frequently but hugged me more frequently still. And she was as generous with her kind words as she was with her cuddles. She always called me 'My little love' even when I was a grown-up and a full head taller than her. Generally, Nanny was a level-headed, no-nonsense sort of West Country girl, but she did tend to get in a bit of a tizz when she was pushed for time. I remember I had to change out of my uniform into my best clothes in the corner of the draughty waiting room on the platform at Bath Spa station before we caught the train to Paddington. Nanny said we didn't have time to go to the Ladies.

Still, it seemed to take an age before the Brunswick Green locomotive trundled into the station from Bristol.

I adored train journeys as a child. I had ridden in the Flying Scotsman and the Cornish Riviera Express – first class, of course. But I was impatient for this journey to be over. I pushed my forehead against the cold window pane and made myself dizzy by staring at the tracks until I couldn't work out whether I was travelling backwards or forwards any more. I memorised the route on the map on the back of the carriage door and I willed each stop to go by quickly – Chippenham, Swindon, Reading. Finally the fields, hedgerows, lakes and forests of the English countryside gave way to row upon row of grubby red-brick terraces and the pale blue sky became increasingly murky and grey. I saw huge factories belching out black smoke and roads so busy that I wondered how people avoided crashing into each other.

We came to an unexpected stop at Ealing Broadway. I stared impatiently out of the window and came face to face with a little girl of about my age. She was sitting on the filthy platform with her mother, their backs to the station wall and an upturned hat in front of them. The girl was pale and thin and her dress and cardigan were threadbare and torn, but what shocked me most was that she wore no shoes at all. Not even stockings! Her feet were entirely bare and almost black with grime. I smiled at her and didn't understand why she glowered back.

'What are they doing, sitting there like that?' I asked Nanny, perplexed.

'Begging, my little love,' she replied, sadly. 'Some people have so little money that they have to beg just so as they can buy food.'

'No food? Oh, that poor girl!' I exclaimed. 'No wonder she's sad. She doesn't even have any stockings on and it's frightfully cold today. I wish I could throw her my new shoes out of the window. Daddy wouldn't mind at all. He's terribly fond of the poor.'

I looked up at Nanny just in time to see her shaking her head at me as if I was quite stupid. I kept my new shoes firmly buckled to my feet and sulked until the train grumbled to life again and began to pull slowly out of the station. I stole a quick glance back at the beggar girl and threw her one last winning smile to cheer her up. To my dismay, she stuck her tongue out at me. I stared in disbelief as she continued to waggle her tongue in my direction until the train pulled too far away for me to see her. I remember thinking that she deserved to be poor and hungry seeing as she had such frightful manners!

Finally, we trundled into Paddington. From there we caught the Underground. Nanny said that it was too dangerous to catch a taxi with all those fast cars on the road in London. Unfortunately, the map looked terribly complicated and Nanny (who had rarely visited London) got a little confused. We ended up getting the first train that arrived on the first platform we found.

'I don't think this is the Bakerloo Line,' she whispered to me as we disappeared into the tunnel. 'I do hope we're not late.'

It turned out we were on the Circle Line. Nanny started to panic as she tried to make sense of the map in the carriage. Her cheeks flushed pink and her pouty bottom lip began to wobble. Thankfully, a kindly young man, dressed in a fashionable suit, took pity on us and prevented us from travelling round and round in circles for the rest of the day. I'd noticed that kindly men – both young and old – frequently came to Nanny's rescue. Eventually we disembarked at Sloane Square, where Nanny asked a gentleman for directions, and then we hurried through Hyde Park (where my shoes got dirty), across Park Lane and into the heart of Mayfair. Nanny kept muttering, 'We're late, we're late ...' under her breath, and I didn't help matters by adding, '... for a very important date' every time she said it. Still, I was only eight years old, and Alice's Adventures in Wonderland was my absolute favourite bedtime story. In some ways, it still is!

Finally we arrived at Papa's favourite hotel, Claridge's on Brook Street. I could feel the remainder of Nanny's floundering confidence evaporate as we entered the majestic foyer with its black and white polished floor. Claridge's was quite the most fashionable place to see and to be seen in those days and it heaved with the smart London set. Poor Nanny seemed to shrink with every step we took towards the front desk and, even at eight, I understood that this was my world, not hers, so I squeezed her hand tighter to reassure her and told her that she looked awfully pretty. It was true. I remember distinctly that she had her finest camel coat on over her uniform and a navy cloche hat covering her blonde curls. Even at that tender age I was quite used to being taken to upmarket hotels and I felt perfectly at home with their stylish guests, marble floors and glistening chandeliers.

It pained me to see Nanny so apologetic when she told the man behind the desk that we were here to meet Lord Beaumont. He was only a member of staff and I could see from his badge that he wasn't even the concierge! Why was she so intimidated? And it irked me even more when the clerk replied to me, not to Nanny, even though she had been the one who had addressed him and I was so tiny I could barely see over the desk. It was the first time that day that I noticed how very young Nanny was. When that desk clerk ignored her, she looked almost more childlike than I was.

'Ah, you must be Lady Matilda,' the clerk grinned at me, doffing his hat. 'We've been expecting you. His Lordship is in the Reading Room. Please, wait here. The hotel manager will be with you directly to accompany you to your father's table.'

I spotted Papa before he saw me. It had been several months since I'd last seen him but there he was, unmistakable, languishing on a sofa, perusing The Times, with his legs crossed lazily in front of him and a forgotten cigar smouldering in an ashtray on the coffee table. He was a tall man, over six feet, and broad too. He'd played rugger for the firsts at Cambridge but, as Mama always said, 'thankfully they didn't ruin his nose'. He had thick dark hair, cut in a short back and sides and slicked back, Clark Gable style, and a permanent tan from all his overseas trips. He was always quick to keep up with the latest fashions but he was never in much of a rush to do anything else. He really was a most unhurried sort of a man: agreeable, mellow, and easygoing.

He was twelve years my mother's senior but he was always the more playful of the two. One could see the child within the man and even when he was discussing something awfully grown-up like politics, or history, or which wine to have with dinner, I always imagined he might break off at any moment and suggest a game of hide and seek instead.

'Papa!' I called across the room.

As he put down his newspaper his handsome face broke into a warm, lopsided smile. He untangled his legs and stood up with his arms open ready to embrace me.

'Tilly!' he shouted as I propelled myself into his arms. 'My precious little Tilly!'

He lifted me up and squeezed so hard that the tweed of his jacket scratched my cheek and the odour of cigars and French cologne tickled my nose.

'I am so terribly sorry, Your Lordship,' said Nanny, grovelling again. 'I'm not at all familiar with London and I'm afraid I got us quite lost on the way here.'

'Are you late?' Papa asked nonchalantly. 'I hadn't noticed. There really is no rush. We have all afternoon and evening.'

'But we must leave on the five o'clock train,' Nanny replied, her cheeks flushing pink. 'I have to get Matilda back to school before lights out.'

'Nonsense,' Papa scoffed, placing me down on the sofa. 'We shall all stay here tonight. I've arranged rooms. You can catch a train in the morning.'

Nanny looked perplexed at this sudden change of plan.

'But the school is expecting her and we don't have any overnight things with us, and Her Ladyship will wonder where I am,' said Nanny, her face turning crimson.

'I'll telephone the school and the house. Although I doubt Her Ladyship will notice anything after cocktail hour,' laughed Papa. 'And as for your overnight things, here ...'

Papa got out his wallet and handed Nanny some notes. 'Buy yourself and Matilda anything you need. Get a taxi to Selfridges and spoil yourself. I believe a lady can find everything her heart desires there. And there's a café in the gardens on the roof if you get hungry or tired from all that shopping. Enjoy yourself. Have an afternoon off. You deserve it.'

Nanny stood there, open-mouthed in the Reading Room, staring disbelievingly at the notes in her hand, as her plump cheeks burned scarlet.

'I can't accept this, Your Lordship,' she said, trying to hand back the money with shaking hands. 'It really is too much.'

'Twaddle,' Papa disagreed good-humouredly, shoving his hands firmly into his pockets.

'And I can't stay in a place like this,' Nanny continued, blushing profusely. 'It's far too expensive and I'm in my uniform. I'll be mistaken for a chambermaid!'

'Balderdash!' argued Papa, still grinning. 'There should be enough there to buy a pretty dress too. You'll need one for dinner tonight anyway. You're eating here at the hotel with Matilda and me. It's all arranged. Besides, Tilly wants to stay here tonight, don't you, darling?'

'Oh yes, please, very much, Papa,' I replied.

'There,' announced Papa, sitting down beside me. 'It's final. You shall go to your room and freshen up, and then you'll catch a taxi to Selfridges, and you'll shop, and then you'll change into some charming new gown and meet us in the dining room for dinner at seven-thirty sharp. And no one will mistake you for staff, Nanny Miller!'

'Very well, Your Lordship,' said Nanny, bobbing a curtsy, finally defeated. 'If that's what you wish.'

'It is,' Papa confirmed. 'Now, run along. Matilda and I have a lot of catching up to do.'

Of course, Nanny did exactly as she was told. As I said, Papa was used to getting his own way.

Papa and I had afternoon tea in the Reading Room – cucumber, ham, and egg and cress sandwiches, Victoria sponge cake, chocolate éclairs and scones with jam and cream – and then Papa announced that we too would do a little shopping. I had never known my father to shop as such. He always came back from his travels with marvellous gifts, and although I had often imagined him haggling in bazaars in Marrakech, or bartering over carpets in Constantinople (or Istanbul or whatever it is called now), I had never seen him do such a thing with my own eyes. We had staff for that.

I felt incredibly proud, strolling through the streets of London, hand in hand with my father that day. I noticed how people stared at him. One couldn't help but notice Papa. He was so tall and fashionably dressed, with an unintentional air of being someone of great importance. I suppose he may have been recognised by some passers-by. He and my mother were often photographed at parties that appeared in the Tatler or the newspapers and I'd heard Mama say that Papa was, 'Quite the man about town in London these days.' She said this with a sniff which implied she didn't approve and muttered something about him thinking himself still a bachelor, which seemed a little hypocritical, even to an eight-year-old, considering all the gentlemen friends Mama went riding with. Anyway, I was as proud as punch to parade down Regent Street with him that crisp, autumn afternoon.

First, he took me to Hamley's and, after at least an hour's deliberating, bought me a small brown teddy bear wearing wire-rimmed spectacles and a red bow tie.

'Look after him carefully and perhaps one day you can give him to your own little girl. What are you going to call him?' Papa asked.

'Freddie the Teddy of course!' I replied, and we both smiled, because Papa's name was Frederick.

We meandered slowly down Old Bond Street, stopping every now and then to look at the extraordinary windows of the shops and galleries. When we got to New Bond Street Papa announced that he needed to buy a little gift for someone special. For some reason, as the doorman opened the heavy, grand front door of Asprey and ushered us in with a nod of recognition to my father, I thought that he meant to buy a present for Mama. How naive I was!

I had never been into Asprey before although I had heard of the store. I adored looking at all my mother's jewels – which she allowed me to do very occasionally as she got dressed to go out. I would fire questions at her as she applied her make-up and chose her outfit for the evening. Where does this ring come from, Mama? What kind of stone is this red one? Who gave you this gold bangle, Mama? Did this brooch belong to Grandmama? She would reply in a distracted, offhand manner until I became too irritating and she would start swatting me away from her dressing table as if I were a wasp buzzing around her martini. Then she would ring for Nanny to come and take me away. Still, over time I had developed quite a good knowledge of fine jewellery. I knew which rings, tiaras and chokers came from where, and how many carats of diamonds, rubies or emeralds they boasted. I was also well aware that perhaps, if I behaved, one day I would be allowed to wear some of Mama's exquisite gems. Two of Mama's favourite pieces had come from Asprey – a company who I knew had also made some of the royal jewels – so I was very excited to be inside the famous store.

'Oh look, Papa, that's just like the one you have!' I exclaimed, rushing over to a large teak trunk with a blue velvet interior. 'But yours is a little bashed up and the inside is red.'

In fact I was very fond of Papa's travelling trunk. When I saw it being carried into the house by the servants it meant two things: firstly, that Papa would be home for some time, and secondly, that there would be gifts for me inside.

'You should get yourself one of these,' I added, picking up a silver cigar box. 'You only have a gold one, don't you?'

'Oh, I think I have one like that somewhere,' Papa replied casually. 'Besides, it's so much more fun to buy gifts for other people, don't you think, Tilly? Especially when one is fortunate enough to have so many beautiful possessions already.'

My mind flitted back briefly to the ragged girl at Ealing Broadway station but then I remembered the way she'd stuck her tongue out at me and I pushed the image of her torn clothes and dirty bare feet from my mind. I had heard Mama talk of the 'deserving poor' in the village and decided that the Ealing urchin must have been one of the undeserving poor. I was glad I hadn't thrown her my shiny red shoes.

'May I be of assistance, Lord Beaumont?' a middle-aged gentleman in a pinstripe suit asked my father. He had a slight limp and yet he moved gracefully, like a dancer.

'Mr Fitzroy, it's so very nice to see you again,' my father replied jovially, shaking the older man's hand enthusiastically. 'I would very much like to look at your ladies' wristwatches, if I may.'

'Of course, Your Lordship.' The gentleman bowed a little and ushered my father towards the stairs. 'Carter is our best watch man. He will give you all the assistance you need. Please, follow me.'

Papa hesitated for a moment and glanced back at me.

'This is my daughter, Lady Matilda.' He introduced me to Mr Fitzroy.

'It's a pleasure to meet you, Lady Matilda,' he said and he bowed at me with a theatrical flourish.

I giggled. I decided I liked Mr Fitzroy very much. He wasn't like any man I had ever met before. He was terribly elegant, with a well-oiled moustache and he smelled of orchids. His fingers were unusually long and slim and he wore an enormous ruby ring on his left pinkie. Of course, I had seen men wearing signet and wedding rings before, but never anything nearly as flamboyant as a ruby.

'Matilda is very keen on rummaging through her mother's jewels,' Papa explained to Mr Fitzroy with a wink. 'And I believe she would very much like to look at some of your jewellery while I continue my business upstairs. Would you be kind enough to look after her, Fitzroy? Perhaps she could try on one or two pieces. She's a little young to own an Asprey necklace yet but it's never too early to start planning for the future.'

'It would be my absolute pleasure,' Mr Fitzroy smiled. 'I see that Lady Matilda has inherited her mother's swan-like neck. I expect that our necklaces will look divine on her.'

Mr Fitzroy ushered me down a dark corridor and through a heavy mahogany door. Once we were inside the private room, he surveyed me closely with his head on one side. He appeared to be concentrating very hard.

'And so, Lady Matilda. How old are you, young lady? Let me guess. Hmm ... Ten?'

I blushed then, like Nanny did, because no one had ever mistaken me for being older than my years before (although I had recently had a growth spurt).

'I'm only eight and three quarters,' I told Mr Fitzroy, a little shyly. 'I'll be nine on January the first. Mama says I totally ruined her New Year's Eve celebrations to welcome in 1930.'

'She must have been joking with you,' smiled Mr Fitzroy kindly. 'I should think your arrival positively made her year.'

I smiled at his kindness but of course I knew my own mother, and her penchant for a good party, a lot better than Mr Fitzroy did.

'Please call me Tilly,' I told him.

'As you wish, Tilly,' he bowed again. 'So, you're a fan of fine jewels?'

I nodded enthusiastically.

'Well then, I think you're in for a treat,' grinned Mr Fitzroy.

And that was when my near-perfect day got even more wonderful. I spent the next hour sitting on a velvet chaise in a small private lounge, sipping fresh lemonade from a crystal glass, while the adorable Mr Fitzroy laid out countless pieces of priceless jewellery in front of me on the couch. His knowledge of rare gems and stones was incredible. He showed me rubies from Burma, sapphires from Ceylon and emeralds from Egypt. He allowed me to touch crowns and tiaras that had been commissioned by European royalty and their beauty transfixed me. But there was one necklace that took my breath away completely. It was a seven strand, opera-length necklace of priceless natural Persian pearls with an ornate gold clasp, which had been commissioned by an Indian maharaja for his maharani (or so Mr Fitzroy told me and I had no reason to doubt him). The necklace was finished but had not yet been paid for so, as Mr Fitzroy explained with a mischievous wink, for now it still belonged to Asprey of London.

'I think you should try it on, Tilly,' he suggested, lifting up the perfect pearl necklace for me to admire more closely. 'You are such a beautiful little girl. When you are older that neck should always be adorned with the world's finest jewellery. And I do hope I am still around to help you decorate it!'

I can still recall how cold the pearls felt on my bare neck as Mr Fitzroy secured the gold clasp and how surprisingly heavy they were. I also remember that they were far, far too long for me and, although an opera-length necklace is supposed to fall to the wearer's breastbone, on me it cascaded down to my waist. But oh, how mesmerising I found those pearls. To me they were so much more beautiful than any of the rubies, diamonds or emeralds I had seen that afternoon. I stared at my reflection for ages, turning this way and that, admiring myself from every angle. I lifted up the necklace and stroked the perfectly smooth round pearls, amazed at how cold they were to my touch.

'Do you see how each one is absolutely the same size and yet ever so slightly different?' asked Mr Fitzroy. 'To make a necklace like this takes years. Each one of these pearls is almost identical in size, symmetry, lustre and colour. To find one perfectly round, exquisitely iridescent, champagne-coloured pearl in an oyster shell at the bottom of the ocean is almost a miracle. To collect three hundred and eighty-nine ...'

'There are three hundred and eighty-nine pearls in this necklace?' I asked, my eyes popping out of my head. 'And each one was found in an oyster? The grey, knobbly things that grown-ups eat?'

Mr Fitzroy nodded gravely. His love of pearls was as clear as the lustre in the gems themselves.

'Each one of these pearls is a little miracle of nature. A flawless gem formed in a mollusc. I cannot abide the new cultured pearl industry. It's wholly unnatural and it's bringing down the value of real works of art like this,' he sniffed, shaking his head in disgust.

Of course I had no idea what cultured pearls were at the age of eight and three quarters but Mr Fitzroy seemed such an expert on the subject that I felt ashamed to admit my ignorance. Instead I asked a more obvious question.

'But how does an oyster grow a pearl?' I enquired. 'Oysters are yucky! They look ugly and they taste of the sea. Papa tried to make me eat one when we were in Cornwall this summer and I was almost sick all over Mama's cream dress.'

Mr Fitzroy laughed then.

'A pearl is a beautiful accident formed when an intruder enters the oyster's shell – a minuscule grain of sand, perhaps, or a tiny parasite. The oyster is irritated by the intruder and creates a sac around the area, which eventually, over time, becomes a pearl. It is very rare that the pearl is round and perfect like this though.'

He fingered the necklace lovingly and although I didn't fully understand what he'd said I did adore the idea of these gorgeous gems being 'beautiful accidents'.

'And how do the pearls get out?' I asked, wide-eyed. 'How do they come to be here, made into a necklace?'

Mr Fitzroy's eyes shone with excitement.

'My dear, that is the most amazing bit of all. Each one of these pearls was collected by hand from the ocean bed by a diver. And each diver has to collect over a ton of oysters to find just one pearl. And of all the pearls they find in a lifetime perhaps only one, or two, will be half as perfect as this. And yet here we have three hundred and *eighty-nine flawless pearls of almost identical size, lustre and colour. Is it any wonder this necklace is practically priceless?'*

But I wasn't interested in the necklace's worth. I was eight years old, spoilt and indulged, I had no concept of the value of money. What I was fascinated by was the idea of these perfect translucent pearls being collected by hand from under the sea in far-flung, exotic places.

'Who are these divers?' I asked, fascinated. 'Where do they live?'

'You really are inquisitive, aren't you, Tilly?' Mr Fitzroy laughed.

I apologised profusely. Mama was forever telling me off for asking too many questions.

'No, no, that's not a criticism,' he said, waving his hand dismissively. 'Let me tell you something that will amaze you. There are pearl hunters all over the world – in the Indian Ocean, the South China Sea, the Persian Gulf where these pearls came from, off the coasts of Venezuela, Korea, Australia, Japan. But the most astonishing part is this: a lot of the divers are women, they have no modern contraptions to help them dive, they dive fifty, sixty, maybe even a hundred feet on one single breath and some of those girls are not much older than you.'

I stared at the pearls in disbelief and their beauty seemed to multiply. It seemed to me the most magical story I had ever heard and I was utterly spellbound.

'Like real mermaids?' I asked, wide-eyed.

'Yes,' smiled Mr Fitzroy. 'Just like real mermaids.'

We were interrupted then by a knock on the door and Papa entered, carrying a small, beautifully wrapped gift box, which I assumed was Mama's present.

'Well I never,' he said, smiling broadly. 'Look at you, Tilly! That's quite some necklace you're wearing!'

'It's a seven-strand, opera-length, Persian pearl necklace,' I told him proudly. 'And each one of these pearls was collected from the bottom of the ocean by a real mermaid.'

'Is that so?' laughed Papa. 'Well, much as I love you, my darling, I'm not sure I can stretch to buying you that today. I'm afraid you'll have to make do with your teddy bear.'

'Oh, I couldn't possibly have it anyway,' I reassured him, still ridiculously unaware of the necklace's extortionate value. 'It's already been bagged by an Indian princess. Her husband is buying it for her as a wedding present. Besides, it's a little long for me, although I would love a pearl necklace one day, Papa. A choker, I think ...'

Papa laughed out loud and retorted, 'Sometimes, Lady Matilda, you are alarmingly like your mother.'

He turned to Mr Fitzroy then and said jovially, 'Thank you so much for entertaining Matilda, Fitzroy. And at least now I know what to get her when she comes of age!'

'It's time to take the necklace off, darling. We have to get back to the hotel now,' Papa said to me then. 'Nanny will have to get you bathed and changed before dinner and you know how she frets about time.'

Reluctantly, I allowed Mr Fitzroy to unclasp the necklace and as he did so I glanced at my reflection one more time. I wished silently that one day I would own a pearl necklace of my own.

On the walk back to the hotel, Papa gave me a piggyback because my new shoes were giving me blisters. I hugged his neck with my arms, rested my head against his hair and inhaled the familiar smell of Brylcreem and cologne. I wanted to imprint the aroma on my brain and lock it away with all my favourite memories, somewhere safe, so that I could get it out and remember it again when he was gone. My sore feet made me think about Mr Fitzroy's limp and I asked Papa why he walked that way.

'Fitzroy was a captain in the navy during the Great War,' Papa explained. 'His battleship was torpedoed by the Germans and he was badly injured.'

'Oh, poor Mr Fitzroy,' I exclaimed, hugging my father closely. 'That sounds frightful!'

Papa was quiet for a long time before he replied, 'Some people believe there will be another war soon if Hitler continues to cause trouble.'

I had heard of Hitler before. Papa and his cousin Aubrey (who disagreed on everything other than Mama's beauty, evidently) had had the most enormous stand-up shouting match during a 'fun' croquet match on the lawn that spring. I had never heard my father raise his voice in anger before and the incident had shocked me. A lot of the argument had been way over my head but I had understood enough to gather that my father despised this Hitler chap, whereas Cousin Aubrey was a huge admirer. I didn't understand why some little man in Germany was causing such a commotion on my croquet lawn in Wiltshire. But the subject clearly incensed Papa. At one point, I actually thought he was going to hit Aubrey over the head with his mallet. I rather hoped he might, actually, because I'd always found Aubrey to be an odious man.

Mama had made things much worse by siding with Aubrey and announcing that, 'Unity and Diana Mitford say Hitler is tremendously charismatic.'

Papa had marched off the lawn. I had run after him, keenly aware that he was only home for the weekend, but he had been so angry that he had asked me to leave him alone for a while so that he could calm down.

'Do you think we should go to war with Hitler?' I asked Papa nervously.

'War must always be a last resort,' Papa replied gently. 'Let's hope it doesn't come to that. Now, here we are back at the hotel.'

He lifted me off his back and planted me back on the pavement.

'The last one through the revolving doors is a rotten tomato!' he shouted.

I threw my head back and laughed as I chased him along Brook Street towards the entrance to Claridge's. Naturally, he let me win and by the time we flew into the foyer and collapsed giggling into each other's arms, all thoughts of war had been forgotten. For now.

We had a lovely dinner that evening. Nanny had bought me a delightful canary yellow pinafore and herself a gorgeous baby blue silk dress from Selfridges. Nanny's dress hugged her curves and I thought she looked even more like Betty Grable than usual. I noticed that Papa had started calling her Polly, rather than Nanny Miller, and I found myself hoping that the other diners would mistake us for a proper family. And what a lovely family we made! The thought made me feel guilty and disloyal to Mama but still I glanced around the room, welcoming admiring stares.

I made Papa order oysters, just in case there was a pearl inside, but there was nothing but grey, soggy mush. I held my nose and swallowed one down because Papa dared me to do so – I was never one to shirk from a dare! It tasted just as disgusting as the one I'd eaten in Fowey that summer and I announced that I would never try an oyster again.

'Oysters,' I declared, 'are only good for finding pearls, not for eating!'

Papa indulged me terribly and let me order anything I desired. He and Nanny drank champagne while I drank hot chocolate smothered in whipped cream. After dinner Papa allowed me to stay up for one drink of Coca-Cola in the bar. While he ordered my drink and Nanny's martini, an elegant American man approached our table. He told Nanny that she was 'an absolute doll' and asked her if she was with anyone. (Which I thought was rather insulting seeing as she was quite obviously with me!) Before she had time to answer, Papa reappeared and practically bit the poor Yank's head off! Nanny blushed to the same colour of scarlet as the velvet armchairs in the bar!

As Papa and Nanny chatted, I curled up on Papa's lap and drifted off to sleep, deliriously happy. Either Papa or Nanny must have carried me to bed at some point because the next thing I remember is waking up at dawn and seeing Nanny sneaking back into our shared room in the dim half-light. I remember she was carrying her shoes in her hand and tiptoeing in an attempt not to disturb me. I pretended to be asleep but I saw everything: the way her hair was messed up, and her lipstick was smeared and her beautiful new dress was crumpled and creased. I saw the look on her face which was a strange mix of pleasure and pain and I saw her take off a dainty gold wristwatch from her wrist, kiss it once and then hide it guiltily back in an Asprey case.

Although I was terribly naive in some ways, I was quite an unshockable child in other respects. I had witnessed a great deal of hedonism and debauchery while spying on my mother and her friends over the years. I didn't question things that other, more cosseted children, might have found disturbing. Of course, now I understand exactly what had happened in the next room to mine but back then it didn't tarnish my perfect day at all. In fact, it felt quite natural. I watched Nanny sit on her bed for the longest time. Her lovely face was framed by the light that seeped through the cracks in the curtains, and I wondered why on earth a stray tear was trickling down her cheek when we'd all had such a marvellous time in London.

Sophia had become utterly lost in her grandmother's childhood. She remembered how often Granny had talked about her father when Sophia was young, and now she thought she understood why. The pair had utterly adored each other. Sophia envied her grandmother that paternal bond. She couldn't imagine her own dad taking her shopping on Bond Street or, God forbid, out for dinner at Claridge's. Maybe that was why Granny had always been a bit sniffy with her dad. Perhaps she found him a terrible failure compared to her own father. And then Sophia remembered hearing what had happened to Sir Freddie and suddenly she felt very sad for her grandmother. Oh God, how could she have ignored all these letters? Maybe, just maybe, it was time to be brave. She started to read the letter again from the beginning, savouring every one of her grandmother's words.

When Hugo finally burst back through the door, half an hour later, Sophia almost jumped out of her skin.

'I'm so sorry,' he said breathlessly, tripping over the debris on the floor.

She looked up, surprised to be back in the real world, dropped the letter almost guiltily and hoped that Hugo hadn't noticed she'd been reading it. But Hugo carried on preening himself in the mirror and talking, obliviously.

'I really didn't mean to take so long. What do you think?'

'Super-hot,' replied Sophia, taking a deep breath and trying to ground herself back in the present. 'So let's get out of here.'

On her way out she picked up the business card from the floor and shoved it in her coat pocket. Just in case ...

Chapter Four

Lower East Side, New York, 2012

Dominic lit another cigarette and let himself out onto the roof terrace. A wall of noise hit him the minute he opened the doors. The racket of Manhattan on a Friday night roared in his ears and he couldn't quite believe that only forty-eight hours ago he had been lying in a tent, in one of the most uninhabited and remote regions in the world. The Yasuni National Park and the Lower East Side were not only in different countries; it was as if they were in different worlds.

There was nowhere to sit on the terrace – the garden furniture had gone too – so Dom leant against the glass balustrade and gazed down at the street far below. Yellow cabs drove, bumper to bumper, hooting each other for no obvious reason, drivers yelling out of their windows expletives that dissolved before they reached Dominic's ears. The sidewalk heaved with couples, arms entwined, on their way to romantic restaurants. Co-workers, finally finished for the weekend, were loosening their ties and their tongues, as they dropped in to their local bar for a quick beer before hitting the subway home to their wives. Trendy tourists from Europe held guidebooks in their hands, trying to figure out their way back to their hotels.

Dom drank it all in. These scenes had been familiar to him all his life. These were his streets, his city, his home. So why did it all feel so alien now? Things moved fast here. He had no idea which restaurants the couples were going to, or where the new hip joint was. The bar across the street was 'Under New Management' again – and the building had been remodelled for the third time in as many years. Dom sighed and felt suddenly very alone. Alone in a city of over eight million people. The New York way of life had escaped him somehow.

Could three months in Ecuador really have had such an impact? His job as a documentary film-maker had taken him all over the world. He had seen mind-blowing places and met hundreds of amazing people but he had always felt pleased to come home before. He'd found himself under enemy fire in war zones, he'd traipsed through deserts, hiked over melting polar ice caps and he'd even lived on a naval submarine, completely submerged for six weeks. He'd met paupers, princes and people from every walk of life in between. Dom had globetrotted, but wherever he'd been, New York had always retained his heart and his soul. He had never felt like this before.

Even by Dominic's standards, his time in Ecuador had been special. He had spent the last twelve weeks living with a local guide, a tracker and an interpreter, deep in the jungle, trying to find the elusive Taromenane – or Red Feet – one of the last two uncontacted Amazon tribes. He had seen how other tribes had now embraced modernity and struck up deals with not only oil companies and the government but with the Ecuadorian mafia to survive.

The thought that people still lived here, deep in the jungle of Yasuni, oblivious to modern life, and its constraints and laws, utterly fascinated Dominic – and he knew that his boss back at the TV company and the viewers of his show would be just as intrigued. These people were still utterly untamed – wild, dangerous, living off their wits. The danger involved thrilled him. As his guide kept warning him, the Taromenane wouldn't hesitate to attack any outsider they perceived to be a threat. But while the treacherous nature of the project didn't worry Dom, it did trouble his conscience. If he exposed the tribe, and captured them on film for the whole world to see, then wouldn't he be the one ultimately destroying them? Still, he had been desperate to see the Taromenane with his own eyes. Whether or not he would actually film them, if he got close enough, he hadn't quite decided. Eyewitnesses told him that they continued to live a nomadic existence, they were almost entirely carnivorous and they were also completely naked. Money, the mafia, violence and nudity – what more would an American audience want? In the end, fate intervened. Dom only caught brief glimpses of the Red Feet. There wasn't a hope in hell of his having time to get his camera out before he and his guide scrambled back through the jungle towards safety. And so the Red Feet remained as enigmatic as ever.

Instead, Dominic had interviewed environmentalists and zoologists. He had talked to elderly members of the neighbouring Huaorani and Kichwa tribes about how life had changed since the outside world invaded. But even the Kichwa described the Taromenane as 'savages' and warned Dominic that he would be killed if he tried to get any closer. 'You have your story. Leave them be now,' his wise Kichwa guide told him after eleven weeks of tracking and filming. 'That's what we do. They do not want to be civilised. We tried to get in touch with them but they threatened us. It's fine this way.' In the end, even Dominic, the dogged documentary maker, had conceded that it was best to leave the Taromenane alone. Who was he to disturb a way of life that had worked for them for hundreds of thousands of years?

And so, a couple of days ago, Dom had finally left the fearsome defenders of their rainforest, made his way back to the capital, Quito, and got on the first flight home to JFK. So why did he feel like going straight back to the airport and jumping on the first available flight, destination Anywhere-But-Here? The answer was simple: Calgary. It wasn't his trip that had made him feel like an alien in New York. It was what had happened in the days before he left. The world he'd inhabited simply didn't exist any more.

Calgary had never been a particularly tactile sort of a woman, which Dominic had found difficult sometimes, coming from an argumentative, demonstrative and sentimental family himself. Calgary was none of these things. Her own background had taught her to be as cool as a New England breeze. She watched herself closely and checked all her emotions thoroughly, before carefully baring only tiny glimpses of her true feelings. She never lost control. She never raised her voice. She got her own way not by stamping her feet like Dom's little sister, but through passive aggression. She huffed, sulked, walked away and put the phone down mid-conversation. Her biggest weapon was withdrawing all affection whenever things didn't go exactly to her plan.

At first, Dominic had had no idea how to deal with someone like that. His mother, his sisters and his ex-girlfriends were all passionate, hot-headed women. He was used to being shouted at and lavished with kisses in equal measure. Love had always come easy to Dom until he'd met Calgary. But this new girl's studied indifference had made him work harder than he'd ever had to before. He was putty in her perfectly manicured hands. The cooler she was, the more desperate he became to impress her. Maybe that's why he'd fallen so hard in the first place.

She was a fellow New Yorker but she was so different, so exotic, and so upmarket, Dom couldn't quite believe he'd ended up with her – the perfect Park Avenue princess. Sometimes, when he caught their reflection together in a window, walking hand in hand down Broadway, he would have to take a second look. They made a handsome-looking couple all right, but they were clearly not from the same tribe! He made excuses for her coldness, just as she did for his lack of class. She was repressed because she'd never been shown much warmth from her parents, Dom figured. But she had a big heart underneath the armour. She just needed to learn how to let it out. And he could help her with that, right? He could teach her to wear her heart more on her sleeve. Just like she'd taught him which cutlery to use in swanky restaurants.

Sometimes he'd felt as if he was breaking down her barriers, just a little, and it warmed his heart to see her smile. And on the rare occasions when Calgary allowed herself to show her real emotions – when she laughed, or grinned, or wept, or kissed him full on the lips – it felt like the most precious and rare gift in the world. He'd always thought it was worth the effort for those few fleeting moments of joy. At least he had done until a few weeks ago.

His best friend, Dave, had never been a big fan. He once said that Calgary tossed Dom the scraps, and that Dom acted like a grateful, starved puppy, thankful for anything he got. But men in love don't listen to their friends, and there had been a time when one smile from Calgary had made everything right in the world – whatever Dave said.

'Buddy, even your dog's unsure of her,' Dave had warned, early in the relationship. 'All I'm saying is this: perhaps it takes a bitch to know a bitch, huh?'

It was true; Blondie and Calgary had never been comfortable bedfellows. Ironically, Blondie had been the one responsible for Dominic's first meeting with his future wife. It was the summer of 2007 on a hot, July day. His beloved golden retriever had just turned one at the time and, although almost fully grown, she was still very much a puppy in her head. And so, Dom's big, beautiful, blonde baby had been a little out of control in Central Park that sunny summer's afternoon. He'd found a quiet spot where he'd thought he could let her off the leash and practise some training methods in relative safety. Dom was trying the basics – sit, stay, heel, come – with the help of a bag of dog treats. Everything was going pretty well until Blondie spotted a seagull land a few feet away and decided to chase the bird. Of course the seagull took off and flew away at high speed across Central Park with Blondie following and Dominic sprinting behind.

'Blondie!' he kept calling as he negotiated joggers, benches, kids on bikes, teens making out and nannies with strollers. 'Stop! Wait!'

But the dog kept running so Dom kept shouting. Finally Blondie stopped at a bench in the distance and lost interest in the seagull. As he ran closer Dominic could see that some kid had dropped an ice cream and Blondie was clearing up the leftovers. But he didn't trust her to wait for him so, as he approached the bench at full speed, he kept calling to her angrily.

'Blondie!' he hollered at the top of his lungs. 'Stop!'

Blondie looked up, saw her master and Dom could have sworn she smirked. She looked over her shoulder at a pack of dogs playing in the distance and for a moment Dom thought she was about to bolt again. He was boiling hot, sweating, pissed off and totally out of breath from running.

'Wait, Blondie! I swear, you take one more step away from me and I will not be held responsible for my actions,' he yelled as he reached the bench. 'Blondie! Blondie! You wait right there, you dumb bitch!'

It wasn't until an icy female voice said, 'Is that your idea of a pick-up line?' that he realised there was someone sitting on the bench. 'Stop, Blondie. Wait, Blondie. Did you really think that was going to work?' said the clipped Upper East Side voice. 'Really? You're repulsive. You really are. Excuse me.'

Dominic was still panting, with sweat dripping down his face, when he looked up and saw the most exquisitely beautiful blonde standing up from the bench where Blondie had stopped.

He stared with incomprehension at the look of utter disdain on the beautiful girl's face.

'Huh?' was all he could manage to say.

But the girl just tutted loudly, turned on her high heels and clipped off down the path towards the exit onto Fifth Avenue. It took a few moments for the reality of the situation to seep into Dom's brain. The girl had long, pale, poker-straight blonde hair. She was a total hottie: the type of girl who had men wolf-whistling her and calling out to her constantly. And Dom had run up to her, covered in sweat, and shouting. Oh shit.

'Blondie,' he said to his puppy. 'You see the trouble you cause? That girl was gorgeous! Come on. We need to go explain.'

Dom and Blondie trotted off after the girl, out onto Fifth Avenue and down the street. Thankfully, she was wearing a bright red shift dress and, with her long white-blonde hair, it was easy for Dominic to spot her in the crowd. It didn't take long for him to catch up with her.

'Hey,' he said, tapping her on the shoulder. 'I need to explain.'

The girl spun round and stared at him with a look of terror.

'Are you crazy?' she asked, backing away, holding up her handbag in front of her for protection. 'What do you want? Leave me alone!'

'No, no, no,' said Dom desperately, holding his hands up in a gesture of submission. 'Just give me a minute to explain. This is Blondie.'

He pointed at the dog. Blondie barked just to emphasise the point.

'Blondie,' repeated the icy blonde. 'You expect me to believe that your dog is called Blondie. What the hell kind of jerk calls his dog Blondie?'

'I do,' nodded Dom.

'Why would you do that?' demanded the girl. 'There are lots of perfectly good names for dogs without resorting to one that's insulting for half the female population of Manhattan.'

She had a directness, verging on rudeness, that Dominic found both intriguing and terrifying in equal measure.

'It's not an insult. It's a compliment. She's Blondie, as in Debbie Harry. My dad was always a huge fan, I was brought up listening to *Parallel Lines*,' Dominic explained.

'I guess they are quite cool,' conceded the girl, grudgingly.

'It's still a dumb name for a dog though.'

'I thought it made sense,' said Dominic, glancing down at his dog. 'I got this puppy and she was the most beautiful blonde I had ever seen ...'

He looked up at the girl and his stomach did a flip. She was absolutely breathtaking. Dom found himself saying, 'Until today anyway.'

The girl tutted again, as if she'd heard the line, or a line like it, a thousand times before. Which she probably had. But Dominic was not one for corny chat-up lines, or for running after strange girls he'd accidentally insulted in parks. There was something about this girl. She was fascinating.

'Sorry,' he said. 'You must think I'm a total schmuck. Anyway, I just wanted to explain.'

He held out his hand by way of apology. She accepted it warily, and then shook it with a much firmer grip than he'd expected.

'Calgary,' she said brusquely. 'Calgary Woods.'

'Dominic McGuire,' he said, grinning, and then, because he couldn't help himself he added. 'Calgary Woods? And you think my dog's name is dumb!'

She snatched her hand away.

'I was going to suggest you buy me coffee to apologise but you're obviously far too childish to waste any more time on, Mr McGuire. Goodbye.'

And with that Calgary Woods turned on her heels and clipped away from him for the second time that afternoon.

'Oh come on, Calgary,' said Dom, trotting behind her. 'It was a joke. Don't you like jokes?'

'I like funny ones,' she replied without pausing or turning round to face him but he could tell by the way her cheeks twitched that she was trying not to smile.

He and Blondie followed her all the way down Fifth Avenue for five blocks and then down East 75th Street to Madison, where she stopped abruptly outside a grand office block.

'I have an appointment now,' she said tartly. 'But you can take me out to dinner tomorrow. It's the least you can do. And choose somewhere decent. I can't abide bad food. I'll meet you at eight. Text me. I don't have time for calls.'

She handed him a business card and disappeared into the

building without a goodbye or a second glance. Dominic read her card.

CALGARY WOODS
SENIOR FASHION ASSISTANT
LUSH

It figured. *Lush* was *the* hottest new fashion magazine to hit the newsstands that year. Calgary Woods looked like she'd work in fashion. Dominic had never really been into blondes. He couldn't stand uptight Park Avenue princesses. And he'd certainly never been into precious fashion types before. But there was something about Calgary that drew him like a moth to the flame. As he walked away from their first chance encounter, somehow he already knew she was dangerous. He suspected there might be a block of ice where her heart should have been. But it didn't stop him thinking about her. Dominic was already hooked on Calgary. He remained hooked for the next five years.

Life with Calgary was not exactly easy. Her family were a nightmare, she didn't feel comfortable hanging out with his loud, lively friends, and she downright refused to visit his family in Yonkers. Although his career was going from strength to strength and he was actually bringing in more money than she was, there was always an implication that it was Calgary's career that mattered more.

Looking back, Dominic realised, she'd always been the one wearing the trousers in the relationship – even though she preferred skirts (no point in spending seven hours a week in the gym if you don't show off your legs).

Even during their early days together, Calgary had spent most of her time in the office, or on shoots in exotic locations, or at shows in Milan, Paris or London. It didn't take Dom long to figure out that Calgary was a complete workaholic. But again he made excuses for her: wasn't it great that his girlfriend was so independent and driven? At least she didn't expect him to keep her in Jimmy Choos – she was more than capable of buying them for herself. She was quickly promoted to Fashion Editor, then Fashion Director and then Creative Director of *Lush*. And pretty soon she was earning more than Dom.

By the time they'd been dating a year, she'd become the darling

47

of the New York fashion set. She always got front seats at the big shows, she styled everyone from Rihanna to Madonna, and she couldn't go anywhere without being followed by a pack of adoring fashion bloggers, snapping away with their iPhones to report exactly what bag she was carrying, or shade of lipstick she was wearing, or brand of jeans she was sporting (if it was the weekend). The more successful Calgary became, the more Dom started to feel like he was trotting behind in her shadow. She would invite him to parties and events but more often than not, Dominic felt that his only role there was to hold her champagne glass as she schmoozed with important clients.

Two years into their relationship he was starting to wonder what she saw in him. And he'd even started to wonder what he was getting out of the relationship – other than free designer clothes and the envious stares of other men. When he touched her, he could have sworn she flinched sometimes. Other times, he would catch her looking at him with a look of such disappointment on her face that it made him want to shake her. What was wrong with him? Why was she even in a relationship with him if she thought he was such a failure? But of course Dominic would never shake Calgary. He would never raise his hands to a woman. He might not be from the Upper East Side, but he sure as hell had been brought up better than that.

Very, very rarely, Calgary's mask slipped. And that was when he loved her most. He would sometimes find her curled up in bed, or locked in the bathroom, with tears streaming down her gorgeous face. She would never let him know what had made the Ice Maiden cry, but she would allow him to hold her until her shoulders stopped shaking and the tears subsided. Afterwards, she would always say thank you, but if he dared question her about what had upset her, she would retreat even further into her beautiful shell.

He got used to the put-downs that were often sugar-coated in Calgary's own brand of caustic 'humour'. ('Oh, don't look so hurt, baby. It was a joke,' she'd often say.) But he never got used to the lack of physical closeness. They had sex quite regularly, but it was always when she felt like it. She barely kissed him and when they were finished she would push him off her, turn her back and go to sleep. Sometimes it felt as if she hated him for loving her.

So, when she suggested that it might be time he proposed to her, he almost fell off his chair. She wanted to marry him? She must love him then! In her own, weird, uptight, rich girl way. It didn't even cross his mind *not* to propose after that. He went through the terrifying ordeal of asking her father's permission and then, after Mr Woods gave his blessing (grudgingly), Dom found himself pretty much redundant in the wedding plans. Calgary made it quite clear that organising a wedding was the bride's prerogative – particularly if the bride happened to work in fashion. So it was all up to her: the venue, the guest list, the rings, the outfits, the flowers, the catering, the cake, the bridesmaids, the ushers and even the groomsmen (she reluctantly allowed him to invite his close family and for Dave to be best man but that really was it). All Dom had to do was enjoy his stag party (no, not Vegas, over Calgary's dead body) and turn up at the family church in East Hampton on time. Which, of course, he did. And when Calgary said, 'I do' Dom could have burst with happiness. Looking back now, it was difficult to understand why he was so elated on his wedding day. He guessed that it was human nature to want what you had to work hardest for. And he sure as hell had worked hard for Calgary.

Calgary had never said she wanted children. But she had never said she didn't want them either. And Dominic was a Catholic. He was one of five kids, his Italian mother was one of seven and his Irish father was one of ten. In the McGuire family, everybody had babies – lots and lots of babies! He just kind of assumed everybody wanted kids, right? He was thirty-two when they got married. Calgary was twenty-nine. They were young, comfortably off, healthy and well educated: prime candidates to go forth and reproduce, or so Dom had assumed. Their sex life ended the day Dominic asked if Calgary wanted to try for a baby. They'd been married less than a year.

She threw herself even more thoroughly into her work, went out with her friends whenever she could and avoided him as much as possible. With both their careers taking them overseas frequently, and both of them working long hours when they were in New York, it was easy to share an apartment without sharing much of a life. They did still share a bed, three times, maybe four times a week, but Calgary always turned in before Dominic and, no matter how quickly he tried to follow her, by the time he got in beside her she would have her back turned towards him and she would be asleep. Or at least she would be doing a great job of pretending to be asleep. If he tried to touch her, she would shuffle even further away from him in the vast bed, and continue her pretence of being asleep.

Dominic ached to hold his wife, to kiss his wife, to make love to his wife like they used to. And, more than anything, he yearned to be a father. He dreamed of moving to a brownstone and raising a whole brood of crazy kids. Occasionally he'd try to raise the subject with Calgary but she'd give him the silent treatment and he was so frightened of hearing the definitive word 'no' that he didn't push it. Not until this summer. By their third wedding anniversary he'd had enough. He'd just turned thirty-five and he was sick of listening to his mom going on and on about when he was going to produce a grandchild. He was sick, too, of going to his friends' kids' christenings. He wanted a christening of his own! So he started putting the pressure on.

'I want to be a father, Calgary,' he told her bravely. 'You don't have the right to take that dream away from me. It's too big a deal.'

'And you don't have the right to enforce motherhood on me,' she replied coldly and walked out.

He tried again a few days later, more gently this time.

'We could get a nanny or I could be a stay-at-home dad,' he suggested, hopefully.

'And would you get fat, throw up, get stretch marks and tear your perineum too?' she asked sarcastically.

'Well no, but there's always elective caesarean, if you can't face a natural birth. I've been reading up on it ...' he said hopefully.

'WOW,' replied Calgary, flatly. And they both knew what that meant. WOW was his wife's abbreviation for Waste of Words. She used it frequently. She even had a Markus Lupfer sweater with the word WOW emblazoned on the front: never had an item of clothing been more suited to its owner.

'I really want a kid,' he ventured one last time.

Calgary stared at him for a long time. Her features softened a little into, what was that look exactly? Pity? He was sitting on the rug on the floor, cross-legged, with Blondie lying in his arms.

'You don't need a baby, Dom. You already have a child,' she

said, nodding towards the dog and trying to force her features into something that resembled a smile. 'You talk to her in that dumb baby voice, you brush her hair and take her to the park. You fix her up special dinners and you have a photo of her as a screensaver. What more do you want?'

'I want to be a dad,' explained Dominic, one last time.

Calgary shook her blonde head. 'I'm sorry, baby, but there's no way. I can just about tolerate Blondie. She's entirely your responsibility and at least she's toilet trained! But I do not want children. End of. I thought you understood that. Let's not waste any more time arguing about it, huh? Right, Marion and I have theatre tickets. I'll be back late. Don't wait up.'

Dominic tried to wait up on the couch for her but he fell asleep some time around three a.m. and when he woke up, still on the couch, it was morning and she was safely tucked up in their bed.

'Good play?' he asked her when she finally surfaced for breakfast.

'Play?' she asked, looking much more dishevelled and hungover than she'd ever done before.

'You said you and Marion had theatre tickets.'

'Oh, yeah, we blew that out,' Calgary explained. 'The tickets were freebies anyway. I got invited to a party in Tribeca at the last minute so we went there instead. It was fun.'

'Good,' said Dom, not meaning it for a moment. 'That's real good. I'm glad you had a fun time.'

The following week, he tried a new tack. Perhaps if they did more together as a couple, things would be better between them? He took her to her favourite restaurant, dressed in her favourite Prada suit, the one she'd bought him for that awards ceremony last year, and went to the barbers for a really close shave to please her.

'Look, honey,' he said as they waited for their starters. 'I know having a baby is a scary prospect for a woman, especially a woman with such a successful career as you, but I'd be here with you every step of the way. I want to be a hands-on kind of dad. I don't mind doing most of the childcare. I'll get up in the middle of the night, I'll put my job on the back-burner. We can afford it. Or, if you don't like that idea, we could get a nanny. Please, Calgary, at least consider the idea.'

'Or what?' she asked, eyeing him warily, like a deer with its back to the fence and a hunter's rifle in its face.

'Or ... I don't know, baby,' he said, desperately. He didn't want to make her feel trapped but he didn't want to sacrifice his own dreams either. 'How do I give up the desire to be a father? It's such a big sacrifice. Christ, if I'd known you didn't want children I'd—'

'What?' she demanded, firmly, but without raising her voice. 'You'd never have married me?'

'I didn't say that,' he replied, tears welling up in his eyes. 'I don't know what I would have done. How do I know? You never mentioned it. You never once said you didn't want to be a mother.'

'You never asked,' Calgary pointed out. She bit her lip and frowned, concentrating hard on staring anywhere but into her husband's eyes.

'Oh come on, Cal, most people want to get married and have kids. It's the logical next step. It's what most people do,' he continued.

'I'm not most people,' Calgary muttered.

A brief flicker of pain flashed across her face and then disappeared again. She rearranged her features in their usual perfect position and continued staring over Dom's head. The less emotion she showed, the more upset and angry Dominic became.

He took a deep breath and said, as calmly as he could manage, 'Cal, you're my wife, I love you, but I want to have kids. Can't you understand that? What would be so bad about us having a family together? Why don't you want to have my baby? There's nothing I want more than to see you pregnant, and watch our baby being born, and see what he looks like. Or she, obviously. I don't mind which, a boy or a girl ... Please, honey, say you'll at least think about it. I can't bear the thought of a future with no children.'

Dom put his hand on hers and tried to catch her eye, to implore her to see things from his point of view. Calgary sighed deeply and stared out of the window for the longest time. Then she pulled her hand out from underneath his and finally, she allowed herself to look at him. The minute she did so the tears began to fall. She opened her mouth, as if she wanted to say something of great importance, but the words seemed to choke her. Dominic could see in her ice-blue eyes that she was being eaten up by something. But what? And although she was obviously trying to find a way to express herself, Calgary Woods was too repressed – or too scared – to open the floodgates. Instead, she swallowed back her words, dabbed her tears away with her napkin and took a deep sigh.

'I'm so sorry, Dominic,' was all she could manage as she took off her wedding ring, placed it neatly on the white tablecloth and stood up. 'I never meant to hurt you,' she said quietly, calm now. Her mask was firmly back in place and Dom had a sick feeling in the pit of his stomach that this time she was never going to let it slip again.

'But we're both here under false pretences,' she continued, pushing back her chair. The cornered deer was about to bolt. 'It was never going to work, was it? We don't want the same things and we certainly don't make each other happy any more. So, you're free now. Free to go forth and multiply with the next girl who comes along. I think it's for the best. You'll be happier without me. I'm not what you need.'

And then she walked out of the restaurant, with her tears dried, and her head held high, as if she was going to visit the washrooms. She never came back. Calgary had always had a way of shocking Dominic, but he hadn't seen this one coming at all. The room spun, his heart pounded with panic, he thought he might throw up. Dominic had to send back the starters and with his cheeks burning with shame and despair, he had to explain that his wife had felt suddenly unwell, pay the bill and leave the restaurant without breaking down in front of all those people. She wasn't at the apartment when Dom got home and she wouldn't answer the phone, or reply to texts, emails or Facetime requests. Finally, two days and two sleepless nights later she sent him one message.

I'm sorry if I've upset you, Dominic. But I'm not sorry for my decision. It's the right one for both of us. I believe you're going to South America tomorrow. I'll collect my things while you're gone. My lawyer will arrange for my name to be taken off the lease for the apartment. I suggest a quick divorce. There's nothing to contest. I won't be seeking alimony and we have no financial ties. I told you it was best to keep separate bank accounts. Obviously you're welcome to the dog. Goodbye, Dominic. I wish you well in the future. Please don't reply or try to call me. I won't respond.

The next morning Dominic left for Ecuador. He sat by the window with his face hidden from his fellow passengers, and curled up under a blanket all the way from JFK to Quito.

Chapter Five

Mayfair, West London, 2012

Sophia had rounded the corner into Berkeley Street, arm in arm with Hugo, and walked straight into trouble. And trouble didn't come in a much more toxic package than Hannah Louise Lovell. Not that the girl *looked* like trouble. In fact, that was her most powerful weapon. She was five foot two and a half of blonde curly-haired, wide blue-eyed cuteness, with a mega-watt smile and dimples. She spoke with a slight lisp, feigned weakness and innocence regularly (although she had a business degree from Cambridge and had coxed the male rowing team there) and she could make herself cry on demand: a skill she had shown off to Sophia when they had first met, aged eight, as first-time boarders at prep school, and one which she had used to get herself out of trouble, and Sophia into trouble, with teachers, housemistresses, friends, boyfriends (and even, on one occasion, the police) ever since.

They had been thrown into the same social circle at a young age, and mutual friends and family connections had meant their lives had been uncomfortably entwined for most of their childhoods and early adult lives.

'Be nice,' whispered Hugo. 'Face the frenemy with a smile.'

'So-phi-ah!' Hannah sing-songed. 'How *are* you?'

'Fine thanks,' she muttered, keen to keep the exchange brief. She was a grown woman now, this was not the Year 8 locker room, she did not have to put up with Hannah any more.

'If you're going to Funky Buddha, I wouldn't,' Hannah said, still smiling dazzlingly, her voice dripping with faux kindness. 'It's a very young, vibrant crowd tonight. Lots of overachievers under the age of twenty-five. The paps are going wild there are so many "somebodies" there. You might feel a little uncomfortable, Sophia.'

Sophia tried to walk past without reacting, but just as the girls were shoulder to shoulder, Hannah muttered, 'I used to be envious of you. Did you know that?'

Sophia frowned. But Hannah was on a roll.

'You always did think you were something special,' she continued. It sounded like a speech she had been waiting to deliver for years. 'With your legs up to your armpits and your hair down to your waist. And your ever-so-famous granny who'd send you food parcels from Fortnum's. That's the only reason you always got the lead in school plays, by the way – because of your grandmother. It had nothing to do with talent and everything to do with the teachers being star-struck and trying to suck up to your diva of a grandmother. And then there was the way you used to lord it over the rest of us when the boys from other schools always asked you to their proms ... "Oh, haven't you got a date? I've got seven. I just don't know which one to choose."

'But we all knew you were only so popular because you'd give up the goods for a ride in a sports car and a vodka and coke.'

The venom in her voice made Sophia shudder.

'But life's got a funny way of dishing out just deserts in the end, hasn't it?' she continued, coldly. 'You're not getting any younger and you certainly aren't getting any prettier. You'll be too old for miniskirts soon and then what use will those legs be? You've never used the brains you were born with. You were quite happy to act like a bimbo as long as it got you noticed, got you laid and got your face in the press. But nobody's asked you to be on TV for years. When was the last time you got papped, eh? 2005?! You're a nobody now, *Lady* Sophia. And you're certainly no lady!'

Hannah took a step even closer to Sophia. She smelled of orchids and vanilla, the sweet scent sharply at odds with the sour words. 'But you go to Funky Buddha with the kids and pretend nothing's changed. Your parents won't take you back this time, from what I hear. And you can't live at Ben's place much longer. I heard his father was putting the Hackney house on the market ...'

Hugo and Sophia shared a panicked glance at that but Hannah

didn't pause for breath. 'You're not going to find yourself a rich man to look after you. Not now. You're with a different guy every week, by all accounts. The whole of London knows what a slut you are. And do any of them call you the next day? Do they hell! But you go clubbing. You enjoy yourself. Because I'm telling you this, Sophia, the party's almost over. And when you finally fall out of your ivory tower, there will be no one there to catch you.'

Sophia opened her mouth to defend herself – she didn't live off her family name, she never even used her title these days! – but before she could find the right words Hannah Louise Lovell had spun on her silver heels and sailed off down the street in a waft of vanilla. Hugo and Sophia wandered towards the club in silence. Not one of the waiting paparazzi lifted their cameras as Sophia walked by.

'Let her think what she likes,' shrugged Sophia. 'I'm past caring what people think of me.'

This was another downright lie, of course. Sophia was reeling from what Hannah had said. And to make matters worse, the party atmosphere of the VIP area in Funky Buddha was just not doing it for her any more. The venues changed – KOKO, Mahiki, Notting Hill Arts Club – it didn't really matter where. Despite what Hannah had said, Sophia still walked straight past the queues of waiting 'plebs'. She still got a kiss from the door staff. The owners and promoters still knew her by name and always sent over a drink on the house. But Sophia had been a regular fixture on the London club scene for over a decade now and the truth was it was beginning to not just bore her but depress her. Tonight, the fakery seemed worse than ever. She kept finding herself thinking about her grandmother's letter and wondering what Tilly would think of Sophia if she could see her now. Not a lot, she reckoned.

'You'll amount to nothing, young lady,' her dad had warned her every time she got a bad report from school.

Maybe he'd been right. She certainly hadn't achieved much to be proud of. There had been a time when Sophia lived for these nights but recently she often found herself locked in the toilet, not to have a line of coke, as she'd sometimes done when she was younger, but fighting tears of frustration and hiding from the people she used to admire.

But the worst part always came later, sometimes after it was light, as Sophia lay alone in her bed. Sleep evaded her like a lost memory. She would crave it so badly – the pure, innocent oblivion of slumber – but every time she tried to capture it and embrace it, it would dart out of her reach, her mind would be filled with a new worry, or a familiar doubt, and she would find herself tossing and turning, wide awake again. She would lie there, watching the light creep through the cracks in her curtains, illuminating her sordid world. Empty wine bottles overturned on her bedside table, overflowing ashtrays spilling onto mounds of dirty designer clothes: the debris of a vacuous party girl.

And then Sophia would see all that she had become and her skin would crawl with the unbearable itch of self-loathing. It wasn't self-pity. It was self-hatred. She was the one who had got herself here. But how could she get herself out? The truth was that Sophia wanted to get up, climb out of her skin and walk out of her life. Sometimes she brought men back and slept with them, just to relieve the loneliness of the dawn. Like a drug, these brief sexual encounters made her feel better for a moment. The feel of naked skin on naked skin and the sweet, kind lies that were whispered into her ears, soothed her. But when they'd gone, she only had further to fall, and the next day she'd feel even cheaper and more worthless than ever.

Which turn had been the wrong one? She knew it was her life, her responsibility, but how could she have stopped it all from ending up here? Where was the pivotal moment? Had she been too vain? Too impressed by the superficial and the trivial? So worried about being cool and 'on trend' that she'd neglected to develop anything more substantial than a 'signature look'? That's what her parents thought.

And hadn't she thought she'd known better? She remembered with a wince how smug she'd been when she'd got her first TV presenting job. She'd thought she'd outsmarted the 'good girls' at schools, still poring over their textbooks and living by the rules. It was a silly, fluffy, empty-headed gig on a fairly obscure satellite channel but, hey, it was better than finishing her A levels, wasn't it? For a few years Sophia had hovered on the verge of celebrity, living off her family name and her grandmother's fading fame. She'd been photographed a lot, dancing on tables in nightclubs, snogging rock stars, smoking cigarettes with minor royals and falling out of parties on the arms of professional football players.

Now Sophia was thirty. She had no job and she was basically squatting in a dilapidated house. Hannah had been right: nobody took her photograph any more. And, while Sophia lay alone night after night, the schoolfriends she'd once branded as nerds were safely tucked up with their husbands, in their warm, snug beds, in some lovely Victorian terrace in Clapham or Chiswick or Blackheath. In the morning they'd get up for work. Or they'd look after their babies. They'd do something productive and meaningful. What did Sophia have to get up for?

A man – another vague acquaintance – nudged her out of her dark thoughts and handed her a mojito.

'Oh, thanks,' she said, dispassionately, taking the cocktail from the young man whose name she couldn't remember. Maybe she'd never known it in the first place.

'How do you do that?' asked Hugo, nodding towards the table in front of them. 'You have five drinks lined up. You didn't buy one of them yourself. You haven't spoken to any of the men who've bought them for you. All you've done is sit there, sulking, and still the free drinks roll in. I've been smiling seductively at every camp man in here and not one of them has bought me so much as a mineral water. What have you got that I haven't?'

'They're called breasts,' said Sophia flatly. 'Here, have a drink. There's no way I can get through all these on my own anyway.'

Hugo took the cocktail gratefully.

'Well, if Hannah's right about us getting thrown out of Hackney before long, we have no choice now, do we?' he announced, his eyes lighting up.

'What are you talking about?' asked Sophia, once she'd downed her second Jägerbomb. Although she knew exactly where this was heading; Hugo was nothing if not transparent.

'Granny is our only answer,' he nodded firmly. 'Tomorrow we go to St John's Wood, you make it up with Granny, get back in with the family and back in that will and by Christmas we'll be back here in West London where we belong.'

Sophia looked around herself again. She was suddenly acutely aware that she no more belonged in West London than she did in Timbuktu. She shook her head firmly.

'No, Hugo,' she said. 'Let's leave Granny out of our mess. I don't want anything to do with my family and I'm certainly not going to emotionally blackmail my grandmother into leaving me her money. It wouldn't feel right. She's the only one I actually like.'

'She can't take it with her, Soph,' he pleaded now. 'And you've always been her favourite. She would want you to have it. You even changed your name to hers.'

This was true. Much to her father's horror, Sophia had added her grandmother's 'Beaumont' to her surname as a teenager, believing Lady Sophia Beaumont Brown made her sound more sophisticated than just plain Sophia Brown. She had never understood why her mother had willingly sacrificed both her name and her title when she got married.

'I was Granny's favourite when I was six,' Sophia reminded her friend firmly. 'When I was sweet and cute. I haven't seen her in two years. I'm not on speaking terms with my parents. I can't be trusted. I am the great family embarrassment. What on earth makes you think my granny would leave me a penny even if I did visit her?'

'She writes you those letters,' Hugo reminded her. 'She still loves you, even though you've ...'

Hugo trailed off, realising he'd accidentally strayed into dangerous territory.

'Even though I've what?' asked Sophia.

She downed a tequila, slammed the empty glass onto the table and looked Hugo straight in the eye, willing him to speak the truth.

'Even though you've had a few minor disagreements with your family,' offered Hugo.

'A few minor disagreements?' scoffed Sophia. 'I suppose that's one way of putting it. What was it Daddy said last time I spoke to him? Oh yes, that's it. "You're on your own now, Sophia. You have no one to blame for your predicament but yourself. I am ashamed to be your father." And he was right! You know he was right! As cold and condescending as the man is, about that, he was right.'

'It wasn't that bad ...' started Hugo lamely.

It only took one warning look from Sophia to shut him up. They both knew it had been 'that bad'. And however low

Sophia had been feeling, there was no excuse for what she'd put her family through. How could she face her grandmother now? How could she face any of them? No amount of alcohol could take the edge off the shame she felt when she remembered the events of two years ago.

Tilly Beaumont's granddaughter in sex and drugs shame, as one of the kinder broadsheets had put it. *Spoilt aristocratic heiress had drug-fuelled orgy in her parents' multimillion-pound mansion!* screamed a less salubrious tabloid. The facts had been twisted and exaggerated almost beyond recognition, of course, but the truth had been bad enough: Sophia had had a party, a big party, in her parents' house while they'd been on holiday. Things had got out of hand. Thanks to her own big mouth and the wonders of Facebook, half of London's party crowd (and their dealers) had turned up on the doorstep and Sophia had been too drunk, and too busy having a good time, to care. She'd let it happen. She'd turned a blind eye to the cocaine being snorted off her mother's granite work surfaces, she'd laughed at the naked supermodel paddling in the pond and she'd simply closed the door again when she accidentally walked in on the threesome taking place in her parents' bed.

OK, so the next day she had panicked, big time, at the mess left behind. But once she and her friends had spent two days tidying and cleaning, and had bribed a local handyman to keep his mouth shut about the emergency repairs he'd had to do to the house and garden, she'd run back to London thinking she'd got away with it. Except no one gets away with that sort of thing any more. Not when everyone has a smartphone. All it took was one 'friend' to email a few pictures to a news desk and boom, Sophia's world was shattered. Her parents returned from the South of France on the Saturday evening to find everything exactly as they'd left it ... Until the Sunday paper dropped onto their doormat the following morning and nothing was ever going to be the same again. Sophia hadn't seen them since. Other than one horrific phone call that Sunday, she had had no contact with her parents for two years. She had been completely disowned. And, if she was honest, she didn't blame them. For all their faults, they were her parents, and she was their only child. She couldn't have done a much better job of humiliating them if she'd tried.

'They'll come round,' said Hugo, patting her arm. 'Eventually. Your dad's always cutting you off and then changing his mind again.'

'Only because Mum makes him, usually,' Sophia reminded him. 'And it's been two years this time. No, I think my dad was relieved to have an excuse to wash his hands of me. I've never exactly been a daddy's girl, have I?'

Hugo shook his head sadly. Not even he could convince Sophia that her father doted on her. If he kissed her, he did it woodenly, awkwardly. Yes, he'd paid for her education (that she'd squandered), and bought her cars (that she'd written off), and flats (that she'd abandoned for parties in Ibiza) and until that party he'd continued to pay several thousand pounds a month into her bank account. But she couldn't remember him once telling her that he loved her, or that he was proud of her.

'He's a different generation, that's all,' said Hugo, kindly. 'Your dad's a bit Old School. He's not into all that touchy-feely stuff, is he? Don't take it personally.'

Sophia nodded but she knew Hugo was wrong. With her dad, it *was* personal. He just didn't like her. He'd wanted a boy. She knew that. She'd been a disappointment to him from the moment she was born. A long-forgotten memory popped into her mind suddenly and replayed in vivid Technicolor. Sophia, aged about seven, dressed in her ballet clothes, dancing around her dad's armchair, trying so hard to be the prettiest, most perfect ballerina in the world. 'Watch me, Daddy, please.' 'See what I've learned.' 'Watch me pirouette.' 'See my jeté.' Her father sitting there, with his newspaper open, studiously refusing to look at his daughter. Sophia getting upset, desperate. Spinning and turning and jumping, frantically trying to catch his eye. And then crash, she stumbles into the table, knocks over his Scotch, breaks the glass. Naughty Sophia. Bad Sophia.

Maybe if her parents had been able to have another child things would have been different. If her dad had got his beloved boy then he'd have been happy, less angry with Sophia, less critical of her mum. And then her mum wouldn't have been so distant and depressed and Sophia wouldn't have felt so lonely and ... but what was the point in wondering, what if?

'I don't want to talk about my family,' she told Hugo firmly. 'I just want to have a good time.'

Hugo nodded but they both knew it was a lie.

A familiar little niggle buzzed around her brain like an angry wasp. She shook her head to clear the feeling but it wouldn't leave her. Maybe she'd imagined it. It was such a long time ago now. Perhaps it was something she'd made up over the years, or imagined at a time when she was feeling particularly dissatisfied with her parents. A false memory.

She knew she'd raided her mum's handbag. That was a fact. Aged thirteen, fourteen maybe, desperate to steal the train fare to London after a particularly nasty argument with her dad. It was a sticky day. July or August. She was home for the school holidays. Bored and trapped and hot as hell. She was climbing the walls. Needed to escape. She hated that house; her prison. Hated her parents; her jailers.

In her mum's bag, deep in her oversized purse, wrapped in shopping receipts, tucked between the store cards and the books of stamps, she'd found them. The memory felt utterly real. She could feel the packet crackle between her fingertips as she turned them this way and that, trying to make sense of ... Tiny little pills. The days of the week clearly marked. Every one carefully taken, right up to that day. Not any pills. *The* Pill. She'd had sex education at school. She read *Cosmopolitan* by torchlight in her dorm. She wasn't a kid any more. But why did her mum have them in her purse? And why were they hidden so very thoroughly? She couldn't have any more children. It was no secret in the family. It was often hurled like an accusation by her father. Alice hadn't been able to give him the son he so craved. So why on earth would her mother need to be on the Pill?

Sophia had never mentioned what she'd found to her mum – or to anybody. She'd replaced them, exactly where she'd found them, and helped herself to the loose pound coins as planned. She'd run out of the house and all the way to the station. She'd escaped that horrible house and its silent secrets and she'd tried her hardest to forget that she'd ever seen those pills.

She was still trying to forget it now. Sophia downed another tequila slammer. Comfortably numb. That's what she strived for now. That was all the ambition she had left.

Chapter Six

Virginia Water, Surrey, 2012

Alice Brown lay still and silent as she listened to the floorboards creak on the landing outside her bedroom. A light went on somewhere in the house and crept its way under the door until she could clearly make out the ghostly shapes of her wardrobe and dressing table; the pink roses in the vase; the portrait of her mother as a young woman taunting her from the opposite wall; the silver-framed photograph of an angelic Sophia, wearing white broderie anglaise and a slight frown, aged around three. Everything in the room, and indeed in the house, was as familiar to Alice as her own reflection. This was her home. So why did she feel so on edge? She wasn't in danger: she knew there was no stranger in the house. Alice knew perfectly well that the midnight prowler was her own husband. Still, the thought wasn't entirely comforting.

The mattress beside her was empty but still warm. She heard a door close down the corridor and the light dimmed a little. Philip was in the study. She knew what he was doing. That's why she had been so careful. It was also the reason she hadn't taken her usual sleeping pills before bed.

The house was so eerily quiet that she heard the musical tone of the computer being switched on quite clearly. Alice ran through it all once more in her mind. Yes, she had deleted the history. Not all of it, that would look suspicious. Philip had no idea how computer literate Alice had become recently.

It was inevitable that he would catch her on the computer eventually. She had planned her reaction to being found, sitting at the mahogany desk in the office that had always been *his* territory, many times. Forearmed was forewarned. Still, she had jumped this afternoon when she had heard his footsteps at the top of the stairs. She should have been paying more attention rather than listening to Radio Four. She hadn't heard the car pull into the drive, or the front door slam. But she had had enough time to close the tab, and by the time he'd entered the room she was innocently perusing the Marks and Spencer website which she'd kept open and ready, just in case.

'What are you doing in here?' he'd asked suspiciously.

She had tried to keep her voice light.

'Well, I bumped into Margot at the post office and she told me that M&S have twenty per cent off today, but only if you shop online. So I thought I'd give it a whirl. It's remarkably easy actually. Even a luddite like me can do it!'

She'd forced a smile. Philip had nodded curtly, but his eyes remained distrusting.

'I hope you're not getting carried away, Alice,' he'd scolded. 'A sale is only a bargain if you're buying something you need.'

'I thought my mother could do with some more nightdresses for the hospital,' she'd replied, truthfully. 'And a warm dressing gown. Perhaps even some sensible slippers. When I went to her house to collect her things, everything she had was made of silk or lace. The only slippers I could find had kitten heels. And she doesn't appear to own a dressing gown, unless you count her collection of kimonos. We can't have her wafting around the wards in flimsy negligees, can we? It's distasteful.'

Philip nodded again, this time more agreeably. 'Quite right, quite right,' he'd muttered. 'Well, if you're sure you know what you're doing, and you're not going to bankrupt us, I'll have a shower before dinner. Dinner will be ready by eight, won't it, Alice? I'm famished.'

'Of course it will, Philip,' she'd replied dispassionately. 'Dinner is always ready by eight.'

She'd deleted her search history the minute he'd disappeared, paid quickly for her mother's clothes, and sent the computer to sleep. But now it was awake again. And so was Alice. She slipped silently out of bed towards the door, she gently turned the handle and tiptoed down the landing, knowing exactly which creaky floorboards to avoid. Being married to a man like Philip for thirty years taught a woman how to become invisible. She was almost at his shoulder before he realised she was there, his drawn face, shocked and guilty, illuminated by the neon blue of the screen. She could see that he had found only what she had wanted him to see. A Google search for 'cancer of the bones' was all he had uncovered.

'Oh Phil, you big softie. You're worried about my mother too,' she said, surprised at how easily she could play the charade.

Alice knew that Philip had absolutely no concern for her mother. He had merely been spying on his wife.

'Um, yes, yes, of course. I thought perhaps the consultant had missed something,' he replied, more flustered than she was used to seeing him. 'You read about these things, don't you? Miracle cures in the US. New treatment not yet available here ...' he trailed off, not even convincing himself.

'She's in the best hands,' replied Alice, realising she was allowed to be the lecturing adult for once. 'I don't think they have her prognosis wrong. It's natural to search for a miracle – I've done it too! But she's an old woman and the cancer is particularly aggressive.'

Philip nodded, grateful for the charade and the chance to compose himself. It didn't take him long to regain his usual superiority. Or to lose any pretence at being concerned about her mother.

'She's been writing to Sophia, you know,' he said, lifting his chin defiantly, crushing his wife with the news. 'Meddling as always. Tilly might be sick but she's still up to her old tricks. Why can't that woman stop playing God with other people's lives?'

Alice shivered. She hadn't known her mother had been writing to her daughter. No one had told her. As usual, her life did not feel like her own. Philip – and her mother – were back in control. It didn't surprise her that her mother had tried to contact Sophia, or that her husband had known and chosen to keep it from her, but it worried her a great deal.

'How do you know?' she asked, trying to sound less vulnerable than she felt. 'When ...?'

'I saw the letter,' sniffed Philip. 'Last week. She was knocked out on pain relief, remember? I don't know how you missed it. She'd left it half-written on the bedside table. "My darling Sophia, I love you so much. I need to see you. I know your parents don't understand you but I do. I have things I must tell you before I die ..." That sort of thing. You can imagine the emotional blackmail, the drama, the hyperbole!'

Alice nodded and swallowed the lump that had formed in her throat. Why hadn't she noticed the letter? She had been too busy staring at her mother's frail body and wondering how someone so powerful could suddenly appear so fragile. Any tiny sense of her own power dissolved into the gloom of the dark night.

'Do you think she'll visit?' she asked, trying to keep the tremor from her voice. 'Sophia?'

Philip tutted and shook his head. 'Of course,' he snapped, his temper rising. 'If Sophia gets a sniff of any inheritance, she'll run barefoot across London if she has to.'

Alice nodded and tried not to look pleased at the prospect of seeing her daughter again, even if she feared what Tilly might tell her.

'The last thing we need is Tilly and Sophia joining forces now,' Philip continued to rant.

'Mother wouldn't cause any trouble,' said Alice, quietly, trying to convince herself as much as Philip. 'She knows what's at stake.'

'Are you sure?' demanded Philip. 'She's dying. What does she have to lose?'

Alice swallowed hard. She wondered what any of them had to lose any more.

'Your mother is no angel, Alice,' Philip warned her coldly.

'I know that,' replied Alice.

Christ, if anyone knew that it was her! But she was still her mother and Alice loved her deeply.

'If Sophia turns up at the hospital, we must retain a united front, Alice,' warned Philip sternly. 'Do you understand? That girl burned her bridges with us. She will never learn to stand on her own two feet unless we teach her the hard way.'

Alice stared at the carpet, feeling the horrible familiar sensation of her heart being ripped in two.

'Do you understand?' he demanded more loudly.

She nodded, feeling suddenly overwhelmed.

'I forgot to take my tablets before bed,' she said quietly.

Philip sighed in exasperation and rolled his eyes heavenwards.

'No wonder you're wandering around the house like some ghostly apparition,' he said. 'Well, go and take them now. There's a good girl. Get some sleep. I'll see you in the morning.'

He patted her awkwardly on the arm and gave her a slight shove towards the door. Alice left her husband in his office, checking her browsing history. She felt suddenly naive for ever having thought she could escape her life, even for an hour or two, in the fantasy of the Internet. This was her reality. For better or worse.

She took her tablets like a 'good girl'. Not because Philip had told her to, but because she knew that within ten minutes she would be lost in a dreamless sleep. And then she wouldn't feel a thing.

'Take the pill and make yourself small,' Alice murmured to her reflection in the mirror.

Chapter Seven

The hours passed, the drinks flowed, the music pounded in Sophia's ears and buzzed around her brain. She told jokes, she flirted, she got up on a chair and strutted her funky stuff. At some point they stumbled out of the club and got a taxi elsewhere. Sophia wasn't even sure which club she was in now. They had all merged into one heady, noisy mass over the years. At one point Hugo hugged her and told her he was so glad she'd cheered up and was back to being the Sophia they all knew and loved. The prickle of self-hatred started to crawl under her skin but she drank more cocktails until the itching stopped and the numbness set in.

She was spinning around the dance floor now, head thrown back, breasts thrust forward, long legs strutting in high, high heels. Her hair had long since fallen out of its bun and was whipping around her head so that she only caught glimpses of what was going on around her. She felt dizzy, out of control, wild, free. And then she saw him. Nathan. *Her* Nathan. Sophia stopped dancing and froze on the spot.

It was him, wasn't it? There, in the pale blue shirt, leaning against the bar with the same floppy dark hair and lopsided grin. A few years older maybe, he'd filled out a little bit and he had faint laughter lines around his gorgeous brown eyes but it was definitely him. And if anything, he looked even more dangerously handsome than ever. Sophia's heart lurched and her stomach did an involuntary somersault. She grabbed Hugo's arm.

'Don't look now,' she shouted excitedly in his ear. 'But you'll never guess who's at the bar!'

'Who?' asked Hugo, immediately spinning towards the bar to see.

'No!' yelled Sophia, grabbing Hugo's face and turning him back towards her. 'Don't look. He'll see us watching him.'

'Who?' demanded Hugo, still trying to peek.

'No!' replied Sophia in exasperation. 'It's him. *Him.* He's here.'

Slowly Sophia watched the penny drop. Hugo's look of excited anticipation turned into one of grave concern.

'Are you sure?' he asked. 'It's definitely Nathan?'

Sophia swallowed hard, glanced once more over Hugo's shoulder and nodded firmly.

'It's definitely him,' she said. 'What do I do, Hugo? Do I look OK? Should I go over?'

'You look amazing,' replied Hugo, frowning. 'But maybe we should just leave? You know how you get around him. I thought he'd disappeared under a rock somewhere. I thought he was working in Singapore. Shit! I thought you were over him. It's been years!'

'I know!' said Sophia, barely able to breathe. 'I can't believe it. I haven't seen him in over three years. It's fate, Hugo. Don't you see? Of all the clubs in London, he's here.'

'Maybe we should leave,' Hugo suggested again.

'Don't be ridiculous!' Sophia yelled in his ear. 'This is my chance. We never really talked after we split up. I still don't understand. We're older now. Things have changed. Maybe ...'

'Maybe what?' asked Hugo, his eyes narrowing. 'Maybe he's grown a heart since he called off your engagement?'

Nathan Roberts was the one true love of Sophia's life. She'd gone out with him for two years in her mid-twenties. For those two years Sophia had felt safe and loved and worthwhile. Nathan had been a hotshot up-and-coming lawyer, with a glittering future in front of him, a lovely family and nice friends. When she'd been with Nathan, Sophia had become almost respectable herself. She'd furnished their flat in Ladbroke Grove beautifully, she'd shunned her old party-girl ways and happily stayed in with him on Friday nights, snuggled up on the sofa. She had learned to cook and she'd thrown dinner parties for Nathan's nice, respectable friends. She'd practically stopped doing drugs altogether, she'd cut down on her drinking and even started dressing more conservatively. Well, a bit. At weekends the couple had visited friends in the country or rented coastal cottages in Devon and Cornwall. Sophia had never been happier.

Her family had been surprised but delighted by her good catch. Even her dad had approved of Nathan. In fact, he had more than approved: he'd positively adored him. He'd even let Nathan call him Phil, rather than Mr Brown or Sir. Sophia remembered with a pang the pride she'd felt in finally doing something that made her father proud. Her dad had hung on Nathan's every word, he'd given him career advice and shared his extensive knowledge of wine. He'd bought him golf clubs for his birthday and a membership to his golf club for Christmas and the pair had often spent Sundays together on the green.

At Christmas, during the second year of their relationship, Nathan had proposed. Sophia couldn't have been more excited, not only for herself, but for the whole family. She had even felt happy for her dad. He'd never had the son he'd wanted so badly, but now she'd delivered the next best thing – a son-in-law he could love instead. A delighted Sophia had begun to try on wedding dresses, visit churches and reception venues and she'd even tasted cakes. She'd googled Ten Best Honeymoon venues and dreamt up baby names for boys and girls. She and her mother had shared a new closeness as they made wedding plans together while 'the boys' played golf and sampled fine wines. For three months, Sophia had known a contentment that she'd never experienced before.

And then, one rainy Thursday in March, completely out of the blue, Nathan had announced that he'd changed his mind and Sophia had watched her future crumble into dust. He said he realised he wasn't ready to settle down. He wasn't even sure he was the marrying kind. He still had places to go and people to see. He'd been offered a job in Singapore and he was going to take it. He didn't want Sophia to join him.

Sophia had been too stunned and devastated to ask the right questions. She'd been struck dumb by the shock and it wasn't until after Nathan had gone that the endless whys had started plaguing her mind. She'd handed back the stunning diamond ring, she'd had to move out of his (had it even been their?) beautiful flat and when she tried to call Nathan his phone was dead. He never replied to her endless emails. When she called his nice friends they were vague and unhelpful. When she called his family they wished her well but said a very firm goodbye.

For months Sophia did little but cry. She didn't eat. She couldn't sleep. She refused to go out. She didn't bother washing, or getting dressed, or even getting out of bed. But little by little, with the help of her friends – and Hugo in particular – she had managed to piece her life back together. It wasn't as neat or as lovely as it had been with Nathan. It was like a broken vase that had been glued back together in a slightly chaotic, higgledy-piggledy way. It had lost its value but it was still intact. Just. Sophia had survived losing Nathan. But she had never really got over it. Like the smashed-up vase, she was still damaged and the cracks were visible for everyone to see. And now he was here, propping up the bar, looking as heart-stoppingly gorgeous as he had done the day he'd caught the taxi to Heathrow and disappeared out of her life leaving her sobbing on the cold kitchen floor of their flat.

'I'm going to talk to him,' said Sophia, firmly.

'Be careful. Please,' was all Hugo could say.

Sophia's legs shook as she tried to walk confidently towards her ex-fiancé. Her mouth went suddenly very dry so that her lips snagged on her teeth as she smiled in his direction. Her heart pumped so hard in her chest that she was surprised her fellow clubbers couldn't hear it beating over the noise of the music. Nathan was talking to a guy on his right. He hadn't seen her yet. It wasn't until she was a couple of metres away from him that he turned his head and looked her straight in the eye. 'Be cool, be cool, be cool,' she told herself but just as she got within striking distance of the great love of her life, Sophia tripped over her high heels and stumbled towards the bar. She watched, in horror, as her Cosmopolitan jumped out of its glass and threw itself all over Nathan's pale blue shirt. And then she collapsed in a heap in his arms.

'Oh shit,' was all she could manage by way of an apology.

Nathan grinned – sexy, amused, confident. Sophia melted into his arms and stayed there for a moment, breathing in the delicious smell of the man she'd pined over for almost four years.

'Well, I guess I deserved that,' laughed Nathan, casually.

He propped Sophia back up onto her feet and mopped himself down with a napkin from the bar.

'You haven't changed, Soph,' he said, still grinning. 'You're looking as hot as ever – and as pissed!'

He winked at her and her legs almost buckled.

'I'm not pissed,' she replied, lamely. 'I tripped. That's all. I was a bit surprised to see you.'

'I'm not surprised to see you,' replied Nathan casually. 'You always were a permanent fixture on the club scene. I've been expecting to bump into you for ages. I thought you'd be the first person I ran into when I got back.'

'When did you get back?' asked Sophia, hoping she sounded interested rather than desperate.

Nathan shrugged. 'A few weeks ago,' he said nonchalantly. 'I'm just reacquainting myself with the old stomping ground.'

Why are you back? Where are you living? Did you think about calling me? Did you hope to bump into me? Have you missed me? Do you think about me? Do you still love me? All these questions ran through Sophia's mind but she kept her mouth clamped shut. She didn't trust herself to speak.

'So who's this hottie?' the guy standing next to Nathan enquired. 'Aren't you going to introduce us?'

'This is Sophia,' said Nathan. 'We went out with each other when we were younger. Many, many moons ago. Sophia, this is my friend Jez. We work together.'

Sophia managed a vague hand gesture of hello to Jez but her mind was reeling. Went out with each other? They were engaged to be married!

'It's a pleasure to meet such a beauty,' said Jez, who was no great beauty himself, and obviously a sleaze. He leered at Sophia's cleavage.

'She is very beautiful, isn't she?' Nathan continued, watching Sophia carefully with his head on one side. 'Beautiful but dangerous.'

'I'm not dangerous!' argued Sophia, trying to work out what Nathan meant by the comment. 'I never did anything to hurt you.'

Nathan frowned slightly.

'I didn't say you'd done anything to hurt me, Soph,' he replied. 'I wasn't talking about me. I was merely informing Jez, here, that you're a bit of a wild one. In case he was thinking about taking a punt himself.'

Nathan laughed and nudged his friend. Jez laughed back. Sophia's stomach was in knots. She didn't understand what was going on at all. Was Nathan trying to set her up with his dodgy mate? Was he so totally over her that he thought he could trade her like a piece of meat? Was he joking? What did he think of her now? Why did he say she was dangerous? What was going on? Her head spun with a thousand unanswered questions. For four years she had wanted to sit down with Nathan and ask him why he had left her so suddenly but now, as he stood in front of her, she didn't know what to say.

'Shall we dance?' asked Nathan suddenly. 'For old times' sake? You always were a good dancer. I warn you, though. I'm a bit rusty. I don't think I've hit the dance floor since my crazy days with you.'

Sophia nodded. He wanted to dance with her. That was a good sign, right? Nathan put his hands on her hips and pushed her towards the dance floor. The feel of his hands on her body brought back a rush of longing so powerful that Sophia had to close her eyes for a moment just to stop the world from spinning. The one thing she was sure of, when she looked back on her relationship with Nathan, was that they'd had great sex. She had never worried that he didn't find her attractive. And, as he slid his hands over her hips now, she was pretty sure he still felt that attraction. But what did he mean by 'crazy days'? Her two years with Nathan had been the most settled and stable of her life. Those had been her 'sane' years! Their life together had been tame – they'd only gone out once or twice a week.

As Nathan pushed her deep into the throng of pulsating bodies, Sophia's mind continued to whirr with confusion. All those questions buzzing around her head! But how could she ask them here? Now? With the music pumping and her head spinning with alcohol? For years she'd been dreaming about the moment when she'd finally see him again and have her chance to get answers. She'd rehearsed this moment so many times and yet, now, when he was right here, breathing the same air, in the same room, Sophia couldn't find the words. How long did she have? An hour? Maybe two? In a noisy, sweaty nightclub? It wasn't how she'd planned their reunion. How did she explain the depth of her pain? How did she describe the years of longing? How did she find the right words to make him love her again?

But Nathan's arms had crept round her waist now and he'd turned her to face him and his hips were swaying against her own to the music. He was smiling at her and his brown eyes were twinkling with mischief and desire. Sophia's mind calmed as the music became more frantic. Perhaps they didn't need words after all. Maybe the base animal attraction that had always been there between them would be enough to answer her questions. Nathan's hands slipped to the base of her spine, he pulled her trembling body towards his own until her breasts were pressed hard against his chest. She could feel his breath in her ear and it was all she could do not to faint with the heady mixture of pleasure, anticipation and fear. He began to kiss her neck. Not softly. But in hungry, greedy bites. And then they were kissing on the dance floor, oblivious to the seething mass of other clubbers surrounding them. Sophia lost herself in Nathan's embrace.

'God, I've missed you, Sexy Sophia,' he whispered into her ear. 'Let's get a cab.'

She nodded obediently as he grabbed her hand and started leading her towards the exit.

'I need my coat,' she remembered suddenly as they got to the door. 'Wait here. I'll be two minutes.'

Nathan nodded but Sophia felt nervous letting him back out of her sight for even a second. What if he disappeared? What if none of this was real? She searched the club frantically for Hugo and found him, finally, chatting to a cute Asian boy in a pink suit.

'Sorry to disturb you boys,' she said hurriedly. 'But Hugo, I need my coat.'

Hugo pursed his lips disapprovingly.

'Where are you going in such a hurry?' he demanded.

'With Nathan,' she grinned. 'I told you! It's not over. I'm not mad. He can't take his hands off me.'

'And we all know that sex and love are entirely the same thing, don't we, Soph?' he retorted, shaking his head.

'My coat please,' repeated Sophia, impatiently. 'Quickly, Hugo. Please!'

'You've been waiting for him for three and a half years and yet you're worried that he might not wait five minutes for you to find your coat?' enquired Hugo.

'Hugo!' snapped Sophia in exasperation. 'Just give me my bloody coat, will you?'

'OK,' said Hugo finally, standing up and bending over the back of his chair. He reappeared with the coat. 'But don't say I didn't warn you.'

She leant over and kissed her best friend on the cheek.

'I'll be fine, Hugo,' she reassured him. 'Nathan's a good bloke. He used to make me happy, remember? We're older now. He's back from Singapore. He's got his wanderlust out of his system.'

Hugo didn't smile back as he kissed her tenderly on the top of her head. 'Take care of yourself. I'll see you tomorrow.'

Sophia barged her way through the packed club. All she could think of was that Nathan was waiting for her by the door. She looked frantically around the exit but she couldn't see him. She checked the cloakroom and felt tears of frustration and panic prickle her eyes. Had he changed his mind and gone? Was that it? Their brief encounter? What if she didn't see him again for another four years? She paced frantically around the foyer but he didn't reappear. Finally, in despair, she ran up the stairs to the street. Nathan was leaning casually against a wall, smoking a cigarette. Sophia's panic subsided. Of course, he'd waited outside. It was no big deal.

'So you're still smoking,' she said and then immediately kicked herself for stating the bloody obvious.

He laughed. 'And you still drink and go clubbing until four in the morning. You'll never change, Soph. That's who you are.'

Sophia felt her cheeks burn with shame. How could Nathan think that about her? Surely he of all people knew that that was just a front? It wasn't who she really was. She'd escaped it once.

'That's not true,' she said, trying to keep the hurt from her voice. 'There's more to me than that.'

'Oi, Soph, don't get all touchy on me,' he laughed, pushing her playfully on the arm. 'It's not a criticism. There are worse things to be than a party animal. Come here.'

He stubbed his cigarette out on the pavement, pulled her towards him by the lapels of her coat and kissed her hard on the mouth.

'Right,' he said, finally coming up for air. 'Let's catch a cab. I believe you and I have unfinished business, young lady.'

Chapter Eight

Hackney, London, 2012

They went back to Sophia's place. She'd hoped Nathan might suggest going back to his, where there were no housemates to contend with, and no sulking Hugo to face in the morning, but when he hailed the taxi, all he asked was, 'What's your address, Soph?' And so it was decided.

'Hackney?' he laughed. 'What the hell are you doing in Hackney? I thought you had an umbilical cord that kept you permanently attached to the Portobello Road?'

'I cut it,' Sophia giggled. 'See, I have changed! All the cool kids headed east, so I went too.'

'I thought you were a leader, not a follower,' he teased her. 'And, anyway, you're thirty now. How much longer can you call yourself a kid?'

'Youth is a state of mind,' Sophia reminded him.

'Well, you certainly still look as youthful as ever,' he replied, slipping his hand under her coat.

He rubbed her breasts gently with his right hand, found her erect nipples through the thin fabric of her dress and squeezed just hard enough for Sophia to flinch. She let out an involuntary sigh of pleasure. Nathan had always known how to handle her body. It was as if he had read the user's manual.

'Bloody hell, you are so sexy,' he whispered into her ear, kissing her neck, pulling her head back, with his left hand lost in her thick hair, kissing her throat, her collarbone, her décolletage. He pushed her breast up with his right hand, so that her flesh oozed over the top of her dress and her bra and with his tongue he searched for her bare nipple. His left hand was on the inside of her thigh now. God, she wanted him. She groaned loudly. The cab driver turned up the radio. Years of longing built up in her as she touched his chest. And then her hands were reaching for the bulge in his jeans and, as he moaned with desire, she knew he was hers tonight.

Later, Sophia slept more soundly than she had done in years. She was woken, at some point, by Nathan, and they'd made love again lazily in a half dreamlike state before drifting back to sleep in each other's arms. When she finally woke up properly, and found Nathan's arms still wrapped around her naked body, she felt she might die of happiness. She snuggled into his perfect, soft flesh, kissed his chest and ran her fingers through his dark hair. This was it: the turning point.

'I love you,' she murmured dreamily.

'Don't be daft, Soph,' he muttered back sleepily. 'You don't love me. You're just on a nostalgia trip.'

But she did love him. She had never stopped loving him and now that she had him back in her arms there was no way she was going to let him go. She squeezed him tighter. Nathan pushed her gently off him, sat up and stretched like a lazy cat.

'What time is it?' he asked, fumbling for his watch on the cluttered bedside table.

'Elevenish, I think,' replied Sophia, who'd been awake for some time already, happily breathing in the smell of Nathan. 'It's still early.'

'It's after eleven?' Nathan shouted, sitting bolt upright. 'Shit! I've got to get home.'

'Why?' asked Sophia, confused.

It was Sunday. What could Nathan possibly have to rush home for?

'I thought we could go out for brunch somewhere?' she suggested. 'We've got so much to catch up on.'

Nathan looked at her as if she was the most stupid person he had ever seen in his life.

'Sophia,' he said slowly. 'Have you completely lost what's left of your mind?'

Sophia had no idea why he was talking to her in this way but the happy, tingling sensation was quickly turning back into a nasty sense of panic. She didn't trust herself to speak so she just shook her head lamely.

'You do know I'm married, don't you?' he asked, with his head on one side and his forehead wrinkling into a frown.

He had a strange expression on his face. His words took a long time to penetrate Sophia's brain. Married. Nathan was married. Her Nathan. Nathan who'd jilted her because he wasn't ready to commit. Nathan who'd had sex with her not once, but twice in the last six hours, was married. Her body began to shake uncontrollably. The dream was turning back into a nightmare. And this time it was worse than ever.

'I have a wedding ring on,' he said, lifting up his left hand. 'I was hardly keeping it from you.'

'I didn't notice,' she managed to whisper. 'I thought ...'

But Sophia couldn't say what she thought. The huge lump in her throat rose up into her mouth and came out as a strangled, agonised sob.

'Oh shit,' said Nathan, almost kindly. 'Oh, shit, shit, shit. I assumed you knew, Soph. I have a wife and a son. And another baby on the way. We moved back to the UK together a few weeks ago. We've just bought a house in Wimbledon. She's American. I met her in Singapore. We've been married for more than two years. I thought someone would have told you – we still have mutual friends – and, failing that, I thought you'd have noticed my ring. How on earth could you miss a wedding ring?'

'I wasn't looking for a ring. I assumed you were single,' Sophia whimpered. 'You stuck your tongue down my throat two minutes after bumping into me. It wasn't such a dumb assumption.'

She pulled her knees up to her naked chest as she tried to comprehend what she'd just been told. He got married over two years ago? But ...?

'You got married the year after we split up?' she asked in utter dismay and disbelief. 'After you'd said you weren't ready to settle down?'

Nathan sighed heavily and rubbed his handsome face with his hands.

'I wasn't ready to settle down with you,' he replied. 'No! That's not entirely true. You weren't ready to settle down with me. That was the problem. You were too wild for me. The thing is, you scared me, Sophia. I couldn't imagine you with kids, or a mortgage, or ironing shirts, or remembering family birthdays. You're just not the right type of girl to be anybody's wife or mother. Imagine you at an NCT meeting. Or on a PTA committee. Come on, you've got to see my point!'

He laughed, nervously, but Sophia didn't see anything funny in the joke. Why would she? *She* was the joke. She felt her heart freeze and then shatter into a million tiny pieces as he spoke.

'What's wrong with me?' she asked, shakily.

'There's nothing wrong with you, Soph,' said Nathan, shaking his head. 'Not really. You're stunning and you're horny, and you're funny and you're fun. But you're the type of girl men want to screw, not the type of girl men want to marry. I mean, look at this place ...'

He pointed at the chaos of her bedroom and wrinkled his nose in disgust.

'You're thirty now and you're still living like a student. It's shambolic. You're never going to grow up, are you? Seeing the way you're living now, it just shows me that I did the right thing to leave. We weren't right for each other. We weren't what each other needed.'

His words slammed her like a battering ram. She wouldn't have been living like this if they'd got married. This was his fault. He'd left her here in this bedlam.

'So why did you come home with me last night?' she asked, tearfully. 'If I'm such a disaster.'

Nathan shrugged. 'Can you blame me?' he asked. 'You're still the sexiest woman I've ever known. Sex was never a problem between us, you know that, Soph. That's never going to change – the physical attraction. I couldn't help myself. And don't tell me you didn't enjoy yourself too ...'

Sophia shook her head in disbelief. She lit a cigarette with shaking hands. He couldn't help himself? What a selfish bastard! What about helping her? Christ, what about helping his poor, pregnant wife?! Sophia wondered if, over in Wimbledon, another woman was crying over Nathan right now. What must she have thought when he didn't come home? Sophia was suddenly freezing cold. She shook violently and tried to push the image of Nathan's wife out of her head. But it was impossible.

'What's she like?' she asked, despite herself. 'Your wife?'

Nathan sighed.

'Helen? She's nice. She's a good wife and a brilliant mother. She's smart. She went to Harvard and her family are really well respected in Washington, where she comes from.'

'I bet she doesn't smoke,' said Sophia, trying to smile through her tears, although she had no idea what she was smiling at: the ridiculous sadness of the situation perhaps? She certainly wasn't smiling at Nathan. She wanted to stub her cigarette out right between his eyes.

Again, Nathan shook his head. 'Nope,' he replied. 'She doesn't smoke, she barely drinks, she's never done drugs in her life. And, as responsible and as reliable as she is, she never makes me laugh like you did. So, does that explain why I wanted to come back here last night? I do miss you, Sophia. And I do, *did*, love you very much. But it would never have worked between us. You must see that.'

'You didn't love me enough,' she said, blowing smoke rings into the air and watching them disintegrate like her dreams. 'You didn't love me enough to see past the front. I changed for you. That wasn't fake. I was genuinely happy when we were together. And I was good to you, Nathan. I learned to cook, I was nice to your friends, I made jam for your dad's birthday remember? I even ironed your fucking shirts so …?'

Nathan was getting dressed now. He paused, bare-chested, and met her eyes. She could see that he felt sorry for her. But she didn't want his pity.

'How long would it have lasted?' he asked. 'You were like a little girl playing house, Soph. It didn't feel real. And every time we did go out, you still got completely wasted. I was always having to save you from lecherous blokes you'd been flirting with and bundle you into taxis when you were half unconscious from downing shots. It was embarrassing!'

'I was twenty-five,' Sophia reminded him, defensively. 'I would have grown up if you'd given me a chance.'

Nathan shook his head as he picked up his crumpled shirt from the floor and pulled it on. The stain from Sophia's Cosmopolitan was clear to see. There were lipstick marks all over the collar too. She wondered how he would explain the stains to his wife.

'There's no point in going over old ground, Soph,' he said. 'We loved each other once. But we were very young. We grew up – well, *I* grew up at least – and we grew apart and it didn't work out. It's sad but it happens all the time.'

'Bullshit,' said Sophia. 'You were happy too. I know you were. It's driven me mad for years, wondering what made you pack your bags and run away like that. What happened, Nathan?'

He was putting on his socks now. Sophia could feel time running out. In a couple of minutes he'd be gone and he'd take his explanation with him.

'Nothing happened,' he muttered, tying his laces.

But she could see he was lying. He refused to meet her gaze.

'Nathan,' said Sophia, in a voice so cold and calm that it belied the stabbing pain in her heart. 'Tell me why you left, or I will track down your wife and tell her all about what you did last night.'

This was a lie. Sophia would never dream of telling Nathan's poor wife what had happened. It wasn't Helen's fault that her husband was a philandering bastard! And, anyway, Sophia hadn't even known Helen existed until ten minutes ago. Nathan's wife was his responsibility and his problem, not Sophia's. Why would Sophia want to shatter the poor woman's world? She didn't want anybody else to feel as wretched as she did right now. But threatening to tell her what happened was the only weapon Sophia had. And she needed the truth.

Nathan stood up, fully dressed now, and smiled at her fondly, as if she was a cute but silly toddler.

'No you won't,' he said, lightly. 'You're a fuck-up, Sophia, but you're also incredibly kind. That I do know about you.'

'Maybe I'm not so kind any more,' Sophia warned him. 'It's been almost four years. A lot of stuff has happened to me – like being dumped by my fiancé! Maybe I've changed.'

'Like I said before,' replied Nathan, calmly putting on his watch. 'You'll never change. You're no bitch. You won't tell Helen.'

Sophia felt her only weapon slip out of her hands. Her shoulders slumped. 'Please, Nathan. You've got on with your life but I haven't been able to move on because I still don't understand why. Why did you end things like that? When we were getting married? Why did you change your mind so suddenly?'

She knew she was being pathetic but what else could she do? Nathan sighed deeply and sat down beside her on the bed. He took her hand in his and squeezed it gently. His tenderness only made Sophia cry more.

'You really need to know the truth?' he asked.

Sophia nodded but didn't trust herself to try to speak. Her heart was in her mouth.

'People always made comments,' explained Nathan. 'Your friends, my friends, total strangers. They'd always talk about what a wild child you were and about the crazy things you'd done. But they did it fondly and they didn't mean to put me off. And then there were those stories in the paper about guys you'd been out with and what you'd done together. That wasn't easy to deal with. But I could handle that. Just about.'

'I stopped behaving like that,' Sophia managed to say weakly.

Nathan nodded but carried on.

'My parents thought you were great but they did have their reservations,' he admitted. 'Actually, Dad was on your side – he adored you – but Mum was more nervous. She was the one who made me imagine you at a PTA meeting. That niggled me but it wasn't what made me leave.'

'So what was it?' Sophia pleaded. 'Tell me so that I can understand.'

Nathan swallowed hard and glanced at her nervously.

'It was your dad,' he said finally.

'My dad?' asked Sophia, utterly confused. 'What did our relationship have to do with my dad? I know he's a difficult bastard but he always loved you. Christ, he doted on you, Nathan. He thought the sun shone out of your arse! Was it too much? Was it creepy the way he tried to father you? But you could have put up with him, surely? It was me you were marrying, not him.'

'No, no, Sophia, you've misunderstood. It wasn't your dad's personality that was the problem. Actually, I really liked Phil. He was good to me. And even you were getting on better with him at that point. Well, you were being civil to each other at least. It was OK. It was all OK until that day. Do you remember we went to your parents' place for lunch the weekend before we split up?' he asked.

Sophia wracked her brain and eventually found a vague memory of a slightly stilted but superficially pleasant Sunday lunch in Surrey. She nodded.

'When we'd finished lunch, you and your mum were looking at wedding magazines in the living room, do you remember?' he asked.

Sophia shook her head. She didn't like thinking about those days. It hurt too much.

'Your dad said he wanted to show me his new car in the garage, so I went out there with him, and I oohed and aahed at his shiny Mercedes and did the whole perfect son-in-law act,' he smiled at her fondly. 'I did care, Sophia. I did try.'

'And then what happened?' asked Sophia, nervously.

Where the hell was this heading? What could her father possibly have done to ruin her relationship?

'Oh God, do you really want to know?' asked Nathan.

'Yes!' snapped Sophia. 'Tell me, Nathan.'

'Your dad said he needed to have a word with me,' Nathan finally admitted. 'He said that he admired me greatly and that he thought I had great prospects.'

Sophia nodded. Yes, she knew this. That was why her family approved of Nathan so thoroughly.

'And then he told me that if I married you, I would be throwing it all away,' Nathan continued.

Sophia felt her mouth fall open in shock. At least Nathan had the heart to wince at her pain.

'He told me that you had behavioural problems, that you always had had. He said you'd been a really difficult child, always throwing tantrums and causing a scene. He said you were impossible to discipline and utterly selfish: that you thrived on being the centre of attention and that you would never support me properly because you'd be too self-obsessed.' Nathan squeezed her hand tighter. 'He said that you'd made their lives hell and that, if I married you, you would destroy me too. He said you'd never stop going off the rails. He told me to get away while I still had the chance. He advised me to find a nice respectable girl to marry instead.'

'But ...' Sophia said, trying to grasp what Nathan was saying, while feeling as if she'd been punched in the guts. 'But why would Dad say that about me? It's not true. None of it's true. Why would he do that to me? I know we're not close but he said he thought you were a really good catch. And why would he tell you to go, when he liked having you around so much? I thought I'd finally done something right. I gave him a son-in-law he loved.'

'I know,' said Nathan gravely. 'That's pretty much what he said himself, that he saw me as the closest thing to a son he'd ever had, and that because he cared about me so much, he had to tell me the truth about you. He said he would miss me immensely but was doing it for my benefit. He said you were beyond saving so I should save myself. And he also said that the Beaumont women had destroyed enough men in their time, and that he didn't want me to be the next victim.'

'I don't believe you,' shouted Sophia, snatching her hand from his and shuffling backwards on the bed, away from him, until her back hit the cold wall. 'He wouldn't do that to me! He's my dad. He loves me. And that's nonsense, about the Beaumont women. He wouldn't say that. What has my mum ever done to destroy my dad? He's the scary one! What did my granny do to destroy my grandpa? They loved each other for over fifty years!'

Nathan sighed heavily. 'I know it's hard to take in, Soph,' he said gently. 'And I don't know what he meant by that either. But it's the truth. I swear. That was exactly what he said. What your father told me put the fear of God into me. If your own dad didn't think you were going to be a good wife, how could I believe in you?'

'If it is true, you should have stuck up for me!' screamed Sophia. 'You knew me better than he did. You should have trusted me. You should have trusted your heart.'

'But that's the thing, babe,' replied Nathan, standing up. 'I obviously had doubts, didn't I? Otherwise I'd have fought for you.'

'And I'm not worth fighting for?' asked Sophia, looking up at him through damp eyes. 'I'm so worthless that my own dad warns off my future husband who walks out on me the minute things get tough?'

Nathan leant forward and put his hand on the top of her head, like a priest blessing a wayward member of his congregation. And then he ruffled her hair affectionately. The gesture only made her feel worse.

'I'd had a job offer from a bank in Singapore that week – a really attractive corporate law position,' he continued to explain. 'The salary was twice what I was earning in London. I was going to talk to you about it to see whether we should relocate, together, as a couple. But after your dad said that, I was scared. And I had a really easy way out. I panicked and ran. It felt like the right thing to do.'

'The ... the ... the right thing to do for you, maybe,' stuttered Sophia, shoving his hand roughly off her head. 'What about me? You just left me here, alone and reeling. And then you have the nerve to turn up years later, fuck me senseless all night and then in the morning tell me that you're married and then ... then ... you drop this bombshell.'

'Look, I'm sorry, Soph. I know what I've just told you must hurt and I realise that last night was a mistake. I should have made it clear I was married. I shouldn't have reopened old wounds.'

He paused halfway out of the door and glanced back at her with his soulful brown eyes.

'We will bump into each other again, Sophia,' he promised. 'London's not such a big place. This isn't goodbye.'

'What?' Sophia reeled up off her bed in anger. 'Are you suggesting we have casual sex next time we meet in a club in the middle of the night?' she asked, squaring up to him, wild-eyed.

'Well, it's never going to be sex without feelings with us, is it, Soph?' said Nathan, stroking her arm, trying to soothe her.

Sophia took a very deep breath and tried to stay calm. She slowly removed his hand from her arm and took half a step backwards. It was all she could do not to slap him in the face. But she wasn't going to lose it. She was going to prove to him that she could be a grown-up.

'Let me make this very clear. I am never going to be your mistress. I was supposed to be your wife!' she spat. 'I hope you and your wife are very happy together. Goodbye, Nathan.'

She gave him a gentle shove so that he stumbled over the threshold, and slammed the door firmly shut in his face. And then Sophia threw herself back onto her bed and pulled the duvet over her head. She didn't budge from that bed for over a week.

Chapter Nine

Dominic ordered a pizza from his favourite Italian place a few blocks away and decided to pop out to the store across the street to buy some beers while he waited for it to arrive. Guido had finished for the day and a new night porter, whom Dom didn't recognise, had taken over the desk. The man was much, much younger than Guido, maybe even a college student working nights to pay for his tuition. Dom made a mental note to find out what his situation was. If he was a student, Dom would tip him regularly and generously. He'd been that guy working nights himself, once upon a time. On his way back in, he introduced himself and asked the new guy for his post.

'Have you been away, sir?' asked the porter. The guy was polite and friendly. 'There is a lot of mail here. Mostly junk, by the looks of things, but there are a couple of official-looking envelopes here too. This one looks important. It's been signed for.' He squinted at the letter.

Dom was usually a friendly, easygoing sort. He'd talk to anyone, about any subject, anywhere in the world. And maybe tomorrow he would stop and chat to the new night porter. But tonight he was just desperate to get back to his apartment, close the door, drink his beers and wait for his pizza. Alone.

'I've been working overseas for a few weeks,' he told the porter. 'So I'd better get back up and deal with this. Thanks.'

It wasn't until much later that evening that Dominic started to half-heartedly sift through the mountain of post. Most was junk that went straight in the recycling pile. Then there were the usual stacks of bank statements, mobile phone bills, credit card bills, work correspondence and store card discount vouchers. Dom didn't know why they bothered sending this stuff to him.

Calgary only every shopped at Whole Foods and Dom was more of a diner or a takeout kind of guy. Oh, he knew how to cook all right. Over the years his mom had made sure both her sons were just as efficient in the kitchen as her daughters. But despite her best efforts to teach him how to cook fine Italian cuisine, her youngest son still chose convenience over effort every time.

Finally he came to the official-looking letter that the night porter had pointed out. He held it warily in his hand as if it was a letter bomb. He had that same knot in his stomach that he used to have as a student waiting to open his exam results. Dominic already knew where it was from. The envelope was stamped quite clearly with the name of Calgary's family solicitor. And he knew what was inside too: divorce papers. His wife had obviously not had any change of heart since he'd been away. Quite the opposite. The fact that she'd cleared out most of the furniture as soon as his back was turned showed that she'd found a new nest pretty damn quickly. Dom had googled the subject of 'Quickie Divorce NYC' extensively over the last three months. Calgary had been right; with no kids, no real estate, no joint assets, and no joint bank accounts between them, the divorce could be finalised in a matter of weeks. Calgary, being Calgary, hadn't even changed her name. It was as if the whole marriage had never happened.

Her parents must be delighted, Dom realised. No doubt Mr Woods had arranged for the divorce papers to be filed ASAP. Now all Dominic had to do was sign these papers and the marriage would be washed away like an irritating stain on a silk blouse.

Dominic threw the unopened letter across the room. He'd been Calgary Woods' puppet long enough. He wasn't going to jump now just because she wanted him to. Christ, how could he have been so blind? So damned stupid? Who would fall in love with a woman that cold and unfeeling and convince himself that she was just repressed? He'd thought he could save her from herself and that if he showed her enough love and kindness she would eventually melt. He'd written a whole stupid love story around the little glimpses of affection she'd shown him. What an idiot! And the worst bit was that here, sitting on his lonely leather chair in their empty apartment, he still missed her like mad.

Dom must have cried himself to sleep. He was awoken with a start when his phone vibrated in his pocket. He jumped, looked around in the dark, confused about where he was and why he was so cold. It took a few moments for him to realise that he was back in New York, alone in an empty apartment with all the lights off and that he'd left the doors to the roof terrace open, letting the icy wind blow right off the Hudson River and into his living room. He shivered, stretched his stiff legs, stood up, turned on the lights and closed the doors. He knew he should check his phone. He hadn't told his mom that he was back yet, or even his producer at the TV company. The only person he'd told was Dave and that was only so he could arrange to collect Blondie tomorrow. Dom wasn't quite sure he was ready to let the real world back in. Tentatively he checked his cell phone. What he saw made him smile. There, wearing Dave's backpack on her back, and a Yankees cap on her head, was a picture of Blondie.

All packed and ready to come home

Dominic read the message and laughed out loud. What a big kid Dave was! The guy was thirty-four years old and he was still dressing dogs up for kicks. Well, for kicks, and to cheer up his best buddy, Dom realised. He had good friends, a loving family and the world's best dog. OK, so he didn't have his wife any more. But Dom would be all right. He'd been all right just him and Blondie before Calgary came on the scene, and he'd be all right again now.

Had it been a waste of five long years? Five years of anguish and insecurity and now there was nothing to show for it. Dominic had been brought up to believe that marriage was for ever, but to Calgary it had obviously been a fleeting fad, like puffball skirts or high-heeled sneakers. Marriage had been something that suited her for a while but now she'd grown bored so she'd moved on to the next big thing. Whatever that might be. Dom found himself wondering, for a second, if she already had a new guy, but the image of Calgary naked in another man's arms was still too painful to think about.

Dom got his sleeping bag out of his backpack. It still smelled of the rainforest and was still damp, but with no duvet or sheets, he had no choice but to crawl back inside it for another night. The blinds weren't quite shut, and the glow of the New York street lights half-illuminated the empty bedroom. Dominic stared at the empty space on the mattress beside him. He could still imagine Calgary there now with her white-blonde hair framing her angelic face like a halo.

And then he remembered the way she flinched when he touched her under the covers, and how she would always turn away from him. He could still feel the silent determination in the set of her shoulders and the steely resolve in her rigid back. Dom wiped one last tear from his eye and the image of Calgary disappeared. And it hit him then: it had been lonelier to be here in this bed, staring at his wife's back, than it was now to be here alone. The thought was a revelation. It soothed Dominic's troubled mind and moments later he was sleeping soundly, under a New York sky, with eight million others.

The next morning he calmly signed the divorce papers.

Chapter Ten

Sophia woke up suddenly and squinted in the harsh light. Hugo's willowy form was silhouetted against the bay window.

'Right, Sleeping Beauty,' he said. 'Time to rise and shine.'

While she'd been in bed, October had turned into November, the trees in Victoria Park had lost their leaves and London had got a lot colder.

'Here, I bought you a latte from the deli. With an extra shot,' he said, thrusting the cardboard cup into her hand. 'And one of those Portuguese custard tarts you love.'

Sophia sat up and rubbed her eyes. She suddenly realised she was starving.

'Thanks,' she said, lamely, accepting the pastry.

'Nathan's not worth it,' he said. 'He never was. I know it hurts. I know he's made you feel wretched, but you've wasted enough of your life pining over him. It's time to start living again. By the way, this arrived this morning.'

He placed another of her grandmother's letters onto the bedside table. Sophia noticed that this time he hadn't opened it.

'I'll leave you to it,' said Hugo, glancing meaningfully at the letter. 'I'll come and check on you in a bit. Don't go back to sleep!'

'I won't,' promised Sophia. And she meant it.

With every sip of coffee and nibble of tart, Sophia felt a little stronger. She stared out of the window and watched a flock of pigeons circle the park in perfect formation. Why had she trapped herself in here? She knew Hugo was right. Nathan was not worth this. And neither was her father. It was time to stop making mistakes. And it was time to stop letting other people make her feel small. Sometimes hitting rock bottom was the only way to start climbing back up.

She opened the letter and read her grandmother's short note that came with the latest sheaf of memories and recollections.

Sophia felt the tug on her heartstrings. Could she trust her grandmother? Wouldn't Granny's loyalty always be towards Alice, her daughter, first? Finally, Sophia could admit to herself that she did want to see her grandmother, but there was no way she could face the pain of seeing her mother at the same time. Her mum had had two years to get in touch, to defy her father and to contact Sophia, but she'd done nothing.

But while she'd slept, something had shifted. Sophia felt as if a great weight of darkness had lifted. In its place a gentle sense of hope settled tentatively. She drained the last of her latte and began reading the latest instalment of her grandmother's memoirs.

Beaumont House, Wiltshire, the war years

Beaumont House was never the same after World War II. No bombs were dropped on our part of rural Wiltshire, although we saw the German planes flying low over our land on their way to attack Bristol and Bath. In many respects we were the lucky ones, but our lives and our landscapes were nonetheless changed for ever.

Papa had volunteered to fight very soon after war broke out in 1939. Mama had begged him not to go, telling him he was crazy to take such a risk when Cousin Aubrey had so kindly arranged a desk job for him at the Home Office. But Papa had insisted, saying that if the local boys from the village were willing to serve on the front line then the very least he could do was join them. And, besides, Cousin Aubrey had been an avid supporter of Hitler only twelve months prior to war breaking out, how could Papa take any offer from that man seriously?

No, he had made up his mind. He joined the RAF and was made Group Captain. I thought he looked frightfully handsome in his blue uniform and peaked hat. I was incredibly proud of my brave father as I waved him off to do his officer's training. He came home briefly for the Christmas of 1939, but before we could celebrate my tenth birthday, on the dawn of 1940, my darling Papa disappeared out of my life once again. I was only to see him twice in the next five years.

1940 was a dreadful year. Most of our male staff left to fight and many of them never came back. Tony, the gardener's son, my childhood friend, was the first to die. A few days later Papa's valet, Simon, died too. They were both not even twenty-five. I remember peeking around the corner into the kitchen and seeing a dozen of the staff huddled around a telegram at the oak table, crying their hearts out. That was when the reality hit me. I cried for Tony, and the valet too, both had been kind to me, but it was Papa I was most worried about.

As well as the men who had signed up or who had been called up, or who had already died, some of the younger female members of staff decided to join the Wrens or to become Land Girls. Mama declared they were insane to want to roll their sleeves up and get their hands dirty but I admired them greatly for seizing this opportunity to help the war effort and to do something more adventurous than be a scullery maid or a cook. Much to Mama's annoyance, it seemed there was not a soul left in Wiltshire to replace the lost staff. At the beginning of 1939 we had twelve live-in staff; by the end of 1940 we had just four.

Our housekeeper, Mrs Ashton, and butler, Mr Wise, tried very hard to keep the vast old place from falling apart at the seams but, like a lot of our boys on the frontline, they were fighting a losing battle. The manicured lawns and rose gardens began to resemble jungles, buckets were placed on landings to catch drips from the leaking roof, the polished wooden floors became dusty and dull and the windows rattled in the wind. We stopped using the entire west wing. Most of the house was simply shut up and left to become damp and cobwebbed. I became scared of my own home.

But worst of all, my beloved nanny had suddenly been asked to leave the house. I wasn't even allowed to say goodbye. I simply came home from school one weekend to find her gone. I begged Mama to tell me why she'd had to leave but she remained very tight-lipped about the subject and merely told me that Nanny Miller was a 'dreadful woman with no moral fibre at all' and then she stormed off towards the stables muttering what sounded like, 'Floozy', followed by, 'Trollop' and then 'Jezebel' under her breath. I asked Mrs Ashton, who was normally very sweet to me, where Nanny had gone but she told me quite sternly that she wasn't at liberty to say. Mama said I was too old for a nanny now anyway and that I would just have to entertain myself from now on. She ordered me to forget that Nanny Miller had ever existed but there was no way I could do that. I missed her so dreadfully that I cried myself to sleep for weeks and I vowed that one day I would find her again. I began to loathe coming home to the increasingly cold and dilapidated house at weekends. I'd rather have been at school than at Beaumont House without Nanny or Papa to look after me.

In the autumn of 1940 my prep school in Gloucestershire was commandeered by the government for the Air Ministry and all the boarders were relocated. Any girl whose parents lived nearby had to move back home and become a daygirl instead. And so, just as Beaumont House began to fall apart, I found myself back there permanently. Those were a lonely few months. The house, which had once been so full of life, felt deathly quiet now, as if it barely had a pulse. I even began to miss Mama's wild parties.

Mama did not cope well with the beginning of the war either. As you can imagine, she wasn't much good with austerity measures, and the mantras of the day – Keep Calm and Carry On, Make Do and Mend, Loose Lips Might Sink Ships – were completely at odds with her own philosophy on life. Mama loved nothing more than causing a scene, buying new clothes and gossiping. She must have felt that the war had been sent to personally persecute her. Her friends no longer had time for weekend house parties and, besides, where was one to find a decent fillet of Scotch beef? Or Italian ice cream? Or French wine now that rationing had started? While the rest of the nation was at war with Germany, Mama seemed to be at war with the war itself. For a few months she appeared to be defeated. Her cashmere jumpers became a little bobbled, her stockings sometimes had runs in them, she ran out of her favourite red lipstick and had to wear a coral colour instead and her afternoon cocktails were replaced by gin and tonics (without lemon, oh, the agony!).

But Mama, for all her faults, was a fighter, and it didn't take her long to rise to the new challenges before her. In 1941 she managed to find a new estate manager called Foster who was young and strong (if a little menacing). Despite being six feet four and a frightfully good shot, Foster had somehow managed to escape the call-up – even though he looked as if he could easily murder an entire German battalion with his bare hands. Officially, Mama employed him to look after the grounds, the gardens, the livestock and the wildlife. Unofficially, we all knew that he was at Beaumont House to save our bacon.

Foster placed metal traps all over the woods and warned me, in a gruff, unfriendly voice, to stay away 'or else!'. He wore dead rabbits draped around his neck like a scarf and he would slam bloody pheasant carcasses onto the kitchen table, much to Cook's irritation. I didn't much care for Foster but I was very fond of his Jack Russell terrier, Badger.

Under Foster's watchful eye, Mama's friends began to return to the house at weekends for shooting parties. None of them hunted for foxes any more though. They shot anything that couldn't outrun them – rabbits, deer, pheasants, grouse, hares – and by doing so they were inadvertently working for Mama and Foster, even though none of them had knowingly done a day's work in their lives. On Saturday evenings they'd eat like pigs, drink like lords (because that's what most of them were) and party like there was no tomorrow. On Sunday afternoon the guests would leave, hung-over and bloated, and they could never eat everything they'd caught – any leftovers were kept in the enormous cold store behind the staff kitchens. Therefore, despite rationing, there was no shortage of fresh meat at Beaumont House from then on.

Mama's parties were just part of the plan though. Her friends could never kill as many wild beasts in one weekend as Foster could in a week. Soon, the walk-in cold store resembled a morgue. I remember peering in there and shuddering at the sight of row upon row of skinned deer. There were birds and rabbits in there too but what really surprised me was the sight of cows and pigs. We only had a smallholding at Beaumont House, with two dairy cows for milking, a dozen chickens for eggs and a couple of goats which Papa had bought, I think, just for my amusement. Where had these animals come from?

I asked Mrs Ashton about the livestock in the cold store and she turned a funny shade of purple. Later I heard her shouting at Foster in the kitchen.

'Why should the entire nation be on rations when the likes of you are making a fortune from the black market? If you do this one more time I shall have no choice but to tell Her Ladyship, who I have no doubt will inform the police!'

I heard Foster cackle with laughter.

'Whose bloody idea do you think it was, woman?' he guffawed. 'If you think I'm a wrong 'un you want to take a closer look at that mistress of yours. She's missed her calling in life, that one. She's the best bleeding crook and con artist I've ever met. She's a right firecracker when she gets started too, let me tell you.'

'I don't believe you,' Mrs Ashton shrieked in a strangled voice.

'What an absurd accusation! You are the most vile man I have ever had the displeasure to know.'

I thought it very loyal of Mrs Ashton to stick up for Mama in that way but I remember thinking, even at the tender age of eleven, that Foster was probably telling the truth. Mama could not function without money and nice things. She would have done anything to maintain her lifestyle. The war she was fighting was not the same one that Papa, and the rest of our troops, were fighting overseas.

On Thursdays Foster would load up his green Bedford van with fresh meat and game and he would disappear off, who knows where, until the following day. I had become quite an adept spy by now. Unfortunately, my tender years meant that I could not help the war effort but had to make do with spying on my mother, her friends and what was left of the staff. One Friday, shortly after I watched Foster's van chug back up the long drive to the house, I decided I needed to find out more about his weekly trips away from Beaumont House.

I ran out of the house and hid behind a bush near his parked van. I watched him take a fat wedge of pound notes out of the glove compartment. He counted the money twice, creamed off about a quarter and then folded the remainder up neatly and put it in his jacket pocket. He hid the smaller bundle in his underwear. Next, I followed him to the stables. Badger was at his ankles, as always. He went round the back of the block, leant against the wall and lit a cigarette. He was obviously waiting for someone. I climbed a tree that overlooked the yard and waited too, never taking my eyes off Foster. He was an unmistakably handsome fellow, with broad shoulders and strong thighs. He had the same square jaw and dark, swarthy good looks as the American actors who played cowboys in the movies I'd seen at the cinema in Chippenham. But there was something missing: Foster had not one ounce of kindness in his face. The man was dead behind the eyes. Just watching him made me shudder. He paced like an impatient, caged tiger. He looked around in an edgy, intolerant manner, threw his cigarette butt angrily into the horse's trough and immediately lit another one.

Eventually my mother appeared on horseback with her red lipstick back in place, her jodhpurs as white as ever and what looked like a brand new pair of riding boots. Where did she find the money for those in these times of austerity? The minute she arrived, the angry tiger turned into a docile little pussy cat. She smiled provocatively down at him and asked, 'So? How did we do this week?'

'Pretty good,' replied Foster, taking the notes out of his jacket pocket and handing them to my mother like an obedient child. 'I've got a new hotel in Bath on board. The chef said he hadn't been able to get fresh beef in weeks. Paid me double what the bloke in Bristol offered too.'

'Clever boy,' simpered Mama, slipping the notes into the breast pocket of her riding jacket. 'Be a love and pass me a cigarette, will you?'

Foster lit a cigarette from his own packet and passed it to Mama obediently. The man was practically a giant but with Mama on her favourite stallion, Ebony, he had to crick his neck just to see her beautiful face. I noticed that he couldn't take his eyes off her as she slowly smoked her cigarette and stared off into the distance, showing her best side.

'I need to stable Ebony,' Mama announced finally. 'Will you help me, Foster? It's such terribly hard work looking after the horses now the groom and the stable hand have gone. It really is most inconvenient. I could do with a strong pair of hands right now.'

Most inconvenient, indeed, I remember thinking, particularly for the groom and the stable hand who were, at that moment, fighting for our freedom in Crete and El Alamein respectively. Besides, Mama had never needed any help looking after her horses. She loved horses so much more than she did human beings.

They disappeared round the side of the stable block, Foster on foot, Mama still looking down on him from a great height, Badger trotting behind. I had to shimmy down the tree quickly to keep up. I peered round the corner of the block just in time to see Mama, Foster and Ebony disappear into one of the stalls. Badger waited patiently outside. I crept slowly and silently past the other stalls, ignoring the horses who leant out and snorted at me, wondering where their sugar cubes were today, until finally I was outside Ebony's stable. I stroked Badger gently, hoping he wouldn't bark and give the game away. I could hear Mama's sing-song, mocking voice coming from inside the stall.

'Were you trying to hide something from me, Foster?' she was saying. 'That wasn't such a clever place to put it now, was it? I was bound to find it there.'

With my heart in my mouth, I peeked through the open stable door. Foster stood with his back to the wall and a half-terrified, half-excited look on his face. His trousers were at his ankles. Mama had dismounted Ebony and was standing about a foot away from Foster, with the stolen notes that had been hidden in his underpants in one hand and her riding whip in the other. I wondered how on earth she'd known to look there for the money.

'You have been a very, very, bad boy, Foster,' she was scolding him. 'And bad boys need to be punished.'

'Yes, Your Ladyship,' murmured Foster obediently. 'I'm so sorry, Your Ladyship.'

'Turn round!' shouted Mama so firmly that it made me jump.

I watched just long enough to see Mama horsewhip the young gamekeeper several times. My mother had made him drop his underpants and it looked awfully painful, so I couldn't understand why, every time she whipped him, he was begging her for more punishment. After a few moments I couldn't bear to look any more. It seemed so degrading for a woman to do that to a huge big hulk of a grown man. Still, he had stolen from her, I supposed. Badger obviously agreed with me though, because when I turned heel and ran back towards the house he followed me.

Mama and Foster's lucrative business arrangement carried on for several months, as did their clandestine meetings in the stable block. Until, that is, one Friday when the police arrived at Beaumont House to inform my mother that her estate manager had been arrested for poaching, stealing, selling illegal meat on the black market and also for dodging his conscription to the army. Mama played the part of the horrified employer rather well, I thought, and the police didn't stay long. She didn't appear to take Foster's departure very badly but she did get terribly depressed about the sudden lack of income. Within weeks Mama's stockings had begun to ladder again and she was running low on gin. It was time for her to come up with a new plan. We never saw Foster again – and I certainly wasn't sorry to see the back of him – but I'm delighted to say that Badger, the Jack Russell, stayed with me for another ten years.

Hugo knocked quietly on the door and popped his head into Sophia's room.

'You OK?' he asked, hopefully.

Sophia smiled and nodded.

'Is there any hot water left?' she asked Hugo. 'I need a shower. I can't go and see my grandmother looking like this, can I?'

Chapter Eleven

Tokyo, Japan, 2012

Aiko Watanabe awoke in a cold sweat and for a moment she had absolutely no idea where she was. She wasn't at home in her own bed, she knew that. She fumbled for the bedside light switch and winced as the unfamiliar room was suddenly, painfully, illuminated. Slowly, sense seeped back into her sleep-deprived mind. Of course, she was in Tokyo for a business conference, staying at the Imperial Hotel, just as she had always done ever since the new building was opened in 1968. She had once frequented the old Imperial Hotel too. It had been demolished decades ago to make way for this new, high-rise vision of modernity, but she had been there, in another life and another world. Tomorrow she had to make a speech to over two thousand of Japan's brightest and keenest young business minds. The clock told her it was just after four in the morning. She needed to be asleep. What was wrong with her these days?

Aiko did not normally suffer from anxiety or insomnia. Well, not for many, many years at least. Her mind was old, it had weathered many storms, but it was strong. Old age had given Aiko aching bones and grey hairs but, until now, it had also brought her wisdom and peace. Aiko was often held up as the matriarch of modern Japanese business. She had been born into a different world, a different time. The Japan of her childhood was full of mysticism, ritual and rules that no longer existed. But unlike many of her contemporaries, who resisted and resented the great tides of change, Aiko had embraced the new world and its ways. As the decades passed and the twentieth century turned into the twenty-first, she had become its poster girl. Often she was listed in the newspapers' top ten Most Influential Women in Japan. Which was silly really, because she had left

Japan a long, long time ago and now only returned for business trips. Aiko felt more American these days than she did Japanese but, still, it was nice to feel admired and appreciated by her motherland.

As she grew older, the press treated her with increasing wonder and awe. They marvelled at her ability to keep up with the latest technology, political ideas and social trends. This made Aiko laugh. Why would she, of all people, cling on to the past? The old world had been brutally cruel to her. As it crumbled to rubble, the old Japan had torn down Aiko's world and taken all those she loved with it. She had found herself standing alone in the ruins. As the new Japan had emerged, blinking uncertainly into the light, she had been among the first to nurture and embrace it. Why wouldn't she have done so when the old world had stripped her of her family, her dignity and almost her life?

No, Aiko had never lived in the past. It was such a waste of time. It wasn't as if she could go back and change one, darned thing (as her husband would have put it had he still been alive). Over the years, she had kept her head high. She had been strong. The ghosts she had known had long since been banished to the very back of her mind and they'd flickered from view. So why was she suddenly having these vivid, disturbing dreams?

These dreams were not exactly nightmares, they were more akin to strange, dismembered flashbacks. They were stories she had been told by her father, her grandmother and great-grandmother when she was a very young girl. Stories she hadn't thought about in years. But the dreams were startlingly real. And they all ended the same way: with Aiko drowning. Unlike most dreams, these visions didn't fade and disappear in the daylight. She had no difficulty in remembering every last detail. The problem she had was shifting them out of her mind and getting on with her real life. Her great-grandmother would have called them premonitions. She would have insisted they were a warning of something significant that was about to happen. But then her great-grandmother, Haruki, was a very superstitious lady. Aiko was not. She must wipe them from her mind. But as she drifted off back to sleep, a few precious words escaped her mouth.

'Manami ...' she murmured. 'Manami ... My mother, Manami.'

'I saw you yesterday, Manami,' said Haruki from her perch in the corner.

A baby sat on the old lady's lap, gurgling happily, with her chubby fingers clamped around Haruki's faded linen robe. The robe had once had a willow pattern printed on it in bright indigo but the pattern had long since faded to a dull grey-blue. The bond between the flawless infant and the crumpled old woman was as clear as it was incongruous. A shaft of early morning sun broke through the clouds and cast a yellow light through the screen, bathing the small room in molten gold. The old woman's voice was stern and it stopped Manami in her tracks.

'You saw me doing what, Granny?' asked Manami, pausing at the door, one bare foot on the wooden floor, the other already on the dirt path outside.

She was intrigued. What had she done to displease her grandmother this time? Manami knew she was Haruki's favourite grandchild but with favouritism came criticism. She hesitated and waited for her grandmother's words. She could smell the sea. She could feel the spray on her cheek as it was blown up onto the cliff by the wind. She was already late but she had no desire to leave. Here, in this tiny little wooden house that clung to the cliff edge like a limpet, were two of her three favourite people in the whole world: her grandmother Haruki, and her baby daughter Aiko. Her other favourite person, her husband Yoshiro, was already out on the ocean in his boat.

Manami returned her attention to her grandmother. Haruki's face was as worn and wrinkled as an ancient treasure map, but her eyes still twinkled like stars reflected in the ocean. Manami was unsure how old her grandmother was. Haruki claimed not to remember (although she did recall that she was Year of the Rat). One thing was certain though, there was more life and more wisdom in those eyes than in any other living creature Manami had ever encountered. She thought that Haruki must be very ancient indeed to have learned so much without ever having left this tiny village.

'Aiko and I went for a walk yesterday. We were watching you from the cliffs. You are staying under the water too long,

Manami. You are still only young. You have more to learn than you realise,' Haruki warned.

Manami grinned at her grandmother affectionately. 'I am quite safe, Grandmother,' she insisted. 'I am your granddaughter and my mother's daughter. I was taught by the very best. I've been diving since I was eight. It is in my blood. If I cannot dive, then show me an Ama who can!'

'Oh, you can dive, my Manami-chan,' replied Haruki, her voice softening. 'You can dive better than any of my other granddaughters. You were born for the sea – our very own mermaid. You are better than your mother was at your age. Perhaps even better than I was.' Her eyes twinkled again with mischief at her own lack of modesty. 'But you are not cautious, you are not patient and you are not wise.'

'Not wise?' asked Manami, indignantly, taking a half-step back into the tiny house.

Manami prided herself on being smart. She knew she was clever. Just as she knew she was beautiful and strong.

'Who, of the young girls, has made the most money this season, Grandmother?' demanded Manami. 'Who has collected the most abalone, the most oysters, the most mother-of-pearl? Who found three pearls last season? Which young Ama keeps Nishimoto-san wealthy and fat? And ...' Manami swung her long black hair over her shoulder defiantly, 'which Ama caught the most handsome husband on the Shima peninsula?'

Haruki threw her head back and laughed. Little Aiko joined in with delighted squeals as if she understood what the women were saying and began to bounce on her great-grandmother's lap in excitement.

'I did not say you are not talented. I do not deny that you make Mr Nishimoto very wealthy and, yes, even fatter every year. Or that you have snared yourself the most handsome husband in the prefecture. I have told Yoshiro many times that if I were a younger woman I would have wanted him for myself!' Haruki grinned. 'I said, Manami-chan, that you are not cautious, you are not patient and you are not wise.'

The old lady held the chubby baby up like a prize, so that Aiko danced on tiptoes on her great-grandmother's knees.

'I do not think you realise what you are risking.' She nodded towards Aiko and then kissed the baby's black hair tenderly.

'You have so many blessings already but, my Manami-chan, you always want more. How many times do I have to tell you, child, patience is a life-long blessing. Before you ride a horse, you must ride an ox.'

'I am bored of riding oxen!' announced Manami. 'Besides, were you patient when you were young? I have heard your stories, Grandmother.' Her grandmother ignored her and continued.

'What are you now? You were born in the Year of the Rooster so you are how old? Not quite eighteen, Manami-chan. And in such a rush to live your life. You had to marry young, you defied your father, you brought shame on the family, you had a baby while still only a baby yourself and now you dive to depths far too deep for a girl your age. Your heart might be big enough to love but your lungs are not ready to dive to the bottom of the ocean. You will not be a fully trained Ama for many years yet. You still have so much to learn. Do not try to dive to the depths your mother can reach, Manami, or even your older sisters. What is the rush to get to the bottom of the ocean? What do you think you are going to find down there?'

'Exactly the same thing that you found when you defied your own mother and father and Mr Nishimoto Senior!' answered Manami defiantly.

Her grandmother frowned and the lines in her face deepened.

'I do not know what you are talking about,' she spat, angrily. But her eyes gave her away.

Manami sighed. She knew Haruki was lying. She knew her grandmother's secrets, just as her grandmother knew her own. But Manami also knew better than to push Haruki when her eyes were filled with rage. She counted to ten in her head, as her father had taught her to do when the red mist descended, and she tried to swallow the words that had formed in her mouth. She did not want to argue with her grandmother. It was never wise to disagree with an elder, particularly one as revered, respected and opinionated as Haruki. Besides, Haruki had a temper as wild as Manami's own. Manami might be almost eighteen now, and a wife and mother, but she knew from experience that she was not too old to receive a slap from Grandmother.

Manami adored her grandmother, but she had no desire to follow in her footsteps. She did not want to be an Ama diver all her life. Nor did she want to find herself still here, in this village, as an old woman. She didn't have the time to patiently learn every breathing technique. The best Ama were in their thirties and forties. There was no way Manami was waiting that long. Like all Ama, Haruki had started diving in the shallows as a girl. She had continued diving until she was a grandmother. Manami's mother had done the same and was down there now, waiting on the beach for her daughters. The Ama women of Ise Shima had been diving for a thousand years.

It was not that Manami did not love to dive. She never felt as free as she did when she disappeared under the waves. When she dived into the icy water her heavy mind became as weightless and unburdened as her body. It was the only place she felt at peace. There, and in Yoshiro's arms. She had dived right up until the day before Aiko was born – it was what all pregnant Ama did. A whale is more graceful in water than stranded on the beach, after all! But Manami did not want to dive to make somebody else rich. Yes, Ama made good money for women. And, during the summer diving season, they enjoyed a freedom from domestic drudgery that very few other women experienced. But it was only their boss, Mr Nishimoto, who got rich.

Manami wanted to be mistress of her own destiny and her own fortune. Over Manami's dead body would Aiko grow up to become an Ama. The divers of Ise Shima had more freedom than most, Manami was well aware of that. They had the comradeship of the Ama hut, they earned their own money and they had time away from washing, cleaning, cooking and child-rearing. Manami had heard stories of Ama who enjoyed their freedom so much that they had run away from their husbands and children altogether. But Manami did not want to be free of her husband and daughter. What Manami wanted for Aiko was the freedom to love and to live differently. As she gazed lovingly at her beautiful baby daughter her heart burned with a longing for a better life, a bigger life, away from this tiny village.

Nishimoto-san boasted about riding in trains and automobiles. He told tales of geisha girls, theatres, factories and aeroplanes. He'd visited Kyoto, Kobe, Osaka and even Tokyo. Manami had only ever visited the next town – a ramshackle port, splattered with misshapen, thatched houses. It was an ugly town that stank of poverty and rotten fish. Manami wanted to go to glamorous places, she wanted to dress in silk kimonos and travel in automobiles. She wanted a house for herself, Yoshiro and Aiko. She liked her parents-in-law, and she respected them greatly, but she did not want to live in their house for ever – whatever tradition dictated. For six months of the year, when the ocean was too cold to dive, Manami was little more than a housemaid for her mother-in-law. Her sisters and friends thought she was lucky because, unlike their own mothers-in-law, Yoshiro's mother was a soft, warm sort of woman, who rarely hit Manami or scolded her unduly. But what did her friends or sisters know? Just because her life could have been worse, did not mean it shouldn't be better. Manami had dreams that were bigger than their world, dreams that her grandmother could never understand, dreams that could become a reality for Aiko if ...

'I see the fire,' said Granny, nodding as if she could read Manami's mind. 'You have always had too much fire, Manami. You'd better go to work now. Perhaps the ocean can put out those dangerous flames! But heed my warning, child. Do not stay under too long. Do not go too far down. Here ...'

Haruki stood up, slowly, resting Aiko on her hip, and took what looked like a dusty old rag from the top of the cabinet and shuffled with a slight limp towards her granddaughter.

'This was mine. It will bring you luck, Manami-san. And wisdom, I hope.'

Manami unwrapped the dusty rag and saw that it had been protecting an old *tegane* – the tool that the Ama divers used to prise stubborn abalone and oysters from the rocks.

'I never had a better *tegane* than this one,' explained Haruki, patting Manami on the arm affectionately. 'May it bring you good fortune, child.'

'Thank you, Grandmother,' replied Manami, gratefully, bowing to her elder. 'I'm honoured that you think I am worthy.'

'Here,' said Haruki, holding up Aiko to her mother. 'Kiss your daughter goodbye and get to work before Nishimoto-san arrives. Your mother will be looking for you.'

Manami planted a wet kiss on her baby's damp lips, tapped her tiny upturned nose gently with her finger and said, 'I will see you later. Look after each other!'

'We will be quite safe,' called Haruki from the door as Manami rushed down the cliff-top path towards the beach. 'It is you who needs to be looked after!'

The old woman's words were whipped up by the wind and seemed to echo around Manami's ears as she descended the steep track towards the sea. And then they were blown away for ever.

Haruki stood at the door and watched her granddaughter disappear down the cliff path. She clutched the baby to her face and kissed Aiko's porcelain-smooth cheek.

'Following happiness is like chasing the wind, or clutching the shadow,' she whispered into the infant's ear. 'Do not clutch shadows like your mother has done, Aiko.'

And then the image faded and the old woman and the young diver and the baby fragmented into nothing.

'Mother!' screamed Aiko, waking herself once again as she did so.

She was damp with sweat and the bedclothes were twisted around her arms and legs. She did not believe in ghosts.

She sighed deeply. This was ridiculous. It was beginning to get light outside. It was time to give up on sleep. She switched on the light and the television and sent a message to room service ordering strong coffee and breakfast. She watched the international news channel while flicking through her emails and she used every ounce of strength she could muster to keep herself firmly grounded in the modern world. She would not let the ghosts of the past haunt her. Not now. Not ever. She had closed the door on them many decades ago. There was no way Aiko was inviting them back in now.

Part Two

The Bends

From birth, man carries the weight of gravity on his shoulders. He is bolted to earth. But man has only to sink beneath the surface and he is free.

Jacques Cousteau

Chapter Twelve

'Where is it?' asked Sophia, resting her nose against the cold, damp window until it clouded up with her hot breath.

She stared out at the street below. Still no taxi. It was murky and damp outside. The last of the leaves had fallen off the trees in the fierce wind, the park was empty of children playing, or dogs walking, or couples kissing, and the whole world seemed to have taken on a deathly greyness.

'I only ordered it five minutes ago,' Hugo reminded her. 'Don't be so jittery! Your grandmother will be ecstatic to finally see you. Think of all the wonderful time you spent together when you were younger.'

It was true: Sophia had loved the weekends she'd spent in the huge house in Hampstead, away from her disappointed parents. She had always felt safe and loved there and her granny would lavish her with the sort of attention that she rarely received at home.

Granny would take her shopping and buy her ridiculously overpriced clothes from Harrods, which her mother would tut at and say, 'What use is a red velvet coat to a child?' or, 'You can't wear pink suede boots in the rain.'

Entire afternoons were spent wandering around Highgate Cemetery looking at the graves. Granny would always stop and buy two beautiful bunches of seasonal blooms from the flower shop in Highgate Village on their way there. As they looked round, Granny would stop and place a single flower from the first bunch of blooms on each of her friends' graves, mainly actors and actresses. The second bunch was the most important though. It was for Grandpa. He was buried beneath a simple white headstone, under an oak tree in the West Cemetery. His headstone read:

IN LOVING MEMORY OF
FRANK PERRY JUNIOR
ACTOR
BORN IN MASSACHUSETTS 5TH MAY 1928
DIED IN LONDON 30TH JULY 1987
BELOVED HUSBAND OF MATILDA 'TILLY' BEAUMONT,
FATHER OF ALICE AND GRANDFATHER OF SOPHIA

Beneath this transcription was a quote by Oscar Wilde. It read: *Keep love in your heart. A life without it is like a sunless garden when the flowers are dead.*

Granny said it was Grandpa's favourite saying and that Grandpa was an extraordinarily clever man and that Sophia should always remember that quote. She promised that she would. Granny would place the flowers carefully in the vase by her husband's grave and then she would chat to him for a while, quite naturally.

'Hello, my darling Frankie,' she'd say. 'I have little Sophia with me today. Except she's not so little any more! I wish you could see her. She's growing into such a beautiful girl. Everybody keeps saying how much she looks like me but they're only trying to flatter me, I know. When I look at her, I do so remember Alice at that age though. Alice really was the most adorable child, wasn't she, Frankie? Do you remember that summer in Florida in 1973 when she had had a growth spurt and she reminded us of a fawn because she was suddenly so tall and gangly? Her hair was down to her waist and her legs were up to her armpits and she kept tripping over her feet because she wasn't used to her new height? Well, that's how Sophia looks right now – but minus the Sarasota tan! Sophia and I are going to go for a walk on the Heath next. I wish you were here with us. I do miss you so. I love you, Frankie. I'll be back soon.'

Sophia would watch Granny very closely when she spoke to Grandpa. She would see how Granny's pale blue eyes lit up as she lost herself in love. It's true what they say about eyes never growing old. In the presence of Frank, all Sophia could see was the young actress who'd fallen head over heels for an

American movie star. Sophia would try to imagine them to-gether – young, good-looking, rich and glamorous. She couldn't really remember her grandfather. She'd only been five when he'd died suddenly and prematurely of a heart attack. But there were pictures of him all over Granny's house – photos taken on sets of movies, photos taken at film premieres, photos with presidents and starlets and musicians and photos taken at home with Granny and Sophia's mother, Alice, as a child. God, how Sophia had loved those photos!

It had felt, to Sophia, as if he might just walk back in at any moment. His panama hat had still hung on the coat stand in the grand hall of Granny's house, his leather slippers had remained neatly placed at his side of the bed and his Oscar had pride of place on the marble mantelpiece in the drawing room beside Tilly's own. Sophia had always wished that she had known him better.

These idyllic visits to Granny often followed major family fights. Sophia would be sent away to 'think about her behaviour' and although they were supposed to be a punishment, they were more of a reprieve. Sophia had always had terrible arguments – especially with her dad. Her mother would disappear into her bedroom whenever Sophia caused a scene, but her dad never walked away from a fight. He would get angry but in a very controlled way, a vein would pulse in his neck but he never raised his voice. He always remained eerily dispassionate, even when Sophia was weeping and wailing and throwing things about. Being sent away to boarding school at eight had been a direct result of a game of Monopoly that had ended up with Sophia hurling the board across the living room.

There was also the time she'd thrown a metal biscuit barrel at him – he'd ducked and it had smashed through the bay window. It had taken Sophia months to pay back the money for the new glazing from her pocket money. On another occasion she'd tried to climb out of her dad's sports car while he was driving along the M25 at eighty mph. She must have been about eleven. They'd been on their way to Sophia's boarding school in Gloucestershire after half term and she'd been begging her father not to make her go back there. Even though she argued with them, she'd hated being away from her family. She'd wanted to go to a day school closer to home, like all their friends' daughters did. Sophia had felt constantly lonely, homesick, rejected and miserable.

'Please, Daddy,' she'd begged. 'There are plenty of good girls' schools in Surrey. I want to stay at home with you and Mummy. I'll work hard, I promise. I won't cause any trouble. I'll be a really good girl. Please don't send me away again.'

But her dad had just got annoyed with her when she'd cried and pleaded and begged. He'd called her a spoilt brat and told her she was an ungrateful little madam not to appreciate the money he was spending on her education. He'd reminded her that her grandmother and her mother had gone to Westonbirt and that they had understood what a privilege that was. Whereas she, Sophia, was nothing but an ungrateful, self-centred little cow.

'What if my parents are there?' asked Sophia again.

'They won't be,' Hugo reminded her again. 'They visit on Tuesdays and Fridays. Your grandmother made that clear.'

Sophia sighed. The butterflies in her stomach were getting worse.

'I got everything out of perspective, didn't I?' she was telling herself more than she was telling Hugo. 'It doesn't matter about any inheritance. It doesn't matter what my parents have done. She's my grandmother. She was always there for me when I was a child. And what have I done? She's terminally ill, lying in hospital, sending me letters, writing me her memoirs, and I've ignored her. I've been more worried about Nathan than I have about Granny. What have I become, Hugo? Who does that?'

'We all make mistakes,' Hugo said gently. 'And you're doing the right thing now.'

The old, familiar prickle of self-hatred itched her skin. Granny was the one person in her family who had never let her down. And Sophia felt wretched that in return for all that love and loyalty, she'd abandoned the old lady in her dying days. Why the hell had she taken so long to visit? It was weak and selfish. She'd been so self-obsessed.

And now she had to get there, fast, before it was too late. How would she live with herself if Granny died not knowing that Sophia loved her? What if she died today, before they arrived, never knowing that Sophia had been on her way to the hospital?

'I need to fix everything. I've screwed up, haven't I, Hugo? I've really made a mess of things.'

Hugo walked over to her and draped his long arms over her shoulders. He kissed the top of her head tenderly and said, 'No, baby, you haven't messed up. You've taken an unconventional journey, I concede, but who wants to be conventional? Was your grandmother, the Hollywood sex symbol, ever conventional?'

Sophia found herself smiling.

'No,' she replied. 'But my mum is as conventional as they come,' she reminded him.

This was true. Alice was the archetypal Surrey housewife. And she didn't even partake in the more interesting suburban activities: she'd never been to an Ann Summers party, let alone a key-swapping party.

'And my mum's a winner,' Sophia reminded Hugo, suddenly feeling sad again. 'She's always been safe and looked after by my dad. She's never had to worry about anything more important than which roast she's going to make on Sunday. Maybe the unconventional gene is overrated.'

'Well, you can ask Tilly for her opinion on that when we get to the hospital. I doubt she'd agree. She's had an amazing life.'

A horn sounded outside.

'Our carriage awaits!' Hugo announced, taking Sophia's hand and pulling her down the stairs.

'Do I look OK?' asked Sophia, as she climbed into the taxi. 'For Granny, I mean? Do I look nice?'

She was wearing an old black cashmere sweater of her mum's, with tight-fitting black cigarette pants, bright red ballet pumps and a vintage Burberry trench coat.

'You look gorgeous,' said Hugo. 'And very sophisticated: every inch the respectable aristocratic heiress.'

'Hugo, you can't come in with me today. You do understand that, don't you?' she told him firmly for the umpteenth time. 'You can wait for me in the café.'

Usually Sophia relied on Hugo hugely for moral support but something told her that facing her grandmother after all these years was a lone venture. It was time to woman up.

She gazed out of the window and saw that the taxi had barely got to Dalston. The traffic crawled slowly through the rain-drenched streets. There was plenty of time to read the latest of Tilly's letters.

Chapter Thirteen

Beaumont House, Wiltshire, the war years (continued)

Papa came home for an all too brief visit early in 1942. He brought me gifts – a gold scarab beetle brooch from Egypt and a beautiful pencil sketch of a young girl that had been drawn by an Italian prisoner of war my father had met. The girl was the soldier's fiancée back home in Capri. Papa said the Italian was not only a very talented artist but a fine young man and that war was a complicated business because the enemy were only people, like us, too. Papa looked healthy and well. He had escaped injury and he told me that in many ways he was enjoying the war. It had given him a sense of purpose and meaning that he had not known before. He lamented that his only real pain was his long absence from me. We took the horses out and went for a glorious gallop through the grounds. The house looked as grand and magnificent as always from a distance and Papa promised that after the war he would get it back on its feet. He told me I mustn't worry, that this war was just a blip, and that soon life would be back to normal. And then he was gone again.

During the summer of 1942, Badger and I were sent off to stay with Mama's Aunt Ophelia in St Ives. Aunt Ophelia was a spinster who fancied herself as a sculptress. She was perfectly kind but utterly incapable of looking after a twelve-year-old girl. She rarely woke up until after noon and then she would spend the rest of the day locked in her artist's studio. I had no choice but to fend for myself.

I was a spoilt, unworldly child, but I did have one thing on my side – I was sociable. Mama called me a terrible chatterbox, but whatever the correct term, I was completely lacking in inhibitions. I marched straight up to the first girl I saw in the High Street – a tiny blonde with long pigtails and a face full of freckles – and introduced myself.

Despite my posh accent and grand clothes, I found myself quickly accepted by my new best friend, Patricia Trevallion, and soon we were inseparable. We spent our days on the beach, or exploring caves, or climbing cliff paths, or crabbing, or building campfires in the woods, with her shy, but rather beautiful, older brother Peter – and Badger, of course. It wasn't a particularly hot summer but it was dry and sunny and we rarely went indoors. There was a brief heatwave at the end of July and we spent those few days swimming in the ocean. I told Patricia and Peter all about the pearl divers that Mr Fitzroy had told me about and we practised holding our breath and diving under the waves. Unfortunately, we failed to find even one oyster between us.

It was an idyllic summer in many ways. Patricia's family's harbour-side cottage was very small and they certainly weren't wealthy. Her father, a fisherman by trade, had joined the navy and was away at sea, so I never had the privilege of meeting him. But despite their circumstances, they were very generous people. Patricia's mum, Mrs Trevallion, fed me three square meals a day for two entire months. When I fell over and tore my stockings, she darned them for me. When my shoulders turned beetroot from sunburn during the heatwave, she smothered them in calamine lotion. When I got a fever the following week, she nursed me for three days until the colour returned to my cheeks. I'm not sure Aunt Ophelia even noticed that I'd gone.

I missed the Trevallions dreadfully when I had to go back to Beaumont House. As a leaving present Mrs Trevallion knitted me a cornflower blue cardigan with beautiful tiny pearl buttons. I had told Mrs Trevallion about my day at Asprey and about my obsession with pearls and I thought it touching that she had remembered – although the pearls on my cardigan had come from Woolworths and were plastic, of course. I have kept that cardigan to this day. Patricia and Peter saw me off on the train platform when it was time to leave. Patricia and I hugged for the longest time and promised to keep in touch for ever and ever and ever. Peter, who was fourteen, kissed me briefly on the lips as he bid me farewell and then blushed to the colour of his scarlet pullover! That kiss made me smile all the way back to Chippenham station. It was my first.

After the war, when Mr Trevallion returned from the navy, the family emigrated to Canada and we lost touch. Patricia tracked me down years later, through my agent, after my career had taken off, and in her letters she told me that, although her brother was a happily married father of four, he never tired of telling people that his first true love had been Tilly Beaumont, movie star. It still makes me smile to think of the Trevallions and so many happy days, right smack bang in the middle of that horrendous war. I wonder how Patricia and Peter are now. I think they must still be alive. I have a feeling that if either of them died, the other would find a way to tell me somehow. I do hope they are contented in their old age, their days spent surrounded by loving family. It's what we all dream of in the end.

When I got home, Mama had turned the house into a hospital. Well, not Mama herself – it was the army who had moved in and taken over, turning the ballroom, the grand dining hall, the library and the lounge into infirmaries and the bedrooms into smaller wards for the most badly injured men – but it was entirely her idea to open the doors to the armed forces. The sweeping drive was filled with parked trucks, military cars and ambulances and when I opened my own front door (already baffled by the fact that Mr Wise had ignored the arrival of my taxi from the station and failed to meet me at the bottom of the stone steps that led to the front entrance) I was greeted not by the butler, but by a stern-looking military matron who informed me, brusquely, that I was trespassing on army property and demanded I explain myself immediately. I was so shocked that I could barely stutter the words out to explain that I was Lady Matilda Beaumont and that this was my home – or at least it had been when I'd left it eight weeks earlier.

I was incredibly keen to help the war effort and I hugely admired our boys fighting on the front line, but nobody had prepared me for arriving back at my family home and finding over a hundred badly injured soldiers in residence. All the old furniture had disappeared, the portraits had been taken down from the walls and the familiar smell of fresh flowers, candle wax and furniture polish had been replaced by the smell of iodine, bleach and, underneath it all, the lingering taint of disease. Mama, who eventually appeared running down the sweeping central staircase carrying armfuls of bandages, had taken to wearing her own version of a nurse's uniform (although her skirt was rather tight and her stockings were still black) and was rushing around the house with a sense of pride and purpose that I had never seen before. As I stood, open-mouthed, in the hall, with my suitcase at my feet, she informed me briskly that we had moved into the disused gardener's cottage in the grounds and that I mustn't even think of going to my old bedroom because it had been commandeered as a makeshift morgue for 'the poor dears who haven't made it through the night'.

'Where's Mr Wise?' I asked, hopefully, once I'd got over the shock of the thought of dead bodies in my old nursery.

'Dismissed,' said Mama, casually. 'There's no need for staff now. Only medical staff.'

'Mrs Ashton?' I enquired desperately.

'Oh, yes, Mrs Ashton, she's still here somewhere,' replied Mama, absent-mindedly, brushing a stray hair back under her white hat. 'She's running the kitchen, I think. Our brave boys still need to eat, after all!'

I sighed with relief. If anybody could explain to me what was going on round here it was Mrs Ashton. I staggered across the grounds, lugging my heavy case and trying not to stare at the soldiers, smoking cigarettes in the garden, some in wheelchairs, some with horrifically burned faces, some with missing limbs. I had always thought of the workmen's cottages as tiny little things – mere Wendy houses in comparison to a 'proper' home, like Beaumont House. I'd been amazed that the head gardener and his entire family had managed to live in even this, the biggest of them, until their departure at the beginning of the war (they left when poor Tony died).

But now, as I dragged my case up the stairs and dumped it on the floor of the blue bedroom (which would be mine for the next few years), I found myself comparing it to the Trevallions' seaside cottage and realising that it was actually rather lovely. What's more, it still smelled of flowers: peonies, to be exact. Pink ones, placed prettily in a yellow vase on my window sill with a note from Mrs Ashton that read, Welcome home, my dear Tilly. I realised that my clothes had all been folded neatly into drawers or hung in the small wardrobe, my favourite doll and Freddie the Teddy sat waiting patiently for me on my pillow and my old, battered copy of Alice's Adventures in Wonderland rested quietly on the bedside table beside a framed photograph of Papa. Someone had gone to a lot of effort to make me feel at home in the cottage and I knew it hadn't been Mama. I had not yet got over losing Nanny, but in that moment, I understood that I still had one true ally at Beaumont House.

It was a sticky, hot, late August day. I quickly changed out of my travelling clothes, threw on a clean, thin, summer dress from the wardrobe and ran back across the overgrown lawn towards the kitchens.

'Your mother has gone stark raving mad,' explained Mrs Ashton, in clear frustration, as she stirred an enormous cauldron of vegetable soup violently with a huge ladle. 'I used to stick up for her when people complained about her wilful ways, and her inappropriate friendships, and the parties, and the drink, and the … Well, no need to go into details ... But this time, she's gone too far. Three different boarding schools asked if they could use this house – yours included. Not to mention the navy, looking to house some Wrens. We could have taken in evacuees, but no, your mother does not want children in the house – all that giggling and squealing would give her a headache she said. So, why not the Wrens? I asked. Lovely, hard-working young girls. But no, women in uniform, trying to be like men, it just isn't dignified, says Her Ladyship. Or we could have used the land to grow vegetables and raise livestock, I suggested. Take on some Land Girls? Oh, she wouldn't have that for a moment either. Women wearing trousers and getting their fingernails dirty. Shocking! Worse than the Wrens, she cries! But I know what she was really thinking: heaven forbid, a houseful of attractive young women who might steal her limelight. So much better to fill the house with young men, who've been through hell, and haven't seen their young ladies in months. I don't buy that Florence Nightingale act for one minute. It's all about Lady Beaumont being the centre of attention and absolutely nothing about the war effort. I'm sorry to talk about your mother in this way, Tilly, but you're almost a teenager now and with your father away, you're the only Beaumont left with an ounce of common sense. This is your house, your future, your inheritance, so I think it's your duty to know what's been going on round here.'

I wasn't remotely offended by what Mrs Ashton had to say about my mother. I knew perfectly well what Mama was.

Mrs Ashton had been at Beaumont House since she'd first been sent here as a fourteen-year-old maid. She'd worked for my grand-parents and known my father as a boy. She had always taken great pride in her work and her life's ambition had been fulfilled when she'd finally been promoted to Housekeeper. It was difficult to see her now, demoted to general cook and dogsbody, and I thought it terribly cruel of Mama to have done this to such a proud woman. Mrs Ashton had been here far longer than Mama and her respect for, and loyalty to, the house of Beaumont was much stronger than her mistress's. She stared at me intently.

'I hope your father comes home soon, Tilly,' she said. 'I worry about you here on your own with her.'

I shrugged and waved my hand dismissively. I had very little respect left for Mama, but I certainly wasn't scared of her. Not yet.

'I'll be fine,' I reassured her. 'Besides, I still have you to look after me.'

'I'll do my best but it's not right you being here with all these young men.'

I didn't exactly know what she meant but I guessed she was saying that the soldiers might think I was pretty. I rather liked the idea, to be honest. My brief kiss with Peter seemed to have awakened a new vanity in me. I wanted boys to notice me! Perhaps I wasn't so different from my mother after all.

Mrs Ashton turned her attention back to her dinner duties but I could still see the dark shadows crossing her face.

'She's not going to deal with growing older well, Matilda,' she warned me. 'Women like your mother do not age gracefully. And they do not like to be upstaged by their own daughters. I've seen it happen before. You have to be careful, dear. Very careful.'

'What's happened to the furniture and the paintings?' I asked her, trying to change the subject. The idea of my mother being jealous of me made me suddenly very uncomfortable.

'Gone,' replied Mrs Ashton, abruptly. 'Sold mostly, to pay for the upkeep of the house – and your mother's black market silk stockings, I expect. There are a few bits in the cottages and poor Mr Wise stored some of the more valuable paintings in the barn before he was dismissed but otherwise your mother has got rid of it all. Oh, apart from her jewels. She made sure she kept hold of those. They were the first things she squirrelled away under her bed when she moved into the cottage. Her wardrobe's full of furs and gowns too, although what use those are to her with a war on, the Lord only knows!'

'What on earth will Papa say when he comes home?' I asked, shocked at my mother's behaviour. 'Those are his family's belongings, not Mama's!'

'Beaumont House has never needed a master so badly in all its history! Right,' she said suddenly, picking up a tray. 'You and Badger better scarper. A hospital kitchen is no place for children and it's definitely no place for dogs!'

I yearned for Papa to come back too and that desire became more and more desperate as the weeks passed and I realised exactly what had happened to my home. Many of the soldiers were badly injured both physically and emotionally. At night the old house echoed with the screams and shouts of those reliving their worst nightmares as they slept. I imagined I could hear their cries through the open window of my bedroom in the gardener's cottage. By day the house groaned with the sound of men in excruciating pain. Every week the mortuary van drove bodies, some belonging to those not much older than I was, out of our drive to be repatriated with their heartbroken families. Those poor boys had got back to Britain alive, but they never made it home. It broke my heart. Meanwhile, trucks and ambulances full of wounded men, fresh from the front, arrived every single day. Even as they arrived, I knew that some would be in the mortuary van come Friday. It was a harsh lesson for a twelve-year-old to learn.

The grounds were full of convalescing men and boys. Some were friendly and made me laugh with their silly stories and funny jokes. But most were too badly wounded to see the joy in life any more. I made myself look at their wounds, even though it pained me to do so, knowing that they had sacrificed everything for my safety and freedom.

There was one man in particular who fascinated me. I couldn't tell how old he was, or how tall he was, or what he might have looked like before he was injured. He was in a wheelchair because both legs had been amputated above the knee. His skull had been broken in an explosion. He had very pale blond hair, like Peter's, and I found myself wondering if he had been beautiful, like Peter, just a few weeks ago. His name was Jim and he was always in the garden even when it rained. He didn't speak to me. He spoke to Badger. My little Jack Russell would hop up onto Jim's lap and lie patiently for hours on the tartan blanket. It was as if the dog understood how much the man needed him. After Jim left one Friday in that dreaded mortuary van, Badger became a little less bouncy and a little more subdued. None of us escaped those years at Beaumont House without lasting scars.

Mama had struck up one of her special friendships with a brigadier with a bad leg. He was a loud, blustering, self-important bore called Wilfred Scott-Thomas and, in comparison to Mama's usual type, he was awfully ugly. At least Foster had been a handsome thug. Scott-Thomas was a stout, squat, toad of a man, with a weak chin and a prominent nose, covered in purple broken veins. Every time he touched my mother it made me squirm. Not only because she was being disloyal to Papa – I had seen Mama touched by many men over the years – but because his ugliness was at such odds to her beauty. Mrs Ashton and I secretly started referring to the brigadier as The Beast.

By Christmas of 1942 I had got quite used to The Beast being in the cottage. He seemed to be entirely well again, and he barely limped on his bad leg any more, so quite what he was still doing at the hospital I had no idea. Not that he spent any time in the hospital as such. No, he spent his days boring Mama and me with his endless tales of heroic deeds in France, or else he would put his feet up on our chaise, read the papers and eat his way through our week's rations. At night I could hear his grunts and the creaking of the bed coming from my mother's room across the landing. It made me sick. I despised him. And I gradually began to despise my own mother too.

Christmas was particularly depressing that year. There was no money for presents and the cold, damp weather was not good for the soldiers' health. Three men died in Beaumont House on Christmas Day. I couldn't bring myself to rejoice and sing carols that day. Mama had tired of her role as Florence Nightingale and she rarely worked on the wards any more. Gone was her nurse's uniform and instead she was back to her usual wardrobe of riding clothes, well-fitted tweed suits, fur and velvet. Her supply of Chanel red lipstick showed no sign of drying up any time soon.

She and The Beast shared a private little Christmas for two in the gardener's cottage. They asked me to join them but I could tell the invitation came more from a sense of duty than any desire to actually have a child at their table. I politely declined. I would eat Christmas lunch with Mrs Ashton and the nurses in the kitchens of Beaumont House. As I left the cottage I glanced back and saw my mother and The Beast sitting at the grand dining table, which had been squeezed into the cottage's modest dining room. She was dressed up to the nines in a silk gown and a ruby necklace. He was wearing his full military uniform and a smug look on his face. They held hands as they clinked their wine glasses. Mama threw her head back and laughed at something he had said. The brigadier leaned forward and kissed her long lily-white neck.

Perhaps my mother's undoing was the making of me. On the first day of 1943, I turned thirteen. Mrs Ashton had somehow found the ingredients to make me a delicious Victoria sponge cake and the soldiers in the main infirmary sang me a hearty rendition of 'Happy Birthday'. There were no jewels, no new pony, no shiny bicycle or trip to London. But it felt like a fitting tribute to the end of my childhood. I was in my teens now. I decided it was time to grow up.

For the remainder of the war, I worked. On weekdays I went to school, in the evenings and weekends I helped out as much as I could in the infirmary or in the kitchens. I washed sheets, scrubbed filthy floors, chopped vegetables, boiled water and generally did any chore that was asked of me. As my heart closed on my mother, it opened on the men and boys who were suffering on my doorstep. I learned to look beyond their burns and scars and to really get to know them. Many of the soldiers came from vastly different backgrounds from my own, and I became fascinated by their tales from back home, wherever that home was. They teased me about the way I talked 'with marbles in my mouth' but I think they rather liked me. That year, I stopped being a spoilt, snobbish, ignorant brat and, I am proud to say, I grew into a much kinder, better-educated and more well-rounded young woman. Heaven knows what I would have been had the war not saved me from myself and from my upbringing.

The Beast had finally been given a clean bill of health, although the shrapnel wound to his leg made him unfit for active service. He had been given a desk job in Warminster, which, unfortunately, was far too close to Beaumont House for comfort. He remained a firm fixture in the cottage. When Mama was not with The Beast, she was a recluse. Her friends had stopped visiting the moment the army arrived. I noticed that her breath had started to smell of gin before lunch. Although she remained beautiful, and exquisitely dressed at all times, her elegant features had begun to take on a mask-like quality. She rarely laughed or smiled or showed any emotion or expression. There was no life left in her eyes. She had never been much of a mother, but now she seemed barely a human being at all.

Chapter Fourteen

St John's Wood, London, 2012

Sophia stared out of the window at Regent's Park on her right.

'We're almost there,' she said, quietly. 'I don't know why I didn't come before.'

'Well, you're here now,' said Hugo, as the cab pulled into the car park of the Wellington Hospital. 'And that's what matters. Now go!'

Clutching the business card, with the details of her granny's room on it, Sophia followed the signs to the oncology unit. It was one of those smart private hospitals that looked more like a hotel. Only the smell of disinfectant, the rubber-soled shoes and the hushed voices gave the game away. Sophia approached the desk, still clasping the letter, and smiled nervously at the nurse behind the reception desk.

'I've come to see my grandmother,' she said.

The nurse looked up, stared at Sophia for a moment and then her face broke into an ecstatic smile.

'Sophia!' she exclaimed. 'You're Sophia!'

Sophia nodded, a little confused by the warm welcome.

'Oh, I'm sorry,' apologised the nurse, who was about the same age as Sophia, but a proper adult thirty-year-old rather than an overgrown teenager like Sophia. Her name badge said *Linda*.

'Your grandmother is going to be overjoyed to see you,' Linda continued. 'She has a photograph of you by her bed, and she spends all her time writing letters to you. Come, come.' Linda ushered her along the corridor. 'The morphine makes her a little drowsy sometimes but today is a good day. We all adore Tilly and this is exactly what she's been waiting for.'

Linda knocked on a wooden door at the end of the corridor.

The muted sound of a television could be heard through the door.

'Come in!' came a cheerful, well-to-do call.

Sophia recognised Granny's voice immediately and in that moment it all came flooding back – the cuddles, the days out, the fancy tea parties, the funny stories, the warmth, the joy, the glorious feeling of being loved and safe and understood.

'I have a surprise visitor for you, Tilly,' said Linda, as she opened the door.

Sophia patted down her trousers, picked a stray thread off her cardigan, pulled her fingers through her hair and, with a deep breath, stepped into the room. Her grandmother stared for a moment, blinking, mouth open, as if she'd seen a ghost.

'Sophia,' she said eventually, her voice shaking with emotion. 'Oh, come here, let me look at you. I can't believe you're finally here.'

Granny beckoned her, smiling and crying simultaneously. As Sophia threw herself into her grandmother's arms, her own tears poured down her face. She took in the familiar smell of Granny's perfume (Je Reviens by Worth, Sophia immediately recalled), and the softness of her silver hair. The old lady simply held her and whispered in her ear, 'Shhh, Sophia, everything is all right now.'

In an instant Sophia was back in Waterloo station. It was 1992 and she was ten years old. She'd had a dreadful fight with her parents – the worst she'd ever had. She couldn't even remember now what it was that she'd done but she did remember that it was the first time her father had used the word 'worthless' to describe her. She had been packed off to Granny's in disgrace and for the first time she was made to travel on the train by herself. Sophia had cried all the way from Virginia Water station to London, filled with shame and self-loathing, and when she arrived on the platform, Granny had been there, arms open wide, huge smile on her face, ready to embrace her and love her no matter what she'd done at home. Why had she left it so long to see her?

'I'm sorry, Granny,' she wept. 'I'm so sorry, I should have come ages ago. I should never have stopped seeing you in the first place. I wanted to come. But I was ashamed. I thought after what I'd done, and what Mum and Dad thought of me, that you'd think badly of me. I couldn't bear to see the disappointment in your eyes. But I missed you, Granny. I missed you so much.'

'It doesn't matter,' said her granny gently, stroking her hair. 'You're here now, my angel. And let me tell you something important. Look at me, Sophia.'

Sophia looked up into her grandmother's clear blue eyes.

'You will never see disappointment in these eyes when I look at you,' she stated with absolute certainty. 'I'm the one who's let you down. You have nothing to be sorry about.'

'But you've never let me down, Granny,' said Sophia.

Her grandmother sighed deeply and there was a hint of a shake of her head. For a moment Sophia felt confused, as if she'd missed something, but in an instant Granny had regained her warm smile.

Tilly ordered some tea. Sophia sat on the side of the bed, holding her grandmother's hand and grinning like an idiot.

'You look well, Granny,' she told her. 'Hugo said you'd look like a ghost!'

'I feel remarkably fine,' Granny replied, cheerfully. 'I've had this blasted stomach tumour for years. It was slow growing and they kept it under control with drugs for a long, long time but recently it's grown and the cancer has spread to my bones. I certainly couldn't dance a tango but I don't feel as bad as you might expect. And today, seeing you, I feel on top of the world!'

Sophia swallowed the lump in her throat and squeezed her grandmother's hand tightly. She hated to think about her granny's condition. Everyone said she was dying but she looked very much alive: old, frail and painfully thin, but her eyes still sparkled and her smile still lit up the dark November day.

'Did you read my letters?' she asked, once she'd pulled herself together.

'Yes,' nodded Sophia, relieved that she could tell the truth. 'Actually, if I'm honest, I only just read your last one in the taxi on the way here but that's a long story involving Nathan – but … anyway, he's not important. I realise that now.'

'I never liked Nathan,' said Granny, frowning. 'His eyes were too deep-set.'

Sophia spluttered. 'Granny, everybody loved Nathan. I think Mum wanted to marry him herself!'

'That may be so but your mother doesn't have much experience with men,' continued her grandmother. 'The eyes are the windows to the soul, and if you can't see a chap's eyes, you can't possibly know how they feel. Your grandfather had gorgeous eyes. He could never hide any of his emotions. That's why he was so successful. When Grandpa was on the big screen, every woman watching truly believed that he was in love with her.'

Granny's eyes misted over and Sophia knew that she'd lost her for a moment. But it didn't take Tilly long to pull herself back into the room.

'Actually, I had just finished writing some more of my memoirs, darling,' Granny smiled. 'Would you like to read them?'

Chapter Fifteen

Beaumont House, after the war

The telegram arrived on 7th April 1945. Just a month before the end of the war. I was the one who answered the door and I knew, the minute I saw the young boy in his uniform, that it was bad news. He knew it too. We were about the same age. Our eyes met for a moment as he handed me the telegram and without speaking he told me he was sorry. Papa was missing in action. His plane had been shot down over the Rhineland. Nobody knew what had happened to him.

'Well, he's clearly dead, poor chap,' The Beast blustered, patting Mama on the back. 'Such a damned shame at this stage. We've got the blighters now, I'm sure. It's all over bar the shouting match.'

He handed her a stiff gin. I have never wanted to hurt another human being as badly as I wanted to hurt Brigadier Wilfred Scott-Thomas that day. I am ashamed to say that I wished him dead. Why was he alive and well and standing in my sitting room, when Papa was missing presumed dead? And there was Mama, showing no emotion at all, sitting like a shop mannequin in her armchair, sipping her gin and saying nothing.

I ran out of the cottage to seek solace in the arms of Mrs Ashton. She was my rock during the next few dreadful weeks. As the rest of the nation celebrated the end of the war on 8th May, I was in the worst kind of limbo imaginable. There had been no confirmation of Papa's death. No body had ever been found. He remained officially missing in action. But neither had there been any contact, or sighting of him. In the chaos of the end of the war, there was no way of knowing what had become of him. I had hope but I was holding onto it by the very tips of my fingers. No one else believed there was even a chance that my father had survived but as I lay on my bed, cuddling Freddie Bear, I prayed and I prayed and I prayed.

It was a further six weeks after VE Day that the second telegram arrived. Papa was alive. Just. He had survived the plane crash although he had been badly injured, and then he had immediately been captured by the Germans as a prisoner of war. But fate had been on Papa's side. As the victorious Allies approached, the Germans had fled, and Papa had been left to die in their abandoned camp. Thankfully, he had been discovered, unconscious but still breathing, by a US Army patrol and taken to a US hospital camp, where he had been treated. He'd remained unconscious for weeks and all the Yanks could tell was that he was an RAF officer. His personal documents had gone missing, and so nobody had known who the mystery airman was until he finally regained consciousness several weeks after the German surrender and managed to whisper his name.

My jubilation at Papa's survival was short-lived. The man who finally arrived home at Beaumont House in July 1945 was not my father. Nothing could have prepared me for the extent of his injuries. I had seen similar burns, scars and disfigurements on the men in the army hospital, but I had not known those men before they were hurt and I could not miss what they had been. With Papa it was completely different. I had known his handsome face, better than I had known my own. I had had endless piggybacks on his strong shoulders, I had clung to his long legs, and gone to sleep soothed by his deep, melodic voice. All the different elements that went together to make my father my father had been dismantled and destroyed. There was a body, and a pulse, and eyes, and arms, and one remaining leg, but the sum of those parts was not my papa.

He sat silently in his wheelchair without a flicker of recognition for me or a word of hello. He stayed in that comatose state for months, as I fussed around him, spoon-fed him soup, bathed his wounds, read him stories and told him lame jokes. Mama ignored him completely and The Beast continued to visit on a daily basis as if the master of the house had not returned at all. They even spoke about Papa in front of him, as if he wasn't there.

'Blasted Germans,' The Beast would say. 'To do this to such a fine man.'

'Freddie would prefer to be dead,' Mama would announce. 'He must hate being like this. He was always such a physical man. Did I ever tell you what a skilful tennis player he was, Wilf? And of course he played rugger for the firsts up at Cambridge ... poor soul.'

It made me sick to hear Mama talk about him like that: as if he was just somebody she used to know, rather than her husband, who was still here, still alive, sitting in the same room. I stopped going to school.

I made a bed up for Papa in the sitting room and I slept on the floor beside him, terrified that he might stop breathing in the dead of night. Sometimes The Beast stayed for the night and Papa and I would have to endure the torture of listening to his grunts and Mama's groans through the floorboards. I spent every waking moment caring for my poor father and finally my hard work was repaid. One morning, after I had fed him his porridge with golden syrup, Papa stared at me and said, quietly, but quite clearly, 'Thank you, my darling Tilly.'

The army hospital had shut now and all the soldiers and staff were gone but we could not move back into Beaumont House. Like its master, the place had been all but destroyed by the war. The holes in the roof had never been fixed and six years of rain had dripped into the house. The walls and floors were cracked, scratched and decayed. There was no money to pay for repairs, no furniture left, no staff. Even Mrs Ashton had left to run the grocery shop in the village. She said she could no longer afford to work for the Beaumonts for free. Papa was oblivious to our state of affairs and Mama seemed not to care. In early 1946, she and the brigadier disappeared off together to 'get over that ghastly war' and visit friends in Barbados. They did not return until the autumn. Nobody missed them. Least of all me.

With Mama gone, Papa began to make a marvellous recovery. He was in no way his old self, but the colour returned to his cheeks, and although he would remain wheelchair-bound for the rest of his life, he regained the strength in his arms and shoulders and he became quite adept at whizzing around the grounds. But most importantly, he was talking again.

'Would you like to see Polly?' he asked me one mild April afternoon.

'Nanny Miller?' I asked, excitedly. 'Do you know where she is? I tried to contact her. I wrote to her at her parents' address in Malmesbury several times but she didn't reply. I'd love to see her. How I've missed her!'

Papa nodded. 'She wrote to me often during the war. She's moved to Bristol and is working as a primary school teacher. I believe she's very well. And so is her son ...'

He trailed off then and allowed my mind time to catch up with the conversation. I remembered the night at Claridge's and the way Nanny had sneaked back into our room. I remembered the Asprey wristwatch and the crumpled dress. I thought about the way she'd been so suddenly and cruelly dismissed while Papa was away at war and I was away at school and I remembered Mama's muttered words, 'Floozy', 'Trollop', 'Jezebel'. I was old enough now to make sense of it all.

'How old is her son?' I asked, catching my father's eye.

He did not look away. He was not ashamed or embarrassed. Perhaps the war had broken some of the constraints and chains of polite society.

'Five,' said Papa. 'Thomas is five years old now. He will be six in September.'

I did my sums. The child had not been conceived at Claridge's. He was too young. He must have been conceived when Papa came home on leave at Christmas in 1939. I wondered how long the affair lasted. I wondered if Papa loved Polly still. This was the first time he had suggested venturing off the Beaumont estate since his return from Germany. But I knew better than to pry further. In those days, a father did not have to be held accountable to his daughter. He nodded curtly.

'We shall visit them next week,' he announced. 'I cannot visit them without your help, Tilly. Not in this blasted contraption. Can you drive yet?'

I nodded. I was only sixteen but I had learned to drive not only cars but also military trucks and ambulances while the hospital was at the house.

'Are my motor cars still in the garage?' he asked.

I shook my head.

'Mama sold them,' I explained. 'But Foster left his Bedford van. I've driven that to Chippenham and back before and there's plenty of room in the back for your chair. There's a can of petrol in the garage too. That should get us to Bristol.'

The subject was closed. We never spoke of my father's affair openly again. There was no need. He knew I understood. Had my mother been an honest, loyal wife, I am sure I would have been horrified by my father's infidelity, but how could I judge my father when my mother was living with another man right under his nose?

Nanny had not changed at all. When we arrived at the front door of her smart terraced townhouse in Clifton she embraced me. If she was shocked or appalled by Papa's appearance she did not show it. She kissed him warmly on the cheek, told him how well he looked and wheeled him into her drawing room where she'd laid on tea and cakes. Her hair was still blonde and curly, her eyes sparkly and blue and, despite being a mother now, her waist was still as tiny as ever. The house was grander than I had anticipated and I was surprised to see wedding photographs framed on the mantelpiece. Nanny caught me staring and squeezed my hand.

'That's my husband, Martin,' she explained. 'We were married two years ago. He's a headmaster and I am a teacher now. Are you proud of me?'

I nodded. Nanny Miller, or Mrs Williams as she now was, had indeed done very well for herself. I glanced at Papa, deeply concerned at how he would be taking this news of his lover's marriage, but he was smiling fondly at Polly and seemed quite unsurprised.

'You knew Nanny was married?' I whispered to him while Polly went off to fetch Thomas from the nursery.

'Oh yes, of course,' replied Papa. 'Isn't it wonderful? A headmaster. And a jolly decent chap he is too. I'm delighted for Polly. She's made a good life for herself and Thomas. She deserves nothing less.'

'But ...?' I struggled to find the words. 'Isn't that ... you know ... rather awkward?'

My father smiled at me.

'You're young, Tilly,' he said. 'I'm sure your head is full of romantic notions of love and of living happily ever after. And I hope one day that is exactly what you find. But life is complicated, and the world has been a very cruel place lately. I thank God for small mercies. I have you. I have Polly as a dear friend. I have little Thomas to visit now and again. It's probably more than I deserve. It's enough for me, Tilly, really, it is.'

When Thomas ran into the room there was no doubt who his father was. He was the image of Papa, and so happy and strong and full of life that I couldn't help but cry to remember how my father had once been. It felt good to realise that, after sixteen years as an only child, I actually had a half-brother: even if he was one that I must keep secret.

But as I drove back in the dark, with Papa asleep beside me, I felt a melancholy shadow cross my heart. The war had sent everyone and everything flying into the air. Now that the war was over, things had settled back into an uneasy, unfamiliar calm. But nothing had landed back where it should be. Nobody seemed to be in their rightful place. No one lived with those they really loved. I had a brother I barely knew, my father had a lover who was married to someone else, and my mother ... well, she had lumbered herself with The Beast and that was exactly what she deserved, as far as I was concerned. I made a vow that night, as I drove Foster's battered old Bedford along the potholed country roads, that I would never settle for second best when it came to love. I wanted the whole fairy tale and I would stand for nothing less.

The world as I had known it had crumbled and decayed. The wealth, money and privilege I had taken for granted meant nothing any more. The war had taught me that I could not only survive, but thrive, without material possessions. What mattered were people: flesh, blood, hearts and minds. And if that flesh was bleeding and those hearts were broken, then only love would mend them. Yes, love was all that mattered now. Love, freedom, peace and happiness. And from that moment on I made it my life's mission to find those things.

Papa and I spent a lot of time listening to the radio together. Or else I would read to him from the newspapers. I was particularly fascinated and horrified by the reports coming out of Japan a year after the atomic bombs were dropped on Hiroshima and Nagasaki. During the war, I had thought of the Germans and the Japanese only as 'the enemy' – nameless, faceless, frightening foreigners. But now, as I read the stories of 'real' Japanese people, something shifted in my conscience. I cried for those people. I tried to imagine 200,000 dead – but it was too much to picture.

'I hate war,' I announced to my father. 'I pray there will never be another war again. I pray with every fibre of my body that something like this never, ever happens again.'

Papa smiled then. He placed his scarred hand gently on my knee, squeezed gently and said, 'Then I did not fight for nothing, Tilly.'

Chapter Sixteen

Sophia swallowed, placing the letter neatly on the bedside table. 'How can you bear to remember?'

Granny shrugged and half-smiled. She seemed suddenly very tired, like a child who'd struggled to stay awake until the end of her bedtime story.

'It's my life, darling. It's not as if I can ever forget. Besides, it wasn't so bad. I was lucky to have such a wonderful papa. The war was a messy time but some good did come out of it. I'm jolly glad Thomas was born, for a start. He's a wonderful man. Never got what he deserved from us Beaumonts but ...' Her words came slowly and stutteringly and then dissipated into the sterile air. 'Anyway, you haven't finished the story yet. There are a few more pages.'

'I know,' said Sophia. 'But perhaps I could read them later. When I get home? There's so much to take in. I mean, I didn't even know about Thomas ...'

'Of course you didn't,' replied her grandmother sadly. 'He was yet another family secret. Your parents consider his existence an embarrassment and your father won't even acknowledge that he's my brother. In fact, he's convinced your mother that my half-brother is a con artist and a gold-digger. So Thomas was never going to be invited for Christmas dinner!'

'But you've been in touch with him all these years?' Sophia probed gently.

'We don't see each other very often but we've always written to each other regularly in painstaking detail and with great fondness,' replied Granny. 'He knows all about you, Sophia. Oh, and he visited me last week. Quite out of the blue. Which was divine. I hadn't seen him in years. Such a wonderful surprise.'

'And you're sure he's your brother?' Sophie found herself asking, almost despite herself. She already knew the answer.

'Quite sure,' said Granny firmly, almost irritably. 'And he's the opposite of a gold-digger. Thomas has absolutely no interest in my money.'

Sophia felt immediately guilty for having asked. Her grandmother looked exhausted suddenly and she wondered how many times Tilly had had to defend Thomas in the past.

'I'm sure you'll meet him soon and then you can judge for yourself,' said Granny, her voice softening again. 'You'll like him. I have no doubt about that.'

Sophia swallowed hard. Her grandmother was referring to her own funeral. Where else would Sophia finally meet her long lost great-uncle?

'You look tired,' she told Granny gently. 'Besides, they won't let me stay here all night! But I'll come back tomorrow. There's so much we still have to catch up on. I've wasted too much time already.'

'And, of course, you must be curious to know about your inheritance ...' Granny paused, watching Sophia carefully under heavy lids.

Sophia felt her forehead crumple into a frown. Her fingernails bit into the flesh of her palms. Why did that statement sting so badly? Was it because the truth hurt? She understood that her grandmother was testing her motives. And she didn't blame her. She'd stayed away for years and fallen out with the rest of the family, and everyone knew she wasn't earning any money or getting any help from her father. Any inheritance would obviously be much appreciated. And yet, money was not the reason for her visit. She needed her grandmother to know that.

'I'm not here for money,' said Sophia, simply but with conviction.

She met her grandmother's gaze for a second and noticed the older woman give a tiny hint of a nod. Sophia unclenched her fists.

'That's what I thought,' smiled her grandmother, weakly. 'And hoped.'

The sparkle was dimming in her eyes, the colour in her face was fading and her voice was becoming quieter. She lifted her thin arm and clutched Sophia's wrist. Her grip was still surprisingly strong.

'I need you to find something for me,' she said, almost desperately. 'I have to set things straight ...'

'I don't understand,' said Sophia. 'What do you need me to find?'

'Just promise me you'll read the rest of this letter tonight,' said her grandmother, fumbling for the pages and thrusting them back at Sophia.

'Of course. Now, you need to sleep,' Sophia told her gently, placing the letter carefully into her handbag. 'Get some rest, Granny.'

'From Papa,' Granny was mumbling quietly, with her eyes half closed. 'From Papa to me. And then to little Alice and now to you. But I don't know where it is. Your mother knows. She says she doesn't but ...'

'Mum knows what, Granny?' asked Sophia, trying to catch hold of the fragmented words and make sense of them.

'Everything ...' whispered her grandmother and sleep swept over her like a gentle tide.

Sophia sat on the bed in silence for a few moments, trying to make sense of what she'd just heard and watching the rise and fall of her grandmother's chest as she slept. As she watched, Sophia vowed that whatever it was that was missing, she would help find it. Even if it meant facing her mum.

She reluctantly left her sleeping grandmother and wandered back through the maze of hospital corridors knowing that come hell or high water she would be back to get to the bottom of the family mystery. She eventually found Hugo, still in the café just as he'd promised. He didn't notice her approaching. He was sitting at a cosy table for two with his hands clasped around a latte and his blond head bowed coquettishly to one side. Sitting opposite him, hanging off Hugo's every word, was a handsome, dark-haired man of about thirty. What a gorgeous couple they made! Sophia grinned despite herself. Hugo had actually managed to pull in the hospital.

'Hello, boys,' she said, disturbing their tête-à-tête and making both Hugo and his companion jump. 'Are you going to introduce me, Hugo?'

'Oh, hi! Sophia, Damon,' said Hugo obligingly. 'Damon, this

is Sophia, my best friend, the one I've been telling you about.'

'Hi, Sophia,' said Damon, half standing and shaking her hand. He had a faint Essex accent, a firm handshake and a quietly confident air about him. 'I do recognise you now. Hugo said I would.'

Sophia's cheeks burned. She didn't like it when people said they recognised her. Recognised her for what, exactly? Flashing her knickers in the tabloids? Presenting a tacky dating show on an obscure late-night satellite channel a million years ago? For getting questioned by the police over the party at her parents' house? It wasn't anything she was proud of.

'So how's Tilly?' asked Hugo, dragging his eyes away from Damon for a moment.

'Pretty good actually,' replied Sophia truthfully. 'And God it was so good to see her, Hugo ...'

'Do you want a coffee, Sophs?' asked Hugo, hopefully.

Sophia could see that her friend was desperate to stay with Damon for as long as possible, and she could understand why. But she felt utterly drained by her visit to the hospital. She hadn't been prepared for the overwhelming feelings that had swamped her. There were so many unanswered questions buzzing around her brain. What she wanted more than anything was to get back to her room, curl up on her bed and read the next instalment of Granny's memoirs. She needed to know what Granny had been talking about. She had to start unravelling the mystery before it was too late.

'No thanks, darling,' she told Hugo, trying to ignore the injured look he flashed her in response. 'We need to go home. It's getting late and it'll take us ages to get back.'

'Where d'you live?' asked Damon, cheerfully.

'East,' said Hugo, vaguely, clearly trying to imply Hoxton or Shoreditch.

'Hackney,' said Sophia, more specifically, knowing she was being naughty.

'Hackney. Brilliant,' stated Damon matter-of-factly, draining his coffee and standing up. 'I'll give you a lift then. I live in Wanstead so it's more or less on my way. I've got a van full of gear – I'm a painter and decorator – but as long as you don't mind climbing in with a few dust sheets, it's got to be better than the bus, right?'

'Oh, you really are our knight in shining armour,' gushed Hugo, squeezing Damon's arm.

As he drove through the dark, rain-drenched streets of north London with two virtual strangers beside him, Damon chatted away comfortably about his work and his family, and the band he played bass in and the football team he played for every Saturday, without an ounce of self-consciousness or awkwardness. As Hugo gazed adoringly at him with their knees touching, Sophia could almost feel the fairy dust of attraction being sprinkled on the van.

Hugo had been in love many times. Sophia always missed him when he disappeared off to live (very briefly) with the latest aging art dealer, or fashion designer, or creative director, but what she really wanted was for Hugo to be happy. Even if that meant she would end up alone.

And then the van pulled up outside their horrible house of horrors, and with a shudder the engine of Damon's van cut out.

Sophia leaned over Hugo and kissed Damon on the cheek, thanking him for the lift and telling him (with a lot of conviction) that she really hoped she'd see him again soon.

Eventually, Hugo appeared out of the van, grinning broadly. And Damon drove off, blowing a kiss at Sophia from out of his open window.

'So?' she asked Hugo hopefully. 'Did you get his number?'

Hugo nodded and grinned.

'A goodbye kiss?'

Hugo continued to nod.

'A date?'

'We're going out for dinner on Tuesday. Can you believe it? But what happened with Tilly?' asked Hugo, eagerly. 'How was she? And the big family secret? The "thing" she had to tell you?'

'I'm not exactly sure,' said Sophia. 'She wants me to find something for her. It has something to do with my mother. She says that my mum knows where it is but won't tell. It was all a bit weird.'

'You see, I was right,' said Hugo, confidently. 'There's some huge inheritance for you. It's a secret Picasso, isn't it?'

Sophia shook her head and laughed.

'No, Mr Gold-Digger, I don't think so,' she said. 'I don't

think it has much to do with money at all, actually. There's something else going on here. Something I don't understand. Yet.'

Something had shifted today. For the first time in years, Sophia felt the tug of hope pulling at her heartstrings.

Chapter Seventeen

Manhattan, New York, 2012

'What do you mean my film is too "earnest"?' asked Dominic, trying to keep the growing irritation out of his voice.

'Your job, Dominic,' said his new Head of Documentaries at ISN Media, 'is to entertain. And to get viewing figures up! These days everything has to be "sexy". Or did you miss that memo?'

The young upstart (whose name was Felicity) cocked her head and smirked to show that she was 'joking'. Except that they both knew she wasn't. She was enjoying her new power.

'I understand that documentaries have to engage the viewer,' he continued, patiently. 'My films report life as it really happens, not people playing up to the camera in an attempt to grasp their fifteen minutes of fame. I understand there's a place for that but that is not what this company does, is it? At least, it wasn't. And it's not what *I* do.'

'No ...' said Felicity. 'No, that's certainly not what you do.'

Dominic's old commissioning editor, Miles, had been sacked (or encouraged to take early retirement at least) while Dom had been busy filming in Ecuador. Which left Dominic in a rather sticky situation because Miles was the one who had sent him to Ecuador in the first place. In fact, Miles was the one who had commissioned Dom's last seven projects. In theory, Dominic was freelance, but in reality he had been working exclusively for Miles for the last five years. Now, suddenly, Miles was no longer in fashion, and that meant that Dom was screwed.

Miles had been old-school: a fiercely intelligent, Harvard-educated, liberally-minded conservationist and human rights campaigner who commissioned worthwhile, groundbreaking and insightful documentaries. In his heyday, he'd been considered the best in the business. But Miles was not what modern television needed, apparently. And now Dominic had to deal with Felicity. Felicity looked about twenty-five and had the attitude of someone who had been plucked out of media college and fast-tracked through the system without ever having had the time to gain any real experience. She was looking at Dominic as if he was a dinosaur. For the first time in his career, he had a horrible feeling his film was about to be dropped from the schedule. It felt like only five minutes ago he was a young hotshot who could do no wrong. Now, suddenly, he was being treated like an old has-been who didn't understand the world he was living in.

'What did you expect me to find in the Yasuni jungle?' he asked her, baffled. 'I uncovered mafia involvement and corruption. That's "sexy", isn't it? And don't forget I was chased by a naked indigenous tribesman with a spear. That's dangerous. It must be pretty "entertaining", surely?'

'That bit was good,' Felicity conceded, reluctantly. 'But the rest was a bit disappointing really. I mean, you didn't actually speak to these uncontacted tribespeople, did you?'

She flicked her glossy, dark hair and fixed Dominic with a bored stare. He half expected her to pop the gum she was chewing any moment.

'The Taromenane do not speak English,' Dominic explained to her slowly. 'In fact, they do not speak to anybody outside their own tribe at all. That's the whole point of my film. They have had no contact with the outside world and they do not want any contact with the outside world. It's mind-blowing! Don't you find that fascinating?'

He looked up at her hopefully.

'I'm afraid we're going to have to can the whole project, Dominic,' she said, getting stern.

She pushed her glasses up the bridge of her nose and glared at him like a disillusioned teacher scolding a lazy pupil.

'What?' said Dom, finally letting his frustration show. 'Oh, come on, I spent three months of my life out there. I shot footage no one has ever seen before, I've just spent a month editing that footage and—'

'And this company has spent thousands of dollars bankrolling a project that's never going to see the light of day,' she retorted.

'So I guess that makes us both feel a little ... pissed, huh?'

A little pissed? That was the understatement of the year! Dom stared out of the window above Felicity's head and concentrated hard on biting his tongue. There was no point in getting into a confrontation here. He had to keep Felicity onside. He would need another commission.

'Look, Dominic, I understand you're having some personal problems at the moment ...' Felicity lowered her voice to a more 'understanding' tone.

What the hell did his personal life have to do with work? And how did this jumped-up little madam know about his marriage break-up? Then he remembered that Calgary had written about 'Single Girl Dressing' in her latest fashion blog and that the whole of New York knew about his divorce.

'Maybe you need to take some time out and then, when you're feeling better, why don't you come up with some new programming ideas for me? A completely new direction though. Times are changing, Dominic. I'm after more human-led material.'

'The Taromenane are human,' Dom reminded her tersely.

'I mean humans, *people*, that viewers here, in the States, can relate to. I want glamour, entertainment, fashion, excitement, and an element of surprise. Yes, I want "sexy", Dominic! And I'm not ashamed to admit it. So go, have a few weeks off. Enjoy the holidays at your leisure. And if your creative juices start flowing again ...'

She smiled at him disingenuously.

'So, let's pencil in another meeting for the New Year, shall we? I'll get my secretary to call you when she has my diary in front of her. Oh, and Dominic. Have a very happy Christmas.'

'Sure,' said Dominic, standing up and shaking Felicity's hand. 'You too.'

When she stood up he realised she was barely five feet tall. He felt as if he'd just been told off by an eighth-grader.

Dominic decided to walk back downtown rather than catch the subway. Have a happy Christmas? What a joke! It was a cold, crisp November day and after the meeting he'd just had he could do with some fresh air. Since when did Christmas start in November anyway? He walked past the shops with Christmas decorations in the windows, and past the street sellers offering wicker reindeer and bunches of mistletoe. He tried not to let the Christmas songs that poured out onto the street from every building he passed seep into his head. When he was a kid, no matter how broke the family were, Christmas had always fixed everything, temporarily at least. But this year the magic was gone.

Chapter Eighteen

Beaumont House, Wiltshire, 1947

When Mama and Wilfred finally arrived back from the Caribbean, they sold a couple of the few remaining paintings that had been cheering up the walls in our modest living room where Papa slept, and used the money to move to the cottage next door to our own. They had the entire place redecorated and bought brand new, fashionable furniture from Heal's in London. When I complained to Papa that this was preposterous he just shrugged and told me that he was beyond worrying about such things as family heirlooms or money and that he certainly couldn't give two hoots where, or with whom, his wife lived.

To say my teenage years were unconventional would be a dreadful understatement. While my wounded father and I lived in the gardener's cottage, quietly and modestly, my mother and her lover lived lavishly in the remodelled blacksmith's cottage next door. With the war over, the parties began again. But even I could see that there was no joy in these soirées. My mother and her friends were simply going through the motions because they didn't know what else to do if they weren't getting dressed up, eating, drinking, gossiping and telling frightfully funny stories. As we tried to sleep, or read, or listen to a play on the radio, we would often be disturbed by the noise of a raucous dinner party spilling out of Mama's cottage. Meanwhile, the rotting carcass of Beaumont House loomed over us, reminding us all of what we had lost.

Sometimes men in suits from London would come to talk to my father about his businesses and the house. The Empire had crumbled after the war. As entire nations were bought, sold, bartered over and exchanged, overseas business interests like my father's simply evaporated. There was very little left. Any money Papa did recover from abroad was a pittance in comparison to what he would have needed to save Beaumont House. I overheard the gentlemen from London offer to buy the place. But Papa did not want to be rid of the burden.

'I was born here, and I shall die here,' he told me. 'Let me live out my days at Beaumont. After that I couldn't care less what happens to the place. Do whatever you like with it, Tilly. It will be yours by then, after all.'

The last party ever to take place at Beaumont House was my eighteenth birthday on New Year's Eve 1947. As the clock struck midnight, I would come of age. Papa had persuaded Mrs Ashton to rally the old troops and for one day only – on the eve of the New Year – the Beaumont Estate buzzed with staff. They swept the cobwebs out of the ballroom and dusted off the chandeliers. They hung bunting and balloons from the walls and laid white linen tablecloths over any old tables that they'd found stored in the cottages, barns and stables. Mrs Ashton reopened the kitchens and, once again, the old place was alive with the sound of chattering voices. The walls were scarred, the floors creaked and the windows rattled with the howling wind, but none of us cared. For one night only there was joy in our home and our hearts.

Nanny came, her husband Martin too, and Mr Wise and dear Tony's parents. In fact, so many of the old staff turned out for my party that it felt like more of a family reunion than an eighteenth birthday celebration. Mrs Ashton had even managed to get in touch with my old chums from Westonbirt and they had all made their way to Beaumont House despite the storm that raged outside. Batty old Aunt Ophelia had somehow travelled all the way from St Ives and my only regret was that the Trevallions had not been able to come too. When I asked Aunt Ophelia where my dear Cornish friends were, she remembered that they had emigrated straight after the war but couldn't recall for the life of her which country, or even which continent, they'd moved to.

Mama wore a ridiculously opulent purple taffeta ball gown, a fox fur stole and a diamond tiara she'd had hidden under her bed. She got stuck into the champagne long before dinner was served and was completely blotto by nine p.m. I was mortified but did my best to ignore her as she flirted with boys my age and tripped over the long skirt of her dress. Wilfred sulked in a corner for the remainder of the night and that suited me just fine.

Papa looked remarkably debonair in his best suit. His scars would never heal but his hair had grown back rather well, he had colour in his cheeks and a wide smile on his face. It was the best birthday present I could have wished for. He had bought me the most extraordinary dress for my birthday – it was made from the plushest red velvet, with a decadently full skirt, a tiny, cinched waist and a sweetheart neck. The dress was part of Dior's 'New Look' collection, which had taken the fashion world by storm earlier that year, and Papa had had it shipped over from Paris especially. It wasn't like the good old days, before the war, when Papa could pick up couture clothes whenever he was in Paris. It had taken him months to get his hands on the dress this time but he told me it was remarkable what one could achieve with a telephone, and a few old contacts left in Paris from the good old days! There were shoes too – shiny, black, patent-leather pumps with a vicious, spiky high heel. I was in heaven! After years of wearing drab, patched-up clothes, stepping into my new outfit felt like stepping into a new world. Which I suppose I was. I had reached adulthood and was stepping out of my childhood for good. I even borrowed Mama's red lipstick and felt rather pleased with myself that it suited me so well. Papa said I reminded him of Katharine Hepburn, which really was the biggest compliment ever. I was obsessed with films, actors, actresses and anything to do with Hollywood and the movies. I went to bed every night dreaming of becoming a famous actress, not that I would ever have admitted that to Papa. I'm not sure he would have approved.

I drank champagne and danced the jitterbug until my head spun. Mrs Ashton had found a wonderful band from Bath who played all the latest tunes. By the time midnight approached I think I was a little tipsy because I remember thinking that I might rather like to kiss my friend Amelia's brother, Bernard, at midnight. And, in hindsight, Bernard really wasn't much of a catch! Thankfully my father intervened just before the bells rang for my birthday and the New Year. He insisted I had to come with him for one more little surprise. I followed, as the men carried Papa in his wheelchair to the half-landing on the grand central staircase and from there he clinked a glass with a spoon until everyone had turned to look at us. The ancient grandfather clock on the landing upstairs rang, once, twice, three times ... until finally 1947 was over. Once everyone had calmed down, Papa spoke.

'I would like to present my darling daughter, Matilda, one final token of my adoration on this, the occasion of her eighteenth birthday. As you all know, Tilly has sacrificed a great deal for me over the last two years. She has given up her studies and her social life to nurse me full time. To look at me you may think I am not a lucky man, but you would be wrong. I have Tilly, the most wonderful gift of all, and for that I am truly blessed. And so, here, I have a rather special gift that I know she will love and cherish for ever. It's something that Matilda has dreamed of since she was a very little girl. So, without further ado, Mr Fitzroy ...?'

My head spun. Fitzroy? It was a name I hadn't heard in years, although I had remembered him on occasion with great fondness. He appeared, beaming, from the top of the staircase above me carrying a blue velvet Asprey jewellery case.

'Happy birthday, dear girl.'

He handed the box to my father with a lavish bow. By now my heart was in my mouth. How could it be? I could barely allow myself to hope that ...

'For you, Tilly,' said my father, handing me the box.

I opened it with shaking hands and when I saw what was inside I couldn't help but let out the loudest gasp imaginable. Everybody laughed and clapped.

'Pearls!' I exclaimed. 'The most perfect pearls!'

'A choker,' grinned Papa, proudly. 'Just what you wished for before the war. Do you remember, darling?'

Did I remember? How could I ever forget? Papa clearly had no idea what a special day that had been for me.

'It's the most gorgeous thing I have ever seen, Papa,' I gasped. 'Thank you. I shall cherish this necklace always.'

I bent down, kissed him and hugged him.

'They're from Japan,' he told me. 'Hand-picked by mermaids as you said! Sixty-seven perfect, round, champagne-coloured pearls. And this one ...' He fingered the centrepiece of the necklace; an enormous luminous pearl of breathtaking beauty which sat proudly in the middle of the central strand. 'This one is something else. Isn't it, Fitzroy?'

Fitzroy nodded.

'It's the most perfect gem I have ever had the privilege to work with,' he said.

'It has taken Mr Fitzroy and his colleagues many years to find the right pearls for your choker, Matilda. In fact, he only got his hands on them a few weeks ago, didn't you, Fitzroy? It's rather difficult getting gems out of Japan these days. We thought you might have to wait until your twenty-first birthday. And look here,' Papa continued, 'he's had them fixed with a special clasp. You see, darling? It's platinum, studded with twelve more tiny pearls, and on the back it has your initials engraved. Including the Lady!'

He laughed, a little embarrassed at the gesture, and shrugged.

'A little indulgent perhaps, pretentious even, but it wasn't meant that way. It's just you really have proved yourself to be a lady of the very highest calibre these past few years, my darling, and I wanted to mark that. You are no longer my little girl, Tilly. You are undoubtedly a Lady. Do you like it?'

I was almost lost for words.

'I love it, Papa, and whenever I wear it I will think of you.'

'It's my pleasure, Tilly. Absolutely the least I can do to repay you for all you've done for me these past two years. Here, bend down, my darling. Let me put it on you.'

Everyone cheered as I stood up straight to show them my wonderful present. The huge, central pearl sat perfectly on my throat and I thought I would burst with pride as everyone applauded. Everyone, that is, except my mother, who I saw downing another glass of champagne before she glared at me once and then flounced off out of the ballroom. Mrs Ashton watched her exit too, and then she caught my eye and smiled a little sadly. I remembered what she'd said about Mama not coping well with me growing up and I finally realised what she'd meant. But even my mother could not have brought me down that night. Papa had made my childhood dreams come true and, as I stood at the top of those stairs, wearing my beautiful pearls, I felt as though I was on top of the world. I wish I could have captured that moment for ever.

In the weeks that followed I took my necklace out of the box and tried it on at least ten times a day. It really was exquisite but my dowdy country-girl clothes really didn't do it justice. I wondered if I would ever lead the life that went with my new necklace. I had started to worry about how exactly Papa had managed to buy my birthday present. I had sixty-seven perfect saltwater pearls (seventy-nine if I counted the tiny ones in the clasp!) in my possession, one of which was so large it made my eyes water, and yet my father could not afford to re-roof his house. But when I asked him about the expense he told me not to worry. He said he had first mentioned the necklace to Mr Fitzroy long before the war started and that he had insisted on giving Asprey a large deposit to buy the pearls at the start. He said he had wanted to secure the very finest pearls for my necklace. And, he added, it was a good thing he had done so too, otherwise my necklace wouldn't have been ready until my wedding day. Papa insisted it was money from another time and another world. It jarred with me slightly but I knew there was no point in offering to give up my new necklace. We could have sold it and used the money to start repairs on Beaumont House but a new roof would never have made Papa as happy as he was when he gave me that necklace.

That winter, Papa fell ill with influenza. He developed pneumonia and died in his sleep on 13th February 1948. I cried every day for three months. Mama cried a lot too, but that was because Papa had changed his will after the war. He had left Mama a modest lump sum of money but he had left Beaumont House, all the land and the cottages to me. She barely disguised her hatred for me after Papa died. She tried to contest the will, arguing that Papa wasn't in his right mind when he made those changes, but she couldn't get anyone to take her seriously and the case never got to court.

That summer, she and Wilfred moved to Dorset and bought a spacious modern bungalow on the beach near Poole in some up-and-coming area called Sandbanks. She took with her the jewellery that rightfully belonged to me but I decided she was welcome to it. No amount of diamonds would ever bring her happiness. She wrote to me from time to time, more to boast about her fabulous new life than to ask after my well-being. She and Wilfred had made such marvellous new friends; she was quite the talk of Bournemouth and Poole apparently. The truth was, she'd started drinking her way into oblivion. I was not to see my mother again for many years.

Papa had been the heart and soul of Beaumont House. With him gone, the house was nothing but an old, decrepit, empty shell. I was the only Beaumont left and I could never fill that house on my own. I was eighteen years old, an only child, with few friends and no experience of business. The men from London, who had visited my father, explained to me that there was no way I could afford to keep the house on my own. They advised me to sell up and start again and explained that, for an eighteen-year-old, I would be very wealthy indeed. I sold Beaumont House to a young entrepreneur from Birmingham who had made his money in steel. He seemed likable enough and was awfully enthusiastic about the house and grounds but I had no interest in knowing what his plans for the place were. The new owner would have to spend far more on the house to restore it than he had paid me to buy it. I remembered what Papa had told me: that once he was dead I could do whatever I liked with Beaumont House and that made my decision far easier.

I fancied London, but I was an unworldly country girl and needed to

be somewhere relatively quiet and green, so I bought myself a delight-
ful Georgian townhouse in Hampstead that overlooked the Heath.
That is where I headed, in the ancient Bedford van, with Badger on
the passenger seat, as I left Beaumont House. When I drove out of the
drive for the final time in December 1948, I did not look back.

Hackney, London, 2012

'I know what it is,' shouted Sophia excitedly, banging on Hugo's bedroom door.

Sophia had been right. Something had shifted yesterday. Here she was up (if not dressed in anything more than an oversized T-shirt) at the crack of dawn, with energy, purpose and maybe even the beginnings of a plan. She was starting to feel a lot more positive about life: not exactly full of the joys of spring, but then it was a particularly wet and miserable November, her grandmother was dying and she had recently had her heart broken by both her ex-fiancé and her own father.

She tried not to think too much about what her dad had done. It made her spin out and lose focus. At first, when Nathan had told her, she'd wanted to call her dad and scream at him, demanding to know why a man would want to destroy his own daughter's life. But she'd taken to her bed instead. Now the pain had faded a little. Oh, it was still there, locked in a tight angry ball somewhere deep in her heart, but she had buried it for the time being. The wound was a little less raw than it had been a couple of weeks ago but she still had no desire to face her father. Not yet. She had Granny back in her life and for now that was all the family contact she needed. Besides, it was obvious why her dad had done it: he thought she was worthless. Nothing Sophia did would ever change his opinion, of that she was sure.

Somehow, this morning, she had managed to shrug off Nathan, and instead she felt utterly focused on the future. She could hear Hugo's voice drifting through the door, soft and low, less cutting than usual, and she wondered if he was talking to Damon. She hoped he was. Good men were few and far between and Hugo would be crazy to let that one slip away. But that didn't mean she didn't want him to hang up and let her in – right now!

'Hugo!' she said again. 'Let me in! I know what it is that Granny needs me to find.'

There was a thump from inside and then the door swung open. He was already immaculately dressed and cleanly shaved. The whiff of expensive aftershave wafted out of his room. Hugo told whoever was on the phone that he would see them later.

'What? What is it?' he demanded.

'It's my inheritance,' she told him, handing Hugo the letter.

His eyes skimmed the letter quickly, greedily.

'A nineteen-forties choker of Oriental pearls made by Asprey of London. And belonging to Tilly Beaumont, Hollywood Legend. I wonder what they're worth?'

Sophia shrugged.

'I have no idea,' she admitted. 'I'm more confused by how they went missing in the first place. They were her eighteenth birthday present from my grandfather. They must have meant the world to her. How on earth would she lose her most treasured possession?'

Chapter Nineteen

Tokyo, Japan, 2012

Aiko's speech at the conference had gone exceptionally well. Later, once all the delegates had finally left, she had met up with her son, Ken, and his wife, Suki, for dinner at the Imperial. Ken and Suki lived in the Tokyo suburbs and ran the Japanese arm of the family business. She Skyped Ken often but it was not the same as seeing him in the flesh and it had been a wonderful evening.

She had fallen asleep easily at first, exhausted but content from her busy day and the broken sleep she had suffered the night before. She had been firm with herself. No more ghosts. Tonight she would sleep like a baby. And yet here she was, wide awake again, in the dead of night, with her heart pounding. Perhaps she was losing her mind. Aiko certainly didn't seem to be in control of her own thoughts any more. Although she was half awake, her dream continued. It played like a horror movie in her head and Aiko had no power to turn it off.

Ise Shima, Japan, 1927

The Ama hut, or *amagoya,* was already buzzing with activity and the voices of twenty or so women when Manami arrived for work.

'Good morning, Manami-san!' shouted her friends, sisters and cousins. 'You are late. Were you too busy brushing your hair?' they teased. Manami was known to be vain.

'Is Yoshiro late today also?' teased another voice. 'His sister tells me you lovebirds would stay in bed all day if his mother didn't beat you out with her broom!'

Manami took her friends' teasing in good spirits. Her family were revered as the oldest and best diving family in the region and, although they were not rich in terms of wealth, they were certainly fruitful in terms of talent. And Manami – beautiful, passionate, fiery Manami – was considered the ultimate Ama princess. As such, she was forgiven for being a few minutes late in the morning. Yoshiro always said that Manami was an entirely different species from the other girls in the village – a full head taller than most, her limbs were long and graceful, her hair fell down her back in a braid as thick as a rope and her eyes had so much fire in them that they were more amber in colour than brown.

A few months before, a stranger had turned up on these shores carrying strange machines. He was dressed in a dark linen suit and a hat. He looked as alien as the foreign men Manami had seen in the pages of Mr Nishimoto's newspapers and yet this man, Mr Fanaki, claimed he was from Tokyo! It turned out that his machines were photographic equipment – he was here because he had heard of the Ama and he wanted to take photographs of them and ask them questions so that the whole world would know of their extraordinary talents.

Some of the Ama had refused to have their photographs taken – especially the older women. Mr Fanaki did not seem particularly upset when they refused. He preferred to photograph the younger, prettier girls. Manami did not blame him. Besides, of all the Ama, it was Manami who Mr Fanaki seemed most interested in.

'It's not only that you are beautiful, it is because you are naked and beautiful,' Yoshiro had laughed at the time. 'In the cities, girls do not walk around in their loincloths as you Ama girls do.'

'If they get pleasure from looking, then let them,' Manami had laughed back. 'Who am I to deprive a businessman in Tokyo his pleasure? Besides, I am nursing Aiko. My breasts have never looked so fine. It is right that they should be admired!'

Manami had loved posing for the photographs. She had never felt shy – she had spent her entire working life naked. Manami had loved answering Mr Fanaki's questions too.

'No,' she had laughed. 'A boy cannot become an Ama. Women have an extra layer of fat. We can stay in the water much longer than men and collect a bigger catch. I have heard that there are male divers in some villages but not here. It's silly! They cannot cope with the cold waters. Men should stick to their boats and their fishing nets.'

Mr Fanaki had seemed surprised at the Ama's lack of respect for their menfolk.

'We do respect them,' Manami's mother, Umiko, the undisputed matriarch of the *amagoya*, had insisted, 'but they respect us too. We can make more money collecting abalone than they can from catching fish.'

'So you are not Dragon Wives?' Mr Fanaki had probed. 'I heard the Ama are known as Dragon Wives because you are so dominant!'

The amagoya had filled with the sound of laughter and shrieking then.

'Yes, we are Dragon Wives!' Umiko had said. 'And proud! But it does not put men off! It's a blessing to be an Ama. We can choose whichever husband we want. We make money. We support our families. We are valuable assets to our husbands and if we nag a bit? If we have our own opinions? So be it! They are lucky to have us.'

Mr Fanaki had continued. 'Divers can get very sick from going so deep. Do you ever worry about drowning?'

'We have breathing techniques,' Umiko had replied with a frown. 'Only novices are in danger and only then if they do not concentrate or listen to their elders.'

The *amagoya* had become deathly quiet. All the Ama knew that this was a lie. Women had died during dives. Many women over the years. Some of them very experienced and very wise. They all knew this. And then there were the older Ama who could only work in the shallows now, who had got sick after one particular dive and who had never been quite the same since. There was one woman of about Umiko's age who couldn't speak any more and another whose right side was paralysed. One of Manami's cousins, who was almost thirty, now behaved like a five-year-old child. Common was the sight of an Ama coming out of the sea with blood pouring from her ears after her eardrums had burst with the pressure. And hadn't they all suffered headaches sometimes? Hadn't they all felt the pain in their chests? But even Manami had known better than to talk of these things with Mr Fanaki. It would have been bad luck to say those things out loud.

Sensing the Ama's discomfort, Mr Fanaki had changed the subject. 'And what about the pearls?' he'd asked, his eyes shining with excitement.

At that, some of the women had rolled their eyes in Manami's direction.

'We collect shellfish, urchins, seaweed,' Umiko had replied abruptly. 'But we make the most money from abalone. That's what the seafood company wants. Not pearls.'

'But I thought Ama were pearl divers? Pearls can be worth a fortune,' Mr Fanaki had continued, looking a little disappointed.

'Yes,' Umiko had replied patiently. 'Very rarely you find a pearl. But you would have to collect tons of oysters to discover just one. And then? Then most would be too small, or mis-shapen, or a bad colour. Maybe once or twice in a year an Ama will find a pearl that is worth something to the fishing company and that is a blessing, indeed. But we do not spend all our days searching for pearls. What sort of gamble is that? To waste our life on a maybe? Perhaps in the past our ancestors were diving more for pearls. But that was before the fishing company arrived. We can collect seaweed, urchins and abalone every day. That is our job. Besides, Man has found a way of making pearls now. Real pearls are dead. They belong to our ancestors.'

'But real pearls are priceless,' Mr Fanaki argued. Umiko had flashed a warning look in Manami's direction. Manami had known what her mother's look meant. But the fire in her belly had risen then and she could not swallow her words.

'I still look for pearls,' Manami had blurted out. 'And I find them. I gave Nishimoto-san three last year.'

Again, the small hut had filled with the sound of laughter.

'One day I am going to find a pearl so huge and so perfect that I will be able to live like an empress,' Manami had boasted.

Umiko had walked off then, obviously angry with her young-est daughter, and the other Ama had continued to giggle and tease, but Mr Fanaki had leaned in closer to Manami, eager to hear her words.

'Ever since I was a tiny child I have dreamed of finding a pearl. It is the largest, most perfect pearl anyone has ever seen. And it is going to save me: me, my husband Yoshiro, my baby Aiko and any of my family who want to come too. We will build a big house with a pond full of koi carp. We will have peacocks in the gardens. I will dress in beautiful silk kimonos and Yoshiro will eat like an emperor. We will have servants. Then I will travel to all the fancy places I have heard of. I will visit the theatre and the mountains and the lakes. Perhaps I will even visit you in Tokyo, Mr Fanaki, and you will be able to show me your world just as I have been able to show you mine.'

'But would you not miss the ocean?' Mr Fanaki had asked, wide-eyed. 'If diving is in your blood, then how could you leave the water behind?'

Manami had thrown her head back and laughed then. What a stupid question to have asked!

'I will never leave the ocean,' she'd replied. 'We'll build our house right on the beach and I will dive every day. But I will do it for the sheer joy of it. I will do it so that I can feel as wild and free as a dolphin. Not so that I can collect abalone for the fishing company.'

Mr Fanaki had written down all of Manami's words in the small, black leather notebook he carried with him. Manami was fascinated by the way his smooth, clean hands made their delicate little strokes so swiftly on the pages. She had never seen a man with such unblemished hands – not even the doctor had hands like that. Not that Manami could read the words he wrote. She had never been to school.

Mr Fanaki had stayed in the village for five days, much to Mr Nishimoto's annoyance as there hadn't been much time for diving with all the posing and boasting that had gone on that week. (Although rumour had it that Mr Fanaki had paid Mr Nishimoto a handsome sum for the Ama's time and that Mr Nishimoto had pocketed this money for himself, rather than passing it on to the fishing company.) When Mr Fanaki finally left, he had bowed before Manami and said, 'It was an honour to meet you, beautiful Manami-san. I will pray that all your dreams come true and that one day you will come to Tokyo and find me.' He had handed her a little card with some writing on it. Manami had had no idea what it said but she'd taken it home with her that night and put it in her box of special things. Just in case it should ever come in useful.

'Hurry up, Manami,' Umiko called impatiently from across

the wooden hut. 'Stop daydreaming, child! There's work to be done!'

'Sorry, Mother, I was thinking about Mr Fanaki,' said Manami. 'I was wondering if our photographs have appeared in newspapers in Tokyo yet.'

'What does it matter if they have or have not?' Umiko asked. 'If we cannot see them they might as well not exist.'

'Just because you can't see something doesn't mean it's not important, Mother,' retorted Manami. 'We cannot see Tokyo but we know it exists. And we cannot see the abalone from the beach, can we?'

'No, we cannot, Manami,' snapped Umiko impatiently. 'So get diving before one of the others beats you to the day's best catch.'

Although there was a real camaraderie in the Ama hut, there was also a great deal of secrecy. No Ama would let slip if she'd discovered a particularly fruitful diving ground – not even to her mother, or sister, or best friend.

But Manami had learned as a very small girl that if she sat quietly in a corner and pretended to be very busy cleaning knives, or listening to her friends chatting, or humming to herself, the older women would forget she was there and sometimes they'd let a little nugget of information slip out within her earshot. By the age of six, she was observing the older women's diving habits with the focus of a heron stalking fish. Little by little the young Ama had amassed a great deal of knowledge and stored it in the library of her mind. By the time she was old enough to dive in the shallows, she knew how the tides affected the crops of abalone and oysters. She knew which waters were more fruitful in spring and which were more giving in the autumn. She understood that a cold snap changed the water temperature and therefore the depth of the crop. She knew exactly where the seaweed and shellfish would end up after a storm and she knew exactly how long a diver had to stay under to collect the biggest catch. And that is how Manami came to be the most successful young Ama in Shima province.

At first the older women proclaimed that she was simply lucky and that the sea spirits must be on her side. Her mother boasted that it was in Manami's blood to be naturally gifted. Haruki insisted that it was because she herself had taught her youngest granddaughter her techniques. But the simple truth was that Manami was as bright as a magic lantern. While the other little girls had been playing, she'd been sucking up the older Ama's knowledge like a sea sponge and now she was reaping the rewards. Needless to say, the older, more experienced Ama were very tight-lipped around Manami these days. Even her own mother seemed a little guarded about where she was planning to dive.

But Manami had her secrets too. Oh, she talked often to the others about her plans to make money from pearls and to escape this life but they did not know the truth. The truth was that while the other girls her age scavenged for abalone, Manami had already amassed a private collection of pearls. She had found the first one when she was only a child. It had been a stroke of luck; a freak oyster in a rock pool just offshore that happened to be hiding a beautiful secret. She had not handed that pearl over to the fishing company. Nor had she given it to her mother. She had hidden it in her loincloth, sneaked it home and kept it safely in a small silk pouch which she hid under a loose floorboard. Over the years there had been many more finds. The smaller ones, she gave to Nishimoto-san. But the best ones she kept for herself. Now Manami had a collection of over twenty pearls. But she needed more. The bigger the collection, the more it would be worth. And most of all, she needed a really, really big one. She needed to find the pearl of her dreams.

She knew that Haruki had a secret collection too. Manami had found it once, rolled up in her grandmother's silk wedding kimono in the dusty old *tansu* that nobody ever opened any more. Haruki's secret had fed her own. But unlike Haruki, Manami would not keep her collection hidden until she was old and grey. She would use it while she was still young. She would buy herself, her husband and her child a better life with those pearls.

'Have you seen Yoshiro this morning?' she asked Umiko hopefully as she slipped off her robe. 'I was thinking about work. I thought maybe it was time that I went out on his boat?' she suggested, not for the first time.

Umiko shook her head even more firmly. 'You are not ready, Manami. How many times do we need to discuss this? Perhaps next season.'

Yushi laughed at her younger sister and said, in her best Haruki impression, 'Before you ride a horse, you must ride an ox, Manami-chan.'

Manami shot Yushi a warning look. How dare her sister belittle her like that! Everyone knew that Manami was the more talented of the two. Just because Yushi was older, it meant she could go out on her husband's boat with him and dive with weights attached to her waist. Yushi could dive to the bottom of the ocean but Manami could not. Plus Yushi could spend all day with her husband. And those two didn't even like each other. What she and Yoshiro would give to have that time together! It simply wasn't fair. Manami could feel the anger smouldering in her belly.

'Be calm, Manami,' her mother warned. 'Yushi is simply teasing you. Why must you always burn with rage like this? When will you learn? A firework might light up the night sky but it only glows for a moment and then it's gone. You are not even eighteen yet,' she continued, patiently. 'And besides, you and Yoshiro cannot be trusted to work together. You would get distracted. We have Aiko to prove that fact!'

Manami blushed. Her mother was a stubborn woman, and there was no way she was going to give in on this subject. Not today, at least. But she had another plan. If she couldn't get out into the open sea on Yoshiro's boat, she would swim there herself. She began to unwrap the tool Granny had given her.

'What have you got there?' Umiko asked.

'Grandmother's *tegane*,' replied Manami. 'She gave it to me. She said it would bring me luck. She seems to think I need it!'

Manami saw a shadow cross her mother's face.

'She gave you that?' asked Umiko, her voice shaking a little. 'Give it to me,' she continued, gravely.

Manami frowned, confused, and held the *tegane* to her chest. 'No, Mother,' she replied. 'Grandmother wanted me to have it. It's a gift. It belonged to her and now she wants it to be mine.'

'And before it belonged to your grandmother, it belonged to someone else,' continued Umiko sternly. 'That *tegane* is cursed. Grandmother should have thrown it in the ocean years ago. I don't understand why she's given it to you.'

'What do you mean, Mother?' asked Manami.

Umiko was quiet for a very long time. She held her head in

her hands as if she was battling a great war in her mind. Finally she spoke.

'You're right, Manami. I cannot take away a gift from your grandmother. Perhaps she knows something that I don't. I would rather you left that here in the *amagoya* but it's your choice.' Umiko's shoulders slouched as if the battle had defeated her.

'You worry too much,' said Manami, trying to lighten the mood. 'Go. I'll see you later.'

Umiko was not a tactile woman. Over the years she had shown her love for her children through clean clothes and bandaged knees rather than by showering them with kisses. And so it took Manami by surprise when her mother held her face gently in her hands and kissed her forehead tenderly.

A bewildered Manami watched her mother leave. Sometimes her family was crazily superstitious! They saw mystery and meaning and blessings and omens in everything. It could be exhausting. Yoshiro's family was more grounded. His people came from earth and wood while Manami's came from water and fire. Manami loved Yoshiro's strength. His roots kept her tied firmly to solid ground. Of course, Grandmother saw things rather differently.

'You are fire and Yoshiro is wood,' Haruki had stated, gravely, on the day of their wedding. 'Be careful your flames don't burn down his tree, Manami-chan.'

Chapter Twenty

This time Sophia marched confidently through the hospital corridors, waved hello at the nurses, knocked on the door of Granny's room and waltzed straight in with a smile on her face.

'Darling, you're early!' announced her grandmother, grinning. 'Wonders will never cease.'

Sophia smiled back, kissed her granny's soft cheek and handed her the box of lavender shortbread she'd bought on the way.

'You look well,' she said, making herself comfortable on the bed beside her grandmother.

'Looks can be deceiving,' grimaced Granny. 'I felt wretched when I woke up this morning but it's amazing what a dose of morphine and a bit of make-up can do.'

But Sophia was staring at the silver-framed photograph on her grandmother's bedside cabinet. She had seen pictures of her grandmother in her youth so many times before but now, having read the letters, it all seemed much more real. Granny looked amazing in her Dior dress and there, wound around her swan-like neck, were the exquisite pearls: three strands with an enormous centrepiece, just as Granny had described. Sophia was mesmerised.

'My necklace,' said Granny, noticing Sophia's eyes being drawn to the pearls. 'Isn't it beautiful?'

Sophia picked up the photograph and looked closer. The pearls were larger than she had imagined and even in the old black and white picture their lustre shone out.

'It's gorgeous,' she said. 'Your dad must have loved you so much.'

'He did,' replied Tilly with a certainty that Sophia envied. 'Which is why this is all so terrible.' She placed her hand on

Sophia's forearm. 'The fact that they're missing, darling. It won't do. How can I rest easy until we have them back in the family? Papa gave me those to cherish. Besides, those pearls should be yours.'

Sophia nodded but said nothing. She desperately wanted to know more about the choker, and what exactly had happened to it, but she was reluctant to ask too many questions. She didn't want her grandmother to think that all she was interested in was her inheritance. But Granny did the talking for her.

'Promise you'll help me, darling,' she said. 'There's nothing I can do from here. You're the only one I can trust.'

Granny looked up at her with watery blue eyes, and although it was obvious she did want those pearls back, Sophia found herself wondering whether her grandmother was still playing a role of some sort. But what role? And why?

'Are you sure Mum doesn't have the necklace somewhere for safe keeping?' asked Sophia, trying to be rational. 'Or Dad? You know what he's like. He has all your paintings in secure storage somewhere, doesn't he?'

'Yes,' said Granny. 'But the necklace should never have left the family.'

'How do you know it's actually left the family?' Sophia probed gently. 'Like I said, perhaps Mum has it—'

'No!' replied Granny, her eyes flashing now. 'You must believe me, Sophia. It's gone. And I have to find it before it's too late.'

'But I don't understand, Granny,' said Sophia. 'Why do you need me to find it? Why don't you ask Mum?'

'I have tried,' said her grandmother, her voice breaking. 'But you know what she's like. She's so vague and detached sometimes. She doesn't seem to feel any sense of urgency about anything. And, of course, your father always has to take over and you know how he tries my patience.'

Sophia swallowed hard. This all sounded far more complicated than she'd imagined. How on earth was she supposed to track down a missing pearl necklace? Her mother wasn't talking to her and if her grandmother had no other ideas, she was stuck before she'd even started.

Her grandmother took a deep breath and started again.

'It's quite simple, my darling,' she said, in a forced, perky tone. 'My beloved papa gave me that necklace and I would dearly love to see it again before I die. Besides, I wanted you to have it. You should have had it on your eighteenth birthday, just like I did, just like your mother did. It is your necklace just as much as it is mine. And wouldn't you love to own something so perfect? So exceptional? Not many women have that chance.'

Sophia thought hard. Was this just an elaborate ruse to force her into calling her mother, she wondered? Was her grandmother's greatest wish before she died actually to reunite her daughter and her granddaughter, rather than to track down some missing necklace? She didn't doubt that Matilda's heart was in the right place, but how could she trust her motives? 'Ask your mother. Alice knows,' Granny had said yesterday. Sophia would dearly love to find Granny's choker but the last thing she wanted was to ask her mother anything. Still, it would make her grandmother happy and wasn't that all that mattered now? She didn't have to play happy families. She didn't have to talk to her father. All she had to do was make one phone call to her mum. For Granny's sake. Besides, there was no denying that even the faintest hope of ever owning such a treasured possession was strangely intoxicating.

'When did you last see the necklace?' she asked, playing along with her granny's game.

'Nineteen eighty-one,' said her grandmother with absolute certainty.

'Nineteen eighty-one?' repeated Sophia, trying to keep the disbelief out of her voice. 'You'd like me to find a pearl necklace that you haven't seen for over thirty years?'

'Yes,' said Granny with conviction.

'I thought you meant it went missing recently,' said Sophia incredulously. 'I thought you wanted me to root around in your jewellery boxes, or to check my parents' safe or something. Where do I begin to look for something that's been missing since before I was born? I can't even find matching underwear in my bedroom!'

'I am well aware that your parents don't always credit you with the intelligence you were born with, yes,' replied her grandmother, evenly. 'But I had always assumed that you didn't believe their assessment of you, and that you were as aware of your many skills and talents as I am. I'm certainly not going to treat you like a fool just so you carry on being a ... what does your father call you?'

'A loafer.'

'Yes, that's it. You are far too clever to waste your time doing nothing, young lady.'

Sophia smiled despite herself. Granny had always been the only one who thought she was a genius – even when her school reports had claimed otherwise. If it was another one of her granny's little ploys, then the compliment worked.

'OK, I'm in,' she said. 'But you're going to have to tell me everything about the pearls.'

As the old woman sat quietly for a moment, Sophia could see she was silently seething.

'It didn't used to make me so angry that the necklace was missing,' she said eventually. 'I had so many pretty jewels and fancy gowns. I was spoilt. But now I have so little time left, those other luxuries have lost their shine, this is the one that matters – I can see that now. That necklace was more than a piece of jewellery. It is a piece of history – *my* history, *our* history. It is irreplaceable.'

She lay back on her pillows. She looked worn out suddenly and the colour had drained from her cheeks.

'Silly, I suppose. To long for something from the past, from my youth, when my life's so near to the end ... But ... That necklace was my link to Papa, it was the reason your grandfather and I ever got talking, it was the necklace I wore on my wedding day, and at the premier of my first film, at the Oscars, at your mother's christening ... It was my link to the past and I wanted it to be my link to the future, once I'm gone.'

'I promise you, I'll do everything I can to help find it,' Sophia pledged. 'I'll do anything, Granny. I'll even speak to my mum, OK? I'd love to see you wearing your pearls again. And when we find it, we'll drink champagne. Deal?'

Her grandmother smiled but her face remained tinged with sadness.

'Champagne it is. But we don't have much time, Sophia,' she said gravely. 'You do know the consultant says we're talking weeks, not months?'

Sophia nodded and fought back the tears. This was no time for weakness. Granny needed her to be strong.

'So where do I start?' she asked. 'Can you remember exactly where and when you last saw the pearls?'

Granny looked away for a moment and stared out of the window, as if she was considering carefully what she should say next. Not for the first time, Sophia had the sense that her grandmother knew more about what had happened to the pearls than she was letting on. And now she had reeled Sophia in, she was deciding exactly how much to tell her.

'I gave the necklace to your mother for her eighteenth birthday,' admitted Granny finally. 'And in turn you would have been given it on your eighteenth birthday. Had it not vanished ...'

'And so, then Mummy wore it ...' Sophia urged her granny to go on.

'No,' said Granny. 'That's the strange thing. I never saw her wear it after her eighteenth birthday party. Not once. I thought perhaps it just wasn't her style. It was the nineteen eighties and, believe it or not, she was a very fashion-conscious girl at the time. I didn't mind. I thought she'd keep it safe and grow into it over time. But on her wedding day I asked her if she was going to wear it and she said no. No explanation, no excuses. Just no. And then when you were christened, it was the same thing. No pearls.'

'Weren't you angry with her?' asked Sophia, shocked.

Sophia couldn't imagine her goody-goody mother refusing to wear the family jewels to her wedding. She was such a conformist these days.

'It was her wedding day. I couldn't make a fuss, could I? I wasn't keen on her getting married at eighteen, or her permed hair, or her groom either, quite frankly! But your grandfather made me promise not to make her cry on her special day. She had come back from Italy in a really strange mood. She announced she wasn't going to go to university and that she was going to get married instead. It was as if a different girl came home after her trip. She'd obviously had a hard time and all I wanted was to have my happy, bubbly Alice back. So even though I was sad about her not wearing the pearls, I didn't want to do anything to upset her because I thought, or hoped at least, that her marriage would be the start of a new, happier chapter for her.'

'What hard time?' asked Sophia, intrigued. 'What was Mum doing in Italy?'

She'd thought her mum had never done anything more risky than making a particularly tricky soufflé. She'd assumed she'd never travelled anywhere that wasn't organised by an upmarket package operator. And she'd certainly believed that her mother had never suffered anything worse than a broken nail in her charmed life.

'Your mother went Interrailing in Europe. It was all the rage with youngsters in those days. Frankie didn't want her to go. He said she was too young but I convinced him it would do her good. She was a gutsy girl, full of life, back then, and she was going with a friend from school. I thought it would be just the sort of adventure she needed. I'd moved to London at her age and it had been the making of me. But ...'

'But ...?' asked Sophia, sensing more.

'I think there was some boy,' Granny continued. 'She met some boy in Rome and got her heart broken, that's all. We've all been through it. Why don't you ask her yourself? I'm feeling a little weary – I'm sure your mother will tell you more than I can.'

'Oh, OK,' said Sophia, reluctantly.

Tilly had played her trump card. Sophia knew that when a terminally ill grandparent said they were tired, you had no choice but to shut up. God, she was good! Always the actress.

Chapter Twenty-One

Ise Shima, Japan, 1927

Manami was now the last Ama left in the hut. The little girls were already wading in the shallows and rock pools, collecting seaweed and the odd shellfish or urchin. The younger women, like Manami, were swimming just offshore in the relatively shallow and safe waters close to the beach. Her sisters and her mother had all joined their husbands on their fishing boats now. They were free divers. Free women. And Manami was impatient to join them.

For now, Manami had been practising her own technique. Well, not so much her own technique as one she'd borrowed from her ancestors. She looked around to check she was alone and then gathered what she needed.

With one last furtive glance back at the other Ama, Manami waded swiftly through the waves until she had rounded the headland and was out of sight of the other girls. There, she leant against the rocks and tied a long length of rope around her bare waist. At the end of the rope was a makeshift buoy. It was only an empty wooden barrel but it would work just fine. She then tied the weights she'd 'borrowed' from the *amagoya* to the rope too. And then, with one final glance back at the shore, she started swimming out to sea.

It was still relatively early in the season – late May – and the water remained icy cold. It was difficult to swim with the weights dragging her down but Manami was a strong girl and she knew exactly where she was headed. There was a sharp rock that jutted out of the ocean about half a kilometre offshore and that would be her base for today's dive. She had done many hours of searching under the waves over the years. She'd heard rumours from the ancient Ama of abundant pearl oyster beds off this headland and although the old women claimed that the beds had long since been hunted to extinction Manami wasn't so sure.

The Ama were so busy working for the fishing company these days, collecting shellfish for rich men's dinner plates in Osaka, that none of the women considered themselves to be pearl hunters any more. No one even looked! What if just a few of those pearl oysters had remained? What if the entire bed had been replenished over the years? Last week, she had come here, to this rock, and she could have sworn she'd seen an entire bed of pearl oysters, hidden in a deep crevice, just a few metres deeper than she could reach. She had tried three times to reach the beds but the sea was choppy, the currents too strong and she'd had no weights to aid her descent. Today the ocean was relatively calm. Today she had all the equipment she needed. Today the sea spirits were on her side. Today Manami was going to hunt for pearls.

When she reached the rock, Manami pulled herself up onto a flat platform that was just big enough to sit on. Usually an Ama would dive with weights off a boat. A rope would attach the diver to the fisherman on the boat and when she was ready to resurface, she would simply tug at the rope and the fisherman would pull her back up, weights and all. But Manami had no fisherman to help her. Her plan was to dive down with the weights and then, when she'd been submerged long enough, she would untie them and leave them at the bottom of the ocean. Simple. She would then swim to the surface and be able to rest on the makeshift buoy she was attached to. She checked that the weights were tied on tightly and that her *tegane* was firmly lodged into her loincloth. She tugged at the long rope that secured her to the buoy, pulled on her goggles and began her breathing. Manami took a series of short, sharp intakes of breath, until her head became light and her lungs became full. And then, with one final gulp of air, she dived into the ocean and disappeared under the waves.

Manami swam harder and faster than she ever had swum before until the pale spring sun was nothing more than a faint glow many metres above her. The ocean surged and tried to pull her off course but Manami would not be swayed from her path.

The deeper she got, the darker the water became and the more the pressure built in her head, her ears and her lungs, but nothing was going to distract her today. Finally, she spotted the shadowy shape of the jagged outcrop of rocks she'd seen the week before. Only another few metres and she would be there. Keeping time in her head told Manami that she had been underwater for more than a minute already and the burning pain in her skull told her that she was now deeper than she had ever been before. And still she descended further into the darkness until finally her hand reached out and touched the rough, solid rock.

Manami grabbed at the rocks and pulled herself through a narrow crevice that was barely wider than her naked body. The rocks tore her bare skin, cutting a deep gash in her left thigh. The salt stung the wound but she barely noticed because there, clinging to the rocks, were dozens of rare black-lipped oysters. Manami's head felt as if it was going to explode but the buzz of adrenalin that pulsed through her veins was stronger than the pain. With shaking, freezing fingers, she took out Granny's *tegane* and forced it between an oyster and the rock. She prised, levered and wrestled with all her might until one, two, three oysters were safely tucked into her loincloth. Manami's head was spinning now. She was so cold that she could no longer feel her feet and her fingers struggled to grip the *tegane*. But she couldn't give up yet. She needed to collect as many of these oysters as possible. Four, five, six. Her loincloth was becoming heavy with her catch. Seven, eight, nine. Just one more. This huge one here. Just one more.

Manami struggled to prise the largest oyster from the rock. It was gripping so tightly that she felt sure the mollusc knew it was fighting for its life. The dizziness in her head was beginning to confuse her, she could barely see her hand in front of her face any more and she felt as if a vice was tightening around her chest. Manami no longer had any idea how long she'd been under the ocean, surviving on one single breath, but it was certainly longer than she had ever gone before and she knew that it was time to get back to the surface – fast. Perhaps she and the oyster were both fighting for their lives. With one final surge of strength, Manami managed to yank the last oyster from the rock. But as she did so her grandmother's *tegane* slipped from her hand. Manami reached out to grab the precious tool but it was too late. Her fingertips brushed the tool's handle for a moment but she couldn't quite reach it. Manami watched in horror as the *tegane* disappeared into the depths. There was nothing she could do but curse her own carelessness. How would she tell Granny that she'd lost the precious tool on the very day she'd been given it?

Manami began to panic. And the last thing a free diver should ever do is panic. Now she felt as if her head was floating off her shoulders and she could barely feel her body at all. She thrust the last oyster into her loincloth and squeezed clumsily back through the crevice. The water turned red around her as blood wept from her wounds. With quivering fingers Manami tried to undo the knots that tied the weights to her waist, but she was so tired and desperate to breathe that she had no strength left. She didn't have the *tegane* to cut the ropes and she'd stupidly left her oyster knife in the barrel, thinking she'd have no use for it until she resurfaced.

The pressure in Manami's head was unbearable. She realised that the blood was pouring from her ears as well as her wounds and her head was filled by a strange droning noise that got louder and louder as her heart tried to pump its way through her chest. All she needed was to get back to the surface but the weights wanted to pull her down deeper. Manami thrashed her legs to stay level with the crevice and frantically began sawing the rope with the edge of the sharp rock. It seemed to take an age to fray the rope, and every time she missed the rope, the rock bit into the skin on the inside of her wrists instead, but Manami knew she had no choice. An image of Aiko's perfect face filled her mind as she ripped the rope to shreds on the rock. She would not be defeated. She was doing this for her daughter. Finally the rope snapped, the weights plummeted into the chasm of the ocean and Manami was free.

With all her remaining strength, she swam upwards towards the tiny speck of muted light above. The distant sun pulled her like a magnet towards the surface. Manami felt the temperature of the water rise and she noticed the sea change from a thick black soup to a more familiar murky grey-green. The light of the day beyond the ocean grew vast and close and a moment later she burst through the waves, gasping, bleeding, and in agony but alive. She grabbed the wooden barrel and collapsed over her makeshift buoy. She had been under the water for only a few minutes but it had been terrifying. She closed her eyes and lay there feeling the oxygen refill her aching lungs, and the waves break over her torn flesh. She was cut to pieces, her eardrums had burst and her head still felt as if it was about to explode. She must look like she'd lost a fight with a giant sea serpent. How would she explain this to her mother without getting into huge trouble? How would she explain it to Yoshiro? And how would she break the news to Granny about her *tegane*?

And then she thought about the oysters in her loincloth and Manami felt a wave of strength fill her body. She was far offshore. She would never make it back to the beach until she'd had a rest, but the rocks she'd dived off were not far away. Still clutching the barrel for support, she swam with all her might until her fingers gripped the flat shelf and she scrambled out of the cold water. Manami was shocked at how deep the gash on her thigh was and she could now see hundreds of cuts and grazes all over her legs, torso and wrists. What a clumsy fool she'd been. She hoped she wouldn't have scars.

She still felt shaky and weak and her ears, head, chest and flesh all throbbed but Manami had work to do. Her fingers tingled with pins and needles as she untied the oysters from her *fundoshi* and laid them out on the flat rock where she could admire them. Less than a dozen oysters would not impress Mr Nishimoto but if her gut instinct was right, then the contents of these oysters may be worth more than a ton of seafood for the fishing company. She fished the oyster knife out of the open barrel and did what Ama are never supposed to do: she began opening the oysters. Of course, molluscs are of no value to the fishing company once opened but the last thing Manami was thinking about was Mr Nishimoto and his profits.

Manami expertly slid the sharp blade between the first oyster's lips, twisted the knife, and sliced through the muscle that clamped the shell shut. Nothing.

'*Ku so!*' she shouted above the sound of the crashing ocean. 'Damn!'

She threw the worthless oyster into the waves for the greedy seagulls to squabble over. Manami repeated the process eight more times until she was left with just one oyster on the ledge.

She was beginning to feel very strange. The pins and needles in her fingers had spread up her arms. And even though she was safely out of the water she was finding it hard to catch her breath. Her head pounded and her vision was so blurred that she could barely see the shore. Manami tried desperately to hold herself together as she attacked the final oyster with the knife. Twice, three times she missed the lips and stabbed herself in the hand instead. What was wrong with her? Why was the world spinning? Finally, she managed to stick the knife into the oyster's flesh. It was the largest one, the one she'd had a life-or-death battle with in the underwater cave, and still it did not want to give up its secrets. Manami plunged and twisted the knife deep between the tight lips but the oyster wouldn't budge. She banged it against the rocks and tried again. For a moment, she had to rest her head in her hands because she felt so light-headed. And then with one final surge of energy she attacked the oyster with the knife. It opened. Manami had finally won.

With shaking hands she prised open the shell. She was so dazed that she had to stare for the longest time before she could make sense of what was right in front of her. There, glinting in the pale spring light, was the largest, roundest, most luminous and perfect pearl in the entire world. It had to be! Manami had never seen a pearl so enormous, so beautiful, except in her dreams. Or perhaps she was dreaming now? Everything had become hazy. The grey-blue sky, the murky green sea, the faint May sun, the distant shore, it all swam in front of her eyes, and the rock she sat on began to ebb and flow and surge beneath her, as if it had been swallowed by the ocean. Nothing seemed real. But she had done it, hadn't she? She had realised her dream. Manami grabbed the pearl from the shell and clenched it in her fist; she threw her battered body into the ocean and began to swim in what she hoped was the direction of home. As the waves crashed over her head she had just two things on her mind: Yoshiro and Aiko, her world.

Haruki clutched Aiko to her chest as she hurriedly scrambled down the slippery cliff path. She cursed her stiff old legs and her weak heart. As she half slipped, half ran down the path, she muttered a prayer under her breath to the sea gods.

'Please spare Manami, for she is young and she has her whole life to lead. Her daughter needs her, her husband too. If you want a spirit, take mine – not hers. I am old and I have led a good life. I am ready to go. Not Manami. Please. I implore you. Not my Manami-chan.'

Haruki had been watching Manami again from the cliff tops today. She had been angry at first when she'd seen her granddaughter tie on the buoy and the weights. These were old techniques that were no longer taught and Manami was ignorant of their complexities. And then she'd swum out, far from the headland and safety. Who did that crazy girl think she was, diving so far from the shore with no one to look after her? Haruki had screamed out from the cliff top.

But Manami could not hear. And then, when she had disappeared under the water, Haruki too had held her breath. She had stared and stared at the waves beside the abandoned barrel, waiting and willing Manami to reappear. But as she watched the gulls circling and diving, and counted the sea swells rising and falling, she knew her granddaughter had been submerged far too long.

The wait was excruciating. Haruki was overjoyed to see Manami resurface but she could tell immediately that her granddaughter was injured.

She'd thought her sister's *tegane* would bring Manami luck but perhaps it had been a dreadful mistake. Haruki's older sister, Chiyoe, had burned with the same flames as Manami. She had even had the same fire-coloured eyes. At seventeen Chiyoe had fallen in love but Haruki's father had forbidden the relationship. Chiyoe and her lover had run away together in the dead of night and no one ever saw either of them again. In the morning, Haruki had found Chiyoe's *tegane* discarded on the beach. Even though Haruki's distraught mother had always sworn her daughter had drowned, Haruki still prayed for Chiyoe often and hoped she was safe and happy. Until today, Haruki had felt sure that Chiyoe's *tegane* was a lucky charm. She had used it herself for many, many years and hadn't she been blessed with a fruitful life? But today she had given the *tegane* to Manami, and now Manami was in terrible danger.

Manami had thrown herself back into the ocean and she was trying to swim home. Haruki could see her, perhaps fifty metres offshore. The waves were crashing over her head and she kept disappearing beneath them for what seemed like far too long. Haruki jumped down onto the beach and began to run towards the sea, still carrying the baby. Aiko looked up at her with huge, startled eyes but she did not cry.

From the beach, the old woman could barely see Manami. The shoreline was deserted. All the other Ama were either out on their boats or diving on the other side of the headland. Without hesitation, Haruki waded confidently into the freezing water. She had spent her entire life in the Pacific. And although she had retired seven summers ago the ocean held no fear for Haruki. Her legs were not as strong as they had once been and her robe clung heavily to her old limbs but Haruki strode on without a backward glance. The waves soaked the baby's clothes and sprayed her tiny face but still Aiko did not cry. Manami was only twenty metres from the shore now. Haruki called out to her over the thundering ocean and for a moment she managed to catch her granddaughter's eye. To her amazement, Manami did not seem scared. Instead, her eyes were full of wonder and joy. Haruki held the baby up high, out of danger, and held her free hand out towards Manami.

'Come to me!' she called out. 'Grab hold of me please, Manami-chan!'

As Manami drew closer Haruki could see blood on her face and arms. What had happened out there? Manami no longer looked like the headstrong Dragon Girl who had strutted into her house that morning full of big dreams and grand plans. The waves were battering her like a rag doll, rolling over her head and forcing her underwater. She reappeared, coughing and spluttering with her arms flailing weakly. Finally the ocean dumped Manami's broken body into Haruki's arms.

The old woman carried her grown-up granddaughter in one arm and her infant great-granddaughter in the other and with the strength of a sea serpent she brought them safely to shore. She lay Manami down gently on the sand and knelt beside her, pushing her wet hair from her face. Her eyes were closed now and her chest was so still that Haruki could not tell whether she was breathing or not.

'Manami,' said Haruki, desperately. 'Wake up, my Manami-chan!'

Finally, Manami opened her eyes, and even though she was only half conscious, the fire in them startled Haruki as much as it had done on the day Manami had been born. She held her hand out weakly to her grandmother and smiled.

'For Aiko, Granny,' she whispered. 'Keep it safe for her until the time is right. It must be our secret.'

Haruki could not believe her eyes. In Manami's bloody palm sat the most perfect, iridescent pearl imaginable. It was twice the size of any she had collected herself. She took the pearl and held it up to the light, dumbstruck by its beauty.

'Did I do well, Grandmother?' murmured Manami. 'Have I made you proud?'

She stroked Manami's face and said, 'You have fulfilled your dreams, Manami-chan. I could not possibly be more proud of you.'

'There are more, Granny,' whispered Manami. 'Under the loose floorboard, in a silk pouch.'

'I know,' replied Haruki. 'I have always known what you do, Manami-chan.'

Manami's eyes turned slowly to Aiko.

'May this pearl bring you good fortune and blessings, my precious Aiko,' she managed to say in a whisper.

And then her eyes closed.

Haruki looked around desperately but the beach was still deserted.

Manami was icy cold and her lips had a blue tinge to them.

'Manami! Can you hear me?' shouted Haruki.

Manami's blue lips moved but she did not open her eyes. 'Tell Yoshiro I love him,' she whispered. 'I am tired now, Grandmother. My head is so sore. I need to sleep.'

'Manami! Do not sleep! Manami! Stay with me! Manami!' screamed Haruki. But her granddaughter was deathly still.

Finally, Aiko began to cry. Haruki clutched the infant to her chest. By the time Haruki heard the pounding footsteps and frantic shouts of the Ama, arriving from around the headland, she knew that it was too late for Manami. She closed her fist tightly around the pearl.

'Your mother is gone, sweet Aiko. But this pearl is her gift to you,' Haruki whispered through her tears. 'And one day it will set you free.'

Chapter Twenty-Two

Hackney, London, 2012

All the way home from the hospital, Sophia tried to keep her mind on her grandmother and the necklace, but somehow her thoughts kept going back to her mother instead. Sometimes she felt as if she didn't even know the woman who had given birth to her. If anyone ever asked her to describe her mum, she always used words like 'normal' and 'safe' but was it actually 'normal' to be such an enigma to your own daughter? What did she believe in? OK, so Alice believed in keeping things tidy. She believed in being early for everything. She believed in good manners. She believed in quietness. She believed in Waitrose and Marks and Spencer and in playing bridge and in wearing a lot of navy blue. But was that it?

Sophia felt suddenly guilty that she'd never really asked these questions before. She'd spent years trying to work out her father's motives for his behaviour, attempting to come up with logical reasons for his contempt towards her. But her mum? She was always just there, by her dad's side, looking slightly pained and perplexed. Sophia had always seen her as the silent sidekick. Alice was never the aggressor. She never started the fight. She was polite and quietly spoken. And when things got too loud? Too angry? Too raw? She'd just hidden in her bedroom.

Sometimes, when she was little, Sophia had crept into her mum's bed, long after a fight, when her dad had stormed off to the golf club to calm down, and they would both lie there without talking, holding each other tight. Her mother would stroke her hair and kiss her head but she never said a word and Sophia could never understood why. As she got older, Sophia stopped going to her mum's room.

Now Sophia tried to imagine her mum as a teenager, travelling around Europe, but the image just wouldn't come to her head. Granny had tried to make out that Alice had been wild and adventurous in her youth, but surely that was just an old lady looking back at her daughter through rose-coloured spectacles? She wracked her brain for her earliest memories of her mother.

A car journey late at night. Just Sophia and Alice. Sophia couldn't remember where they were going or why. Perhaps she had never known. But the car was yellow. And Sophia was in her pyjamas. And her mum seemed happy, and her hair was down, and Sophia felt safe, and they played the same songs, over and over again, and Mum sang along, all through the night, as Sophia drifted in and out of sleep, and they drove onwards, for miles and miles, and then in the morning … They were at home again. And everything went back to normal.

Sophia wished she could remember the song her mum had sung that night. All the way back to Hackney she tried to find it in her head.

'Do you want to know what I've discovered?' asked Hugo as soon as she got home.

He was sitting on her bed, cross-legged, with his laptop resting on his knees.

'I left you three voicemails and five texts while you were out,' he said, impatiently. 'I've been doing my research on the necklace and it is completely amazing. The most expensive pearl necklace ever sold went for more than twenty million dollars! And even the cheap ones go for, like, half a million when they're old and genuine and all that stuff.' Hugo looked up at Sophia with huge round eyes, like a kid on Christmas morning.

'Three things, Hugo,' said Sophia, trying to be patient with her best friend. 'Firstly, the necklace is missing. My grandmother has not seen it since the summer of 1981. Secondly, even if she did have it, I doubt very much it's worth anything like the ones you're looking at online. And thirdly, I have absolutely no clue how to go about finding it after all this time.'

She could feel her cheeks begin to burn with the shame of lying to Hugo and she hoped he couldn't see her blushing. Sophia was scared to tell him what her granny had said about Alice being the key. In fact, she wasn't sure she should even tell him that her mother had ever been given the necklace. How could she? He would immediately try to bully her into going straight to her parents' house to confront her mum and that was something she simply could not do yet. No amount of money would make her feel strong enough to face her father after what Nathan had told her. And right now, she wasn't sure she could bear to talk to her mum either.

'This is a choker of sixty-six perfect, champagne-coloured Japanese pearls, hand-collected from the waters off the Shima Peninsula. And your grandmother is one of the best-known Hollywood actresses of her day. I am fairly sure that that necklace is worth a fucking fortune. Plus it was given to her by her father for her eighteenth birthday. I've read every single one of her letters. It's "darling Papa" this and "marvellous Papa" that. There is no way she would misplace the most precious gift he ever gave her. It doesn't make sense.'

Sophia sighed. Sometimes Hugo wasn't quite as blond as he looked. She would have to tell him about her mum and the necklace soon. She would need his help to find the damned thing after all these years. But how could she do it without facing her parents? She watched Hugo closely as he stared at his computer screen, a look of stern concentration on his face.

'And you really think it's worth a lot?' she asked him.

Hugo nodded. 'It's not only the quality of the jewellery that counts; it's who it belonged to. Christie's sold Elizabeth Taylor's pearl necklace last year for over eleven million dollars, Soph."

Sophia let out a deep breath.

'I don't think I could sell the necklace now, Hugo,' she explained. 'If we get it back, Granny wants me to keep it so that when I wear it I think of her, and her dad, and the whole Beaumont dynasty nonsense. I promised.'

'And where are you going to wear your pearls, Sophia?' sniffed Hugo. 'To the local soup kitchen? Honestly, what use is a million pound necklace if you can't afford a Pot Noodle?'

'This is a complete waste of time. We'll never find it anyway,' said Sophia, flopping back onto the bed. 'It's all a fantasy. It's like looking for a needle in a haystack. All I can do is go through the motions of trying to find the pearls to keep Granny happy for the next few weeks before ...' She swallowed hard. '... before she dies. And then we forget about the stupid necklace and get on with our lives.'

Chapter Twenty-Three

Tokyo, Japan, 2012

Aiko sipped her coffee and stared out of the hotel window. Tokyo buzzed with the thrill of money, success, technology and power.

But, this morning, as hard as Aiko tried to focus on the spectacular view before her, and her plans for the day ahead, visions of the past kept barging their way into her head uninvited. At first, they had only invaded her dreams, now they were sneaking into her waking hours too. The longer she gazed at the scene from her penthouse room, the less she saw of what was really there. Instead, pictures of the past seemed to superimpose themselves on top of the view. It was as if Aiko could somehow see the broken, ruined, tangled Tokyo of 1946, still lying wounded beneath the shiny new skyscrapers. She shook her head and willed the ghosts to leave her be. She wanted to remain here, planted firmly in the comfort of the present. But a force more powerful than Aiko was dragging her mind back.

Tokyo, Japan, 1946

'Luck exists in the leftovers,' Aiko told herself as the rickety cart made its way slowly towards Tokyo. She was weak from lack of sleep and lack of food. But she chanted the proverb in her head over and over again to keep her spirits high. If luck really did exist in the leftovers, as her great-grandmother had said, then surely Aiko would find luck soon, because right now, she was living on the scrapheap.

Japan was as broken and shattered as her spirit. It had been a year since the war ended. A year since the atom bombs had been dropped on Hiroshima and Nagasaki. Three million Japanese had lost their lives in the war, a third of all homes had been destroyed, there were no jobs, there was no industry, roads were impassable and the railways were ruined. What was left? Certainly not Aiko's tiny village. During the war the young men had all left to fight: not one of them returned home. Disease and hunger killed most of the women, children and elderly who remained. Abandoned houses rotted like the carcasses of dead birds. The beach was littered with abandoned possessions of empty, broken homes. The Ama stopped diving. There were no fishermen left to take their boats out to sea. When the war ended, anyone left standing packed up their meagre belongings and left. Aiko was one of them.

Aiko didn't think much about her own pain and suffering. It was nothing compared to that of others. The little boy lying beside her in the filthy, rancid cart was getting weaker by the minute. Aiko wasn't sure he was going to make it all the way to Tokyo. She didn't know his name or how old he was or even where he'd come from. No one made small talk on a journey like this. They were all trying to get to Tokyo for their own, private reasons.

She guessed the boy was about five or six. Even though she had not talked to him, he had edged closer and closer to her ever since she'd lifted him up and handed him to his father in the scramble to get onto the cart. Aiko couldn't help but notice he was travelling alone with his father. Like so many other children in Japan, this boy appeared to be motherless. And Aiko understood better than anyone how that felt. Although Aiko was barely twenty years old, and far from being a mother yet herself, she allowed the child to snuggle right up to her. Now he laid his head on her shoulder. His murmuring about the pain and emptiness in his stomach was getting louder and louder.

'Shut that boy up or I'll throw him off!' shouted the farmer, who was driving the cart.

The driver had taken twenty yen from each passenger for the trip. Once upon a time Aiko would have thought him a heartless monster, but since the war she understood more about what suffering did to ordinary people. They were all just trying to survive in horrific circumstances and the survival instinct made people selfish. It seemed to Aiko that there was no such thing as society any more. Or family. She squeezed her eyes shut and tried to banish the thoughts of her old village from her head. It was too painful to remember her father, Yoshiro, her grandparents and her beloved great-grandmother, Haruki.

They were all gone now. Her father had died in the war, or at least, Aiko assumed he had. He had been conscripted with all the other men in the village in 1942 and no one had seen or heard from him since. With Yoshiro – the sole breadwinner in the family – gone, the others had died of disease and malnutrition. One by one they had dropped like flies around a lantern until Aiko found herself totally alone. She could still smell the sea in her nostrils but it had been many months since she had last seen the ocean. She missed it almost as badly as she missed her family.

She shushed the boy gently, telling him that everything would be OK. She told him the beautiful lies that a boy his age deserved to hear. The truth was not for one so innocent as him. To comfort him, she began to whisper a story in his ear that Haruki had told her, time and time again, whenever she asked why her mother had to die so young.

Haruki always said that Manami had left a great gift for Aiko and that she had sacrificed herself so that her daughter could soar as high and free as a mountain eagle. Aiko never quite understood what the old woman meant by this but she liked the sound of it very much. It sounded so much more romantic than the way her father put it. He said that her mother and the other Ama lived a tough life and were under huge pressure to make money for the fishing company. He explained that one day she had simply dived too deep for too long and that the ocean had made her sick and that she had died. But then her father never liked to talk about Manami. He said being an Ama was the worst, most dangerous job in the world, and he forbade little Aiko from ever diving. Still, while her father was out fishing, Aiko and Haruki would sometimes go down to the beach and Great-Grandmother would teach her and watch her dive in the shallows. Aiko needed the ocean like she needed air. But she never let her father know this secret. She understood what the sea had taken from him. Everyone said that his heart had split in two the day Manami died and that he had been living a ghost-life ever since.

But Great-Granny saw things very differently. She used the

fable of Tamatori-hime – the Princess Jewel Taker – to explain Manami's death. The tale had soothed Aiko to sleep on many a stormy night. Now Aiko hoped it would do the same for this little boy in the cart.

'This is the legend of Princess Tamatori,' she told him. 'A long, long time ago there was a great man called Fujiwara no Kamatari. He had sent his prettiest daughter to be the consort of the emperor in China. When Fujiwara died, his daughter grieved terribly, so to honour her dead father, and to comfort his heartbroken lover, the emperor sent three priceless treasures to Japan. But on the way one of the treasures, the most lovely pearl in the world, was stolen by a wicked dragon king during a terrible storm.'

Aiko saw that the boy's eyes had opened and he was looking at her now. She smiled and continued the tale.

'Kamatari's son went in search of the priceless pearl to a distant land. There he met and fell in love with a beautiful pearl diver named Ama. They married and she bore him a son. Ama loved her husband and baby son very deeply, and so she vowed to help recover the stolen pearl. She managed to lull the dragon and his creatures to sleep by playing soothing music, and while they slumbered she stole back the pearl. But she had not gone far when the terrible sea creatures woke and began chasing her. Ama was so desperate to reclaim the pearl for her husband and son that she cut open her breast and placed the pearl inside the wound for safekeeping. Poor Ama was bleeding terribly now but the blood clouded the water and she was able to escape from the dreadful dragon and take the pearl home to her husband. Ama died from her wounds, but to this day she is revered for her sacrifice for her husband and her beloved baby son.'

'Thank you for the story,' whispered the boy, quietly. 'I think my mother was like Ama.'

'Then you are a very lucky boy,' whispered Aiko back. 'And do you want to know a secret?'

The boy nodded sleepily.

'My mother was like Ama too,' she told him. 'So you see, we have something in common. We are two peas in a pod.'

The small boy put his cold hand in Aiko's and squeezed weakly. Soon, he drifted off to sleep with a faint smile on his lips.

'Thank you,' said the boy's father, bowing at her from across the cart. 'No one has shown us such kindness in a very long time. You are an angel.'

It was the first time he had spoken during the journey. His clothes, Aiko noticed, although ragged now, must once have been very expensive – and he spoke with the crisp, clean vowels of the well-educated. She wondered how a man of his standing could have ended up here, in this cart.

'She's not an angel, you idiot,' snapped a woman beside him. 'You men are all the same. She is pretty, that's all. She has the face of an angel, yes, but I'm sure her heart is no more pure than mine – or his!'

She pointed at the farmer's back. But the little boy's father ignored the woman and continued to gaze at Aiko.

When the cart finally arrived on the outskirts of the great city, the farmer ordered the travellers to get off at once. It was the middle of the night. There was no sign of any houses. Despite the shouting and complaining all around, the little boy did not wake up. Aiko handed his sleeping body back to his father.

'Thank you,' he said, taking his son tenderly in his arms. 'May the gods be for ever on your side.'

Aiko wished the man well and watched as he carried his sick little boy off into the dark night. She had no idea whether the boy ever woke up again. She took the weight of that pain and added it to the unbearable weight of pain that had already suffocated her young heart.

Chapter Twenty-Four

Granny, being Granny, had come to life when she'd realised that she had not one, but two visitors that afternoon. She had made a huge fuss of Hugo when they arrived, telling him that he was quite the most handsome man she'd seen since Sophia's grandfather died, and that hadn't he grown into himself wonderfully. Hugo, being Hugo, had lapped up the attention.

Now, Sophia and Hugo sat like obedient children at Granny's feet as she insisted on reading from her memoirs. Granny read with a beatific smile on her face and a tinkle in her voice, utterly lost in her own memories (but checking, every now and then, just to make sure that the sentiment wasn't lost on her audience).

London, 1950s

The fun didn't start immediately when I moved to London after Papa's death. I was terribly young and naive and I knew no one in the capital. At first, I spent most of my time walking on Hampstead Heath with Badger, mourning the fact that I had no friends in the city. Poor, dear Badger died of old age during my first year there. He was the first of my pets to be buried under the oak tree in the garden in Hampstead. I was desperately lonely. I adored fashion, so I would spend a fortune on the latest trends from Selfridges, Harrods and Liberty, but I had nowhere to wear them and no one to impress. I'm rather ashamed to say that, like my mother before me, I would sometimes dress up in a gown, heels, jewels and full make-up just to sit alone in my drawing room: a sad state of affairs for a girl who'd just turned nineteen!

Thankfully, the solitude didn't last long. I had always adored the theatre and now, stuck in the house on my own, I pored over the theatre reviews in the Evening Standard, *I devoured stories about Hollywood stars in* London Life *and* The Lady *and, when I dressed up in my new dresses (with the tags still attached) I pretended to be at the Oscars. Early in 1950 I finally plucked up the courage to join a local amateur dramatics society in Highgate and quickly made friends with two girls called Madeleine and Louisa – or Maddie and Lulu, as they liked to be known. (You must remember Aunt Maddie? She's still very much alive and kicking and living in Marylebone.) They were much better actresses than I was. Plus they were both a little older than me and London born and bred. I thought they were terribly sophisticated, fashionable and worldly wise and anything they wanted to do, I wanted to do too!*

Maddie and Lulu started taking me to Soho with the rest of their bohemian crowd. By day we drank black coffee and discussed poetry behind dark glasses in coffee shops on Wardour Street. At night we walked up dingy alleys and climbed narrow staircases to find obscure nightclubs and jazz bars. I was finally walking on the wild side. For a naive country girl, this new lifestyle was as addictive as the French cigarettes I'd started to smoke.

My mind opened like a spring flower during those early years in London and I'm pleased to say that, along with my innocence, I lost any remaining prejudices and snobbery from my childhood. I met penniless artists and opium-addicted poets. I became friends with black jazz musicians from Alabama. My favourite adoptive 'godparents' were an elderly gay couple who lived above a sex shop on Dean Street.

But the part I loved most about my new life was meeting the actors who came in for a drink at the Colony Room Club, Club Eleven, the Cy Laurie Jazz Club or the Harmony Inn when they finished on stage at the West End. I discovered romance quite late (I was twenty before I had my first kiss since St Ives) but I quickly made up for lost time and dated a series of actors, writers and musicians during this time. I threw myself into the role of Femme Fatale with much aplomb! Men seemed to like me and I liked them very much too but I was never very good at making up my mind. I found myself spoilt for choice so I never went steady and, although I was very fond of my boyfriends, I never fell in love. Not until I met Frankie.

When he walked into the jazz club in February 1951, I spotted him immediately and stood, frozen, with my glass in my hand and my words stuck in my throat.

'What is it?' Maddie asked, turning to see what had caught my attention.

'Aha,' she said, smirking. 'Frank Perry Junior. Isn't he just the biggest stud you have ever seen?'

I nodded, still unable to speak.

'He's American and everything!' added Lulu excitedly.

'He's an actor,' Maddie continued.

'And totally out of my league,' I finally managed to say. 'He looks like a different species to the rest of us.'

I had never been shy before, and I normally waltzed straight up to anyone I liked the look of and started chatting quite happily, but I was so in awe of Frank Perry Junior that I couldn't bring myself to talk to him. Instead, I spent the next hour hanging around near him, flicking my long hair this way and that, blowing smoke rings in his face and saying incredibly witty things very loudly to my friends in the hope that he would hear. I even dropped my purse at his feet so that he could pick it up (he didn't). It was my necklace that got him talking in the end. I was wearing my pearls with a tight, black cocktail dress. He was chatting to another guy at the bar when he suddenly seemed to notice me. He stopped and cocked his head to one side.

'Hey, baby,' he called over to me. 'Come here.'

It was an incredibly bossy thing to say and had he not been so handsome I would have told him to trot off! Instead, I swallowed hard, took a deep breath and went over to him.

'Are those real?' he asked, picking up the pearls and fingering them. I couldn't speak so I just nodded dumbly.

'Are you some kind of heiress or aristocrat or something?' he demanded in his sexy American drawl.

I stammered, 'Kind of, yes, I-I-I suppose I am.'

'So what's your name, Cutiepie?' he asked.

'Matilda,' I managed to reply. 'Lady Matilda Beaumont.'

And then I immediately regretted sounding so pompous and added, 'But just Tilly really. Everyone calls me Tilly.'

'Lady Matilda,' he grinned, ignoring me. 'So you're the real deal? That's crazy! Do you know the King?'

I shook my head solemnly before realising he was teasing. I blushed.

'You're cute. I kind of dig you, Lady Matilda,' he announced. 'You should dance with me.'

At that point, I regained my senses a little, and decided I didn't like his bossy tone, no matter how gorgeous he was. Besides, something told me that Frankie was far too used to having girls jump when he clicked his fingers. And I had no interest in being just another girl. Perhaps I had learned something from my mother after all – how to deal with men.

'I should do no such thing,' I told him, firmly. 'I won't be told what to do by you, or anybody. If I dance, it will be because a gentleman has asked me nicely, and I've been kind enough to accept. Excuse me.'

And then I walked away. I had barely gone five steps when Frankie all but threw himself at my feet.

'Lady Matilda, please do me the honour of dancing with me,' he asked. 'You're the most beautiful girl I've ever seen and I don't know how I'll carry on if you walk out of my life right now.'

He was exaggerating, of course, playing to the crowd, but when I looked at his face, gazing eagerly up at me, waiting for my reply, I knew I could happily stare at that face for ever. And I knew he felt the same.

'Oh well, if you insist,' I replied eventually. 'And seeing as you asked so nicely, I suppose I could spare the time for one dance.'

And that was that. By the end of the week we were dating, by the end of the month we were in love, and by the end of the summer I was leaving London on a plane to LA with the love of my life. I had quickly learned that Frankie's larger-than-life public persona was all a bit of a front. He was a very talented actor, after all, and he had a playboy image to preserve. But beneath the bravado was a kind, thoughtful, generous man. We had got married at Westminster Register Office the week before we left London, but this was no honeymoon: LA was to be our new home. Frankie was about to start shooting his first feature film. It wasn't a big part, but it was a start. He never did call me Tilly. To Frankie, I remained either Lady Matilda, or Cutiepie for the rest of his life.

We moved to a condo in Malibu. It was bliss. The sun shone every day. Frank suggested I start acting classes now I was in LA. He told me that with my looks and a few acting lessons I could be a star. I thought he was biased but, as always, Frankie was quickly proved right. I had just enrolled in an acting workshop in Beverly Hills and was all set to learn my new trade when I got a telephone call from Frank on set one morning.

'My co-star's got herself knocked up,' he explained excitedly. 'She's dropped out. They're casting for a new love interest today. You've got to come, Cutiepie. Try out. I've told them my girl's an actress too and the director says it's cool. Come to the set now.'

I didn't get the part. I had only been in the USA for a matter of days and my feeble attempt at the accent was terrible but I did get asked to audition for another movie. It was a war film, set in occupied Europe, and this time I was auditioning for the role of an English girl, trapped behind enemy lines. I guess Liz Taylor must have been busy that week because somehow I got the part. And it was right up my street: if anyone could play a spoilt, aristocratic daddy's girl, it was me! The movie had a bigger budget than the one Frankie was working on and while he only had a supporting role in his film, I seemed to have accidentally landed the lead. The amazing thing was he didn't seem bitter or jealous at all. He was simply very, very proud.

I think perhaps the fact we were a couple helped both our careers. In 1952 we starred in our first film together and the critics went wild for our 'real, onscreen chemistry'. And the rest, as they say, is history.

Sophia's grandmother paused and looked up, eyes still shining with excitement from the memories.

'Do you want to hear more?' she asked. 'Do you want to hear about Alice?'

Sophia paused for a moment. Did she want to hear about her mother? And then she thought about all the unanswered questions that had been bothering her lately and she nodded.

Her grandmother cleared her throat, turned the page, and continued her tales.

Cannes, France, 1963

Trust me to realise I was pregnant in the middle of a party, on a yacht, moored off the Croisette in Cannes on the last night of the film festival. I couldn't understand why the champagne and the bobbing of the boat were making me so sick when I was quite used to both sensations. I kept lighting cigarettes and then handing them to Frankie half-smoked because my mouth felt dry and the smoke caught in my throat. I'd been furious that my dress had been so tight that morning. I had to lie face down on the hotel carpet and darling Frank had to put his foot on my back just to prise the zip closed.

I'd barely eaten a thing in the run-up to the film festival, knowing that the success of my latest movie would mean I would be photographed extensively, and I'd been so sick with a stomach bug the week before that I couldn't understand why I was so bloated. The dress – a stunning, white, silk, Givenchy creation – had fitted me perfectly back in Paris a month earlier when I had my private fitting. It made no sense at all! Worse, Audrey Hepburn had just turned up at the party in exactly the same dress in black, looking much more beautiful and much, much thinner than I did. There's nothing worse for a woman than turning up at a party and finding someone else wearing the same dress – only better!

I was thirty-three by then, and Frankie and I had long since given up our dream of ever becoming parents. I had suffered a series of heartbreaking miscarriages early in our marriage and the doctors told me there was no chance that I would ever conceive again. For the next ten years we threw ourselves into our careers, our marriage and our social life. We had lots of friends, fabulous holidays and homes in London, Hollywood and Lake Como.

We were lucky. We loved each other deeply and the passion never faded. We had the most wonderful home, high in the Hollywood Hills, with a large pool on the top of a cliff that looked out towards the ocean. Our walk-in closets were full of designer clothes and our diaries were full of exciting engagements. We both won awards over the years. But our lives were never quite complete until that evening in Cannes.

I was in the ladies, feeling as sick as a dog, when I turned sideways and suddenly caught sight of the bump. In my tight cocktail gown there was no denying that it was there. Suddenly it all made sense: the nausea, the exhaustion, the indigestion. The doctors had told me it was impossible for me to get pregnant, so I knew at once that this child was a miracle. I don't know how, but the moment I realised I was expecting, I knew that this baby would be the one to survive. I had no idea at that time that I was already four months pregnant. By the end of October that year, your mother would be born.

When I squeezed my way back into the throng of the party, I slipped my arm round Frankie's back and whispered, 'You're going to be a daddy-o,' in his ear. My dear husband, usually the epitome of elegance, immediately dropped his glass and spilled champagne all over poor Brigitte Bardot. He was an unflappable man and I think that was the one and only time I ever really shocked him.

Of course, these days, thirty-three is a perfectly normal age to have one's first child, but in the 1960s it was considered positively ancient! In hindsight, becoming a mother later in life was a godsend for me though. It meant, when your mother did come along, that I could concentrate on her needs rather my own. I had had my selfish years. I had lived decadently, hedonistically. No one could ever say that I didn't have fun!

I was celebrating my thirteenth box office success in Cannes that night. I had no idea it would be my last for over a decade. But the moment your mother was born, everything changed. Perhaps it was because she was so utterly unexpected and so thoroughly cherished, or maybe it was because I was older, but I couldn't bear to be away from her for one moment. We called her Alice, after my favourite book from childhood. I stopped working and moved back to London so that she could have as 'normal' a life as possible. We could easily have afforded a nanny, of course, but after my own upbringing, I was determined that Alice would be brought up by her parents, not staff. I didn't see it as a sacrifice to give up my film career; I considered it a gift to spend all my time with my daughter.

Dear Frankie doted on her too – she was absolutely the apple of his eye – and he hated having to go away to shoot films. He would fly back from filming in the States at the weekend, just to spend one day with his precious Alice. When he was interviewed, he must have infuriated the journalists and film promoters alike, because all he would talk about was his adorable daughter rather than his new movie! He phoned home every single day, no matter where he was in the world, and no matter how antisocial the time difference. I never once regretted putting my career on hold. I knew I was lucky to be spending my days with my daughter, and that Frankie would have traded places with me in an instant. But I must admit, although I missed my beloved Frankie hugely, I rather enjoyed having Alice to myself when he was away. She was the most adorable, bright, sunshiny child in the world. I loved her so much that I thought my heart would explode. And despite all the wonderful things I'd seen and done in my first thirty-three years, Alice's childhood was by far the happiest time of my life.

Granny looked up and smiled at Sophia and Hugo.

'I wish I could have bottled those days,' she said. 'I wish I could open that bottle now and splash a little of that happiness across this hospital room.'

'It's a pity you can't splash some on Mum and remind her what an amazing childhood you gave her,' muttered Sophia, wandering to the window.

'Alice has her reasons for being the way she is,' replied her grandmother, thoughtfully. 'But yes, I do sometimes think she forgets about the past. She seemed to turn her back on being a Beaumont the moment she married your father. That was why I wasn't hugely surprised when she didn't wear the pearls after I gave them to her.'

Sophia glanced at her grandmother. She appeared to be falling asleep again, with her memoirs still in her hand, but Sophia could have sworn there was a faint smile on her lips.

'I don't get it,' said Sophia as they left the hospital. 'Granny gave her daughter everything. So why is Mum so cold with her now? I've never even seen them hug. Mum greets Granny with a couple of air kisses about a foot from her cheek. Mind you, that's about as affectionate as my mum gets. I don't understand.'

'You're right; it's very odd that she ended up the way she did. She's very, very beautiful – all you Beaumont women are – but she hides it under that hideous hairdo and all those shapeless, mumsy clothes she wears. Even when we were kids she dressed like that, remember? And if you think about it, she was really young – much younger than we are now. How old was she when she had you?'

'Nineteen,' replied Sophia, thinking about it properly for the first time. 'Christ, she was just a baby! Dad's quite a bit older than she is though.'

'Maybe that's why she never stands up to him,' mused Hugo. 'He bullies her almost as much as he bullies you, if you think about it. And what was she ever doing with your dad, anyway? I mean, no offence, but he's no oil painting ...'

'Beats me,' sighed Sophia.

'I know,' agreed Hugo. 'She was born Lady Alice Beaumont Perry, the aristocratic daughter of Hollywood royalty. And she chose to become plain Alice Brown, suburban housewife. Didn't you say she dropped her title?'

Sophia nodded, 'And Beaumont and Perry. She shed her title and both names.'

'It's weird,' mused Hugo. 'She should have a real sense of self-importance, she should be colourful, charismatic, glamorous and a little bit eccentric in that fabulously British way.

Instead, your mum's so uptight and repressed that she makes the Stepford Wives look like free spirits ...'

'They did marry when Mum was awfully young. And Granny tried to tell me yesterday that Mum was a right laugh before Dad came along. Not that I believe her ... I think that's the wishful thinking of a mother who was cursed with a very dull child! Well, I tell you one thing for sure, Hugo. I am never getting married and I am never having children. I mean, Granny was a good parent but my dad? My mum? My great-grandmother? No! My family are just not cut out for parenthood. We don't have the right genes. It must be all those centuries of handing our kids over to nannies means that the nurturing gene has been bred out. Yes, the parenting gene was bred out alongside the work ethic gene, I reckon. And stop smirking, Hugo, because the same thing happened to your family too. That's why we're both incapable of getting proper jobs or sorting out our own lives.'

They walked in silence for a while towards the tube station and then Hugo said, quietly but firmly: 'You're going to have to see your mum soon, Sophia.'

Sophia studiously ignored his comment and watched her feet as they pounded the grimy, wet pavement.

'You can ignore me all you like but the fact remains,' Hugo went on, sternly, 'that you've promised your dying grandmother that you'll find her missing necklace and in order to do that you are going to have to face your mother – and perhaps even your dad.'

Sophia felt her stomach do a flip. He was right, of course. But how on earth could she face her parents now? It had been an uncomfortable enough prospect even before she knew what her father had said to Nathan. The climb up the mountain felt steeper than ever.

They remained in silence as the Central Line hurtled east.

By the time the pair climbed out onto the street outside Mile End tube station, the drizzle had turned into a downpour. They turned up their collars, cast down their eyes, and ran through the park towards home. They were almost back at their street when a black Labrador appeared from the bushes, play-wrestling with what looked like a dead animal.

'Put that down, Duke!' shouted a man, whose face was

obscured by the hood of his anorak. 'What the hell have you got there? Put it down, Duke! Come here!'

Reluctantly, the dog dropped the dead animal and skulked back to his owner. Sophia stopped and stared at the abandoned carcass on the path.

'Is that ...?' Sophia squinted in the dim, dusk light. 'Is that my fake fur coat?'

Hugo didn't even look up.

'Don't be daft, Soph,' he said. 'You left your coat in your room. You said it was too wet to wear it.'

The moment they stepped onto their street, Sophia and Hugo could see that something was very wrong.

'Oh no,' said Sophia. 'I think we've been evicted.'

The front garden of the house looked as if it had been used for fly tipping. Dozens of black bin liners were heaped in a haphazard mound on the grass. Some had split and clothes and books had spilled out onto the muddy lawn. Ben and Amelia were sitting side by side on top of one of the bags, soaking wet, silently sharing a roll-up.

'What happened?' asked Sophia, desperately. 'We only went out a few hours ago. Why is all our stuff out here?'

'My dad sold the house,' said Ben, shaking his head in disbelief. 'I mean, he did say something about doing that ages ago but I didn't think he actually meant it. And some people came round one day, a couple of months ago, I think, with a guy in a suit, and they said something about it being a viewing but ...'

'Didn't he give you any notice, Ben?' asked Sophia, as gently as she could, pulling her fingers through her tangled hair. 'A house doesn't get sold overnight. He could have given us time to find somewhere else.'

'He sent letters,' said Amelia, sadly. 'But Ben didn't open them.'

Sophia nodded, remembering the mountain of post in the porch. None of them were very good at opening letters.

'Then a couple of hours ago, some man came round and said this was his house now, and we had an hour to get out,' continued Amelia, getting tearful now. 'And that's when Ben opened the letters.'

'He's my dad,' said Ben, pitifully. 'He could have phoned me. The letters were from a solicitor. I didn't want to open them. I thought I was in trouble.'

'We are in trouble,' seethed Hugo. 'We're homeless.'

'Calm down, Hugo,' said Sophia, patting his arm. 'It's only stuff. We're fine. We can sort it out.'

'How?' asked Hugo in a high, strangled voice.

'Where are you guys going?' Sophia asked Ben and Amelia.

'A mate of ours knows about a squat in Camberwell,' said Ben. He threw the roll-up into a puddle and stood up. 'Just for a bit. Until something better comes along.'

Ben and Amelia picked up three bin bags each.

'Sorry, guys,' said Ben. 'Stay in touch, yeah. Hope you get something sorted.'

Sophia watched the couple struggle down the street with their belongings. Amelia dropped one of her bags and Ben picked it up for her. Sophia already knew that nothing better was coming along for them.

She took a very deep breath and thought carefully. She was upset, but she was quite calm. And, unlike after Nathan, she didn't feel broken by the situation. She would fix this. She felt sure of it. She sat down on the nearest bin bag and patted the space beside her.

'Sit,' she said to Hugo, who was standing shivering by the gate still. 'Here.' She handed him a cigarette. 'Let's calm down, have a think and then, let's get as far away from this hellhole as we possibly can.' She patted him on the knee affectionately. 'Surely we must know someone who can help us.'

Hugo's frown began to turn into an unexpected smile.

'What? Like a man with a van?' he asked, grinning now.

'Damon!' they said in unison.

Damon was a godsend. He drove all the way from a job in Southend to pick Sophia, Hugo and all their belongings up. By the time he arrived, Sophia and Hugo had managed to repack the errant shoes, knickers and knick-knacks back into the ripped bin bags.

'Look at the guns on that, eh?' Hugo whispered to Sophia as Damon climbed out of his van. 'Have you ever seen biceps like them? I just wish he owned a house in Chelsea rather than Essex.'

'He's gorgeous,' Sophia whispered back. 'And completely lovely. Look what he's doing for us. Maybe you need to stop serial-dating sugar daddies and settle down with someone you actually like for a change. What does it matter if he can't afford to buy you things? Things never make you happy.'

'Maybe,' said Hugo, thoughtfully. 'But I barely know him yet, Soph. Honestly, we shared an egg-white omelette and a superfood smoothie for brunch yesterday, but that is as far it's gone. He could be too good to be true.'

'All done!' said Damon cheerfully, shoving the last bag into the back and slamming the door. 'I can't believe you guys are out on the street. I assumed you were loaded!'

'Has it put you off us?' asked Hugo, nervously.

'Nope,' said Damon, matter-of-factly. 'In fact I think it's made me like you even more.'

Sophia clambered into the front seat beside Hugo and Damon. There was something comforting about being huddled up in a steamed-up van. The truth was, she was glad to be leaving the Hackney house. It had become more of a prison than a home.

'Right, lovelies,' said Damon chirpily. 'Where are we going, then?'

Hugo and Sophia looked at each other. Hugo's face fell.

'I don't know,' he wailed.

Sophia fingered the card in her pocket and wondered if it was the right thing to do. She knew her grandmother would want to help but was it too much to ask of a dying woman? Would she be taking advantage? And what would her parents say about her freeloading again? The truth was Sophia despised feeling like a charity case. Right now, she'd give anything to have a tiny flat of her own, that she paid for herself through a hard day's graft. The thought popped into her head totally unannounced. Did she mean it? Did she really want a normal job, slogging her guts out just to meet the rent each month? Oh. My. God. Yes she did. Sophia wanted her dignity back and it had suddenly hit her that the only way to do that was to start standing on her own two feet. Soon! But right now, she and Hugo were destitute so she was going to have to ask for help one more time.

'Give me two minutes,' she said, clambering out into the rain to make the call to the Wellington Hospital.

'Hampstead, please, Damon,' she said brightly as she climbed back in the van a few minutes later. 'Christchurch Hill.'

'Wow,' said Damon, setting his satnav. 'That's swanky. So you are loaded after all?'

'No,' said Sophia. 'We're just lucky, that's all. Granny says she still hides the spare key in the same place. I hope I can remember where that is.'

'In a jam jar, in the bushes to the left of the front door,' Hugo reminded her.

Chapter Twenty-Five

Tokyo, Japan, 2012

'Are you sure this is the place?' asked Aiko, a little confused by the leafy, suburban street.

'Quite sure,' the driver assured her.

Aiko thanked the driver and asked him to pick her up again in the same spot in one hour.

She tried to get her bearings. None of this had been here. This was clearly now a very affluent area. For some reason she had expected empty fields and perhaps a few rickety wooden houses. It had been silly, of course. They had only driven half an hour out of the city centre.

Aiko looked back down the hill and saw Tokyo sprawling before her: mile upon mile of high-rise buildings, and to the east, the glistening ocean in Tokyo Bay. Yes, this was the right spot. The cityscape had changed and grown beyond recognition, but the distance to the sea was the same.

She spotted a narrow lane that led off the street on her right and without questioning why, she started to follow it. Soon the street behind her disappeared, the path narrowed and Aiko began to feel as if she was lost in a maze. She felt light-headed and dizzy, the ghosts called to her, they shrieked in her head, refusing to be quiet after all their years in exile. Aiko tripped on a tree root, stumbled and fell into a clearing. In front of her stood the shell of a dilapidated barn. The roof had long since gone and a magnolia tree had grown through the place where the floor had once been. Perhaps she would not even have known it had ever been a barn, had she not been there before. Aiko's knees buckled. She held onto the magnolia for support. There was no ignoring the ghosts now. They were here.

Tokyo, Japan, 1946

Aiko slept in a barn that night. She had never been to Tokyo before. She had no idea which direction to go in and it was too dark to see anything, or anybody, in the dead of night. Besides she had no shoes, and the soles of her feet had been ripped to shreds from weeks of walking on bomb-pitted roads. No, better to hide tonight and carry on her journey in the morning. She'd come too far to take any silly risks now. So she waited until all the people from the cart had disappeared and then crept into this dilapidated barn, away from the dangers of the main road.

It was always difficult for Aiko to get to sleep: her muscles ached, her hair crawled with lice, her stomach growled with hunger and her skin itched with insect bites and rashes. But far worse than the physical discomfort were the images that filled her head when she shut her eyes – the emaciated bodies of her grandparents, the sight of Great-Granny's house crumbling into the sea after she died, her father's face as he was dragged away from his only child to fight an enemy he had never seen, the empty village she had left behind. It took all her mental strength to switch off those pictures and concentrate on tomorrow and the future instead. Aiko patted her chest to check that her red silk pouch was still safely tied inside. It was. Knowing that her only valuables in the world were safe, she allowed herself to fall asleep.

She awoke at first light and made her way carefully back down the narrow lane and finally onto the road that had brought her here. What she saw horrified her. She was at the top of a hill with a straight, but almost completely destroyed, road ahead of her. She had wondered last night why the mean farmer had thrown them all off the cart so far from the city itself, but now she understood. The main road from Nagoya to Tokyo simply ended here.

Aiko had heard about the firebombing of Tokyo but nothing could have prepared her for the sight of a city this devastated. It looked nothing like the Tokyo she had seen in newspaper pictures as a child. The city, famous for its timber and paper buildings, had simply turned to cinders and dust. Ahead of her was street after street and neighbourhood upon neighbourhood of burned-out houses, temples, factories and schools. It all merged together into one huge, grey-brown mass of debris. Far in the distance, under a dark, smoggy cloud, she could just about make out the ocean but it looked nothing like the green sea back home in Ise Shima. Worse, she could not smell it. She had been sure she would be able to smell the ocean here in Tokyo but all that Aiko could smell was a rancid reek of charred wood, decay and death.

With a heavy heart and bleeding feet, she began her long walk into the city. There were others walking the same way with their heads down and their shoulders hunched. The old and infirm shuffled painfully slowly while women carried exhausted children. Some men carried large trunks, or small pieces of furniture, or even crates of chickens – anything they had managed to salvage from their past lives, Aiko guessed. Half-dead goats and cows were dragged behind on ropes, while emaciated dogs followed loyally at the rear, trying to keep family groups herded safely together. But the strange thing was, that for every person Aiko saw heading towards the city, she saw another leaving in the opposite direction, trying to escape. One man's sanctuary is another man's prison, she guessed. Aiko passed several bodies by the side of the road but she did not stop and stare. She had seen many corpses already in her short life and they held no morbid fascination for her. Death was just death. It was as much a certainty as the rising of the sun. Her only mission now was to cheat death for as long as possible. Somehow, despite the tragedies that had befallen her, Aiko's strongest desire was to live. It burned like a fire in her belly, pushing her forward. She had no idea what she was living for, she had no friends or family, nor did she know where she was going, exactly. The final destination was more of an abstract idea of happiness and contentment, rather than a physical place. All she knew was that she would not give up until she got there. She whispered to herself as she walked on and on towards the burned city ahead. 'Fall seven times, but stand up eight. Fall seven times, but stand up eight.'

Aiko was still a mile or more away from the outskirts of Tokyo when she heard a loud, low rumbling noise behind her. She looked back warily and saw an American army tank approaching. It was the only type of vehicle capable of driving along such a devastated road. Her heart sank. She was terrified of American soldiers. Not only because of what had happened during the war, but because of how they looked and behaved too. They were so alien to her, so different from the men she knew from back home.

The GIs she had come across since the occupation treated Japanese girls like pieces of cheap meat. She had seen the bars and houses where American soldiers bought young local girls for as little as five yen. They seemed to think all Japanese girls were on sale. Well not this one! Aiko put her head down and walked off the road onto the grass verge to be as far away from the tank as possible when it passed. The sound of its engine got closer and closer but Aiko didn't dare look over her shoulder. She willed it to keep going and to pass her by but, somehow, she already knew what was about to happen.

The tank stopped beside her. Two soldiers sat on the roof, chewing gum and grinning at her. A third poked his blond head out of the top.

Like a rat appearing from its hole, thought Aiko to herself.

'Hey, gorgeous,' leered one of the GIs. 'You're a sight for sore eyes, ain't ya?'

Aiko had been around American soldiers enough to understand what they were saying, but she pretended not to hear them and tried to walk away. Two of the soldiers jumped down off the tank and followed her. The blond one shook his head and stayed where he was with his head poking out of his rat hole.

'Leave her,' he shouted at his friends. 'We don't have time for this. Let's get back to camp.'

Perhaps that one wasn't such a rat after all. But the other two ignored him and jogged to catch up with Aiko.

'Hey, honey, don't be shy,' said one of them, a squat monkey of a man, or boy really, with orange hair and freckles on his skin. He grabbed her arm and pulled her round to face him. 'We're just trying to be friendly.'

'Please leave me alone,' said Aiko, one of the few phrases she'd learnt in English, trying to keep the fear out of her voice. She refused to look up at the soldier and kept her gaze firmly on the ground.

'Well, that's a bit rude, missy,' said his friend, a taller, skinny boy with glasses and a thin moustache (which Aiko decided he must have grown in an attempt to look older). 'That's no way to talk to us when we're here to save your slanty-eyed ass. You Japs would all be dead if it wasn't for us and General MacArthur there, helping you clean up this hellhole of a country of yours.'

Aiko swallowed hard. The first soldier still had his hand tightly around her arm. She hoped her red pouch was secured tightly. She had no idea what was about to happen to her but whatever it was she could not lose her treasured possessions. They were everything she owned.

She could feel the heat of the GI's breath on her cheek. He was standing too close. Aiko's heart raced in her chest.

'She's a real beauty underneath the dirt, this one,' said the skinny one.

'She sure is, Harry,' the freckled one said. 'But she stinks! I bet she hasn't washed in years. You obviously need to be civilised by us, sweetheart.'

He leered at her. She shuddered as she felt his eyes wandering all over her body.

'She's got long legs and nice big titties, ain't you, darling?' the freckled one laughed. His grip on her arm tightened.

'And her eyes are kind of orange,' added the skinny one, Harry. 'They look like they're on fire. Hey, I think this little bitch is hot for you, Duane!'

Aiko would not let them see her cry. She wanted to struggle, to kick him where it hurt, to spit in his ugly face and to run for her life and her freedom, but she was not stupid. There were two of them, three if she counted the one in the tank, and this was a battle she could not win. She allowed herself to glance up and saw that the third soldier had finally got out of the tank and was approaching. Something about his presence made Aiko relax a little. He was young like the other two – only a year or two older than Aiko perhaps – but he seemed to have more authority. He was incredibly tall with very blond hair, pale blue eyes and a deep tan. He didn't wear the same lewd expression on his face as the other two. He glanced at Aiko with a mix of shame and sympathy and then glared at the red-headed one angrily.

'Don't be an ass, Duane,' he told the soldier who was gripping Aiko's arm. 'Let the poor girl go. How would you like it if some

Japanese soldier manhandled your kid sister like that, huh?'

He slapped Duane's arm hard.

'Ow,' he complained, dropping Aiko's wrist, and rubbing his own arm now instead. 'That hurt!'

Aiko did not want to stay to see what happened next. She murmured thank you to the blond GI and started running, as fast as her bleeding feet would allow her, away from the road and the tank and the horrible GIs. When she looked back, the blond man and the one called Duane were shouting and pushing each other around. Maybe all Americans weren't bad after all. She hid behind a tree and watched in shock and awe as the tall, blond, blue-eyed American boy punched his colleague right smack bang in the middle of his ugly face, turned round and walked calmly back to the tank. Harry scratched his head for a moment and then followed his sergeant. Finally, Duane got up, holding his bleeding nose and, still swearing and muttering under his breath, got back into the tank too. Aiko's pounding heart began to calm as the tank disappeared. She had been stupid to get herself into such a situation. She would never rely on a man to save her. Aiko would always save herself.

Chapter Twenty-Six

'What's wrong?' asked Hugo, sitting down next to Sophia on the floor of her grandmother's bedroom in Hampstead. She was surrounded by black bin liners. 'I thought you were going to unpack, settle in and have a nice, long bath. Damon's worked out the boiler for us. Watching the way he can wield a spanner really is quite a turn-on. Anyway, the radiators are on and the water should be hot soon too.'

Sophia swallowed hard. She was not going to cry. But she couldn't find her voice to speak.

'Hey,' said Hugo, softly. 'I thought you were feeling happier about everything since you started seeing your gran? And we're here, in this lovely house now, away from that horrible place. We have carpet beneath our feet and a clean kitchen – I thought this move would make you feel a bit more positive about life.'

'I was feeling better,' Sophia nodded. 'I felt great until about ten minutes ago.'

'So what happened?' asked Hugo, looking perplexed.

'Well, you know how Granny said she'd given the necklace to my mum? And that if I wanted to solve the mystery I had to ask Mum some questions?'

Hugo nodded.

'Well, I thought about what you'd said about how I was going to have to face my mum. And so I texted her and asked her about the pearls,' Sophia admitted.

'Good for you!' said Hugo. 'I'm proud of you—'

'No,' interrupted Sophia. 'It was a stupid thing to do. I knew I shouldn't open the floodgates. I told you.'

'Why?' asked Hugo.

'Because she's just sent me this email in reply,' Sophia wiped the tears away with the back of her sleeve and handed Hugo her phone.

'Sophia,' Hugo read out loud. 'I'm afraid I have absolutely no idea what you are talking about. I have never heard of such a necklace. Had you bothered to visit your grandmother previously, you would have seen her deterioration first-hand. Your father and I are in agreement that she is no longer in her right mind and is prone to fantasy, now her memory is not what it was. The chances are there never was any pearl necklace.

'It does not surprise us that you have been drawn in to such a tale, however. As your father would like to point out, you have never shown any interest in this family, other than when your bank balance requires attention. We have no idea how you are subsidising your dubious habits now that we have cut you off financially but you can rest assured that any ideas you have of inheriting a priceless necklace are complete nonsense.

'We would rather you did not visit your grandmother again. She is a very sick old woman and the last thing she needs is you upsetting her during these, her final weeks. Your father feels it is best for everyone if you stay away from Granny and the rest of the family until you have cleaned up your act. As we have made quite clear in the past, we have all had enough of your childish, immoral and often illegal antics and we cannot cope with the stress or the shame any more. If one day you decide to re-enter civilised society, then perhaps we can begin to build bridges. Until then, we would rather not have any contact with you. Mum.'

Sophia flinched as she heard the words spoken out loud. This was her mother speaking. Yes, Sophia had her faults, yes she'd made mistakes, but was she such a waste of space that she deserved this from her own mum?

'What a witch!' shouted Hugo. 'Click your heels together three times, Sophs, and make a wish that you *never* have to go home.'

Trust Hugo to try to make her laugh at a time like this.

'OK, I know the email sounds harsh but if you read it carefully it doesn't really say anything they haven't told you before. Except the bit about your gran being senile: that's new,' said Hugo. 'And, actually, the nasty stuff is all from your dad. It's "your father feels" this and "we think" that. You know perfectly well your mum doesn't have a mind of her own. She's just written down whatever bile your dad's dictated to her.'

'I guess,' Sophia replied, uncertainly. 'But she thinks I'm only interested in the necklace for money!'

Hugo scratched his head. 'No offence, but that was the main reason you went to see your granny, wasn't it? And we are now squatting in her house so ...?'

'We're not squatting!' Sophia replied, hitting him gently on the arm. 'Granny said we can stay here for as long as we like. She said she'd rather the place was being looked after, anyway. She was worrying about burglars. She said we're doing her a favour.'

'And you bought that?' teased Hugo.

'Yes, I did,' replied Sophia tartly. 'And anyway, my inheritance was not the only reason I went to see Granny. You know that. Those letters had really started to get to me. If anything the necklace gave me an excuse. It meant I could change my mind about seeing her without losing face.'

'Uh-huh,' teased Hugo. 'And maybe if you keep telling yourself that you'll actually start believing it. What? You don't have any desire to own a priceless pearl necklace?'

'Of course it would have been amazing to inherit something worth a load of money but it would also be amazing to put a big smile back on Granny's face before she dies. Anyway, you know I could never sell the necklace now. It's about doing something special to repay her for everything she's ever done for me. That's why I want to find the necklace. Wanted to find the necklace ... If it even exists ...'

'Oh, it exists all right,' said Hugo, with certainty. 'I'd bet my entire collection of original nineteen sixties silk ties on it. Why would your granny lie? Why would she make up all those elaborate stories? Anyway, we've seen that picture of her wearing it on her eighteenth birthday, remember?'

'That could have one of her mother's necklaces, or the pearls could have been cheap copies. Granny has always had just as much costume jewellery as real stuff. I used to try it all on when I was little and I couldn't ever tell the difference between the real and the fake stuff,' Sophia continued.

'So, you think your granny's lying?' asked Hugo, narrowing his eyes, testing her.

Sophia thought long and hard before she answered. Could Tilly really be lying? Were her parents right? Was her grandmother senile? And then she remembered the sparkle in Tilly's eyes when she talked about that day with her father in London, about Asprey and the war, and how she'd cried with joy on her eighteenth birthday when her father had presented her with his precious gift. And she knew, at that moment, beyond all doubt, that Tilly was telling the truth.

'No, Hugo,' she said. 'I'm not sure she's telling me the whole story, but I know Granny's not lying about the pearls.'

'Of course she isn't.' Hugo waved his hand dismissively as if there could never have been any doubt. 'Your parents just don't want you getting your hands on any of the family money in case you piss it up the wall. Your dad's probably got that necklace stashed safely in the attic somewhere, ready to take to Christie's the minute Tilly dies. What we need now is evidence.'

'Evidence?' asked Sophia, wiping her tears.

'Yes, firm proof that the necklace exists.'

'Of course,' said Sophia, feeling suddenly brighter. 'Yes, that's exactly what we need. I wonder if Granny has any old photograph albums.'

'All old people have photo albums,' replied Hugo with certainty. 'It's the law, like all gay men quote *The Wizard of Oz* when trying to cheer up their best friend.'

'I think she keeps them in the dresser in the blue drawing room,' Sophia remembered, standing up and tugging at Hugo's hand. 'Come on, let's go and see.'

An hour later they had all the evidence they needed.

'What a filthy little liar,' said Hugo, lifting up a picture of Alice and waving it triumphantly in the air.

He turned the photograph over and read the back.

'Alice on the Spanish Steps, Rome, July 1981,' and then he added, 'Wearing the necklace.'

He picked up another photo.

'Alice, Charity Ball, Venice, May 1981. Wearing the necklace.'

He picked up the last photograph.

'Alice, Piccolo Bar, Capri, June 1981,' he stated. 'Still wearing the bloody necklace! I mean, what sort of student goes Interrailing with a priceless pearl necklace in her backpack?'

Sophia shook her head.

'She had a really cosseted life, my mum,' she said, aware that she was trying to find excuses for the woman who had lied to her, rejected her and allowed her father to emotionally abuse her. But still, there had to be a reason, didn't there? She tried to put herself in her mum's shoes.

'Her parents were world-famous movie stars. She was an only child. Granny had all those miscarriages before she had Mum so I guess she and Grandpa really spoiled her. Granny didn't make another film until after my mum went to boarding school and, according to my mum, she was the one who wanted to board. Granny wanted her to stay at home but Mum felt suffocated there and wanted to spend more time with girls her own age. It must have been hard for her to grasp any sort of normality. She was at parties with Jack Nicholson and Sean Connery and Liza Minnelli one minute, and then being bundled into cars with a coat over her head the next because my grandparents were paranoid about her being hounded by the press. It must have been weird. She can't have had much grip on reality.'

'And we thought we were the poor little rich kids,' said Hugo, sarcastically. 'Poor, poor Alice, having to hang out with James Bond, eh?'

'I suppose it was ridiculous of her to take that necklace back-packing, wasn't it? Do you think she lost it in Italy and then never had the nerve to own up to it?'

Hugo nodded. 'I bet that's exactly what happened.'

'And now she's denying all knowledge, and telling me I'm immoral!'

Sophia let the reality of the situation seep into her brain. She picked up the photo from Capri and stared at the young girl in the picture, trying to read her mind. The girl looked a lot like Sophia had at that age. She had her mouth wide open, laughing, bright red lipstick on full lips. Her breasts oozed out of a black corset top, her tiny waist was clinched with a thick black patent belt. Her long, tanned legs were barely covered by a tiny, flippy, red miniskirt and her arms were draped around the shoulders of two handsome young men, who were both gazing at her adoring-ly. But Alice was staring right at the camera. Her eyes shone with life, mischief, adventure, and naughtiness. She looked fun. She looked like the sort of girl Sophia would have liked as a friend.

'What the hell happened to you?' she asked the girl in the photo. 'Where did you go? How did you turn into my mum? And what the hell did you do with that necklace?'

Sophia gathered up the photographs, slipped on her boots and grabbed her coat.

'Where are you going, hon?' asked Hugo. 'It's late. It's almost eleven.'

'The last train to Virginia Water leaves Waterloo at eleven forty-five,' she informed him. 'I can't sleep on this. I need to talk to my mum tonight.'

'Are you sure?' he asked, looking anxious. 'They'll be in bed. And what about your dad? He'll go ape!'

'I don't care what they think,' she said, grabbing her handbag. 'This isn't about them. It's about Granny.'

Chapter Twenty-Seven

Tokyo, Japan, 2012

Aiko came round to see a young woman in green staring down at her with a concerned look on her face.

'Do not try to sit up. You are in hospital, Mrs Watanabe,' explained the woman. 'You were found unconscious. We need to run some tests. We are on our way to the recovery room now. Try to relax. You are in safe hands.'

Of course. She was in hospital. The ghosts had proved too strong for her. She had tried to fight them all her life but now they had won. Aiko lay back down. She had stopped fighting. But she wasn't relaxing as the doctor had told her to do, she was merely resigning herself to her fate.

Tokyo, Japan, 1946

'I am looking for this address,' Aiko explained to the elderly woman at the vast, open-air market in downtown Tokyo.

She clutched the faded old piece of card carefully and held it out for the old woman to see. But the woman just shook her head.

'You don't know where it is?' Aiko asked. 'This address?'

'Oh, I know where it was,' nodded the woman gravely. 'But that area, that street, that house, it is gone now. There is nothing left there but cinders. I am sorry.'

Aiko swallowed hard. It had been a crazy plan – to find some man her mother had met twenty years ago, turn up on his doorstep and expect some sort of help. She had prepared herself for the idea that Mr Fanaki might have moved, or that he may not remember her mother, or that he might have been dead, but not this. How would she find him now? Aiko had found Mr Fanaki's card in her mother's special treasure box when she was eight years old. She'd asked her father who it belonged to and he had told her that a famous photographer from Tokyo had once come to take pictures of Manami because she was such an extraordinarily beautiful woman. Father said that those pictures had appeared in magazines all over the world and that when Manami died, Mr Fanaki had found out somehow, and he had come all the way from Tokyo to pay his respects.

'Do I look like Mummy?' Aiko had asked her father.

Her father had stared at her for the longest time and then he had said, with watery eyes, 'You look so much like your mother, Aiko-chan, that sometimes it is like having a ghost in the house.'

Aiko had hoped that her resemblance to her mother would help jog Mr Fanaki's memory, but first she had to find him. He was the only soul she knew of in Tokyo – and she had never even met him. She ran back up to the old lady, who was trying to barter over the price of tea with a market seller.

'What is it now, girl?' the woman demanded, impatiently.

'Where did these people go?' she asked, waving the card frantically. 'The ones who lived in this street.'

The woman frowned and looked at Aiko as if she was insane. 'They died,' she said bluntly. 'They all died in the fires. There is no point in trying to find anyone who lived there.'

'But where am I to stay?' asked Aiko.

The old woman nodded across the crowded market to a house on the corner. Young girls, wearing too much make-up and showing too much bare flesh were sitting on the laps of American GIs at the tables outside.

'There are places for girls like you,' she told Aiko.

Aiko shook her head firmly.

'I understand that everyone must make a living somehow,' she replied, 'but that life is not for me. I would rather starve.'

The old woman nodded and smiled. 'Good girl,' she said. 'You look like a pauper but you have fire in you. I wish you good fortune, my child.'

Aiko bowed at the lady and then allowed her to buy her tea in peace.

That night, Aiko slept in a doorway, huddled up in a tiny

ball, clutching her red pouch for dear life. She slept there the next night, and the next too. She ate scraps she found behind restaurants, and vegetables left on the ground after the market had closed. She was not the only one who lived this way. There were hundreds of them, men, women and children, scavenging for food and shelter. Some people huddled together in bomb craters, others slept cheek to cheek in abandoned subways, but Aiko preferred to be alone. Alone and invisible. Perhaps it was her solitude that saved her. With everyone living on top of each other, tuberculosis spread through the slums as fast as the fires that had destroyed the city in the first place. Aiko had become numb to the sight of dead bodies but with every cart that passed, carrying the unfortunate ones who hadn't made it through the night, her resolve strengthened. She would not die. Not here. Not like this.

Crime and violence were rife, and the market was run by the Kanto Ozu gang, but Aiko kept her head down and avoided the mobsters at all costs. She never got into a fight over food. She knew it was wiser to walk away hungry than to stay and be stabbed. She got thinner and weaker. The nights grew colder. Sometimes the lady from the tea stall would make her a cup of chai, but that was all she had to sustain her.

Every day, from her perch in the doorway, she called out to people from under her blanket, asking whether they knew of a Mr Fanaki – a famous photographer. Most people looked right through her as if she no longer existed at all. But one day, somebody answered. He was about the same age as her father would have been now. Aiko had seen him around, haggling and joking with the market sellers. Sometimes he came to the market with a car full of US military officers. She had seen him introducing them to members of the Kanto Ozu gang. He seemed to know everybody. He dressed expensively in Western suits and looked to be very well fed, which was something of a miracle in Tokyo.

He walked towards her, bent down, and put his hand on her chin and lifted her face up towards his. Aiko would not meet his gaze.

'I do not know your Mr Fanaki,' the businessman told. 'But I do know that you are going to die soon if you don't eat something and put some warmer clothes on. It is winter now. This is no time for a young girl like you to be living on the streets.'

'I have no money for food, or clothes, or a place to stay,' Aiko told the man, finally glancing up nervously to meet his stare.

'Why don't you beg?' he asked, head cocked on one side, probing her with his eyes.

'I will never beg,' replied Aiko proudly, jerking her chin from his grasp.

'Or become a geisha?' he inquired.

They both knew he didn't mean a geisha in the old sense of the word. The GIs did not know the Japanese word for prostitute – *baishunfu* – they only knew the word 'geisha'. In their ignorance, they did not understand the difference, and so in post-war Tokyo, the word had become slang for whore. Now it seemed that half of the young girls in the slums of Tokyo were geisha. But not Aiko.

'I would rather sleep with the rats,' retorted Aiko, getting angry now. She was not a toy for this rich man to play with.

'I have a bar—' he began to say.

'I said I would rather die!' hissed Aiko, backing further into her doorway.

'It's a nice place, respectable, I don't employ prostitutes but I do need pretty girls to work there. I have a lot of important clientele, Americans mostly. They keep me rich! All you would have to do is talk to my customers, charm them, and flatter them. Nothing else, I promise. I'm not trying to take advantage of you. Or offering you charity, before your pride gets in the way! You have a most unusual beauty and I like the fire in your eyes. You have spirit! My customers will admire you greatly. I'm asking for your trust. In return I'm offering you a job, and a roof over your head, and three hot bowls of rice a day.'

'Why should I trust you?' demanded Aiko.

The man looked around the squalid market place.

'I don't think you have much choice,' he replied, reaching out his hand towards her.

Aiko hesitated. She stared deep into the man's eyes. They twinkled with life, and perhaps a little mischief, but there was no evil there. Aiko decided to trust, not so much the man, but her own instincts. She wasn't going to get anywhere sitting here in her doorway. Perhaps it was time to save herself. She took a deep breath and reached her hand out to meet his.

'I am Mr Oshiro,' he said, as he pulled her unsteadily to her feet.

'Thank you, Mr Oshiro,' she replied. 'I am Aiko. Aiko Watanabe.'

'I can tell that you have been on a long and treacherous journey. My wife, Nana, is a kind woman. She'll look after you until you are well enough to start work and move into the boarding house with the other girls.'

Aiko quickly learned that she had been right to trust her instincts. The Oshiros had never been blessed with children of their own and Nana was so full of wasted love and kindness that she was practically bursting with affection. She was a pretty lady in her early forties, who kept herself neat, if a little chubby. Aiko adored her. After three weeks in Nana's care, Aiko could walk without limping, the colour had returned to her cheeks, her hair was free of lice and the rashes that had plagued her body had all but disappeared. What's more, Aiko had learned what it felt like to have a full belly again. Mr Oshiro owned not only a bar, but two restaurants and a grocery store too. Their beautiful two-storey house was brand new. Aiko had never been in a home with stairs before! Every house she had been in had been one-roomed and made of paper and timber.

But somehow Mr Oshiro had managed to build himself a new home in a rich neighbourhood of west Tokyo that had escaped the bombings. His house had several separate rooms, it even had electric lights. Aiko thought the place was a palace. For the first time in years, she felt safe. 'There is luck in the leftovers,' she reminded herself.

When the time came to start work at Mr Oshiro's bar, Nana begged her husband to allow Aiko to stay with them, rather than sending her to the lodging rooms above the bar with the other girls. Aiko stood still as a heron on the stairs and listened to the conversation going on below.

'She can help me around the house,' Aiko heard Nana tell Mr Oshiro. 'I do not have a daughter, or even a daughter-in-law to help me with my chores. She will be doing us a favour.'

And then Nana lowered her voice.

'Besides, it would be a terrible shame if she got in with the wrong crowd, no? Remember what happened to Junko? I hear she is working at the International Palace now, servicing

American soldiers. We must keep Aiko safe, husband. She has been sent to us for a reason. It is our duty to keep her from harm.'

Aiko did not know who Junko was, but she had heard of the International Palace – it was supposedly the biggest brothel in the world. Hundreds of American soldiers turned up there every day to have their way with Japanese girls. Aiko had heard that it was such an efficient operation that the young GIs took off their shoes when they arrived, did whatever it was they did with the girls, and then collected their shoes, freshly cleaned and polished, when they left. Other girls, Aiko had heard, would sleep with soldiers for a packet of cigarettes. And the Americans certainly had a lot of cigarettes! She'd seen them selling cartons of Old Golds to the gangsters in Ozu market, along with liquor, chocolate and even condoms. A lot of those young soldiers were making a fortune on the Tokyo black market. And they were spending a fortune in places like International Palace too. Aiko knew she would never end up there like this poor Junko. Mr Oshiro would never allow it. She had noticed that Nana could wrap her husband around her little finger. It warmed Aiko's heart to see a man so in love with his wife.

Nana had given Aiko some pretty cotton robes, woollen stockings and a pair of shoes when she first arrived but on the day she was to start work, Mr Oshiro presented her with two exquisite kimonos; one in pale aqua blue, the other in a fiery orange-red shade.

'Water and fire,' he said. 'Because you are a mixture of both, Aiko-chan.'

The girls who worked the bars in the poorer areas of Tokyo had taken to wearing Western clothes and make-up. They chewed gum and swore in English. But Mr Oshiro would never allow such behaviour in his establishment. The hostesses dressed traditionally – it attracted a more discerning customer, he explained to her. That first night, Nana helped Aiko into the blue kimono, put her hair up with an ivory comb and applied pale make-up to her face, rouge to her cheeks, black kohl to her eyes and a red stain to her lips.

'There,' she said. 'You are a woman now.'

Aiko stared in disbelief at the sophisticated woman in the mirror. She wished that her father could see her now. Once

Nana had left her alone in her room, Aiko collected the little red pouch from under her pillow and secured it beneath the blue kimono. She trusted Nana and Mr Oshiro with her life but she would never go anywhere without her treasure.

Mr Oshiro's bar was in the wealthy Ginza area. It was called the Peace Palace.

'The Yanks like the name.' Mr Oshiro grinned at Aiko as he ushered her through the door. 'They think it makes my place extra friendly. They think I must approve of the occupation because I've used the word peace.'

'And do you approve of the Americans?' Aiko asked him, warily, unsure whether it was respectful to enquire about such matters. 'I mean, do you like them?'

Mr Oshiro shrugged, unfazed by her question.

'They are just people. I like some of them and not others. But, even if I do not like them, I like the colour of their money, so here at The Peace Palace we are nice to all Americans, Aiko. Remember that and you'll be a great success.'

Mr Oshiro introduced Aiko to the other hostesses. They were all good-looking, well-spoken, respectable girls. Aiko relaxed immediately. Mr Oshiro had been true to his word: his bar was nothing like the geisha houses in the slums. It was opulent with a polished wood floor, red velvet curtains and shiny chrome bar stools. Behind the long bar were rows of glass shelves holding bottles of alcohol, every colour under the sun! The head hostess was a stunning woman of about thirty, who had been a proper geisha in Kyoto before the war. She had hair as black as a raven and eyes as dark as the night sky. Her name was Kira and Aiko was immediately awestruck. Kira taught Aiko which liquor was which. She showed her how to serve sake correctly, how to mix drinks the way the Americans liked them.

And then Kira asked, 'Do you know how to make men fall in love with you, Aiko?'

Aiko blushed. She had never even kissed a man. What did she know of love? There had been no time for her to fill her head with romantic notions, she'd been too busy merely trying to survive.

'No,' she admitted. 'I do not know many men. Only Mr Oshiro.'

Kira laughed. 'My darling Aiko, with your beauty they will

be falling at your feet. I will teach you a few tricks and then they will all be in love with you!'

'But why would I want that?' asked Aiko, confused. She didn't want lots of men falling in love with her, just one nice one would do when the time came. And that wouldn't be for a long time yet. Aiko had too much to do to let romance get in the way.

'Because the more they love you, the bigger the tips they will give you. And presents too. See?' Kira pulled down her kimono to show a delicate gold chain with a diamond pendant attached. 'One of the customers gave it to me last week. Isn't it lovely?'

'Yes,' replied Aiko. 'It's beautiful.'

She felt a little worried again now. All this talk of gifts and making men fall in love sounded a little sordid. Kira saw the concern on her face and smiled.

'I know what you are thinking,' she said, softly. 'But there is no need to worry. All we do here is make the men feel special, interesting and handsome. We do not let them touch us. We do not kiss them. We do not agree to meet them outside the bar. These are Mr Oshiro's rules. We are beautiful works of art for them to look at while they are here. They may buy us gifts but they can never afford to own us. Understand?'

Aiko nodded with relief. She understood. Those rules suited her just fine.

It didn't take long for her to feel at home at the Peace Palace. After just two weeks of work, Mr Oshiro proclaimed she was 'a natural!' and he bought her a third kimono – this time in emerald green. The truth was, Aiko found her new job easy. It hardly felt like working at all. It certainly was nothing like the work women back home in Ise Shima did. She did not have to toil or sweat. Most of the customers were high-ranking American officers. The Japanese clients were all incredibly wealthy and friendly with the Yanks. Mr Oshiro had been right about the Americans too: a few were rude, some were lecherous, but the vast majority were charming, polite and respectable. There was music, laughter, innocent flirting and sometimes a little dancing and singing. Aiko felt happier and safer there than she had felt in many years.

The Peace Palace was more than a bar though. It quickly became clear to Aiko that the bar's purpose was not only to entertain the US officers. Aiko heard the men in the bar discuss a lot of 'business' together but she never intruded or got too close. She needed Mr Oshiro and his important friends to think that their business was none of hers. But Aiko listened and watched intently as she poured sake and handed out Singapore Slings. She stored every little detail in her brain, knowing that one day soon she would be able to use the information she had gathered. Knowledge was power. And power was freedom. And wasn't that what Haruki said Manami had died for? Aiko's freedom.

Nothing escaped her. She saw the dollars and yen that changed hands under the tables. She knew that most of the bar's alcohol came straight from the US military's own supply. And she was well aware that Mr Oshiro had a large safe, hidden behind a picture, in his private office. Everyone knew that the Yanks had recovered tons of Japanese bullion from Tokyo Bay last year, but how some of it had ended up in her boss's safe was a mystery. Aiko also knew that Mr Oshiro had a pistol locked in the top drawer of his desk and another in a cabinet in his home. But Mr Oshiro and his customers had no idea Aiko had noticed a thing about what really went on at The Peace Palace. She smiled sweetly, bowed respectfully, served her drinks, flirted, smiled, laughed and played along.

Haruki had always said that Aiko must have come from the sea because she was like a sponge: she soaked up every little thing she ever saw or heard. It didn't take long for Aiko to learn how to make men fall in love with her and within weeks she was taking home bigger tips and better presents than Kira. She could mix a mean martini or recommend a ten-year-old Scotch. She quickly became fluent in English and could be as swift with a comeback to an American as she could to a Japanese man. They seemed to like her humour.

At home with Nana, she worked much harder than she did at the bar. Nana was no hard taskmistress, and she never asked much of Aiko, but Aiko was so incredibly grateful to the Oshiros for taking her in that she insisted on doing more than her fair share.

'You must have been sent to us by the gods,' Nana would say, when Aiko made dinner or swept the floors without being asked. 'I wish you could stay with us for ever, Aiko-chan. You are the closest thing to a daughter I will ever know.'

'I'm not going anywhere,' Aiko would reply with an affectionate smile. 'Why would I?'

'One day you will, my child,' Nana would say, a little sadly. 'A man will steal you away from me soon. Mark my words.'

But Aiko knew better. She would leave the Oshiros one day, that was true. But it would be for her own reasons, in her own time. No man was ever going to get in the way of Aiko's destiny.

Chapter Twenty-Eight

Virginia Water, Surrey, 2012

'Mum!' Sophia banged on the heavy oak front door of the sturdy red-brick detached house she had once called home. 'Mum!'

She'd already rung the bell twice, she'd seen her parents' bedroom light go on, the curtains twitching and then dropping down again. They knew she was here. The security lights in the driveway had come on the minute her boots started crunching on the gravel. Now they'd be having emergency talks in the bedroom: how to deal with The Problem Child.

Come on, Mum,' she continued. 'I'll keep doing this until I wake all the neighbours if I have to.'

That did it. It was Sophia's never-fail trick to get her mum to answer the front door whenever she was banned from the premises: threaten to embarrass her in front of the good folk of Virginia Water.

'Hi,' she said, as Alice opened the front door in her dressing gown.

Her mother's face was drawn and white. Her hands shook as she clutched her dressing gown closer to her chest.

You'd think I'd returned from the dead, not London, thought Sophia as she walked through into the large hallway. She made her way to the kitchen and sat down on a bar stool by the central island. She got out the photographs and spread them all over the granite work surface.

'It's after midnight. Have you finally gone mad, Sophia?' asked her mum, in a ridiculous shouty whisper.

Who was she being quiet for? They both new full well that Philip was awake upstairs, just waiting for his moment to sweep in and take over in the battle of Alice and Philip Brown v Sophia Beaumont Brown.

'What are you doing here?' demanded her mum. 'We made it perfectly clear that you are not allowed in this house until you prove to us that you can behave.'

'Behave?' asked Sophia. What ammunition did Alice and Philip have left? They'd already disowned her, cut her off and told her what a useless daughter she was. Her father had even scared off her fiancé. What else could they do to hurt her?

'You lied, Mum,' she went on, with adrenalin pumping through her veins. 'That email earlier. It broke my heart. Do you ever think about that? Does it ever cross your mind that you might be hurting me?'

She saw her mum flinch. What was the look that just crossed her face?

'But you're a liar, aren't you, Mum? You made out that I was trying to get my hands on Granny's necklace so that I could make money out of it. But the truth is, you're the one who's trying to pull a fast one.'

'I have absolutely no idea what you are talking about, Sophia. What necklace? I didn't send you an email! And I will not be spoken to like this in my own house. Nor will I be made to feel guilty about the way you've turned out. We tried our hardest. We sent you to the best schools, we gave you ballet lessons, horse riding, piano ... You had every chance, every experience and every opportunity that money could buy,' her mum lectured her. It was a lecture she'd heard a thousand times before.

'But you didn't give me love, did you, Mum?' she replied. 'And that would have been free.'

'We did love you,' whispered her mum.

'No you didn't,' said Sophia, calmly, with certainty. 'You might have loved me, in your own way, when I was little. But Dad didn't. No, don't even try to deny it! And for whatever reason, you didn't love me enough to take my side when Dad was cruel to me. By the time I was a teenager you'd given up on me.'

'You were always such a handful!' her mum cried.

'No, I wasn't,' said Sophia. 'I was a little girl who was desperate for attention because I always felt like I was in the way, superfluous to family requirements.'

'It isn't just us who find you difficult, Sophia,' her mum went on. 'What about Nathan? He loved you but he couldn't handle your behaviour either.'

'Nathan left me because Dad told him to,' said Sophia, trying desperately to stay calm, and not lose her rag. 'Did you know that, Mum? Or is it another little secret you'd like to brush under the carpet?'

'What do you mean secret? What secret?' she asked.

Sophia lifted up the first of the photographs.

'Alice on the Spanish Steps, Rome, July 1981,' she read out. 'And you appear to be wearing Granny's pearl necklace. The necklace you denied all knowledge of earlier today. And, look, here you are wearing it again in Rimini, and Capri! Did you have a good time in Italy, Mum? Did you get pissed and lose your mum's priceless pearls?'

Sophia watched as her mother's face turned from white to bright scarlet. She saw a monster take over her placid middle-aged mother and heard a roar come out of her mouth that made Sophia jump.

'How dare you!' shouted Alice, lunging towards Sophia. 'Don't you ever, EVER talk to me about that again!'

The next thing Sophia knew, her mum had grabbed her by the shoulders and was shaking her hard.

'You don't know what you're talking about!' she screamed. 'You don't know anything about me!'

'Mum, stop, please,' she begged. 'You're hurting me. What are you doing?'

Sophia had never seen her mother so much as swat a fly. For the first time in her life, she was relieved when her dad finally walked in.

'What the bloody hell is going on in here?' he demanded, pulling Alice off Sophia. 'My God! What have you done to upset your mother like this, Sophia?'

Her dad hugged her weeping mum and glared at Sophia.

'She attacked me for no reason,' said Sophia, gathering up the photographs and bundling them into her bag. 'And you tell me I'm mad! Look at your wife, Dad. She's a basket case! What sort of mother attacks her own daughter?'

She wanted to go. She wanted to run away, just like she had when she was ten. But this time she would not feel ashamed. She was an adult now and things were different. Yes, she'd caused her parents pain, but not this time. This time she knew she was not the one who had done something wrong.

'What did you say to her?' asked her dad, narrowing his eyes. He didn't even try to hide the loathing in his voice.

'I told her I knew that she had Granny's necklace when she was Interrailing in Italy. That was all. I pointed out that she was a liar for denying the necklace ever existed and that if she'd got pissed with Italian boys and lost the pearls, then the least she could do was admit it now, thirty-odd years later. It was granny's most treasured possession and she lost it.'

'I didn't lose it!' her mum screamed like a banshee.

Sophia watched in horror as her dad had to hold her mum back from attacking her again.

'I DID NOT LOSE THAT NECKLACE!' she roared, over and over again.

'You're nuts,' said Sophia, quietly. 'You're obviously having some sort of breakdown and you,' she turned to her dad, 'you probably drove her to it. Do you know what?' She headed for the front door. 'This time, I'm disowning *you*.'

She opened the door and ran out before her dad could respond. But, as she ran down the long drive, away from the house, it wasn't her dad she could hear shouting after her. It was her mum, crying, 'Sophia! I'm sorry. Please, Sophia, don't go! It's not what you think. I don't know where that necklace is now. That's the truth. You must believe me. Sophia!'

But it was too late for apologies or explanations. Something in Sophia snapped. She didn't think there was anything her parents could do or say to fix things now. She slept fitfully in the waiting room at Virginia Water station and got the first train back to Waterloo in the morning. This time, as the train hurtled its way towards London, she did not cry.

Chapter Twenty-Nine

Alice Brown stood in her dressing gown at the kitchen window and watched the light slowly creep over the garden hedge. As the sun rose she realised with a jolt that she hated the garden with its perfectly manicured lawn, mowed into neat stripes by Philip on his beloved sit-on mower. She downed the neat whisky she'd poured herself – her third since Sophia had left – and enjoyed the way it burned her throat on the way down and warmed her stomach despite the chilly dawn. Alice rarely drank and never touched spirits. But Alice did not want to be Alice any more. She felt as if she was waking up from a very long dream. She stared at her own home as if seeing it suddenly through new eyes.

She hated the twee summer house with its fake dovecote and the ridiculous ornamental pond with its collection of koi carp that Philip was forever fretting over. And while she was at it, she hated her stuck-up neighbours on both sides (although she had called them friends for years and she often played bridge with them). God, she hated this house with its pompous exterior and its overly neat, chintzy interior. She hated the clothes in her wardrobe and the flowery crockery in her cupboards. She hated her husband, Philip, who snored obliviously upstairs. But most of all, more than anything, Alice Brown hated herself. She hated herself for the bad choices she'd made and the weaknesses that had brought her here. She hated what she'd done to Sophia, and she hated what she'd done to the girl in the photograph that Sophia had dropped as she'd fled.

The photograph was still in her hand. A little crumpled now and damp from tears. Just like Alice's face. She looked at the girl in the photograph in her miniskirt and make-up. Her eyes shone with excitement and her full mouth was open in sheer joy.

'Sorry,' she told the girl. 'Sorry I got rid of you, Alice. I didn't mean to. I thought I was protecting you. Me. Whoever that might be. I'm not sure I know any more.'

Capri, Italy 1981

Lady Alice Beaumont-Perry was eighteen years old, and three months into an Interrailing holiday around Italy with her best friend, Claudia. And, boy, was she having a ball! Freedom had been a long time coming, and now it was finally hers, Alice was devouring it with gusto.

'Adventurous', 'high-spirited', 'brave', – these were all words used to describe Alice in her leaver's book from school that spring. And yes, she had always felt all of these things, but this was the first time she'd actually been able to act upon her urges. She had swum naked at midnight with a bunch of crazy German students in a lake just north of Verona. She had smoked weed for the first time on a crowded bunk bed in a hostel in Milan. She and her friends had been kicked off the train from Florence to San Marino for being too drunk to find their tickets. In Rimini she had tried bridge-jumping for the first time. And last week in Naples, she and Claudia had run out of money and had had to work in a rather seedy nightclub until their parents could wire more funds to them. There was no doubt about it: Alice was having the time of her life.

This summer she had finally become free of her very loving but over-protective father. As the daughter of two Hollywood stars, her life had been ridiculously privileged but also cosseted and claustrophobic. There had always been security guards watching her every move and that was no fun for a teenager. Finishing School in Switzerland had given her a small taste of freedom but only when she and the other girls had managed to sneak out and meet up with the local boys behind the teachers' backs.

But now, finally, she was in Italy. Her mum had sent her off on her travels with her blessing, but her dad had been a bit more nervous. She was still a baby in his eyes! Her mum had finally persuaded her dad to let her go by telling him that every girl needs an adventure when she comes of age – hadn't they only met because Tilly had had the nerve to run away to London? When she got back, Alice planned to study Art History at Oxford, but until then, she had a year to fill with fun.

Alice and Claudia had had a ball in Milan, Florence, Rimini, Pescara, Foggia, Taranto, Messina, Palermo and Naples. Now here she was in Capri, sipping an espresso in a divine little café overlooking the turquoise ocean. She was super-tanned and felt super-sexy. She loved the way the Italian boys and men appreciated her curves. She felt like a woman here! And not like Tilly Beaumont's daughter, either. She finally felt like Alice for Alice's sake. No one here knew who she was. She was free. She savoured the bittersweet coffee and drank in the delicious view. Could life taste any sweeter?

'Hi,' said Claudia, interrupting Alice's thoughts.

She was dragging Javier, her French boyfriend, behind her like a slightly startled puppy as usual. Claudia had picked Javier up in Rimini weeks ago and had barely put him down since. The poor boy looked exhausted.

'Hi, Claud, Javier,' said Alice brightly. 'What are the plans for today?'

'Javier has a friend with a yacht!' Claudia told her excitedly. 'So we can all go for a sail today – and maybe even tomorrow too – but ...'

Claudia's voiced trailed off and Alice realised that her friend was staring at her in a weird, slightly nervous manner.

'What's wrong, Claud?' she asked.

What could possibly be wrong here? In paradise?

'Um, nothing is wrong exactly,' she said. 'It's just that, um, well, I may have a slight change of plan.'

'Change of plan?' Alice didn't understand.

'The, erm, the yacht ...' Claudia was not normally stuck for words.

'My friend, with the yacht, he is going to Monaco at the weekend,' Javier finished for her.

'That's nice for him,' said Alice brightly, wondering if they were about to be invited to Monaco.

They were supposed to be getting the train from Naples to Rome next week and working there for the rest of the season, but they could put that off for a week or two if there was a chance of a trip to Monte Carlo.

'He has asked us to go with him,' said Javier, watching Alice carefully for a response.

Claudia meanwhile seemed very busy concentrating on stirring her coffee.

'And when you say us ...?' Alice asked, getting a little nervous suddenly.

'Me and Javier,' explained Claudia, suddenly finding her nerve. 'I'm so sorry to do this to you, Alice, but Javier is my soulmate. You know that, don't you? You're a romantic. You understand?'

Alice nodded and tried to smile. She was a romantic and she did understand. Kind of. She and Claudia had left England as a tight twosome. Their plan had been to stay together and explore and enjoy Italy until the ski season started, when they would get jobs together as chalet girls in one of the resorts in the Italian Alps and then finally return home the following spring. But Claudia had fallen in love. And love trumped everything, right? Who was Alice to stand in the way of that? If Claudia wanted to go off on her own adventure with Javier, then she had Alice's blessing. Even if that meant that Alice would have to go on to Rome alone.

'That's cool,' she said as brightly as she could. 'I would never stand in the way of love's young dream!'

The relief on Claudia's face was evident.

'I knew you'd understand,' she squealed with excitement. 'You are the best friend in the whole world ever. But just one more thing.'

'Yes?' asked Alice.

'Please don't tell your parents you're not with me any more. They might tell my folks and I would be in massive trouble if they found out I'd gone off with Javier. They wouldn't understand. You know what old people are like. They don't know a thing about love.'

'I promise,' said Alice. And she meant it.

She and Claudia had been covering for each other for years. There was no way she was going to drop her in it now. Besides, her dad would freak out too if he thought she was travelling Italy solo.

'And you'll be OK in Rome, won't you, Al?' asked Claudia, hopefully.

It felt like more of an instruction than a question. It wasn't as if she had a choice now. Alice swallowed a lump in her throat and forced herself to smile and nod with fake enthusiasm. For the first time in three months she felt homesick and for a moment she thought she might actually cry. She was happy for Claudia, really she was, but she was also a little bit scared. Rome on her own. It would be OK, right? What could possibly go wrong in the most romantic city in the world?

Virginia Water, Surrey, 2012

'What are you doing, Alice?' asked Philip from the kitchen doorway.

His voice was quiet and level but Alice recognised the familiar warning tone. She carried on staring at the photograph and sipping her whisky.

'You know you mustn't drink, darling,' he warned her, walking over and taking the glass from her shaking hand. 'Not with your nerves. It doesn't mix well with your pills.'

He smiled at her but his lips were thin and tight and there was no warmth in his eyes. Not that she cared. Whatever he thought of her, Alice was sure she thought less of herself.

'I know that Sophia barging in like that has upset you, Alice,' he continued, slowly, patronisingly. 'But you mustn't dwell on her behaviour. I'm disappointed that you allowed your emotions to get the better of you in front of her. You know she thrives on drama. We've discussed this. Your emotion only feeds hers. That's why we made the decision to protect the family from her. You must learn to detach yourself. Sophia has had countless chances to prove herself to us but she is incapable of behaving responsibly. She's a destabilising influence. We have each other. We have our beautiful home and our friends. We don't need Sophia. She has lost the right to our love.'

'A parent's love should be unconditional,' said Alice, still fingering the crumpled photograph.

'There's no such thing as unconditional love,' he snapped.

And then, realising he'd showed his own real emotions too

freely, he took a deep breath and continued, 'Love has to be earned. It is not free.'

He was trying desperately to appear composed but his words came out in a strangled staccato. Alice did not agree. But she had learned over the years that there was no point in disagreeing with Philip.

'What have you got there, Alice?' he asked her, his eyes shifting to the photograph.

She held the picture up for him to see and watched with a slight thrill as his pale complexion turned pink. She was too weak to fight, but she got a little kick every time she wound him up. It was the closest Alice ever got to danger and excitement these days. Perhaps she was more like Sophia than Philip realised. There was a tiny part of her that wanted to feed the drama too.

'It's me,' she said, speaking finally. 'During my misspent youth. I look good, don't I?'

'You look like a slut!' spat Philip.

His harsh words made Alice jump. She wasn't used to him being so transparent. But then she had just raised a subject that had lain dormant for decades. And an incredibly touchy subject at that: Alice before Philip. He'd never been able to deal with the fact that she'd existed before *him*, before *them*. Unlike his university days or his childhood memories, Alice's past had been airbrushed out of their collective history.

'This is exactly why you shouldn't drink,' he snapped, snatching the photograph from her hands. 'It unhinges you, Alice. It makes you quite uncontrollable.'

Alice watched his face turn from pink to puce and a shiver of fear ran up her spine. Perhaps she had pushed him too far this time. If he hit her she would have a reason to leave. But Philip would never hit his wife. He preferred to use more subtle methods.

She watched closely as he closed his eyes for a moment and forced himself to calm down. His lips moved slightly but no sound came out and it was impossible to make out what he was saying to himself. Alice wondered what mantra he used to restrain his own body and mind in such a firm way. After a few seconds the colour gradually drained from his face, and then Philip walked slowly to the utensil drawer, calmly took out a pair of scissors and snipped the photograph of young Alice into a hundred tiny pieces that fell like confetti to the floor.

'Pick that mess up and put it in the bin,' he told her, as he walked out of the kitchen. 'I'll have poached eggs on toast for breakfast this morning.'

Chapter Thirty

Tokyo, Japan, 2012

'Good news, Mrs Watanabe,' smiled the doctor. 'We have run a series of tests and we can find nothing wrong with your heart. Your blood pressure was a little high when you arrived but it is quite normal now. I understand that you are a very important and busy woman, but you are not young any more. I think you should see this episode as a warning sign to slow down a little, no? You have worked hard your whole life. You should be enjoying your old age. Your son agrees. I have been talking to him outside.'

Aiko smiled and thanked the doctor through gritted teeth. Who was he – a boy, barely out of medical school – to tell her she was working too hard? This had nothing to do with the business. She had been overcome by the power of the past. She knew this to be true but there was no way she would even begin to try to explain that to the young doctor – or to Ken.

'Hey, Mom, how are you feeling?' asked Ken.

He had lived in Tokyo for over thirty years now, his wife was Japanese, and his children too, but he had not lost his American accent and English remained his mother tongue. She felt a little wave of peace as he kissed her on the cheek.

'I'm fine, absolutely fine,' she told him. 'When are they going to let me out of here? I have a flight back to New York tomorrow.'

'They're going to discharge you in the morning once you've had a good rest,' said Ken. 'But you can't fly tomorrow. You must come and stay with me and Suki. We'd love an excuse to have you around a few days longer.'

'No, darling,' she told him firmly. 'I must go back. It has been lovely to see you, as always. You know I miss you like mad. You are still my baby boy!'

'I'm fifty-three!' Ken reminded her, laughing.

'Oh, you will always be three to me, my Kenny-chan,' she teased him. 'But I want to go home. Sometimes Tokyo gets too much for me.'

'Yeah, sure,' grinned Ken. 'Tokyo gets too much for you, huh? Too much for the woman who chose to relocate to New York at the age of seventy-six?'

'I'd had enough of California,' she told him for the umpteenth time. 'Change keeps me young.'

'Oh, I know you're not like other mothers,' laughed Ken. 'I wish I had half your strength. But you still haven't told me what the hell you were doing out there though? In that field.'

'I was visiting a place I went to just after the war,' she told him truthfully. 'I was trying to lay some ghosts to rest.'

'And did it work?' he asked, gently, his blue eyes still a surprise in a face so like her own.

'Not yet,' she admitted.

And then she closed her mouth firmly and shut her eyes.

'You must be tired, Mom,' said Ken, sensing her wish not to dwell on the subject. 'You get some rest and I'll come fetch you in the morning.'

'And take me to the airport?' asked Aiko, hopefully, half opening one eye to watch his reaction.

He smiled affectionately and kissed her again.

'If that's what you want. Who am I to argue with the great Aiko Watanabe?'

After Ken had gone, Aiko tried hard not to sleep. The ghosts had got hold of her now and every time she closed her eyes they were there, desperate to tell their stories, needing to be heard. So she fought them for a while. Watching the television, flicking through magazines, anything to put off the inevitable. But eventually she could fight them no longer. Her eyelids grew heavy and she drifted off into a fitful sleep.

Tokyo, Japan, 1947

Aiko had been working in the bar for six months when he walked in. She recognised him immediately as the blond soldier who had protected her all those months ago. His uniform had changed

233

and he was with some important officers who were regulars at the Peace Palace. Aiko could tell he had been promoted, not only by the way he was dressed, but by the way the officers were slapping him on the back and congratulating him. Aiko realised she was staring. She did not usually find Western men attractive but there was something about this one that intrigued her. With his fair hair, fine features, muscular body, those pale blue eyes and ridiculously long, thick eyelashes, he was by far the most handsome American who had ever crossed the threshold of the Peace Palace. And how could she ever forget that he had saved her? Aiko's stomach did a little somersault. Silly girl! What was wrong with her? There was no time for this nonsense in her life.

'Aiko! Aiko!' called the major general, a jovial, older American who came to the bar most evenings. 'Aiko, you must meet our friend, Captain Bo Anderson. We're celebrating. He has just been promoted for the third time in six months. And he's barely out of diapers!'

Bo blushed a little at what the older man had said. He glanced up at Aiko and smiled politely but there wasn't a flicker of recognition in his face. Aiko blushed too but for entirely different reasons.

'It's a pleasure to meet you, Aiko,' said Bo. 'I'd like a bottle of champagne to celebrate, please. My shout, guys!'

Aiko bowed, and said, 'Yes, sir. Of course, sir,' but she felt a little hurt that he didn't recognise her. Oh, she knew it was irrational. How many starving, homeless Japanese girls must Bo have seen? Why would she be special? Besides, she must hardly look like the same girl now, dressed in her fine clothes and make-up. She barely knew her own reflection in the mirror; why should she expect a virtual stranger to know who she was? Aiko went behind the bar to collect the champagne from the refrigerator and four flutes. As she prepared to open the bottle (the 'pop' still made her jump), she became aware of someone at the bar, watching her.

'Have we met before?' he asked.

Aiko glanced up at Bo and smiled. She nodded her head. So she had made an impression on him, at least.

'We met once but I am not going to tell you where if you can't remember,' she teased. She had learned that men liked it when girls teased.

'Aw, come on, give me a clue at least. That's unfair,' he replied with a broad grin.

'No it's not,' she retorted. 'It is unfair that you do not remember where you met me. You have offended me.'

Bo smiled at her quizzically.

'Don't be offended,' he said. 'It'll come to me. You wait and see. I'm usually pretty good with people and places,' he scratched his blond head, confused. 'I swear, I'll remember soon. In the meantime, call me Bo. Did you call me Bo last time we met?'

Aiko shook her head and laughed at the concept. He obviously thought they'd met in Mr Oshiro's circles, at a party here in the rich part of Tokyo, where people still had fun, blind to the squalor and deprivation all around them. He had made no connection between the glamorous hostess and the ragged girl on the road from Nagoya to Tokyo.

'Bo? It's a strange name,' she said, desperate to keep the conversation going. 'You Americans have lots of odd names but I have never met a Bo before.'

'It's Swedish,' he replied. 'My folks are from Stockholm but I was brought up in California.'

'Ah, California,' replied Aiko, impressed. 'I have heard of California. Sunshine and movie stars and the ocean.'

'That's right,' grinned Bo. 'I miss it.'

'Yes, I miss home too,' replied Aiko wistfully.

'Where are you from?' he asked, meeting her eyes for a moment and making her stomach flip again.

'A tiny fishing village on the Shima Peninsula. It's very beautiful there.'

'Will you go back one day?' he asked.

Aiko hesitated, champagne bottle in one hand, glass in the other. She had never really thought about whether she would go back. Home, as she knew it, no longer existed so what would there be to go back to?

'I don't think so,' she said, swallowing a lump in her throat and forcing a smile. 'Nothing is as it was. Sometimes it's best to leave the past to memories, I think. From now on I am just going to concentrate on enjoying every day as it happens.'

Bo nodded as if she had said something very wise.

'No point dwelling on what's been and gone,' he agreed. 'It's all about the future now, building bridges, creating a better world for our kids so that they never have to go through what we've been through. And if that means never going back, then so be it.'

'So will you never go back?' she asked. 'Or will you go home to California soon?'

Bo grinned. 'You got me, Aiko,' he said. 'I guess I'm kind of a hypocrite. I love Japan. I think it's fascinating and beautiful. But I can't deny that I count the days until my tour of duty is over. I'm planning to change the world from my own little corner of it. There's a lot of world to see out there, but my heart will always be in California.'

Aiko felt her heart lurch when he said that. She liked Bo. But life had taught her that everything was temporary. There was no point in getting attached to anything – or anyone. She flashed one of her winning smiles at the captain and handed him a glass of champagne.

'To California,' she said brightly. 'May you return to your home very soon, Bo.'

The next time Bo came to the bar, a few days later, he looked very pleased with himself. He walked straight up to Aiko and said, 'I told you I'd remember where we met before.'

'I don't believe you,' said Aiko, rather taken aback. 'You must be mistaken.'

'You look very different now,' he continued, trying to catch her eye. 'In your fine kimono and all that make-up. But it was you, wasn't it? On the Nagoya Road? Two of my platoon were being assholes. I had to hit one of them!'

Aiko looked down, embarrassed. So he had remembered her, but now, instead of feeling pleased, she felt ashamed. She didn't want Bo to know that she had been barefoot, homeless and destitute just a few months earlier. She kicked herself for ever having teased him about their previous meeting.

'It was your eyes,' he continued, oblivious to her shame. 'I hadn't forgotten you. I just never imagined I'd see you again – especially not somewhere like this. How could anyone forget meeting you, Aiko? You're the girl with the amber eyes. You were so thin and weak back then, but your eyes burned with life.'

Aiko shrugged, trying to hide her embarrassment.

'So how did you end up here?' he probed.

'I met Mr Oshiro and he gave me a job,' replied Aiko, honestly. There was no point in giving him the long story. Why would he care?

'And how did you end up there? On that road that day? Were you a refugee?' asked Bo.

'My family all died during the war. There was no one left. No reason for me to stay. So I decided to come to Tokyo to find a better life. It took me a long time but I got here,' she explained, as briefly as she could. 'And now, thanks to Mr Oshiro, I have a good life.'

Bo nodded as if he understood. But of course there was no way a boy like Bo, who had been brought up under the Californian sun with automobiles and radios and swimming pools in the garden, could understand Aiko's world.

'I thought all Americans were horrible until you,' she said, honestly, hoping she wasn't being too forward. 'You were the kindest person I had met in a very long time.'

'And I thought you were the most beautiful woman I had ever seen,' said Bo.

It was a corny line but it sounded as if Bo meant it. It was his turn to blush.

He stared at her for a moment, bit his lip and let out a deep sigh.

'And here you are, serving my beer. It must be fate, huh?'

Even the stone upon which you stumble is part of fate, Aiko thought to herself. It was one of Haruki's proverbs again. But she did not share it with Bo. She wasn't sure he would understand. So instead, she passed him a cold beer and told him how handsome he looked in his uniform, just as Kira had taught her to do.

Bo came in frequently after that. He always sat at the bar and talked to Aiko while she worked. Although he was respectful and polite to everyone, he never paid much attention to Kira or the other girls and, after he had gone, they would tease her about the handsome captain who was so clearly smitten with her. But it wasn't Bo's good looks that Aiko most admired, it was his enthusiasm and optimism. Even with the world in complete turmoil, he had nothing but hope for the future. His buoyancy was infectious. They laughed together a lot.

Before long she felt she knew everything there was to know about Captain Bo Anderson. He was from San Francisco but before he joined the military he had been a student in Los Angeles. His father was a university professor and his mother was a housewife. He had two younger sisters, Freya and Kirsten. He was twenty-four years old – older than Aiko had estimated – but not so much older that he intimidated or patronised her. He'd studied science and engineering at UCLA and was an expert in some new thing called computer programming. That's why he kept getting promoted: he was a pioneer in his field and the US military needed him. Bo always said that he would love to tell Aiko exactly what it was that he did in the military but if he told her, he would then have to shoot her, and he couldn't possibly do that to his best buddy in Tokyo, could he?

They shared a love of the sea and Bo was fascinated by Aiko's stories about her mother and the other Ama divers of Ise Shima. He said he had done some deep-sea diving himself and wouldn't it be fun if, one day, when all this was over, they could go diving together? He said it as if it might be possible, but Aiko knew there were limits to optimism and hope. It was a crazy dream, a fantasy, that she and Bo's friendship could last beyond his tour of duty. Soon, he would go home to California, and Aiko would be left here alone. Sometimes she wondered if she could trust him enough to share her secret. Perhaps he could help? But whenever she opened her mouth to mention it, something made Aiko stop. No. Better to stick to Plan A. Mr Oshiro should be the one to help. Soon she would broach it with him, when she was sure.

Bo never bought Aiko presents or left her generous tips like some of the other men. Kira would tut and say that if he wanted to monopolise her time, he should at least pay for the privilege. Aiko told her that friends do not owe each other anything and that she wouldn't feel comfortable accepting gifts from Bo. Kira threw her head back and laughed at that.

'You are so naive sometimes Aiko!' she guffawed. 'You think he wants to be your friend?'

'He is my friend,' Aiko insisted.

But that just made Kira laugh harder. The girls were in the bar, getting ready for the first customers of the day to arrive. Kira was fixing up her make-up in the huge mirror behind the bar. Aiko was playing with a new hairstyle. She had become more vain recently: partly to keep up with the other glamorous hostesses and partly to look nice for Bo.

'Aiko,' Kira said firmly, eyeing her in the mirror. 'Listen to me. Men do not want to be friends with pretty girls. Bo is charming and clever but he is no different to any other man. He is just better at playing the game – the long game. He thinks if you trust him, then you will give him what he wants when he finally makes his move. But he will still go back to the USA and leave you here heartbroken. He probably has a girlfriend back there. Or maybe even a wife! I think, Aiko, you are a little bit in love with the captain. Be careful or you'll get hurt.'

'I am not in love with Bo!' Aiko insisted. 'And I am not as naive as you think, Kira. I am not interested in falling in love with Bo, or any man for that matter. I have more important things to think about than silly romances.'

Kira continued to laugh.

'Yes, yes, whatever you say, Aiko-chan. But listen to one who is older and wiser than you. Next he will try to see you on your own, away from the bar,' she said. 'That's when he'll make his move.'

Aiko swallowed hard. She hadn't told Kira that Bo had already invited her to the beach. As far as Kira was concerned that would prove her point. But, no, not Bo, he wasn't like that ... was he? Had she misjudged the situation? Was she really such a fool?

'Don't let him ruin you,' Kira continued her lecture. 'If an American has touched you, no nice Japanese man will want to know you. And you're going to need a husband one day soon, no? It's too late for me. I am almost forty years old.'

'You're forty?' asked Aiko, incredulously. She had thought Kira was ten years younger.

'Yes, child, I am old now! All I can hope is that I will be a rich man's consort and live comfortably. But you are still young. You are beautiful. Before long you will find a good husband who will take care of you and buy you nice things.'

'I don't need a man to keep me,' Aiko replied. 'I can look after myself. Besides, like I told you, I'm not interested in love.'

'Marriage has very little to do with love. Believe me,' retorted Kira, nodding across the bar to where Mr Oshiro sat going through the books. 'Marriage is little more than a business arrangement. Do you think Mrs Oshiro and Nana are in love after all these years?'

'Mr Oshiro loves Nana very much,' Aiko said, suddenly feeling angry at Kira's insinuation. 'I live in their home. They are very happy.'

'Then why does he come to my room every night after the bar closes?' asked Kira, arching her thin eyebrows. 'It is like I told you, Aiko. Men are not interested in being friends. And even the good ones, like your captain and my Mr Oshiro, are not saints. This is just the way of the world. The sooner you understand that, the better.'

Aiko swallowed hard. She had no reason to doubt Kira's word but what she had said made her feel sick to the stomach; the way she had called him 'her' Mr Oshiro; the knowledge that he visited Kira after hours; the realisation that people were not what they seemed. It felt as if suddenly the world had got darker. How would she look Nana in the eye now? How could she trust Mr Oshiro with her secret? And how could she know that Bo's friendship was true? This new life she'd carved out for herself, this haven, where things made sense, and people were kind ... it was a mirage.

Aiko looked at her friend in the mirror. Even Kira's beautiful face looked different now. Older. Harsher. Suddenly Aiko noticed the dark shadows underneath her eyes, and the pinched lines above her top lip. She saw the sadness and the pain behind the painted smile.

'Everything is grubby,' Aiko snapped. 'I hate this place!'

It had been a long time since the tiger inside her had roared so loud. But Kira's life's work had been to deal with people and she was as good at soothing tigers as she was at soothing soldiers and businessmen.

'Shh,' she said softly to Aiko, taking the comb from her shaking hands and brushing her hair. 'Don't upset yourself, baby. And don't let Mr Oshiro hear you say things like that. He has been good to you, remember. He is no angel, but he looks after his own. Do not ever get on the wrong side of him. But you are right, of course. This place is as sordid as the brothels in Funabashi. At least the International Palace does not pretend to be what it is not. The Peace Palace? It is a front. A uniform or a business suit does not make a man trustworthy or good. This is a place where freedom is traded for dollars, or yen. You must use it to your advantage, Aiko, and then one day, before it steals your soul, you must escape and find something better. Promise me you will do that?'

Aiko nodded obediently at the older woman. She thought she understood what Kira had told her but she couldn't be entirely sure. All she knew was that her heart felt heavier than it had done in a long, long time. Once more, she realised, she was on her own. But at least she had her insurance policy. And now, thanks to Kira, she understood how to use it. From now on Aiko would look after Number One. There would be no more silly daydreams about Captain Bo Anderson.

Part Three

Surfacing

A woman is like tea – you can't tell how strong she is until you put her in hot water.

Eleanor Roosevelt

Chapter Thirty-One

Hampstead, London, 2012

'What the ...?' Sophia stared around in disbelief. 'Hugo, what is this? It looks like a bloody incident room in a low-budget cop show.'

Hugo waved brightly from behind one of his laptops. 'Got your texts. Sorry your folks were so awful. But let's get on with what's important, shall we? Welcome to the centre of operations. D'you like my specs? They were your grandfather's, I expect. I found them in the desk drawer, thought they made me look rather intelligent.'

Hugo had spread himself all over her grandfather's office. The room now had two computers, two mobile phones, a wireless printer, several folders of printed A4 paper, photographs Blu-tacked to the walls, a whiteboard, a desk covered with half-drunk coffee mugs and Labrinth playing loudly from an iPod docking system in the corner. Sophia flapped her hands in a slight panic.

One of the phones started ringing.

'Sorry, got to get this,' he said.

'Good afternoon, Beaumont Productions, Hugo speaking, how may I help you?' he sing-songed brightly. 'Ah, hello, Cleo, lovely to speak to you at last. Yes ... yes ... that's right. Really? Wow! That's amazing ... And that's a definite, is it? This Sunday? Mmm-hmm ... Yup ... Yup ... Fab. Thanks so much, Cleo. Speak soon.'

'Hugo, are you going to tell me what's going on?' demanded Sophia.

Hugo stood up, fluorescent marker in hand and started scribbling on the whiteboard.

'That was *You* magazine, the *Mail on Sunday*: they're running a piece this weekend. *Style* mag are too – so that's the *Sunday Times* covered. I have *Grazia* onboard, *Heat* magazine, *OK*, *Hello!* and, oh yeah, I almost forgot, the *Guardian Weekend* on Saturday,' he said, in a super-efficient tone that Sophia had never heard before. 'And I am waiting for a call back from *This Morning*. You'll have to get up early but it'll be worth it. You would not believe the response I've had to the press release. It's been crazy here today. Crazy!'

'Hugo,' said Sophia in exasperation. 'What the hell are you banging on about? What press releases?'

Hugo grinned at her.

'Project Get Tilly's Pearls Back,' he announced. 'It's well under way. Everyone's going wild for the story – dying Hollywood actress desperately tries to find the family jewels with the help of her stunning but heartbroken granddaughter. I've started a Facebook and Twitter campaign too. Soph, by this time next week, I bet we'll have them in our hands.'

He banged the desk with his fist and slopped coffee all over the paperwork. Sophia stood there as Hugo's words seeped into her brain. Hugo, who was allergic to hard graft, had single-handedly managed to start a national press campaign to get the necklace back. Sophia didn't know whether to laugh or cry.

'You did all this ...' Sophia looked in awe around the room, taking in the photographs of her granny wearing the necklace, the timeline, the dates and the locations. 'You did this for me?'

Hugo grinned and nodded. 'It came to me in the middle of the night. I woke Damon up and asked him his opinion and he totally agreed. He's coming round later, by the way, I hope that's OK ... Anyway, I digress, your gran's a national treasure, your granddad was a megastar, you're a bit of an "It" girl ...'

'I was a bit of an "It" girl briefly in the noughties,' she reminded him. 'I'm no one now.'

'You'd be surprised how much weight the Beaumont name still carries,' Hugo argued. 'Thank God you decided to put Beaumont back in your title when you were a pretentious sixteen-year-old. You and your gran are going to get some hefty column inches over the next few days.'

'You're amazing,' said Sophia. 'I thought you couldn't do anything to surprise me any more but this is mind-blowing.'

She had never seen Hugo look so pleased in her life.

When they got to the hospital later that afternoon, Tilly was in remarkably good spirits. But as Sophia began to fill her grandmother in on the events of the night before, and her parents' reaction to the search for the necklace, what little colour she had began to drain.

'Something is not right,' said Granny firmly, prodding the mattress with her bony finger to emphasise her point. 'I am convinced that your mother and your father are both well aware of whatever happened to that necklace. Did your mum seem strange to you, darling? I worry about her. It's as if she's disappearing before our very eyes.'

'Mum had more personality last night than I've ever seen before,' she told her grandmother. 'It was scary, granted, but she didn't half come alive when she screamed at me and grabbed me!'

'No! Oh, Sophia, no,' said Tilly, looking shocked. 'That can't be right. You must be exaggerating. Alice doesn't have a violent bone in her body. You must tell me the truth.'

Sophia's heart sank. Of course, her grandmother's loyalty would always be to her own daughter. How foolish of her to think she could be brutally honest about her mother. Now Granny thought she was lying.

'It's true,' she said, quietly. 'But I don't expect you to believe me.'

Her grandmother stared at Sophia for an uncomfortably long time. And then finally she said, 'I believe you, Sophia. But things must be going very badly for Alice for her to behave in such a way. She was never a violent girl ...'

'Mum's forty-nine,' Sophia reminded her grandmother a little petulantly. 'She's far from being a girl any more. And people change.'

'Or people *are* changed,' said her granny, thoughtfully. 'By circumstance and fate. The things we experience and the people we meet can alter us for ever, Sophia.'

Sophia thought about Nathan briefly and about how she'd evolved into a virtual domestic goddess during their brief engagement. She wondered if she would still be a domestic goddess now if her father hadn't scared him off. But 'if' was a wasted word. 'If' didn't exist. She shook Nathan from her mind and focused on her grandmother. The old woman looked grey with sickness and worry. It was no way for her to live out her dying days. Sophia shouldn't have mentioned her mother's outburst. From now on she would be more careful of what she did and didn't tell Granny.

'Don't give up on your mother, Sophia,' said Tilly. It sounded more like an order than a piece of advice. 'Talk to her. You can get through to her. If anyone can, it's you. Otherwise, all this ... it's a waste of time. I'll have failed.'

'What do you mean, Granny?' asked Sophia, confused. 'Failed?'

Her grandmother stared out of the window for a moment.

'Ignore me,' she said eventually. 'It's the medication. I'm not making sense.'

'Well, let's forget about Mum and Dad for now,' Sophia forced herself to say brightly. 'Whatever they do or don't know about the pearls, I'm pretty sure they don't have them. Mum loves you. She might have disowned me but she does care about you. Why would she keep them from you? And anyway, it was the last thing she said last night. She doesn't know where that necklace is. And for all her lies, she was telling the truth then. I know she was.

'So, Hugo has come up with an amazing plan,' she enthused. 'He's started a campaign to help us search. He's got loads of newspapers and magazines covering the story and he even thinks he might be able to get me on morning TV. Wouldn't that be brilliant? The more people who hear we're looking for the necklace, the more likely someone is to come forward with information.'

'Oh, Jesus Christ!' squealed Hugo suddenly, tugging at Sophia's arm.

Sophia turned to see what Hugo was staring at. There, through the internal glass window to the corridor, were Philip and Alice.

They were the last people she wanted to see today.

'Good afternoon, Matilda,' said Philip to Granny, as he walked into the room.

He turned towards his daughter.

'And what a surprise to see you here, Sophia,' he said, with a loud sniff. 'You've got your feet quite comfortably under the table here I see.'

'Hello, Dad,' she said, feeling the joy being sucked from the room as he entered. 'Hello, Mum. Feeling a bit calmer, are you? Or shall we alert security just in case?'

Granny flashed Sophia a warning look. *Leave her alone, be gentle with my poor little Alice*, Tilly was saying. Alice stood silently, without flinching, as if she hadn't even heard her daughter's words. Where was the screaming banshee who'd attacked Sophia the night before?

'What is this?' asked Philip, glaring at Hugo now. 'A meeting of Gold-Diggers Anonymous?'

'If you can't say anything nice, Philip ...' warned Tilly. 'What are you two doing here, anyway? You always come on Tuesdays and Fridays at two, I can set my watch by your visits.'

'We're worried about you, Mother,' he said.

'May I remind you, Philip, that I am not *your* mother,' sniffed Granny. 'So would you kindly not interfere in my life. Or what's left of it, at least. I invited Sophia here. Hugo too. Plus they are working day and night to retrieve the priceless necklace that Alice mysteriously "misplaced".'

'None of us have any idea how much that necklace was actually worth,' said Philip, waving his hand. 'And how do any of us know when exactly it went missing? It's all such a long time ago now. What does it matter?'

'That necklace was a gift from my father. Of course it matters!' Tilly reminded him sternly. 'And Alice knew – *knows* – exactly what it meant to me. Don't you, Alice?'

Sophia watched her mother closely. Something was definitely wrong. She couldn't look anyone in the eye except for her husband, who she glanced at every now and then for, what was that? Reassurance? Permission? It was as if he'd written the script for today and she was nervous about remembering her lines. Alice didn't react when Granny asked her about the necklace.

'Well, we'll get to the bottom of it soon enough,' said Tilly. 'Sophia and Hugo have started a press campaign to try to find it.'

'Oh, for God's sake,' said Philip in exasperation. 'The whole business is a ridiculous wild goose chase and nothing more than an excuse for Sophia to get her face back in the papers. I thought we'd got past those days, when there wasn't a weekend that

251

went by without our daughter embarrassing us in a Sunday rag, but no, here we are again, having to face Sophia spreadeagled across the centre pages! You're being duped, Matilda. You can't trust Sophia or her silly little friend. They are extortionists. Pure and simple.'

'Sophia has been a rock to me these last few weeks, Philip. Hugo too,' said Granny firmly. 'They're even house-sitting for me. I trust Sophia and Hugo completely.'

'You've let them in your home, Matilda?' Philip rolled his eyes heavenwards. 'God give me strength!' he muttered in disgust, turning towards his daughter. 'I expect you think you'll be inheriting the house now, too, young lady?' Philip turned on his daughter.

'No,' replied Sophia honestly. 'We're just staying there for a few weeks. We're looking after the place well. We are, Granny, honestly.'

Sophia had given up trying to impress her father but she did care desperately what her grandmother thought of her. She hoped Granny wouldn't be too appalled if she could see what Hugo had done to Grandpa's study.

'I'm sure you are, dear,' said her grandmother. 'You know I trust you. But this is a pointless conversation anyway. Because none of you will be inheriting my house.'

'What?' Alice lifted her head and spoke for the first time. 'Surely I'll get the house, won't I, Mummy?'

'And they've got the nerve to call us gold-diggers,' muttered Hugo.

'No, darling,' replied Granny cheerfully. 'My half-brother Tom will get the house.'

The room fell uncomfortably silent. Alice and Philip looked at each other in confusion. Hugo stared at Sophia. Granny took a sip of her water as if she'd said nothing more controversial than, 'It's raining outside, isn't it?' and Sophia stared from one relative to the other, wondering how she could have been born into such a dysfunctional family. Finally Philip broke the silence.

'With all due respect, you have clearly lost your marbles, Matilda,' he said, his voice trembling with anger.

'No,' argued Tilly. 'I've thought about this long and hard over the years and if you ask my solicitor, you will discover that

I actually put this clause in my will a long time ago. So don't get your hopes up about contesting it, Philip.'

'But you don't even know for sure that Tom is your brother,' said Alice, suddenly finding her voice. 'There's never been any proof. It's all just rumour and the word of some nanny or other that she had a baby by Grandpapa.'

Sophia watched her mother with interest, suddenly animated, suddenly caring about something.

'Of course he's my brother,' scoffed Tilly. 'Papa as good as told me so before he died, Nanny would *never* have lied about such a thing and, besides, Tom is the absolute spit of Papa.'

'There has never been a DNA test,' Philip pointed out.

Granny raised a thin eyebrow.

'Really, Philip?' she said, quietly but sternly. 'Are you sure you even want to go there with me?'

There were obviously family squabbles that had started long before Sophia came on the scene. It was a relief to know that she hadn't started all the Beaumont battles.

'I don't need a DNA test to prove Tom is my brother. All I have to do is look at him. Never, in all these years, has he asked for anything from me. I'd have helped him sooner, but he's far too proud to accept anything more than my friendship. But once I'm dead, he can't argue! He's worked hard all his life, raised a lovely family on a teacher's salary. He is a good man. Papa would have been so proud of him. I bought the house in Hampstead with the money from Papa's estate. Poor Tom never inherited a penny from Beaumont House but he is as much a Beaumont as I am. It's the right thing to do, to finally repay him some of what he is owed.'

'If Grandpapa had so wanted Tom to inherit part of the estate, he would have left him some money when he died, surely?' said Alice.

'He couldn't,' replied Granny with certainty. 'My mother was a bitter woman and she would have caused a terrible fuss. She'd have contested the will – she tried to contest the fact that I inherited the house, so an illegitimate child ... It would have meant an awful scandal for Nanny and her husband and Papa would never have wanted to put them through that. No, this is the right thing to do. After all these years, I am going to compensate Tom for what was rightfully his.'

'And does he know this?' asked Philip, clearly appalled. 'That he's about to inherit a five-million-pound property?'

'No, he has absolutely no idea. And not one of you is going to tell him, either. He's a proud man and he'll try to persuade me not to,' said Granny.

Sophia could see that her father was having some sort of internal dialogue. The veins in his forehead pulsed angrily. Eventually he snapped. It was the first time Sophia had ever heard her father lose control and raise his voice.

'Oh, for God's sake, this is ridiculous,' he shouted. 'You're mad, Matilda. You all are! You, Sophia. And you, you're the craziest of them all!'

He pointed at Alice accusingly and Sophia swore she could see a little flicker of a smile playing on the corner of her mum's lips. What the hell was going on here?

'Philip!' said Alice, rising up suddenly until she looked two inches taller than she had done five minutes ago. 'You can say what you like to me, but don't you dare talk to Mummy like that. For God's sake, she's dying!'

Sophia watched in disbelief as the ties that bound her entire family together unravelled before her eyes.

'You're worse than she is!' Philip screamed at his wife. 'Look at your behaviour last night. I had to drag you off your own daughter! We're all so quick to judge Sophia, aren't we? But look at the stock she comes from. Is it any wonder she turned out like this? You're all lunatics. You should never have been allowed to breed.'

'Oh, do shut up, Philip,' said Granny. 'You're giving me a headache. The truth is you're a frightful bore.'

'The truth? The truth?!' cried Sophia's dad in a choked voice. 'You have the nerve to talk to me about the truth? What does this family know about the truth? It's all affairs, illegitimate children, disfigured fathers and alcoholic mothers. It's the stuff of nightmares. I sacrificed everything for this family and what thanks do I get? I don't even get anything in your will, you old witch! I took on Alice, and this is how you repay me?'

'And what about what Alice sacrificed?' asked Granny. 'She gave up her freedom at the age of nineteen. She sold her soul to you. And you took it gladly. She wouldn't have looked twice at you if—'

'Mummy!' screamed Alice suddenly. 'No! Stop!'

'Would someone please tell me what the hell is going on?' asked Sophia, utterly confused.

'Ask your mother,' shouted her dad and then he stormed out.

'Mum?' asked Sophia, desperately.

Her mother looked like a rabbit caught in the headlights. She shrank back down to her normal size before Sophia's eyes. She turned to Tilly and almost pleaded, 'Mummy? Why did you bring all this up now?'

'If I can't be honest at the end of my life, when can I be honest, Alice?' asked Granny, softly. 'You know what you need to do, darling. The truth is the real legacy – more than pearls, or houses, or any inheritance.'

'Don't talk like that, Mummy, please. I can't bear it,' replied Alice, bursting into tears. 'God, I can't do this. Not now. I need some air.'

Sophia watched her broken mother with a mix of concern and anger. Why couldn't she stand up for herself?

'Alice. We're leaving!' her father's voice boomed from the corridor.

'Stay,' said Sophia, suddenly, surprising herself more than anyone else in the room. 'Stay here with us, Mum. Don't go after him. Think about what he just said. Why do you put up with it? Stay, Mum,' she pleaded more loudly. 'Stay with me.'

Her mother hesitated for a moment at the door; she seemed to be torn in two. She took a half step back into the hospital room and for a moment Sophia thought she'd won. But then Alice stopped again, glanced out into the corridor where Philip was waiting and Sophia watched as the life seeped back out of her.

'I'm so sorry, Sophia,' she said finally and then she stepped out of the room after her husband.

Sophia's heart sank. Of course, her mum had chosen her husband over her daughter. Just like she'd always done.

'Wow,' said Hugo, as if he didn't really know what else to say. 'What was that?'

'Yes, Granny,' said Sophia. 'What was that? Could you please explain what on earth is going on?'

Tilly looked pained.

'For once, my darling,' she said, 'I'm afraid I have to agree with your father. You have to ask your mother.'

'But she won't talk,' said Sophia, in despair. 'She never talks. She won't even stay here with me now.'

'Just give her time, Sophia,' said Granny. 'She knows how important this is. She's been running away from something for a very long time. We all have. But she knows. She knows as well as I do that she can't keep running ... Be patient, my darling. Now I have to rest. This has all been terribly tiring for me.'

'OK, Granny,' said Sophia, knowing that she had to put her grandmother's health before her own questions. 'But I'll be in to see you tomorrow.'

'Please do,' said Granny. 'Oh, and Sophia?'

Sophia turned back from the door.

'You do know that your mother loves you, don't you?'

Sophia frowned and shook her head. 'How would I know that? She never shows it. She just chose Dad over me – again.'

'You have always been her top priority underneath it all,' said Granny weakly. 'You'll see, my darling. I promise you, in time, you'll see.'

Chapter Thirty-Two

Tokyo, Japan, 2012

Aiko sat in the VIP departures lounge of Narita International Airport, and tried to concentrate on the financial pages of the *New York Times* but her mind would not do as it was told. She had never felt sorry for herself. No, Aiko had battled and won. Or so she had always thought. Perhaps she had merely pushed the ghosts of the past aside. And now they had awoken.

She checked her emails, replied to a few, sent an email to her PA back in New York to deal with the others. She tweeted about the conference, replied to the Facebook messages that had been left for her by grateful businessmen and women who had attended her lectures. She replied to Ken's text, fretting about her health. *Yes, Kenny. I am fine*, she reassured him, even though it seemed far from the truth.

The departures board told her that the flight to JFK had been delayed. Aiko was impatient to board, to be back in New York where perhaps the ghosts of Japan could not follow. She folded her coat neatly into a makeshift pillow and propped it against the back of her chair. She would not normally try to sleep in public: it wasn't dignified. But she desperately wanted the next hour to pass quickly. And so she laid her head against her cashmere coat, closed her eyes and stroked the gold and jade ring on her left hand for comfort, as she always did when she wanted to find peace of mind. For the second time in her life, she needed to escape from Tokyo.

Aiko continued to chat with Bo whenever he came to the bar. She flirted with him as usual and she still laughed at all his jokes, but she kept herself in check and when he asked her personal questions, she deflected them so that the conversation became one-sided. Mostly, she succeeded in keeping a careful distance between her heart and her mouth but there was one thing she needed to know.

'Do you have a girlfriend back home in California?' she asked him one evening, being careful not to sound too concerned one way or another.

Bo sighed heavily and stared at the bar.

'I won't lie to you, Aiko,' he said. 'There is a girl back home. We've been dating since my freshman year at UCLA and the thing is ...'

Aiko's heart froze. As the rest of his words washed over her, she took her feelings for the captain and shut them away tightly in a box in the furthest corner of her soul. So Kira was right.

' ... I guess she expects we'll get engaged when I get home. But I don't feel the same now. I was a boy when I left. I didn't know what I wanted back then. Maybe I'm still not sure. But I know I need more than she gives me. She's a lovely girl, but she's not the girl for me. Aiko, you know I have feelings for you. Meeting you has confused me. I know she doesn't make me laugh the way you do.'

'But I am not your girlfriend,' Aiko reminded him with a smile frozen on her lips. 'And I am paid to make you laugh. Do not compare her to me. She cannot compete. She is real and I am just a fantasy. Everything here in this bar is a fantasy, Bo. Do not confuse it with the real world.'

Bo looked up, clearly shocked at what Aiko had said. They'd always been so frank and open with each other and he was obviously confused and hurt by her cold words but Aiko could not let herself care. She turned her back on him and went over to entertain a group of Japanese businessmen at the other end of the bar. When she looked back over to where he had been, she noticed that his beer had not been drunk and that Bo had gone. He didn't come back to the bar for several weeks.

In Bo's absence, Aiko concentrated on watching Mr Oshiro's business closely. She kept one eye on the drinks she was mixing and another on working out exactly what was going on in the Peace Palace. She had long been aware that the huge open-air black markets and the cheap brothels that had sprung up all over Tokyo's slums were being run from the comfort and opulence of places like this. Some of the American officers were involved in the black market too but she realised, from their self-righteous demeanour and their air of superiority, that they did not believe that what they were doing was illegal or immoral in any way. These were not men who would break laws in their own country, and she could tell that they justified their behaviour by telling themselves that Japan was another world, with different rules.

Mr Oshiro oversaw the entire venture with open arms, a warm smile and an infectious *joie de vivre* (Bo had taught her that phrase. She used it all the time. It was the only French she knew). Aiko wasn't sure quite where he fitted in. Was he just a facilitator? Or was he the Big Boss? But it was not Aiko's business to know exactly who Mr Oshiro was. She worked in his bar and she lived in his home. He was kind to her and she knew she could trust him up to a point. That was all she needed to know. Any more knowledge would be dangerous.

Finally, Aiko felt the time was right to make her move. She waited until the bar was quiet and Kira was busy entertaining the major general and his cronies. She knocked on Mr Oshiro's office door with her heart in her mouth. This had been her plan for so many years. It had been her great-grandmother's order and, most importantly, her mother's dying wish. There had been a reason Mr Oshiro had picked her from that doorway and placed her here. It had been fate. Luck in the leftovers, as Haruki would have said.

'Aiko,' said Mr Oshiro, brightly, as she entered. 'How can I help you? Is there a problem?'

Aiko shook her head.

'No, there is no problem. I just need to ask for your help in a certain matter.'

'Ah,' said Mr Oshiro, putting down the pen he was holding. 'Sit, sit, Aiko. I think I know what it is. It's Captain Anderson, isn't it?'

Aiko started to shake her head but Mr Oshiro was on a roll.

'I have noticed we haven't seen him in some time. I know he had grown a little too fond of you, Aiko, and I am aware that he asked you to meet him outside the bar,' continued Mr Oshiro.

How? wondered Aiko. She had told nobody about that, not even Kira.

'I told him it was against the rules,' Aiko said, knowing she needed Mr Oshiro on her side now more than ever. 'I have never met him outside this bar.'

'Oh, I know that, my dear Aiko. You are a good girl. You are like a daughter to Nana and me. I know you would never let me down. But he is a nice man and I can understand that the situation has been upsetting for you. They come here, these Americans, and they think they fall in love with beautiful girls like you, but then they go home and forget all about Tokyo. It is difficult the first time it happens.'

'Has he gone home?' asked Aiko, suddenly forgetting why she was there, in Mr Oshiro's office. The thought that Bo had left without saying goodbye made her want to cry.

'Not yet,' replied Mr Oshiro. 'But he leaves soon, I hear.'

Aiko nodded and tried to push the information to the back of her mind. Right now she had other business to deal with.

'I did not want to talk about Captain Anderson,' she said, bravely. 'I have something of value. A family collection I have inherited. It is all I have in the world and I wish to sell it. I thought, perhaps, you would be able to help me.'

With shaking hands, she placed the red velvet pouch on Mr Oshiro's desk and bowed at him respectfully.

'What is this?' asked Mr Oshiro, obviously intrigued. 'You have secrets, Aiko? You have been holding something back?'

Aiko nodded. 'I had to wait until I was sure you knew the right people to help me, but I think you do.'

Mr Oshiro narrowed his eyes a little and glanced at Aiko warily before opening the pouch. He took the pearls out slowly at first, one by one. With each perfect pearl his eyes widened a little more. The pool of pearls began to roll around on his wooden desk top and he had to shepherd them together with his hands to stop them from escaping and rolling off on to the floor.

'How many are here?' he asked, clearly awestruck.

'Sixty-seven,' replied Aiko.

When the largest, most perfect pearl finally emerged, Mr Oshiro let out an audible gasp. He picked up Aiko's prize pearl and slowly, carefully, he cupped it in the palm of his hand. He stared at it for a long, long time, held it up to the light, twisted and twirled it under the gleam of his lamp, and then, finally, he looked up at Aiko once more.

'This is extraordinary,' he said. 'Do you know what you have here?'

Aiko nodded. She was all too aware of its rarity and value.

'It is the perfect pearl. My mother, as you know, was an Ama,' she reminded him. 'She collected many of these pearls. She died collecting this one. My great-grandmother kept it safe for me along with all the others until I was old enough to understand its worth. It is my legacy, Mr Oshiro. My mother's dying wish was that these pearls, particularly this pearl, would reward me one day. Until now I haven't known who could help me with such an important matter, but I think you can help me.'

Mr Oshiro nodded, still staring at the pearl. Aiko knew she had to keep her wits about her. Her boss was fond of her but he was much more attached to money than he was to people. Whatever he offered her, she knew the pearl was worth at least double.

'This is a very valuable pearl, Aiko,' he stated. 'I might be able to get you quite a lot of money for it but ...' He glanced up at her. 'You are a very valuable commodity to me too. The customers are always telling me that you are their favourite hostess. If I get you this money, you will leave the Peace Palace. And what about Nana? My wife would be heartbroken if you decided to move out of our home. She needs you, Aiko – and not just to sweep the floors. Perhaps it is not in my best interests to help you this time.' In silence, he placed all sixty-seven pearls carefully back in the pouch and offered it back to Aiko.

But Aiko stood firm and refused to take back the pouch. She hadn't expected this response but she was a smart girl and she had watched the men in the bar do business for long enough to understand that there was always a deal to be struck. It was just a case of negotiating the terms.

'What if I promise to stay?' she suggested. 'For an agreed

period of time? Perhaps you could invest the money for me during that time and we will both benefit from me staying longer?'

Mr Oshiro's eyes lit up. He nodded at Aiko with a look of ... what was that? Fatherly pride?

'You are a clever girl, Aiko,' he grinned. 'That is an excellent suggestion. I will sell these pearls for you. I know exactly the right man. He will jump for joy when he sees what you have. And then I will invest the money with a banker I know and trust for ... What shall we say? Ten years?'

Aiko shook her head. 'Two years,' she replied firmly.

Mr Oshiro laughed as if her suggestion was preposterous. 'Seven,' he said.

Aiko picked up the pearls from his desk. 'I cannot sell my freedom for seven years, Mr Oshiro. I am forever in your debt and I humbly apologise if I have offended you but my mother died collecting one of these pearls. Her dying wish was that they would keep me free, that their value would give me opportunities she did not have. She did not die so that I could be imprisoned by them.'

It was Mr Oshiro's turn to nod thoughtfully.

'OK, Aiko,' he said finally. 'Five years. You stay with me and Nana for five more years and I will sell your pearls for you.'

Aiko held on to the pouch.

'Agreed. And I will come with you when you negotiate the sale,' she informed him.

Mr Oshiro threw his head back and laughed as if she had told the funniest joke he had ever heard. 'Do not be silly, Aiko,' he said. 'You are just a girl. You cannot come to a business meeting of that sort. What? Do you not trust me?'

Aiko shook her head. 'I respect you greatly, but I do not trust any man when it comes to the business of money – or beautiful women.'

She knew she was being brave, but was she being stupid? Mr Oshiro looked shocked at what she had said. And a little angry. But it was too late now. This was her future. Aiko needed to use all the ammunition she had. If she allowed Mr Oshiro to do the negotiating alone she felt sure he would rob her of most of the money. Kira had given her some valuable information and she had no choice but to use it against her boss now.

'What do you mean by that?' he demanded. 'That men cannot be trusted?'

'Nothing,' replied Aiko, in her sweetest voice. 'But Kira and I are very close and you know how we girls like to talk. Of course I am becoming quite worldly now. But Nana ... I'm not sure Nana would understand. She is more naive than I am. And certainly far more innocent than Kira ...'

Mr Oshiro's face burned crimson, and his mouth became very narrow and pinched.

'I think, Aiko, that I have underestimated you. If you were a man, I might be very impressed with you at this moment but you are a girl, and despite what Nana likes to pretend, you are not my daughter. You are being most disrespectful talking to me in this way. I do not know whether I am angry or impressed by your bravery,' he said.

'I do not mean to disrespect you, Mr Oshiro,' said Aiko. 'But it is arranged now. I will come with you to sell the pearls, then you will invest my money for five years and after that I am free to do what I like with my fortune.'

'I will need commission for my time,' Mr Oshiro reminded her sternly.

'Of course,' she said. 'Five per cent seems fair.'

'Twenty,' he replied.

'Ten,' said Aiko, firmly. 'Or I take my pearls, I walk out of your bar and you and Nana never see me again.'

Mr Oshiro shook his head but this time he laughed. 'You are a force of nature, Aiko,' he told her. 'I knew you were special when I saw you in Ozu Market, even under all that grime! But I had no idea quite how unique you are. You are as rare as that pearl you are holding. No wonder Captain Anderson is so heartbroken. To meet a girl like you and then to lose her. It must tear him apart.'

'Bo does not love me,' replied Aiko, feeling the balance of power slide back towards Mr Oshiro. She had negotiated a good deal and, worse, she had mentioned his relationship with Kira but now he was reminding her that he was the boss.

'Yes he does,' replied Mr Oshiro cheerfully. 'He has told me many, many times that he thinks about you every moment and that he cannot face the idea of going back to the USA without you. But, of course, that is impossible now. You are tied to me for the next five years. By then he will have forgotten all about his silly little infatuation with the Japanese girl. Life is very strange sometimes. It is all down to fate in the end.'

He smiled at her brightly but he knew what he had just done. He had told her exactly what she wanted to hear – that Bo was in love with her – but he had immediately snatched the dream right back from her grasp. Aiko had sold her soul to the devil: for the next five years, at least.

'I shall arrange a meeting with an associate of mine who is in the gem trade. His name is Mr Sato. He will give us a good price for your mother's pearls,' said Mr Oshiro. 'Now, get back to the bar, Aiko. I do not pay you to chat to me in my office. I pay you to keep the gentlemen happy.'

The next day, Aiko sat silently in the corner of Mr Oshiro's office as he and Mr Sato agreed on a price for her mother's perfect pearl and then for the sixty-six smaller gems. Aiko had traded her heart for her fortune but, as she watched the men at work, she knew she had made the right decision. Mr Oshiro was an expert negotiator and the pearls were worth more than Aiko had imagined even in her wildest dreams. Mr Sato agreed to pay $50,000 for the collection. It was over four million yen: enough to buy a palace fit for an empress. It was the summer of 1947. In 1952 Aiko would become a very wealthy woman indeed. But until then, she would continue to be Mr Oshiro's slave.

Before Mr Sato left, Aiko asked if she could hold the large pearl one more time. He allowed her to do so. She held it in the palm of her hand and felt her mother's love, knowing that Manami's living flesh had touched it too. She kissed the smooth, luminous pearl and tried not to think whose hand would touch it next. Where would it end up? Around the neck of some wealthy woman, no doubt. But the pearl would never be so valuable to anyone as it had been to her. As she handed the pearl back to Mr Sato it felt as though she was saying goodbye to her mother for the last time.

It was a time of many goodbyes for Aiko. Bo finally came back to the Peace Palace a few days later. But he had only come to bid her farewell. He had just received his orders. In two hours' time he would leave Tokyo for good. He took Aiko outside to the little courtyard behind the bar. It was a bright, June morning. The pink roses Kira had planted were in full bloom, the air smelt sweet, the birds sang in the trees and from where they sat in the tiny garden, under the shade of a bowing willow, it was as though the firebombing of Tokyo had never happened at all. Bo had bought Aiko an exquisite gold and jade ring.

'I don't think you meant what you said before,' he told her, his blue eyes imploring her to tell the truth. 'I know you feel the same as I do, Aiko. I see it in your eyes. I love you and you love me. It's not a fantasy. It's real. We can make it happen, my darling. What have I always told you? Anything is possible! The future is ours. Come on, Aiko. Say yes! I want you to come back to America with me. It will take a few months to organise but it can be done, I've asked the authorities, they'll organise a visa for you and then, when you get to California, we can get married. Please, Aiko. Say yes.'

Aiko felt the weight of the perfect blue sky fall on her young shoulders. Why was he saying this now? If she'd waited to hear these words, she could have kept the pearls, she could have taken them with her to America and sold them when she got there. She could have got Bo – honest, trustworthy, good Bo – to help her, rather than Mr Oshiro. If she'd had the courage to wait, she could have had both: the man she loved and her mother's legacy.

But Aiko had not been patient. She had already made her deal with the devil. She could never tell Bo what she had done. How would a boy who had grown up surrounded by wealth understand that she had sold her freedom for fifty thousand dollars? Those who take money for granted value it the least. He would think her no better than the prostitutes and thieves in the slums. And Mr Oshiro was right, she could never ask Bo to wait five long years for her. She knew too well that the whole world could change in five years. With tears falling down her cheeks, and her heart shattering, she pushed the ring back across the table towards Bo.

'I do love you,' she told him, for she had had enough of lies. 'But I can never come to America and I can never be your wife. You deserve someone better than me, Bo. I am broken and damaged. I am as shattered as this sordid city. You must forget me. Go back to your nice, sweet American girl. She will make you happier than I ever could.'

'No,' he said, defiantly, desperately. 'I won't do that, Aiko. I need you. I love you. I'm not going to lose you. You are none of those things – you're the purest, most honest person I've ever met.'

He put his hand on the back of her head and pulled her face towards his. She could feel his hot, sweet breath on her face and, as his soft lips finally touched hers, she thought she would faint with desire. A million tiny fireworks erupted in her heart. For a moment she allowed herself to fall into his perfect embrace, to feel his strong arms wrapped around her and his warm body pressed against her own. It was utter bliss. His love enveloped her and for a split second she felt safe and strong again. It took all her strength to push him away.

'I cannot take your ring, Bo,' she sobbed. 'And we cannot see each other again. I am so sorry.'

Aiko stood up. She couldn't look at him. It hurt too much to see the pain and confusion on his handsome face. He was the last person on earth she wanted to damage, but she had no choice. He tried to reach out to her but she opened the gate that led to the alley behind the bar, and she bolted, away from Bo, and back towards the Peace Palace, her prison for the next five years. He tried to follow her.

'Aiko! Aiko! Wait! We can do it. It will be OK. Please, Aiko. Trust me. I love you …!' she heard him call behind her.

Her heart burned in her chest and for a moment she almost stopped and turned towards his voice. But she could not go with Bo. Not now. She had sealed her fate. Bo did not know the backstreets and alleyways of Tokyo like Aiko did. Eventually, when she looked back over her shoulder, he had gone. She kept running all the way to the harbour, where she sat sobbing on a bench that looked out over Tokyo Bay. Usually the sea brought her comfort. It reminded her of home. But today it only reminded her that before long Bo would be at the other side of that ocean and out of reach for ever. Her great-granny had always tried to teach her patience. She used to say that Aiko was just like her mother in that way – they both wanted it all, and they wanted it yesterday! But what was the point in waiting for something that would never come?

'True patience consists in bearing what is unbearable,' she muttered to herself.

It was what Haruki used to say to her father after her mother's death and it is what the Emperor had broadcast to the nation after Japan surrendered to the Americans. She whispered the proverb to herself over and over again until she was no longer sure if it was the wisest, or most stupid, thing she'd ever heard.

She stayed there, at the harbour, until the sun began to set over the grey-green sea. She knew she would be in trouble with Mr Oshiro for having disappeared but she did not care.

When she got back to the bar, nobody said a thing about her unexplained absence. Mr Oshiro simply nodded politely in her direction to acknowledge that she had returned. Kira smiled at her kindly from behind the bar. How was it that everybody always knew her business here?

'He has gone. But he left you this,' whispered Kira, pressing the ring into Aiko's hand. 'You might as well keep it. I told you it was time he bought you a present. It's the least you deserve!'

'Did he say anything?' asked Aiko, trying to keep the despair out of her voice.

'He said to tell you that he won't give up,' replied Kira, rolling her eyes. 'He said he loves you. But they all say that, Aiko. Forget him.'

But Aiko did not forget Captain Bo Anderson. She wore the jade ring every day for the rest of her life and whenever she looked at it she knew she had been truly valued and loved. But for now ... now Aiko went back to pouring drinks and flirting with men in business suits and uniforms. She smiled a lot. Sometime she danced and sang. Everybody said she was the most charming girl they had ever met. But none of them knew the price Aiko had paid to spend her days in the Peace Palace, and nobody cared to notice the frown beneath her painted smile.

Chapter Thirty-Three

Virginia Water, Surrey, 2012

Alice stopped in front of the post box on her way back from
Waitrose. The letter shook in her hand. She lifted the envelope
towards the mouth of the post box and then pulled it back
again. What was she doing? This letter had the power to change
everything. But wasn't change what she wanted? Not only for
herself, but for others too. Especially Sophia. She raised the
letter back towards the gaping hole.

'It's a bit early for Christmas cards, isn't it, Alice?' boomed
a jovial voice.

Alice jumped. It was Margot, her friend and neighbour of
thirty years, standing right behind her. Margot who knew absolutely nothing about the real Alice Brown.

'Yes, yes, it is, I suppose,' replied Alice, trying to keep the
panic from her voice. 'I think I'm getting a bit ahead of myself.'

She shoved the letter back into her handbag, said a polite
goodbye to Margot and hurried home. It was steak for dinner
tonight.

Hampstead, London, 2012

Sophia did her best to push her mother's strange behaviour to
the back of her mind and concentrate on finding the necklace.
Although she was tempted, she didn't try to contact her mum,
and neither of her parents made any attempt to get in touch
with her. Her grandmother had told her that she had to ask her
mother for answers but she had also told her to be patient. It
didn't feel like the right time. She needed all her mental strength
to help Granny. And besides, if her mum had something to tell

her, why should Sophia be the one making the move?

So Sophia avoided the hospital on Tuesdays and Fridays, knowing that her mum and dad would be there, and tried to forget about it. For now. She had theories, of course. Hadn't her dad said that her mum was 'unstable' when they got married? It sounded like an old-fashioned euphemism for some sort of mental illness. And wouldn't that explain her mum's distance? And the way she always did what her husband told her to do? Maybe Hugo was right, maybe her dad did keep her mum sedated? She wouldn't be the first in the family to be 'unstable'. Everyone knew that after Wilfred's death, Sophia's great-grandmother had ended up alone in a psychiatric hospital for the last twenty years of her life. Sophia remembered visiting her there, in Bournemouth, with Granny when she was a little girl.

Granny had explained that her mother had once been very beautiful but years of alcohol addiction, chain-smoking and obsessive jealousy (not to mention sunbathing on Sandbanks beach) had left her with the face she deserved, rather than the lovely one she'd been born with. To Sophia, as a child, the old woman was like something out of a horror movie: she couldn't help staring, even though it scared her. Even in her nineties, Great-Grandmama insisted on having her thinning hair dyed jet black, she wore thick foundation and bright scarlet lipstick that bled into the deep wrinkles around her mouth. She had plucked away all her eyebrows and drawn them back on in a squint brown line with a pencil. She always dressed as if she was about to go to some sophisticated soirée or other. In her head, it was forever 1929; she was young and beautiful, childless and free, with the world, and a dozen dashing suitors, at her feet. She always smelled of gin, even at ten in the morning, and she was completely and utterly vile to everyone she met, from the staff at the hospital to the family who visited her less and less frequently.

When she finally died, at the age of ninety-three, Sophia insisted on going to the funeral. After years of throwing parties for her 'friends', it was rather tragic that nobody turned up to say goodbye to Lady Beaumont except for Tilly, Alice and Sophia: and they were there out of duty rather than love. Sophia had long suspected that her great-grandmother was some sort of vampire – how else could she explain smoking forty cigarettes and drinking a litre of gin a day, and living to ninety-three? Even as the coffin was lowered into the family plot, Sophia held her breath, half-expecting Lady Charlotte to burst forth, cocktail glass in her bony hand. But eventually even the scariest ghosts are laid to rest.

There was a photograph of Sophia's great-grandparents on her grandmother's mantelpiece. In the black and white photograph, Lord Frederick looked ridiculously dashing in his hunting clothes but it was his wife, Lady Charlotte, who made Sophia stare. She was tall, and stunningly beautiful in her white jodhpurs and black riding jacket. She was terribly young in the picture: perhaps no older than twenty-one. Her spirit and sexuality were almost tangible. Her eyes shone and her strong, athletic body seemed to quiver with excitement. In her eyes was a burning desire for ... For what? Sophia wondered every time she stared at the photo. The young woman in the picture looked full of life, not full of bitterness. What happened to turn that beautiful, young, vibrant girl into the withered, terrifying old witch that Sophia had seen buried? It seemed to Sophia that a lot of lives had been ruined, dangling from the broken branches of the Beaumont family tree. As she stared at her long-dead great-grandmother, Sophia vowed to herself that she would not join that list. She would not make the same mistakes the other Beaumont women had.

And so she threw herself into something more positive: the hunt for Granny's pearls. For the first time in her life, Sophia felt the thrill of working to achieve a goal. She woke up early every morning and trotted downstairs to the office to check her emails and text messages. She appeared on TV, she gave countless interviews to newspapers and magazines. She spoke to television and film companies about the rights to her grandmother's films and was delighted when Sky started showing reruns of her most famous movies every afternoon. She smoked heavily – always in the garden so as not to make the house smell – but she barely had time to drink anything other than tea, she never went out, other than to visit Granny or to do more interviews, and she hadn't touched any illegal substances in weeks. At night, she fell into bed exhausted and slept like a log. The insomnia that had plagued her for years had simply vanished the minute she moved to Hampstead. She started to look and feel healthier and happier than she had done in years. Better still, she felt confident and capable. Finally, Sophia Beaumont Brown had a purpose. And it felt good. Now, if only she could get her hands on those pearls in time for Christmas, life would be amazing!

Sophia was no stranger to the press: she'd filled many column inches with her wild-child antics over the years. At the time she'd thought it was pretty cool to be photographed falling out of a nightclub drunk, on the arm of some rock star, or soap actor, or footballer, or minor royal. Now, those memories made her cringe. She'd embarrassed her parents (not that she cared about them), made Nathan ashamed (not that he mattered any more either, come to think of it), she'd got her friends into trouble with their families just by being associated with her but worst, she'd made herself into an empty shell of a human being. The old Sophia had been no more alive than a cartoon character. She only existed for other people's entertainment. The party-girl front had hidden a depressed, alcohol-soaked, drug-addicted mess. But now ... Now Sophia felt real. She felt alive. She felt as if she could fly off the highest building or dive into the depths of the ocean and maybe, just maybe, come up with a pearl.

Now, when the press wrote about her, they would allude to her past bad behaviour, but they used it as a benchmark for how far she'd come.

The first major breakthrough with the search for the necklace came in early December with an email from a woman called Chrissy Travis-Jones. Sophia skim-read the email and almost fell off her chair with excitement when she realised that this was it: she finally had something concrete.

'Oh my God, I think this is it!' she shouted across the room to Hugo. 'It's the real deal this time. Listen!'

She read the beginning of the email: 'Dear Sophia, my mother, who lives in the UK, sent me some links to newspaper articles about the hunt for your grandmother's pearls. She recognised the necklace immediately and wanted to help. I am now convinced that I owned your family necklace in the nineteen eighties. At first I thought my mum was mistaken. It certainly looked the same, but your necklace had sixty-seven pearls while mine only had sixty-six. I know this for a fact, because I once spent an entire week restringing them by hand. It was the clasp

I remembered most clearly though. It was exquisite and it was engraved with the initial LMB. I always wondered who LMB was ...

'It goes on,' said Sophia. 'But you can read the rest in a minute. First, look at these pictures.'

Her heart thumped in her chest as she showed Hugo the three pictures of the necklace that Chrissy had attached. The first showed a box, containing lots of pearls and the distinct clasp that had once held them together.

'Don't panic. Look at the next one. See, she's wearing it. It's fixed. She explains in her email that the necklace was broken when she bought it, but she fixed it herself. Then, years later, when she could afford it, she had it restrung professionally. That's when she discovered how valuable the pearls were.'

The third picture was of the necklace fully restored, sitting in a black velvet box.

'So, does she still have it?' asked Hugo, his eyes shining with anticipation.

Sophia shook her head. It was a shame but at least this was a lead. It would have been too much to ask for the first person to still have it in their possession, she supposed. Nothing was ever that easy.

'She sold it in 1991,' she told Hugo. 'But at least we know where the pearls were twenty years ago.'

'Where?' asked Hugo.

'New York,' Sophia told him. 'She bought them in London, but she sold them in New York.'

'So, what do we do now?' asked Hugo, chewing his nails.

'We take the story transatlantic,' announced Sophia determinedly.

'Right, boss!' said Hugo, saluting her. 'New York City, look out. The Brits are invading and we mean business!'

St John's Wood, London, 2012

Granny seemed tired today. She smelled different too. It was a strange, sickly sweet odour that made Sophia feel scared.

Sophia had spoken to the consultant when she first arrived at the hospital and the news wasn't good. The cancer had spread rapidly. There were shadows on her lungs now and she was no longer eating very much at all. Soon they would have to consider feeding her through a drip. Sophia thought of the bruises and swellings on her grandmother's arms, where the needles and catheters went in, pumping her body with the cocktail of drugs that kept her alive. Granny already said she felt like a pincushion. Sophia wasn't sure she would agree to a feeding drip. She couldn't bear to think about the weeks to come. But at least, this evening, she had good news for Granny.

'I have something to read to you,' she told her grandmother, once they'd kissed hello. 'Something that's going to put a smile on your face. We're finally getting somewhere. Listen ...'

Sophia took out the printed email that Chrissy had sent, explaining the full story of how she'd come to own and sell the pearls. She began to read.

Camden Town, London, 1982

I was twenty-one when I found the pearls in a second-hand shop on Chalk Farm Road across the street from Camden Market. They were in a mixed box of broken bits and pieces which I assumed was all costume jewellery. That's what I liked at the time, or what I could afford, at least: pretty, but worthless, jewels. I was a real magpie and I used to spend hours rummaging through charity and junk shops.

I'd just finished uni where I'd studied economics but, much to my parents' horror, I was trying to make it as a singer. I was in a band with three guys and we were gigging our way round the seedier pubs and clubs of Camden and Kentish Town. We lived in a disgusting squat in Camden Square and subsidised our music by working part time in the bars where we played. I thought I was very cool and dressed in leather miniskirts, fishnet stockings and Doc Marten boots. My hair was backcombed and hairsprayed and tied up with bits of old lace and I used to wear so much black eye make-up that my dad started calling me Panda. He still calls me that now, even though my rock chick days are long behind me!

When I got this particular box of jewellery home and looked at my treasure more carefully, I realised that the pearls weren't made of glass or plastic. I was beside myself with excitement because I'd only paid a pound for the whole box and now I assumed they must be cultured pearls which were worth a lot more than that! For years, that's what I believed – that I had a string of particularly pretty cultured pearls. And I loved them!

At the bottom of the box I found a dainty clasp that must have come with the pearls. It was studded with lots more tiny pearls and engraved with the letters LMB. Our band was called The Lonely Magpies so I thought this was fate – LMB, the Lonely Magpies Band. I couldn't quite work out how to put it all back together at first – all those pearls and the large central one and the clasp. But once I'd fixed it the necklace became my lucky charm and I wore it to every single gig.

In the days before we had a record deal, and long before I made it to New York, I spent a lot of time making my own clothes and customising outfits. I spent an entire week lovingly restringing those pearls. I'm ashamed to admit that I strung them onto cheap nylon thread and tied the knots in a very unprofessional manner.

That's why I know for sure that there were sixty-six pearls in my necklace. I guess the sixty-seventh must have been lost when the necklace was broken. Pearls are pretty hardy but not completely indestructible. I was careful not to spray them with hairspray and I kept them in a cloth bag when I wasn't wearing them. I remember wrapping the necklace so carefully when I packed to leave for the States. I expect that pearl is still around somewhere. What a sad thought that somewhere in the world is one lonely, perfect pearl that should be in that necklace.

Thankfully, just as my career floundered I met and fell in love with the man who would become my husband, Leroy. He was a dancer who performed on my last ever music video and he was, and still is, the most gorgeous guy I have ever seen! We spent the last of my money on buying a dilapidated house together in Queens. Leroy made enough money to just about keep us afloat but when the babies came along – twin boys! – life got pretty difficult. We were living in a draughty, run-down house with no money to renovate.

Thank God, Leroy recognised my depression and did something about it. He danced in a couple of really cheesy TV ads and put the money aside for our wedding. He knew having something to look forward to and focus on would cheer me up. Besides, we were madly in love and we wanted to be man and wife. That's when he suggested I have the pearls restored properly, so that I could wear my good luck charm on our wedding day. I hadn't taken them out of their cloth bag in years.

I took the necklace to an upmarket jeweller in mid-town Manhattan. I was apologetic when I handed them over. I was a bit embarrassed of my cheap cultured pearls in the opulent store. I will never forget the look on the guy's face when he opened the cloth bag, tipped the necklace out onto the counter and started to take a closer look.

'These are real,' he told me after a few minutes of pained silence. 'And they have some age to them too. I'm not an expert, I'll have to get my colleague to take a closer look, but I think your necklace is rather more valuable than you thought, madam.'

I'm not sure you'll want to know exactly how much money I got for the sale of your grandmother's necklace but it meant a great deal to Leroy and me. But I realise, had the jeweller known that the necklace had once belonged to Tilly Beaumont, that I would have got five times as much! Not that I mind. I paid one pound for a box of junk and ended up with enough money to change our lives.

I wore the beautifully restored necklace at my wedding and I still look at the photos of that perfect day and remember how those pearls felt around my neck. They brought me good luck from the backstreet dives of Camden Town, to New York City, and finally to the altar of Leroy's family church in Queens.

It felt like a massive sacrifice to give them up, but the reality is, those pearls bought back my self-respect. They bought me freedom, joy, success and fulfilment. The money we raised from their sale bought us a disused warehouse off Broadway. Two years later, Leroy and I opened the Broadway Performing Arts Centre, a school for talented kids from underprivileged backgrounds. Maybe you've heard of us? We've turned out some really big names – rap stars, Broadway stars, movie stars and even a ballet star. The money from the pearl necklace changed not only my life, but also the lives of hundreds of kids. I hope that your grandmother would approve.

'So ... do you approve, Granny?' Sophia asked her grandmother.

Her eyes had become watery and although she was obviously very weak she managed a smile.

'Oh, very much,' she enthused. 'It's my business, isn't it? The performing arts! And New York is one of my favourite places on earth. I'm glad my pearls were loved and cherished while she had them. But how on earth did they end up in a second-hand shop in the first place? And what happened to them after they were sold? Does she have any idea?'

'She's given me the name of the jeweller who sold them,' Sophia told her granny. 'Hugo was going to speak to them this afternoon. They should have a record of who bought them and then, fingers crossed, we'll be one step closer to finding your necklace.'

Chapter Thirty-Four

Upper East Side, New York, 2012

Aiko sipped her green tea and watched the comings and goings in Central Park from her penthouse window. It was December now and Christmas fever had hit New York with its usual fervour. Aiko adored New York in the spring when the air was fresh and the park was in full bloom; she didn't even mind it in the height of summer when everyone else complained about the stifling heat. She loved the fall when the view from her window became a rustling ocean of red, rust and gold leaves. But most of all she loved New York at Christmas. No city lit up during the festive season in quite the same way.

Perhaps it was because Christmas was not her own celebration that she enjoyed it so. Oh, she had adopted it over the years – the stockings for the children, the elaborate wrapping of presents, the coloured lights and enormous tree straining under the weight of Bloomingdale's finest decorations. But Christmas remained something exotic and foreign to Aiko and she admired it with a distance that native New Yorkers could never understand.

Tokyo, Japan, 1952

There is a famous Japanese proverb that says, 'Sit patiently for three years, even on a rock.' Over time, Aiko had learned what this meant – although she had already waited for more than four years on her lonely, hard rock, rather than just three. She continued to work for Mr Oshiro at the Peace Palace, she remained his most admired hostess. She still lived in his house too.

He had shown her great kindness and he had probably saved her life but there was no real affection on either side: just a mutual usefulness. Aiko did not take it personally. All of Mr Oshiro's relationships worked this way. She had learned that there was no depth behind his smiles. Nana was a different story, of course. She loved Aiko with all her heart and it took all of Aiko's strength not to love her right back. But Aiko could not afford the luxury of love.

The letters from California arrived at the Peace Palace every month like clockwork. Aiko never replied, but she guarded those letters as fiercely as she had done her mother's pearls. Bo's words always made her smile. He was 5,478 miles away (he had told her this often in his letters and had even drawn a map) but somehow it comforted Aiko to know that, even in a far-flung land, there was someone on her side.

Bo had left the army now and was working in communications. He had moved back to San Francisco and was working doing research and development for Stanford University. He told Aiko excitedly that they were doing wonders with radio technology and that there were all sorts of wonderful new machines being developed now that the war was over.

His ex-girlfriend had wanted to get back together with him when he returned from Japan. His parents had been desperate for him to marry her too, but Bo had stayed true to his word. He did not marry his childhood sweetheart. He never mentioned any other girls in his letters after that. He said in every letter that he knew, one day, she would change her mind, and that then she would come and claim him as her own. He wrote that his friends thought he was crazy when he talked of his true love in Japan. He would show them. She would show them. One day ...

He wondered how she was doing in Tokyo. He hoped she was still at the bar, otherwise how would she get these letters? He hoped she wasn't lonely but he prayed to God she hadn't fallen in love with any other guy. He wondered if she wore his ring.

In 1951, Japan was granted its freedom from US occupation. Aiko's nation was stirring again, like a cherry tree in early spring. But Aiko sat tight on her rock. She entertained at the bar, she swept Nana's floors, she did as Mr Oshiro told her to do. In April 1952, as the cherry blossom bloomed, the US troops finally departed Tokyo for good. The officers had gone from their bar stools but the Peace Palace remained busy with Tokyo's new elite and Aiko continued to paint on her smile and wait. And then, one morning in June 1952, Aiko knocked on Mr Oshiro's door.

'I've been expecting you,' he said, with his usual unreadable smile.

He went to the safe, still hidden behind the painting, and brought out several bundles of notes.

'In dollars,' he said. 'Just as you requested.'

Aiko counted the money.

'Don't you trust me, Aiko-chan?' asked Mr Oshiro, still smiling. 'After all this time?'

'I do not trust anyone except myself,' she replied.

It was a lie. She trusted Bo. But she would never let Mr Oshiro know that.

'It is all there,' said Aiko, placing the money carefully in her new handbag.

'So ... You will leave us now?' asked Mr Oshiro.

Aiko nodded.

'You have said goodbye to Nana?' he asked.

Aiko shook her head.

'I have a letter for her. It explains. Please can you give it to her?' she asked, placing the letter on his desk.

Mr Oshiro nodded. The smile was wavering on his face.

'We will miss you, Aiko,' he said, and for a moment, Aiko almost believed him.

She did not look back as she walked out of the Peace Palace. She bought an expensive Western-style dress from a department store in Tokyo's most elegant shopping district, along with a smart leather suitcase and a pretty pair of shoes. That evening, she boarded a Pan Am passenger plane from Tokyo to San Francisco. Hidden in the bottom of her suitcase was $73,000 – her share of the sale of the pearls plus the extra money made in investment over the last five years. When she finally arrived in California, Aiko caught a taxi to the address on the top of the latest letter. When Bo opened the door he looked utterly and completely delighted but he didn't seem surprised at all.

'I knew you'd come eventually, but you sure did take your

time!' was all he said before throwing his arms around Aiko and kissing her.

This time Aiko didn't push him away. She never pushed him away again. Over the years he had never wavered and never let her down. And he had waited for her. They had both been patient – sitting on their lonely rock – for long enough. Aiko was scared but she was willing to take the risk. Maybe together they would thrive. It was time for the Ama-child to sink or swim.

Aiko stared at the ponies in Central Park until she could no longer focus. Bo had taken her on just such a ride during her first Christmas in the USA. They had flown to New York from California for a long weekend and he had had to buy her a fur coat from a store on Madison Avenue she had been so cold.

Suddenly Aiko found her eyes had filled with tears. For the first time since the weeks following Bo's death, she felt she would collapse under the weight of longing for him. When she thought of all they had had to go through to be together, it still took her breath away. She had been so lucky to find him. A thousand years with that man would never have been enough.

Chapter Thirty-Five

'Bad news, I'm afraid,' said Hugo, a little dejectedly, when she arrived back from the hospital. 'The jeweller in Manhattan does have a record of who bought the necklace. It was a Mr Jack Berman. He paid almost a million dollars for it in September 1991.'

'And?' asked Sophia. 'That sounds encouraging. Why the long face? Have you managed to track him down?'

'Kind of,' said Hugo. 'The trouble is, Sophia, that Jack Berman died in the Twin Towers. He was at a breakfast meeting in the South Tower on the morning of Nine Eleven.'

'That's awful,' said Sophia, horrified.

'I know,' nodded Hugo. 'And the poor guy wasn't married, he didn't have any kids and both his parents were already dead, so who inherited the necklace after he died?'

'Maybe he didn't still have it when he died. He must have bought it for someone,' mused Sophia. 'A woman, I mean. A bachelor doesn't spend a million dollars on a pearl necklace for himself. He must have had a girlfriend, or lover, in 1991 ... How can we find out more?'

'He has a younger brother,' said Hugo. 'It's the only lead I can find. His name is Joshua Berman and he is also a seriously wealthy businessman who lives in Manhattan. He's the owner of some big multimedia publishing house. He owns loads of glossy style magazines, fashion websites, interiors books, that sort of thing.'

'Have you tried phoning him?' asked Sophia.

Hugo nodded. 'Can't get through. His PA is a Rottweiler. There's no way she's going to let me speak to Mr Big about his dead brother. I managed to track down his email address though, so I've dropped him a line, and as long as the Rottweiler doesn't get to it first, hopefully he'll read it. Whether or not he responds is another matter though.'

Upper East Side, New York, 2012

'I got a strange message today, honey,' said Josh Berman, pouring himself a Scotch on the rocks and wandering through to the bedroom where his girlfriend was dressing for dinner.

'You did?' she asked, rolling a sheer black stocking onto a perfectly toned, tanned leg.

'Some English guy wanted to know what happened to Jack's pearls after he died,' said Josh. 'Can you believe it? Now. After all this time.'

His blonde girlfriend stood up suddenly, startled. She was naked but for a pair of tiny black panties and one stocking.

'Why does he want to know about the pearls?' she asked, anxiously. 'You didn't tell him anything, did you?'

'No!' scoffed Josh. 'Of course I didn't. I have no intention of replying and I've told my PA to get rid of him if he calls again. Those pearls are nobody's damn business but mine – and yours! You have more important things to think about right now than some dumb necklace.'

Josh Berman slipped his hands around his girlfriend's bare waist and stroked the smooth skin of her stomach tenderly. They both looked at their reflection in the mirror and admired the growing bump. They'd made a life together, regardless of other lives they ruined in the process.

'I'm starting to show,' said the blonde, proudly.

'You sure are, Princess,' said Josh, kneeling down and kissing her rounded stomach tenderly.

'We won't be able to keep it secret for much longer,' she told him, pushing his head down gently towards her panties.

He lifted his dark head and gazed into her perfect blue eyes.

'It's nearly time,' he said. 'Soon everybody is going to know the truth – that you're all mine.'

The girl smiled proudly at her reflection in the full-length mirror. She stared in awe at her pregnant belly as her lover pulled down her panties and started kissing her tenderly. Life didn't get much more perfect than this. She'd waited so long to get here, and nothing, and no one, was going to get in Calgary Woods' way now.

Chapter Thirty-Six

'This Berman guy is never going to contact us, is he?' asked Hugo, his shoulders slumping over his laptop. 'The story's been in all the papers over the pond. They featured it on CNN and *Entertainment Tonight*. I've had hundreds of emails and tweets from Tilly's fans, wishing us good luck, and sending us more pictures of her wearing the necklace back in the day but there's nothing new. I don't think we're ever going to find the pearls. Not in time ... Not without Berman's help.'

'Granny's not good,' replied Sophia, sadly. 'She refuses to have a feeding drip and she's barely eating a thing. I couldn't even get her to try a violet cream from Fortnum's today. And they're her favourite! There's only two weeks until Christmas, Hugo. I wanted to get the necklace back to her in time but at this rate I don't even know if she's going to make it to Christmas ... Oh God, Hugo, what am I going to do without her?'

Hugo came over and gave her a hug. He felt less like an irritating younger brother now and more like a responsible older brother. He was starting to sound less like an extra from a reality TV show and more like a proper adult every day. He spent most of his time working with Sophia, and the rest snuggled up in his Wanstead love-nest with Damon. Sophia couldn't have been happier for him. Sometimes it felt as though Granny had been the making of both Hugo and Sophia. It just seemed such a shame that it was the end of her life that had jump-started the beginning of theirs.

'Right, one last trawl through the emails before bed?' said Hugo, brightly. 'We will not be beaten. Let's channel some of Granny's wartime spirit and keep the home fires burning.'

Sophia managed a little laugh. It was almost midnight and

they were both exhausted but it was worth going the extra mile for Granny. Especially when there was so little time left. The two friends worked in silence until Sophia's eyes started closing and her head began to bob in front of the screen.

'I need to go to bed,' she said, standing up on wobbly legs and stretching her aching arms. 'I'm done in.'

'Wait!' said Hugo, excitedly. 'I've got an email here, from a woman in Australia. She collects old magazines. She says she's found a picture of the necklace in an issue of Vogue from 1992. She reckons that old supermodel Valerie is wearing it at some society wedding. Probably just another dead end, but let's look at these attachments, just in case, shall we?'

Sophia peered over Hugo's shoulders to look at the photographs that had been sent from Australia. The scanned magazine pictures weren't the best quality and the photographs were quite small on the page but ...

'It does look very like Granny's necklace,' mused Sophia, trying to focus through tired eyes.

Hugo enlarged the photos and zoomed in on the necklace.

'Bingo,' he said. 'Look at this one. You can see the clasp. It *is* the necklace. I'm sure of it.'

'Bloody hell, Hugo, I think you're right,' said Sophia, perking up. 'And she's English, isn't she? Valerie? I'm pretty sure she lives in London. Isn't she some yoga-loving, clean-living do-gooder these days?'

Hugo googled 'Valerie' and 'supermodel'.

'Halle-fucking-lujah!' he exclaimed. 'She lives in Notting Hill. And she's still signed to the same modelling agency. We can call them first thing in the morning. She's a real bleeding heart, that one. She's bound to want to help. Right, let's get some sleep. Tomorrow we're going to crack this. I just know it!'

Chapter Thirty-Seven

'I had a terrible thought,' said Sophia, climbing onto Hugo's bed.

'What the ... ? Sophia, I know you want to get on with things but it's not morning yet.'

'I know, but I can't sleep. Seriously, Hugo, there's a major flaw in our plan that we haven't even thought of,' she said, resting her head on his shoulder. She could feel her heart pumping in her chest. 'Even if this Valerie does have the necklace, we can't get our hands on it.' She was trying not to panic. 'That's what I've been trying to tell you. All the newspapers have had experts giving their opinions about what the necklace is worth. Some are saying a couple of million pounds – one said fifteen million! – and I know it's all speculation but the silly thing is, we've kind of become victims of our own success: the more press attention we get, the more the necklace is worth. It's become a phenomenon. Granny's certainly not short of a bob or two and if she could have bought the pearls back for five hundred grand, or even a million, I'm sure she could have done that. But the problem is, we've created a monster. It's like you said about Elizabeth Taylor's pearls when we first began all this. The fact that they were given to her by Richard Burton and everybody knows their story adds value to the necklace and it becomes worth far more than it would have done if it had belonged to a nobody. People want to buy a little piece of history, of glamour, of romance. I woke up in the middle of the night and realised that even if we do find Granny's necklace, we can't afford to buy it back any more.'

Hugo frowned. 'I hadn't thought about that,' he admitted. 'But are people really that greedy? The whole point of our search is so that your granny can have her pearls back before she dies. Would anybody really deny an old lady her dying wish for the sake of money? Wouldn't they at least lend them to her?'

'Maybe,' mused Sophia. 'Maybe not. Whatever the moral arguments, whoever owns that necklace has the legal right to do what they want with it. It belongs to them, not us. I can't believe that thought never even crossed my mind. I've been so hell-bent on finding the pearls, I lost sight of reality. Hugo, I don't think we're ever going to get those pearls back. We're going to fail.'

She swallowed a lump that had formed in her throat. She felt tired and beaten suddenly.

'People are greedy and selfish, Hugo,' she said, quietly. 'We were greedy and selfish, remember? And maybe I deserve to fail.'

'Sophia, you would never let go of that necklace if we managed to get our hands on it now,' Hugo told her, stroking her hair more firmly. 'Pull yourself together and get on with the job in hand. It's what your granny needs.'

Sophia heard his words but they would not penetrate.

'But I'm Tilly's granddaughter and, at the beginning, all I saw were pound signs. Why would anyone else care? Maybe that's why the present owner hasn't come forward yet, even after all the publicity. Who would want to part with something that's worth so much? If they hold onto it until after Granny dies, it'll be worth even more. No one is going to come forward, Hugo. I just know it. It's all been a complete waste of time and I've got Granny's hopes up for nothing.'

'Get some more sleep and when you wake up I'll make you one of my famous fry-ups and everything will look better. We'll phone the modelling agency on the dot at nine. Look, this Valerie woman is always doing charitable work and it's not like she's poor. If she has the necklace, I'm sure she'll sell it back at a price your granny can afford. Or let us buy it back over time, or something.'

'And if she doesn't have it?' asked Sophia, desperately.

'Then something else will happen,' replied Hugo, confidently. 'Don't give up hope, Sophia. Not now.'

Sophia allowed her head to grow heavy on Hugo's chest, her eyelids closed of their own accord. She tried to catch onto the tail end of hope as she drifted off to sleep, her fingertips brushed it but she could not hold on. Hugo was right, but it would take a miracle. And how could Sophia believe in miracles now?

Upper East Side, New York, 2012

Aiko could not sleep. If anything her insomnia had become worse once she was back in her own bed. But luckily she was in the right town for that condition. It was almost one in the morning but in New York City it was easy to find a coffee house still serving lattes to nightclubbers, shift workers and insomniacs alike. She sat at the bar, balanced a little inelegantly on a shiny metal stool, sipped her too-hot coffee and tried to quiet her mind by staring blankly at the TV screen above the barista's head.

Aiko was not remotely interested in the stories about rappers and models, but when a picture of Tilly Beaumont flashed up on screen, she began to watch more intently. Bo had taken Aiko to a Tilly Beaumont movie on their very first date in San Francisco. Aiko dragged herself away from her memories and stared back at the huge screen. The television was showing a montage of photographs of Tilly Beaumont wearing the same pearl necklace. With every picture they showed, Aiko's hand shook more. The coffee sloshed over the edge of the cup and the ghosts in her head started screaming and banging on their prison walls. As the picture froze on a final close-up of the giant central pearl, Aiko lost her grip on the cup. It smashed to the floor.

'Sorry, sorry,' she mumbled to the barista, throwing a twenty dollar note on the bar and rushing to the door.

'Hey, old lady, your change!' shouted the barista, but Aiko ignored him.

She could hear nothing but the ghosts finally surfacing, breathing, clamouring to be heard. At last she understood why they had returned.

Chapter Thirty-Eight

'If I had those pearls today, I would drive to the hospital this instant and give them back to your grandmother,' said the elegant forty-something, languishing on the white sofa.

Everything in Valerie's house was white. The walls, the floors, the furniture, her silk palazzo pants, her cotton vest, her cashmere wrap, the oriental cat purring on her lap – even the minimalist Christmas tree in the corner was white and so were the tasteful decorations.

'I can't believe I missed this entire story,' she rolled her enormous, cat-like green eyes dramatically, 'when I could have been so much help to you. I am integral – integral! – to the plot. Did my agent tell you why I didn't know? I was in Thailand. I run an elephant charity there. It's one of hundreds I support around the globe. I'm afraid I was quite out of the loop. I turn off my phone, I leave my laptop at home, and I fully immerse myself in the local culture. You should try it some time. In fact, I'll send you all my information; if there's anything you'd like to get involved in, you simply have to ask. There's nothing like a bit of charity work in Africa or Asia to cleanse one's aura.'

Sophia nodded obediently. Valerie talked calmly and softly, and gave the impression of being utterly selfless, but there was absolutely no chance of getting a word in edgeways or changing the subject from her chosen course.

'I do so admire your grandmother,' she continued, flicking her long, shiny black hair. 'When I first started modelling I studied all those classic English actresses – your grandmother, Julie Christie, Audrey Hepburn, Elizabeth Taylor – and I tried desperately to emulate them in my pictures. Such poise! Such elegance! If only I'd known my necklace had once belonged to

Tilly Beaumont I don't think I would ever have given it away. But I had so many precious things when I was younger and still beautiful ...'

She paused, holding her undeniably beautiful face in profile for Sophia to admire and then glanced at her guest expectantly.

'But you're still amazingly beautiful, Valerie,' said Sophia obediently.

'Oh, you're too kind,' she replied in faux surprise. 'Ah well, time is a cruel mistress. Is your grandmother terribly ill?'

Sophia swallowed hard and nodded.

'It's not good,' she replied honestly. 'Her consultant's worried that she won't even see Christmas.'

She blinked hard to fight back the tears. She took a sip of the chamomile and liquorice herbal tea Valerie had served her in a fine white porcelain cup to steady herself. It tasted disgusting.

'I know it's terribly tough when a loved one dies but you do know that it's not the end, don't you? I know a wonderful lady in South Kensington who has a real gift for past lives. I'll give you her number. But I suppose you'd like to know about the necklace. It's a love story, of course ... What other types of stories are worth telling?'

Hampstead, London 2012

'She sounds hilarious!' screamed Hugo, laughing as Sophia did her impersonation of Valerie. 'Doesn't she, Damon?'

'She sounds like a complete pain in the arse,' said Damon.

'So what's the story?' asked Hugo, wide-eyed. 'With Valerie and the pearls?'

'She was Jack Berman's lover in the nineties,' Sophia explained. 'He gave them to her in 1991, just a few weeks after he bought them, so I guess they were always meant to be a present for her.'

'Do tell us all the sordid details about the model and the playboy ...' pleaded Hugo.

Damon nodded his agreement.

'OK, boys, if you're sitting comfortably, then I'll begin ...'

Once upon a time there was a very beautiful, but rather dippy, young girl, who landed herself a modelling contract in London. Her name was Valerie Bull – but her agency wisely decided that she should be known simply as Valerie. And that is who she became. She had black hair and green eyes and she was as tall, skinny and glossy as a thoroughbred filly.

In September 1991, when she was nineteen years old, she attended her first New York Fashion Week and she was declared the new darling of the fashion world. At a party at the Waldorf Astoria, Valerie was spotted by one of Manhattan's most eligible bachelors. His name was Jack Berman, handsome, dashing and worth gazillions of dollars. That Christmas he bought her an exquisite pearl necklace.

Their relationship stumbled on through the 1990s. Although they managed to attend celebrity weddings, the Oscars, Cannes, the Monaco Grand Prix and Glastonbury together, they only ever got to spend time alone in five-star hotels. Valerie was constantly on the move between New York, London, Paris and Milan. Soon, she was drinking Cristal alone for breakfast, injecting heroin with her fellow models for lunch and snorting cocaine with ageing rock stars for dinner. She learned well – inject between the toes and the track marks don't show, you'll stay thin and the photographers will keep shooting you. The poor love survived on nothing more calorific than rocket leaves and beluga caviar for years.

Valerie was still in love with her American Boy but he was a clean-living sort of guy, so she had to hide her bad habits from him when they were together. When he did finally catch her injecting smack in a bathroom in his penthouse apartment on the Upper East Side, instead of throwing her out, he paid for her to go to a swanky rehab centre in Arizona and gave a candid interview about living with a partner who had Addictive Personality Disorder to *The New Yorker* (in which he also managed to mention his latest business ventures several times).

In Arizona, Valerie could paint abstract watercolours, swim in the outdoor pool and attend group therapy with the celebrity friends she'd met there. When she finally left rehab three months later she was clean and, as she told all the glossiest magazines in the exclusive interviews she gave (with a guaranteed front cover, of course), she had developed an avid interest in yoga, homeopathy and transcendental meditation.

The new, shinier, brighter Valerie was over the moon when Jack finally proposed to her at Christmas in 1997, and she began planning the world's most expensive wedding. She had her dress designed in secret by her dear friend Karl Lagerfeld, the couple did an 'at home' twelve-page spread for *Hello!*, she pre-booked the as yet unopened boutique hotel, Babington House, for the following summer and threw herself into organising a seating plan for five hundred of her closest friends.

But it seems the dashing billionaire was not so keen on the new improved Valerie. He didn't like green tea, and he preferred his sex frantic, rather than tantric. Just three weeks before the Big Day, Valerie caught him in bed with a teenage model from the Ukraine. She was utterly devastated (as she told Oprah tearfully) but she did not succumb to her old demons. No, instead she swore off men for ever and threw herself into a life of Doing Good Deeds instead.

She packed up the pearl necklace and sent it back to her ex-fiancé. When Jack died in the Twin Towers, he was still deeply in love with Valerie (she thinks) and he would definitely have kept the necklace as a reminder of their relationship, and not have given it to any of the nubile young models who came after her (she thinks). But doesn't really know because they never talked again after they broke up in 1998.

Valerie is currently single and has dedicated her present life to animal welfare charities, although she is not yet sure what she will do with her next life. The end.

Hampstead, London, 2012

The boys rolled around the floor laughing.

'Was she really that bad?' asked Hugo.

'Yes!' replied Sophia.

'But what about the necklace, Sophia?' he asked. 'Was Valerie any help at all?'

Sophia shrugged. 'I don't really know. She talks so much

bullshit it's hard to extrapolate the truth ... But she believes Jack Berman didn't have any other long-term relationship after he split up with her.'

'She's right,' said Hugo. 'So, the chances are, he either sold the necklace after Valerie sent it back, or kept it as an investment.'

'In which case his brother Joshua would have inherited it,' added Sophia.

'And he's a rude bastard who refuses to return my calls or reply to my emails!' said Hugo, exasperated.

Sophia could feel the pressure rising as the time ran out. They had managed to track a lot of the necklace's story but was it actually getting them anywhere? She was terrified it was all going to be too little, too late.

Chapter Thirty-Nine

Dominic stopped by his favourite diner on the way home from another wasted meeting at a television company. No one seemed to want his Ecuadorian story. What was wrong with them all? He'd left New York for three months and by the time he'd come back it felt like the entire documentary genre had fallen out of fashion. He did not want to give up on the project but he was starting to feel like he had no choice. Maybe he had to find a new story. He'd have to give himself a couple of weeks off and regroup in the new year. He could concentrate on finding himself a new apartment, maybe – or at least getting some furniture for the apartment he was still living in. Maybe a sofa and a plasma screen would make him feel better.

He ordered some dinner and a beer and picked up a bundle of newspapers and magazines to plough through. He'd been back for six weeks but he'd been so busy working on the document- ary and trying to sell it to someone – anyone – that he'd barely had time to catch up on what else was happening in the world. Well, it looked like he was going to have plenty of time on his hands now. In the last five months, he'd managed to screw up his marriage and his job – good going, Dom!

He was flicking absent-mindedly through a glossy newspaper supplement, while shovelling forkfuls of meatloaf into his mouth, and studiously trying to ignore the Christmas songs playing in the diner, when he hesitated on a page to admire a photograph of a particularly beautiful girl. Only the day before, Dave had been teasing him about his lack of interest in the opposite sex. His best friend had been trying to persuade him to try Internet dating but Dom had no interest in trawling through pictures of women on his computer. Nor did he want to meet his mom's hairdresser's daughter or her Pilates instructor's sister. Jeez, if he had a dollar for every time his mom called with a potential date, he wouldn't have to make any more documentaries. He'd be set up for life! No, Dominic McGuire had sworn off women. That's what marrying – and divorcing – a woman like Calgary did for a guy. He had his friends, and his dog, and until recently he'd also had his career. But he was still a red-blooded man and there was no harm in admiring a picture of a girl in a magazine, was there?

He skim-read the caption. *Sophia Beaumont Brown, 30, the granddaughter of English actress Tilly Beaumont, is searching for the family's missing pearl necklace, estimated to be worth around $8 million.*

'I bet you are, honey,' he muttered to himself. 'If my family had lost something worth that much I'd be searching for it too!'

The young woman in the photograph looked strikingly like her grandmother. He and his mom had watched old movies a lot when he was a kid and Dom had a soft spot for all things British. They didn't make movies like that any more. Nor did they make women like that any more. At least, not in Manhattan. In London it was obviously a different story, he decided, glancing at Sophia Beaumont Brown. She had the same classic beauty as her grandmother – high cheekbones, come-to-bed eyes, curves in all the right places and legs that went on for miles – but she was darker. She looked kind of dangerous.

Dom read the article as he polished off his dinner and sipped his cold beer. His eyes slid to the close-up pictures. Dom froze. Tilly Beaumont was wearing Calgary's pearls! He'd have recognised that necklace anywhere. Calgary wore those pearls on every special occasion. She'd worn them on their wedding day. He had secured that clasp around her neck a hundred times. She used to joke that the LMB on the clasp stood for Lady Macbeth! When he asked her where she'd got the necklace she said it had been given to her on some fashion shoot and although it looked real, it was just good quality costume stuff. What a liar!

Dom sprinted back to the apartment clutching the magazine. He ran straight past Guido, calling out a hello as he passed, and then ran up the stairs two at a time. As always, Blondie was beside herself with excitement when Dom entered the penthouse.

He bent down and ruffled her long coat affectionately. She

wagged her tail so hard that she knocked over one of the book towers that were still littering the floor.

'Come on, girl,' he said to Blondie, picking up her lead. 'We're going for a walk.'

Dominic and Blondie jogged down Allen Street and turned left towards Manhattan Bridge, dodging Christmas shoppers as they went. Brooklyn Heights was less than two miles from Bowery. Dom had never understood why more people didn't walk in New York. He didn't have much time for the gym these days but he walked, or ran, almost everywhere and it kept him in pretty good shape. It was already dark when he and Blondie turned into Cranberry Street. The houses were all lit up with Christmas lights. It was the first time that season that Dominic actually felt his heart melting a little. The dog knew where she was going and pulled her owner the last fifty metres before bounding up the steps outside Dave's brownstone.

'Your second home, huh, Blondie?' he said, breathlessly, ringing the bell. 'Sometimes I think you'd rather live with Dave, Ellen and the kids than you would with me.'

She wagged her tail enthusiastically.

'You women have no loyalty,' he teased her.

'Uncle Dom! Uncle Dom! Mom! Dad! It's Uncle Dom – and he's brought Blondie!' screamed Dave and Ellen's eldest, Evie, as she opened the door and threw herself into Dom's arms. She was dressed as an elf.

All three of Dave's kids had his mop of curly auburn hair, his insane sense of humour and their mother's boundless energy. Nobody in this household was ever quiet! Evie kissed Dom on the cheek and then wriggled back out of his arms to hug Blondie. Two seconds later he was bombarded by Sonny and Carly – the younger two. As Dave and Ellen appeared, the hall became a mass of hugs, kisses, high fives, shouts, screeches and a very overexcited barking dog. It took a few minutes for anyone to make themselves heard. Eventually, Ellen ushered the kids off to the playroom with Blondie, and the noise level dropped a little.

Dom grinned. He loved this family with all his heart. It had been one of the things that had been so difficult with Calgary. She didn't like Dave and Ellen much. She called Dave 'hairy, lairy and uncouth' and despaired of Ellen who she said was 'really quite attractive if she wasn't always so exhausted, rag-gedy and unwashed'. Worse, she despised the way they lived surrounded by children's toys, with grubby fingermarks on the walls and the TV always on in the background, blaring out cartoons. She said their house gave her a headache and refused to visit. But his friends' home was everything Dominic craved: it was warm, welcoming and full of love. Who cared if the couch had been scratched by the cat? Who cared if the toilet roll holder was always empty? Who cared if the kitchen wall had Cheerios glued to it?

'So what's with the surprise visit, bud?' asked Dave, handing Dom a beer from the fridge. 'We might have been out. You know, at the opera, or at some swanky dinner party uptown, or catching a play ...'

'I think Dom knows us a little better than that, babe,' laughed Ellen.

'You've got to see this,' said Dom, pulling the magazine out of his backpack.

He brushed away some breadcrumbs and laid the article about Tilly Beaumont out flat on the kitchen table.

'No fucking way!' exclaimed Ellen, who didn't swear often. 'Holy shit!'

'I know,' nodded Dom.

'What?' asked Dave, scratching his head. 'I don't get it. I mean, the girl's hot, I give you that, but there are hot girls in every magazine. What's so exciting about some old dame's necklace?'

'It's Calgary's', said Dominic and Ellen in unison.

'I don't understand,' said Dave, shaking his head.

'Neither do I,' mused Ellen. 'She works in fashion. She must have read this story. So why hasn't Calgary come forward?'

'That's exactly what I've been thinking,' agreed Dom.

'So, let me get this straight,' said Dave. 'Calgary owns a very expensive pearl necklace, that it turns out was lost by some Hollywood movie star in the eighties, and now the family are looking for this necklace and Calgary is keeping shtum?'

'I'm going to call her,' said Dom, reaching for his phone.

'No,' said Ellen, gently. 'Let me handle this, Dom. You two haven't spoken since she split, right?'

Dom shook his head.

'She might ignore you,' said Ellen. 'Let me send her an email. She won't be rude enough to snub me.'

'OK, maybe you're right,' Dom conceded. 'I'm going to get in touch with this Sophia girl then. Give her the good news.'

Dave picked up the magazine and nodded.

'Good plan,' he said. 'And why don't you ask her if she's single while you're at it!'

Chapter Forty

Hampstead, London, 2012

It was less than two weeks before Christmas. Granny was deteriorating rapidly. Hugo and Sophia still got up early every morning and rushed to their computers to check how the campaign was going but they did so with less hope than they had before. The longer the search went on, the less possible it seemed that their dreams would ever come true. But Sophia could not give up now and so she and Hugo were back in front of their computers for another day ...

'Hugo! It's finally happened!' said Sophia, in a voice so shaky that she barely recognised it as her own. 'I know where Granny's pearls are. They're in New York!'

'Are you sure?' asked Hugo.

'Positive,' replied Sophia. 'They belong to a woman called Calgary Woods.'

'How do you know?' he demanded, getting up off his chair so quickly that it toppled over backwards.

'Because I've just got an email from her ex-husband. He's sent photographs of her wearing them on her wedding day. He says he knew the minute he read a magazine article about Granny that his ex-wife's pearls were the ones we were looking for. He would recognise them anywhere. I don't see any reason why he would send this email if he wasn't sure. Hugo, I think we've finally done it!' shouted Sophia, finally letting herself believe the words in front of her on the screen.

She stood up and threw herself into her best friend's arms. Finally, the moment had arrived. For the first time in her life, she had succeeded.

'So what now?' asked Hugo.

'I need to get to New York,' Sophia said excitedly. 'But how the hell am I going to do that? We haven't got any money.'

Upper East Side, Manhattan, 2012

'Dominic's on my case, Josh!' said Calgary. 'I just got an email from one of his friends. Ellen? I told you about them – Ellen and Dave. They live in Brooklyn ...'

She said the word 'Brooklyn' as if it tasted revolting, knowing that Josh was the ultimate postcode snob, but the truth was Calgary had always harboured a secret envy for Ellen and Dave's life. She hadn't had much in common with them but the real reason Calgary had never been able to stand spending time in their company was that she found their obvious love for each other unbearable to watch. What they had was what she'd tried to fake with Dom. She let her hand fall to her rounded stomach. It was what she had with Josh now. Wasn't it? Josh had his back to her. He was putting on his cufflinks, oblivious to the doubt that had suddenly gripped her chest.

'Yeah, frigging Valerie's spilled the beans too,' he said, bitterly. 'I had more messages from that English guy, Hugo, asking about the pearls. Jeez, they're your fucking pearls, Calgary! It's not like we stole them. They were left to me by my brother, I chose to give them to you. Where's the crime in that? Why the hell should we be emotionally blackmailed into giving them back just because some old broad's dying? It's not our fault she lost them in the first place.'

Calgary sighed, and stroked her growing bump. He did love her, didn't he? He'd given her the necklace, he'd been true to his word and now it was all going to be perfect, right?

'Ellen says that Dominic's already been in touch with the granddaughter in England. It's only a matter of time before they find us. Or before Dom finds us. But I can't see Dominic like this,' she said. 'How will I explain?'

Her pregnancy would crush Dominic. Calgary should never have married him, she knew that now, and she was incredibly relieved that the sham was over, but she had never intended to hurt Dom. He wasn't a bad man. And she knew he had loved her. How would he handle the knowledge that she was already pregnant with another man's child?

'He's got to know sometime, honey,' said Josh, wrapping his arms around her shoulders and kissing her neck. 'It's not a crime to have a baby. We've hidden away for far too long. We're going to have to let the shit hit the fan this time.'

'I don't want to lose my necklace,' she said, in the voice of a little girl too used to getting her own way. 'You know what those pearls mean to me, baby. I bet they mean more to me than they do to Tilly Beaumont.'

'I won't let them take away your necklace, Princess,' said Josh, kissing her head tenderly. 'I promise.'

She loved it when Josh called her Princess but what she really wanted now was to be his Queen.

'What do we do if they show up?' she asked him, twisting her hair around her fingers nervously.

'We tell them they can have the necklace but we put such a huge price tag on the damned thing that there's not a hope in hell they'll be able to afford it.'

Of course, Josh wouldn't let anyone take away those pearls. He loved her.

'Hey, did you see the paper, by the way?' said Josh, reaching for the *New York Times*. 'Aiko Watanabe was found unconscious in Central Park yesterday. They don't know if she was mugged or what but you need to be careful out there, baby. Especially in your condition. I want you home before dark from now on. I've met Mrs Watanabe several times and she is a formidable old lady. If that can happen to her in this neighbourhood, it can happen to anyone.'

'Aiko Watanabe?' asked Calgary. 'She's owns Pearl, right?'

'Right,' confirmed Josh. 'No wonder she's one of the wealthiest women in the country. Luckily, she's going to be just fine, according to the paper. But still, when something like that happens on our doorstep you need to take notice.'

Hampstead, London, 2012

Sophia had hoped a long walk around Hampstead Heath would help her find a solution but no matter how hard she tried, she could not see a way of getting her hands on more than two grand in the next twenty-four hours. Last minute-flights to New York, just before Christmas, did not come cheap. Granny's consultant had made it quite clear that they were all living on borrowed time now. If she didn't get to New York and find the pearls in the next few days, it would be too late. She couldn't ask Granny for the money, she was far too weak to deal with anything like that. She couldn't ask her parents, obviously. Hugo had tried asking his but they were on their way to spend Christmas in Barbados and completely out of contact. She'd gone through all her possessions trying to find something valuable enough to sell in a hurry but there was nothing of any real worth. Granny had lots of antiques and valuables in the house but Sophia couldn't sell them. One thing she had learned over the past few months was that she had no claim to what wasn't rightfully hers. Whichever way Sophia turned, she seemed to hit a brick wall.

She let herself back into the house, kicked off her boots, and wandered dejectedly into the drawing room. There, sitting side by side, wearing matching silly grins were Hugo and Damon.

'What?' asked Sophia, a little nervously. 'Why are you two looking so pleased with yourselves?'

Hugo nodded towards the coffee table in front of him. He was sitting on his hands as if he didn't trust himself to sit still otherwise. There, on the table, sat Sophia's passport and some printed sheets of paper.

'What's this?' she asked, picking up the papers.

'Your flight details and boarding pass,' Hugo almost screamed, unable to contain his excitement any more. 'You leave tonight.'

'I don't understand,' she managed to say. 'How? Who paid?'

'Damon,' squealed Hugo, freeing his hands and hugging his boyfriend round the waist. 'Isn't he the best?'

'Damon?' Sophia turned to look at the young man on her grandmother's sofa. 'Damon, this is too much.'

Damon smiled shyly and shrugged. 'I do pretty well with work,' he explained. 'It's not like I have a wife or kids to support. I have money, Sophia. Not millions, but more than enough. When Hugo told me you needed to get to New York in a hurry I knew it was something I could do to help. I want to help.'

'Thank you,' said Sophia, swallowing the lump in her throat. 'I'll pay you back as soon as I can. I promise.'

Chapter Forty-One

'Hi,' said the tall, rugged guy in the diner. 'I'm Dominic McGuire. You must be Sophia.'

Sophia felt herself blushing. He had hazel eyes with cute crinkles at the sides, and ridiculously long, thick eyelashes, and biceps that made Damon's look puny ... Sophia had an internal word with herself. Get a grip, woman. You're here to retrieve Granny's necklace, not to ogle the local talent.

'Are you OK?' asked Dominic McGuire. 'You look a bit spaced out.'

Sophia blushed harder and tried to find her voice.

'I'm sorry,' she managed to say. 'I'm in a bit of a daze. It must be the jet lag ...'

Oh shit, she couldn't stop blushing. What was wrong with her?

'You must be exhausted,' said Dominic kindly. 'Sit, sit. Let's get some coffee and something to eat, maybe? Are you hungry?'

It was Dominic's turn to blush. Sophia felt a weird crackling in the air between them. It was something she'd never experienced before. Was this what people meant when they talked about chemistry? Or was this what jet lag did to you?

'The meatloaf sounds good,' she blurted out. 'Don't worry, I have a really healthy appetite and I'm a real carnivore.'

'I can imagine,' murmured Dominic, grinning.

Their eyes met. Was he thinking what she was thinking? Had the word 'appetite' conjured up images of hungry kisses and winter jumpers being pulled over heads and ...

'You're very beautiful,' he said.

And then they sat in awkward silence for a moment. Dominic broke her gaze. 'What a complete jerk I must sound! I'm sorry,

Sophia. I blame my buddy, Dave. He's been going on about you ever since I showed him the magazine article, and now you're here in the flesh. So now we've got that awkward bit out of the way. Welcome to New York, Sophia Beaumont Brown. Let me order you some of our famous meatloaf.'

Sophia smiled, and then the smile turned into a laugh and the laughter must have been infectious because soon Dominic was laughing too and neither of them had a clue what was so funny. The ice was well and truly broken and before long they were tucking into steaming hot plates of food and sharing their stories.

'So Calgary already had the necklace when you met her?' asked Sophia, finally getting round to the business at hand.

'Yup,' said Dominic. 'She told me it was fake, that she'd got it on some fashion shoot or other. I had no reason to doubt her.'

'We think the necklace belonged to a man called Joshua Berman,' Sophia explained. 'Calgary must have got it from him somehow. Does that make any sense? Do you know him?'

Dominic stopped with his fork halfway to his mouth, and stared at Sophia.

'Josh Berman?' he said. 'Why the hell would Josh Berman be giving Calgary a necklace worth millions of dollars?'

'So you do know him?' asked Sophia excitedly. Maybe they were finally piecing together the jigsaw?

'Josh Berman is Calgary's boss,' said Dominic. 'He owns the whole company. She's the creative director for his fashion magazines but ... It doesn't make any sense. Calgary's had that necklace for years. She already had it when we met. She was just a fashion assistant back then. Why would the boss give a fashion assistant a gift worth that amount of money?'

Sophia flinched. The question hung in the air like a dark cloud. She saw the realisation dawn on Dominic's face. She could feel his pain. Finally he said what they were both thinking.

'She had an affair with her boss, didn't she?' he said, shaking his head in disbelief. 'No wonder she got promoted so quickly. One minute she was hanging up dresses in the fashion cupboard and being sent out to get the fashion editors their skinny soya lattes and the next minute she was running the whole fucking shebang. But she was with me during that time ...'

'Maybe the affair was already over,' said Sophia, feeling dreadful that she'd been responsible for this bombshell. 'Maybe it was more of a friendship? A mentoring thing?'

Dominic laughed but this time there was no joy in his laughter.

'No, I don't think the affair ended at all,' he said. 'I think I've been the biggest fool in history. Josh Berman is married. Sorry. *Was* married. He got divorced this summer – at exactly the same time Calgary walked out on me. What a coincidence, huh? We've been to weekend parties at the Bermans' house in Long Island together. Me and his poor wife, we used to leave Calgary and Josh to it. We thought they had to talk shop. No, if Calgary and Josh had an affair, it never ended. She goes on business trips with him all the time. He takes her to fashion weeks in London, Paris and Milan.'

Dominic went quiet for a minute and took a gulp of his beer. He looked pensive but less angry than he had a few minutes ago.

'If she's with him now,' he said eventually, 'which I would bet my life she is, I know exactly where your grandmother's necklace is, Sophia. I know where Berman lives. We can go and bang on their door and demand they return what doesn't belong to them.'

'It's not that simple,' said Sophia. 'Technically, and legally, the necklace does belong to Joshua Berman. We think his brother left it to him in his will. If I want it back, he'll have to be willing to sell it and I'll have to be able to come up with the cash. And that's a massive catch because, you see, I don't have any cash.'

Sophia blushed again, but this time out of shame. She guessed Dominic had thought that she was loaded – she was the great-granddaughter of a lord and the granddaughter of Hollywood royalty, after all – but now she had had to admit to being penniless. She searched his face for a reaction but he looked thoughtful, not judgmental or even shocked.

'How much is it worth?' he asked.

Sophia shrugged. 'After all the publicity? And now he knows it belonged to my grandmother? He knows how desperate I am to retrieve it, too. Unfortunately, that necklace is worth whatever price tag Joshua Berman chooses to put on it.'

'He's a greedy man,' Dominic warned. 'Ruthless too. I can't

imagine he'll care much about your grandmother in all this. All Berman wants is to accumulate wealth. He gets off on gobbling up smaller companies, poaching staff from competitors, acquiring things that no one else can have. Oh, and he likes stealing other guys' wives too, apparently!'

'You don't know that for sure,' said Sophia, trying to be kind.

'I do,' replied Dominic. 'And it makes me angry because I feel as if Calgary and Josh made a mug of me. But don't think for a moment that I still have feelings for her ...'

'Shall we leave Calgary and Berman until tomorrow?' she asked him, hopefully. 'I'm a bit frazzled after the journey.'

Dominic nodded, still smiling.

'Do you wanna get some air or something?' he asked. 'I could show you a few sights?'

'I should get back to my hotel, really ...' said Sophia, already knowing perfectly well that she wasn't going to make it to her hotel in Midtown.

'Well, it's up to you. I'll get you a cab to your hotel but ...' He brushed a stray hair off her cheek. It was the first time they'd touched. Sophia's skin tingled. 'I'd like it if you came back to mine for a while. Just to hang out.'

'OK,' she managed to say. 'Just to hang out.'

It was a ridiculous charade. Dominic grabbed Sophia's hand the minute they got out onto the freezing street. The warmth of his hand on her own freezing one made Sophia's heart race and her knees weak. She had touched virtual strangers before, in the dark, drunken haze of nightclubs but it had never felt like this. It shamed her to remember now, but she had allowed men whose names she'd never known to caress her body and kiss her. She'd been thrilled and disgusted in equal measure by the baseness of such encounters, by the cold, unemotional, animalistic way she could give herself to a man she didn't even know, let alone like or love. But that was a different time and a different Sophia.

Dom stopped her under a street lamp on the corner, grabbed her cold face in his strong hands and he kissed her. With every moment his lips stayed on hers, Sophia felt more light-headed. She had never felt a physical longing for another human being so strongly before. It wasn't purely sexual, as it had always been with Nathan. It was much more than that. Dom opened his coat and enveloped Sophia inside, so that she could feel the heat of his chest through his jumper. She wanted to melt into his body. When they finally pulled up for air, Sophia felt so giddy she almost fell over. Dom grabbed her hand and laughed out loud.

'Whoa,' he said. 'Well, I've never had a first kiss like that before!'

'Neither have I,' admitted Sophia, blushing as she tried to find her feet again.

They ran all the way back to his apartment, past the man on the desk, who winked at Dominic as they passed. In the lift, they started kissing again and it wasn't until the doors opened and they found themselves still in the lobby, with the porter grinning at them, that Dom realised he hadn't pressed the button for his floor.

And then he was holding her face in his hands again and he was kissing her slowly, tenderly, teasing her with his tongue and her knees were buckling beneath her and ... Ping!

'Shall we get out this time or just keep going up and down in the elevator all evening?' asked Dom, pulling away with obvious reluctance.

He fumbled for his keys and opened the door.

'It's a bit, erm, bare, I'm afraid,' he admitted. 'Calgary kinda cleaned me out.'

But before Sophia could comment on the empty apartment, she was knocked backwards by a huge ball of pale golden fluff that launched itself at her at a hundred miles an hour.

'Blondie!' shouted Dom. 'Blondie! Get down!'

But it was too late. Sophia found herself flat on her back.

'I'm so sorry, Sophia,' cried Dom, desperately trying to pull Blondie off by her collar.

Finally, Dom managed to free Sophia from her canine embrace and she sat up on the floor, covered in dog hair and still laughing her head off.

'That is the warmest welcome I think I've ever had,' she finally managed to say, patting her hair vaguely back into place.

'Oh God,' said Dominic, pulling Sophia back up to her feet. 'She definitely liked you, at least. Here, let me fix you a drink to help you recover from the mauling.'

They spent the evening snuggled together on Dominic's mattress on the floor, watching TV on his laptop and drinking Jack

Daniel's and Coke out of chipped mugs (Calgary had taken all the glasses, naturally). Every now and then they put their drinks down and kissed like teenagers. When Dominic's hand finally reached beneath her jumper and T-shirt and touched her skin for the first time, Sophia couldn't help but let out a gasp.

'Is that OK?' asked Dominic, hesitating.

'It's more than OK,' she reassured him. 'It's heaven. Please don't stop.'

He touched her gently, tenderly, stroking her skin and holding her body as if it was something precious and rare. Sophia could barely catch her breath but it wasn't fear that left her breathless this time. Later, when they had exhausted each other, she lay in his arms and drank in his sweet, musky smell. Blondie jumped onto the mattress and Dominic tried to shoo her away.

'No,' said Sophia. 'It's fine. I don't mind if she sleeps on the bed.'

And Dominic smiled at her and held her ever more tightly and said, 'I think you're my dream woman, Sophia Beaumont Brown.'

When Sophia woke up in the morning, she was alone. The sun was filtering through the blinds and casting a white light on the bedroom. The apartment was eerily quiet. There was no sign of Dominic or of Blondie. Sophia felt a familiar panic in her chest. She was tired, jet-lagged, confused and thousands of miles from home. She'd just slept with a man she barely knew and now she was all alone again, in a strange bed, in a strange city.

By the time she'd found her clothes that were strewn around the floor, and struggled back into her jeans and jumper, she'd convinced herself she'd been stupid, naive, irresponsible, sluttish! Never sleep with a guy on the first night: she knew the rule. She was thirty years old. Would she never learn?

She opened the front door to leave.

'Where are you going?' asked Dominic, frowning.

He was standing outside the door with two fresh coffees and a bag of bagels. Blondie was by his side, wagging her tail enthusiastically.

'I'm not letting you go anywhere. Now get back into bed so I can serve you breakfast ... Blondie! Do not eat those bagels, you greedy mutt!'

Chapter Forty-Two

Mount Sinai Hospital, New York, 2012

Aiko was not one to take no for an answer.

'Mrs Watanabe, I am advising you, with the utmost respect, that it is far too early to discharge yourself from our care,' the doctor was saying wearily for the fifth time. 'You had hypothermia and a bad concussion, it's only two weeks since you were in hospital in Japan, we need to run some more tests to eliminate any serious causes for these falls and blackouts you've been experiencing. It was twenty-three degrees Fahrenheit when you were found in Central Park. You are lucky to be alive.'

Aiko did indeed feel lucky to be alive but there was no way she was wasting any more time in this hospital. She had woken here, in a private room, the morning before last, feeling like a new woman. The ghosts had gone. They had made their point. They were not the enemy after all. They had merely been trying to show her the way back to her ancestors, back to the ocean, back to her mother and back to what was rightfully hers.

'Thank you, but really I have to leave now,' she said firmly but politely to the young doctor. 'I shall visit my own private doctor in due course and have any tests he feels I require but for now I have business to attend to. Believe me when I tell you that I feel better than I have done in years.'

She had spent the last two days finding out everything she could about Sophia Beaumont Brown and her hunt for her grandmother's pearls. Right now, Aiko knew, Sophia Beaumont Brown was in New York, meeting with a man called Dominic McGuire. Mr McGuire's ex-wife, Calgary Woods, was believed to be the current owner of the necklace. Aiko felt her heart racing in her chest. She could see the whole picture now, very clearly, as if she was watching from a great distance. She knew exactly what she had to do but there wasn't much time.

Virginia Water, Surrey, 2012

Alice lay awake, listening to the sound of an owl in the garden and her husband snoring beside her. She shuffled further over to her side of the bed, pulled the duvet over her head and tried to block out the noise. But it was no good. His presence weighed heavily on her, even with a foot of bed space between her body and his. She could feel his breath on her back and the stifling heat of his flesh radiating onto her own

She hated Philip now. The events of the past few weeks had ignited a fire in her heart which burned more fiercely every day. It forced her to think, to remember, to feel. It made her realise what a coward she had been. She felt as if she was waking up from a nightmare. Alice had wasted more than half her life, she wasn't going to waste one more day.

She had begun to hide the tablets he gave her. She would put them into her mouth like a good girl and take a sip of water, but the beta blockers and antidepressants he'd been doling out to her for years were now being stored carefully under her tongue and then flushed down the toilet or the sink. It had taken a few weeks for the chemicals to leave her system. She had felt drowsy, nauseous and weak for a while and her skin had itched so badly that she had made her arms bleed by scratching them. Her muted emotions had come back violently at first and she hadn't been able to control the overwhelming mood swings. Her temper, which had lain dormant for so long, had come back with such ferocity. God, how she despised herself for lashing out at her daughter that way. As if Sophia hadn't been the one to suffer the most in all of this. Guilt had eaten Alice up for days after that. But she had also known she had to move forward from that place, for Sophia's sake as much as her own. Alice was a phoenix rising from the ashes.

She turned to face Philip, stared at his face in the half-light and wondered who the hell he really was. Did she know him at all? He certainly didn't know her. If he knew the thoughts that spun through her head every night as he slept beside her it would drive him insane. He thought he owned her. He had controlled her for their entire marriage. But she was no longer his. She never had been, she realised. She had used him far more than he had ever used her and now she no longer needed him. It was time to end this. The truth was, she had never felt anything more for the man she had married than a slight sense of gratitude and a greater sense of duty. She was indebted to him and he had never let her forget that. He had wrung out every last drop of life from her and she had more than repaid any debt she owed him. Alice no longer felt bound by him. She owed him nothing now.

Philip had noticed the change in Alice and it had made him angry. And there was nothing he hated more than feeling angry, or feeling any strong emotion, come to think of it. He became even more impossible to deal with when he got like that and Alice had spent much of her time avoiding him by finding endless reasons to visit the supermarket, the library, the WI. But Philip had always hated his wife going anywhere without him and had been known to hide her car keys to prevent her. She had tried to visit Mummy in hospital alone last week but it had taken her three hours of turning the house upside down before she found the keys. When Philip had caught her, she had placated him as best she could – there was no point in winding him up even further and making the situation more difficult for herself – and they had visited the hospital together as always. It was all about management now. She knew what she needed to do.

Philip had put her 'difficult' behaviour down to her mother's terminal illness and Alice had been happy to let him think that was the crux of the problem. And of course it was true that Mummy's failing health weighed heavily on her mind every minute of every day. The thought of a world without her mother in it was terrifying. Tilly had always been larger than life. It hadn't always been easy growing up in the shadow of a Hollywood superstar – sometimes Alice had resented her mother's fame, beauty, charisma and flair; it made her feel dull and invisible in comparison. But she loved her mother and she knew that when the hellish moment finally arrived, when Tilly Beaumont ceased to exist, Alice would fall apart. There was so much more to say. So much more to do. And so little time to do it all.

She had been angry with her mother at first for stirring up the past. She had seen what Mummy was doing, enticing Sophia back in, dropping hints and setting her off on a wild goose chase after the missing necklace. Yes, her mother loved those pearls, but Alice had known from the start that what her mother really wanted Sophia to find was the truth. That was the quest. But was it fair? When poor Sophia had no idea what she was going to discover? Alice's heart starting racing at the thought of what was going to happen over the next few days. Her mother had planted a seed. That seed had grown and now it had taken on a life of its own. No one could control it. Not Sophia. Not Alice, and certainly not Tilly.

Philip grunted loudly in his sleep and turned over, taking the duvet with him. Tomorrow she would tell him. Only a few hours more. Alice knew what real love felt like. She remembered it every time she dreamt of Italy. The thought calmed her racing heart and made her smile. She had wasted too many years already. She picked up her iPhone from the bedside table and clicked onto her photographs. She had found the picture on the Internet. There he was. Older, with laughter lines etched around his gorgeous eyes, he was a little fuller-figured perhaps, and his once black hair was now silver-fox grey, but he was as handsome as ever. She had spent so many nights staring at his picture that when she closed her eyes she could still see his face as clearly as if he was standing in front of her. After months of trawling the Internet, she had finally found him six weeks ago. She wondered if he ever thought of her too. Did he remember her? How could she cope if he didn't even remember her? Would he accept an olive branch after so many years? She smiled at his picture one more time. His eyes were still kind. Tomorrow Alice would find the courage to send her letter. She switched off her phone, grappled the duvet back from Philip and finally fell asleep.

Chapter Forty-Three

It had taken Sophia and Dominic two days to work out a plan of action.

'We'll do it Sunday morning. He's sure to be home,' Dom had told her. 'We'll turn up at his apartment, rather than at his office. We'll take him by surprise. Him and my delightful ex-wife ...'

She'd gone back to her hotel briefly to collect her suitcase but otherwise Sophia had barely ventured from Dominic's arms since she'd arrived in New York. They'd shared pizzas, noodles, beers, wines, spirits, endless kisses and all their deepest, darkest secrets. She'd told him all about her wild-child past, about her relationship with her parents, about Nathan, everything! And with every confession all he had done was hug her tighter. Sophia had never felt safer, or more in tune with a man before, but she hadn't forgotten what she'd come to New York for and she knew she had to be quick. Hugo had sent her a text that morning telling her that Granny was barely conscious. He told her she had to come home straight away. But the pearls were tantalisingly close.

They stood outside Josh Berman's apartment on the corner of E57th and Madison with Sophia's suitcase at their feet. She would have to go to the airport to catch her flight back to London straight after the meeting. It was seven a.m. on the Sunday before Christmas and the 'City That Never Sleeps' seemed pretty drowsy. Other than the odd overly keen jogger and dog-walker, the Silk Stocking District was dead.

'Right,' said Dominic. 'So let's make sure I've got this straight before we go in. We're going to appeal to their better natures and ask them to lend us the pearls for a couple of weeks, right?'

Sophia nodded.

'I don't have the money to buy them,' she explained for the umpteenth time. 'I don't know what else to do but beg for kindness.'

'From Calgary and Joshua?' Dominic still looked very sceptical about the plan. 'This is going to take a miracle. But it's Christmas, I guess, so anything could happen.'

She'd explained it all to him. He knew her financial situation inside out.

'And I thought I'd landed myself a rich chick,' Dominic had teased.

'I could probably get a million or so together pretty quickly from Granny if Calgary agrees to it. Granny said she could find that once, a little while ago, before I left. She wasn't very lucid but she definitely said that although most of her money's tied up in property and investments, I could buy the pearls back for a million and that would be OK. You know, if she's still ...' Sophia gulped.

Dominic squeezed her hand encouragingly. 'One million pounds is only 1.6 million dollars, though, baby. That might have been enough to entice a reasonable human being with a heart, but Calgary? I'm not so sure. We can only do our best though. Ready?'

Sophia nodded.

'Ready,' she confirmed.

Dominic rang the buzzer to the penthouse suite.

'Yes,' barked an unfriendly male voice.

'It's Dominic McGuire,' said Dom. 'I think we have some business to discuss.'

'Come up,' barked the voice. 'We've been expecting you.'

Dominic nodded sagely.

'Figures. Guys like Berman are always one step ahead,' he whispered as they got into the lift of the grand old building. 'Who the hell is up, dressed and expecting company at seven a.m. on a Sunday?'

Sophia swallowed hard as the lift to the penthouse opened. Dom squeezed her hand reassuringly again and rang the bell. Joshua Berman opened the door and forced a smile – of sorts. He was the kind of tall, elegantly featured, dark-haired man of about forty that you'd expect to see at a polo match, or on the slopes in Aspen. His tanned face seemed to fall into a natural sneer. He shook their hands unenthusiastically. Sophia thought that Calgary Woods had traded down: he was nowhere near as attractive as Dominic. Unless, of course, you judged a man's attractiveness by the size of his bank balance.

Sophia noticed that Joshua had no problem looking Dominic straight in the face. He had the aura of a man who believed it was his God-given right to inherit the earth – or, say, keep another family's pearl necklace, or steal another man's wife – without the slightest tinge of guilt. His tan brogues squeaked on the polished floor as he ushered his guests into the living room. The apartment was furnished tastefully and expensively. Every cushion, picture and rug had been carefully planned. The place looked more like a boutique hotel than a home.

And there she was; the ex-wife. Calgary Woods sat perched on a piano stool in front of a black baby grand in the window, overlooking Central Park. She was the type of tall, willowy, natural blonde that women have nightmares about. She was dressed entirely in black. And just to rub salt in the wound she was wearing a choker of perfect, iridescent pearls wound around her elegant neck. It was the first time that Sophia had laid eyes on the necklace that was supposed to be her inheritance. She could barely drag her eyes away. It really was the most breathtakingly beautiful necklace in the world.

Calgary didn't bother to get up when they entered the room. Sophia glanced at Dominic to check his reaction to seeing his ex-wife for the first time since she'd walked out on him. But Dominic wore an expression of steely determination and when he glanced briefly at Calgary he showed no emotion at all.

'Dominic,' said Calgary, coolly.

'Calgary,' replied Dominic calmly.

'And you must be Sophia,' said Calgary with a falsely warm smile. 'I've been reading a lot about you lately. You do look very like your grandmother, don't you? It's quite uncanny.'

The icy blonde fingered her pearls. She was marking her territory.

'Hello, Calgary,' said Sophia, stepping closer to Dominic for moral support. 'Pleased to meet you.'

Dominic slipped his arm around her waist in a defiant gesture of coupledom. Sophia watched as Calgary took in the scene, computed the facts and then nodded slowly with a wry smile.

'So Dominic's been making you feel at home in New York, I see,' she said. 'Isn't that sweet.'

Joshua walked round behind Calgary and put his arms around her shoulders so that both couples now faced each other. It was a fair fight, at least – two against two.

'I think you know why we're here,' said Sophia, with a shaky voice.

'Sure,' replied Calgary, casually flicking her silky platinum hair off her shoulders. 'You want to try to persuade me to sell you my necklace.'

Sophia swallowed. Calgary's necklace? She supposed that was technically true but it cut Sophia like a knife that this Ice Queen had more claim to the necklace now than her grandmother.

'My grandmother is gravely ill,' she explained, trying to pull at Calgary's heartstrings. If she had a heart ...

'We're aware of that,' snapped Joshua. 'We've all read the articles. But now's not the time for any bleeding hearts business, we're all busy people, so let's just cut the crap and get straight to the point. We've had the necklace independently valued and, although Calgary is very attached to the piece, under the circumstances we're prepared to sell it for ...'

Sophia gulped and nodded. Here it came ...

' ... twenty million dollars. Take it or leave it. It's our first and final offer. It's not up for negotiation.'

Sophia's mouth fell open. Twenty million dollars? That was ridiculous!

'Don't try to screw Sophia over,' said Dominic, firmly. 'We all know the pearls are valuable – but they're nowhere near that valuable. You're just trying to take advantage of the situation, Berman.'

'I'm afraid you're wrong,' retorted Joshua. 'I've already had an offer from an associate of mine, an Arab prince, who's willing to pay the full twenty million. I'd be a fool to sell something that's so special to both Calgary and myself for a cent less.'

'It belongs to my dying grandmother,' Sophia reminded him, trying to plead with her eyes. 'It's her last wish to see those pearls again.'

'With all due respect, Miss Beaumont Brown, those pearls actually belonged to my dead brother,' Joshua reminded her.

'So, if you want to play a game of dead relative Top Trumps, I guess I win. Again!'

'Josh,' said Dominic firmly. 'Let's cut the bullshit. There is no Arab prince. Don't try to play us like you do the rest of Manhattan. The only person who's going to pay you over the odds for Tilly Beaumont's necklace is Sophia. She's got 1.6 million. Have a fucking heart, man. You can buy Calgary a dozen new necklaces for that. What the hell do those pearls mean to you guys?'

'A lot more than you could even begin to imagine, actually, Dominic,' sniffed Calgary.

That's when she stood up. She unravelled her body slowly. A huge diamond rock sparkled on her engagement finger but that wasn't what Sophia noticed. What made Sophia catch her breath was the small, but perfectly formed, baby bump in Calgary's tight, black silk jersey dress. Dominic had told her that Calgary hadn't wanted children. He'd said that it was the major reason for their break-up. And yet here was Calgary, just a few months later, clearly pregnant.

This time Dominic couldn't hide his reaction. He was standing with his jaw hanging open in shock and confusion. He couldn't take his eyes off his ex-wife's stomach.

'You're pregnant,' he said, stating the obvious. 'But you hate children?'

'Life moves on, Dominic,' said Calgary, eyes shining with obvious excitement at her secret being out. 'Get over it.'

She smiled at Sophia sympathetically as if to say, 'I'm sorry, your boyfriend is still hung up on me.' But Sophia didn't need Calgary to put that thought into her head. She'd seen his shock and she'd had to look away. It felt weird enough being with him in the same room as his (undeniably beautiful) ex-wife, let alone witnessing his reaction to her surprise pregnancy.

For a moment, the room was eerily silent. All Sophia could hear was the sound of the clock ticking on the mantelpiece and her heart pounding in her ears. And then, finally, Dominic broke the spell. He shut his mouth, shook his head as if to clear an annoying memory, removed his gaze from Calgary's bump and, still shaking his head a little, he laughed. Sophia watched him, warily. What was so funny? But then he raised his eyebrows at her and gave her a crooked grin and she got it. Dominic thought Calgary was a total nightmare. He wasn't jealous. He was relieved. He had laughed in pure relief to be free of her. It didn't take long for Dominic to regain his composure.

'Congratulations, Calgary,' he said flatly. 'Joshua. You must be very excited.'

'Aren't you cross though, Dominic?' asked Calgary, clearly disappointed by his lack of emotion.

'No,' replied Dom, calmly, honestly.

'Don't you hate me?' she almost pleaded, desperate for a reaction.

At this, Josh muttered, 'Jeez, Calgary!' and let go of her waist.

'Calgary,' said Dom, patiently, 'what the hell does it have to do with me?'

Calgary's mouth formed a perfect 'Oh', but she said nothing. Sophia remembered something her grandmother had once told her: the opposite of love is not hate, it's indifference. The realisation made her heart soar. Dominic smiled at her reassuringly. A quiet calm seemed to have descended on him. Sophia knew she'd just witnessed the moment when Dominic McGuire realised he hadn't lost anything at all – he'd actually had a lucky escape. She felt a huge wave of relief, not only for herself but for Dom too. Calgary had also noticed the shift. Sophia saw the hint of a frown cross her Botoxed forehead, and the corners of her rosebud lips appeared to be turning down involuntarily. It must be hard for a control-freak like Calgary to discover she'd finally lost control of her ex.

'Right, back to business,' Dom continued levelly. 'We are offering 1.6 million dollars for the necklace. We can have the money in your bank account by tomorrow afternoon but Sophia needs the pearls now. Her flight leaves later today and her grandmother doesn't have much time left. Do we have a deal?'

Joshua Berman laughed.

'McGuire, old boy, there is not a snowball's chance in hell that we're selling that necklace for less than twenty million dollars,' he said, still laughing a little. 'I think you'd better leave now. Calgary needs to rest.'

Dominic didn't even flinch this time at the mention of the pregnancy. A steeliness hardened in his eyes.

'So lend them to Sophia,' he continued. 'Just for a couple of weeks. I'll fly over myself and get them back for you. It'll give me an excuse to spend more time with her.'

He smiled at her warmly before continuing, 'Just let the poor old lady have her dying wish, huh? What harm would it do you?'

'We may never see them again,' sniffed Calgary, who seemed suddenly petulant, and any façade of politeness had disappeared. Her pretty little nose had definitely been put out of joint by Dominic's indifference. 'I don't know anything about this woman.' She flicked her finger in Sophia's direction dismissively. 'Except that she has a rather colourful past and her own parents have disowned her.'

Oh great, thought Sophia, Calgary has googled the British tabloids. With one last, desperate breath, she interrupted.

'If you know all that, then you also know I don't have twenty million dollars,' she managed to say. 'Please can I borrow the necklace? My grandmother just wants to touch it before she dies. She doesn't even have to know it's only on loan ...'

'Perhaps we could hire it out to you,' Josh suggested suddenly.

For a moment Sophia's heart leapt. Yes, that could work. She could give them a deposit.

'I think two and a half million would be enough to cover the rent of such a valuable piece for a two-week period, don't you?'

Sophia's shoulders slumped and her fingertips let go of the tail end of hope.

'You know we don't have that much to buy the necklace, let alone rent it for a fortnight,' she told Josh, no longer trying to hide the contempt for his greed from her voice.

She turned to Calgary and tried with all her might to appeal to the other woman.

'I am begging you, from one woman to another, please sell me back my family's pearls. Or lend them to me for a few thousand, Calgary.'

Calgary held Sophia's gaze for a moment. Her eyes were icy blue and completely unreadable. And then she shook her silky blonde head.

'Go on, Calgary, have a heart,' Dominic said, but his voice sounded defeated. He, of all people, knew how deeply Calgary hid her heart.

'No deal,' she said, brightly. 'It seems our little business meeting is over, Sophia. It was a pleasure to meet you though. Do have a pleasant trip back to England.'

'But ...?' Sophia couldn't believe that was it. Surely there was some negotiation, some chance of a deal?

'You heard my fiancée,' said Joshua. 'There's no deal to be had here. I apologise if you've had a wasted trip. I wish you a very Merry Christmas, Miss Beaumont Brown. You too, Dominic.'

'It's Lady Beaumont Brown to you, actually,' said Dominic.

Joshua ushered them towards the door. Dominic couldn't escape fast enough but Sophia's legs felt like lead. With every step further away from her grandmother's pearls, her heart broke a little more. She had failed. Again.

The pearls had somehow just slipped out of her grasp. How did she go home to Granny without the necklace? She'd swum against the tide with all her might, but now she was drowning and there was no one to save her. She was too numb to even cry. It was over. And then she felt Dominic's arm around her shoulders as he pulled her into his woollen coat and swallowed her up in his big arms.

'It's going to be OK, baby,' he whispered into her ear. 'Your grandmother will understand. The biggest joy you'll have given her is the fact that you tried. She'll be so proud of you, Sophia.'

Finally, the tears came, thick and fast. She knew she had to go home and break the news to Granny. She knew that within weeks, or perhaps even days, she would have to say goodbye to her beloved grandmother for good and before that, in just a few minutes' time, she would have to say goodbye to this wonderful man, whose arms she felt so safe in. And she didn't even know if she would ever see him again. Was it just a holiday romance? She couldn't find the words to ask him.

They went back down to the foyer of the grand building, with Dom practically carrying Sophia. He collected her suitcase from reception, and wheeled it out of the heavy front door. They stood on the pavement outside, neither of them knowing what to say.

'So, I guess this is it,' Sophia said, trying to fight back tears.

'Sophia, you do know this hasn't just been some little affair for me,' Dominic told her. 'You've restored my faith. If there's any way I can see you again, I want to. You do know that, don't you? I really want to.'

'But how?' she almost pleaded with him. 'You live here. I live in London. It's hopeless.'

'I don't know,' he said, pulling her into his body. 'But it's not hopeless. There are flights ...' he added, trying to sound bright, but his voice gave him away.

'I'm not sure Damon will pay for me to fly out here every couple of weeks to see you, I'm afraid,' she said, forcing herself to smile up at him through her tears. 'He's nice, but no one is *that* nice!'

'Then let's try to stay in touch and see what happens, huh?' he suggested.

His words sounded empty suddenly. 'Try to stay in touch.' It wasn't exactly a declaration of undying love, was it? But then they had only known each other for three days. Why would she expect anything more?

'I have to go now,' she said.

She was just about to step away when Dominic grabbed her to him. He kissed her with such passion and certainty that her stomach flipped. When he finally pulled away he said firmly, 'This isn't it, Sophia. I promise. OK?'

'OK,' she managed to whisper. 'Bye, Dom.'

She lifted up her hand and a yellow taxi pulled straight in to the kerb beside her. She got in without looking back. She couldn't do it. She bit her lip hard as the cab pulled away and waited until they had travelled out of sight before she let herself go.

Sophia fished her phone out of her bag. She needed to hear Dominic's voice one more time before she left. But when she pressed the call button the screen went blank. Of all the times to forget to charge her phone. She had no way of contacting him now until she got back to London and recharged the stupid thing. Sophia buried her head in her hands in despair as the taxi sped through New York.

Chapter Forty-Four

'I can see Dominic,' said Calgary, resting her forehead against the cold window pane. 'The Brit chick just left. He doesn't look too happy.'

'Stop watching him,' said Josh, sounding slightly irritated. 'What's your obsession with what your loser ex is doing, anyway?'

'Do you think he's completely heartbroken that I'm pregnant?' she wondered.

'He didn't seem too upset,' sniffed Josh. 'I mean, I'm sure he's pretty pissed about you lying – you've spent the last few years telling him you were never having kids! But I don't think that's why he's heartbroken. He's heartbroken because that beautiful English girl just got in a cab and left him.'

'Really?' asked Calgary, turning to face her fiancé. 'Do you think he likes her? Do you think he's moved on already? Or is she his rebound woman?'

'Honey, you left him six months ago. And your marriage sucked. I'm sure he was upset at first but he's obviously over it now and yes, I do think he likes her. What's not to like? She seems sweet and she's gorgeous.'

Calgary pouted and frowned, from Joshua to Dominic on the street below and back to Joshua again.

'More gorgeous than me?' she asked.

'No, honey, of course not,' sighed Joshua a little impatiently. 'No one is as gorgeous as you.'

'I feel a bit bad now,' mused Calgary, stroking her bump again. 'I mean, we've got it all, right? We've got the baby coming, we've got each other, and we've got the pearls.'

'We're winners in the game of life, baby,' replied Josh matter-of-factly. 'It's just the way it works.'

'But Dom's got nothing,' she said. 'Look at him. He's probably in bits down there. Why is he hanging around? Oh, he's on the phone, that's all ...'

'Probably trying to call Sophia and make her come back,' added Joshua. 'I would if I was him.'

'He looks excited about something now. He's smiling. What's going on?'

'Maybe the girl agreed to come back,' said Josh, sounding bored by the conversation now.

'Oh, he's going,' Calgary continued, feeling almost disappointed. 'He just got in a cab.'

'Let the poor guy get on with his life,' sighed Josh.

'Yeah, you're right. He's not so bad, is he?' she mused, finally walking away from the window. 'He didn't ask for any of this.'

'I suppose not,' replied Josh. 'He was just in the wrong place at the wrong time. You needed a boyfriend, his dog chose the wrong bench in Central Park, that's all.'

'Maybe I owe him something,' mused Calgary.

'What is this, honey?' teased Josh. 'A fit of conscience? I didn't realise you had one! What do you owe him? An apology? An explanation?'

Calgary shrugged, fingering the pearl necklace.

'I don't know. I just feel bad the way it all turned out, that's all.'

Manhattan, New York, 2001

Calgary was twenty-one years old when she arrived in Manhattan from upstate New York, full of dreams and ambition. Her first position, as an intern on a glossy magazine, was everything she'd ever wanted. She was overworked and not just underpaid, but completely unpaid, and she could barely afford the shared apartment she rented in the Meatpacking District (even though it was smaller than her closet back home!) but Calgary was happier than she'd ever been in her life. Her parents had offered her the use of their Upper East Side apartment during her internship. Daddy only used it when he was in town for business and he was close to retiring now so he was there less and less. They said she could stay there rent free but Calgary was determined to stand on her own two feet. No one was going to tell her what time she had to get in at night.

She quickly proved herself to be talented and dogged in her job and was soon promoted to junior fashion assistant with a tiny salary. She was hardly running the show but it was a baby step in the right direction. Her life became increasingly glamorous and exciting and she began to meet the type of wealthy, beautiful, important people that she was determined to befriend and use to accelerate her career path. One man in particular blew her mind. He was twelve years her senior and as handsome as hell. He wore bespoke suits and Italian shoes and he could get the best table at the best restaurant in New York without a reservation. Joshua Berman was everything Calgary Woods desired. Better still, he was her boss, and he owned the whole glossy shebang.

Calgary was a good-looking girl – she'd been voted 'Most Likely To Marry Brad Pitt' at high school and she'd never had any trouble turning heads. It didn't take much hair-flicking for her to catch Joshua's eye. He was clearly as taken with the young fashion assistant as she was with him and soon he started taking her out for 'business' lunches – and even to conferences outside New York. The other girls at the magazine made no secret of their disapproval of Calgary's special friendship with the boss but she didn't give a damn what they thought. She didn't need female friends. She had her own game plan and nobody was going to get in her way. There was just one little catch: Joshua was married with two young children. It was blatantly obvious that the married man was falling for her. He flirted like a teenager and his text messages were getting increasingly saucy; although he hadn't actually made a move yet. But Calgary remained resolute. She'd always enjoyed a challenge and, as yet, she'd never failed at getting whatever it was she wanted.

On 9 September 2001, at 8.46 a.m., a plane flew into the North Tower of the World Trade Centre. Seventeen minutes later, a second plane crashed into the South Tower, where Joshua's older brother, Jack, was having a business meeting. His body was never found. Josh fell to pieces after his beloved brother died and guess who was there to offer a shoulder to cry on? Calgary threw herself into the role of saviour. It was easy to seduce a grieving man into bed and have him believe she was his salvation in an otherwise hellish world. After that, their bond was unbreakable. One day they would be together but until then the lovers needed a plan.

Joshua promised that he would leave his wife and be with Calgary but he explained he couldn't do it until the children were teenagers. His wife had signed a pre-nup, she wouldn't get a cent if he stayed for another ten years, but if he left her before that, she'd get the house, the cars, the holiday homes and half of the business. Calgary was a sensible girl and she understood that ten years of waiting would be worth the return. She saw it as an investment for the future. To prove he meant it, and as a symbol of his promise, he presented Calgary with the pearl necklace that his brother had left him in his will. Calgary wore the necklace whenever she could – she wore it with jeans, she wore it with cocktail dresses, she wore it with sneakers in the park – and every time she looked at that necklace, or fingered the perfect, smooth pearls, she reminded herself of what would be hers one day. Nothing and nobody would ever part Calgary from those pearls.

Calgary had a steely determination and with that came patience. She could wait for as long as it took, as long as she won in the end. Calgary's few female friends told her she was crazy to wait for Joshua but she knew they were wrong. Through most of her twenties she remained 'single', rebuffing male attention and turning down dates. She became known as the Ice Maiden, a tag she rather enjoyed, but no man could, or ever would, come close to her Josh. Being a mistress meant that Calgary had a lot of time to put into her career and by the time she was twenty-seven she was the best-known fashion editor in New York. The fact that she was screwing the boss helped but no one could say she wasn't good at what she did.

Manhattan is a surprisingly small place though, and rumours had started to spread like wildfires through certain media circles that Calgary Woods and Joshua Berman were more than 'just good friends'. Joshua's wife had started to ask awkward questions and he'd caught her snooping through his jacket pockets and his private diary a couple of times. He was a smart man and he took no chances but, still, they had to quash these rumours fast. Josh told Calgary that they needed to protect what they had and to do that, they had to create a smokescreen. What Calgary had to do was find herself a boyfriend and then get married – quickly!

That's where poor Dominic McGuire came in. Calgary thought Dom was OK. He was handsome in a rugged kind of way and he was clever too. His career was pretty cool and he was well respected by his friends and peers. He looked pretty good hanging off her arm and he was easygoing enough that she could just about bear to spend time with him. Within weeks of meeting him, Calgary could see that Dominic was the perfect façade. Besides, he adored her and the worse she treated him, the more he tried to make her happy. Sometimes she hated him for being so pathetic, other times, when she missed Josh, she liked the fact that she could find comfort in Dominic's strong arms. Sex was always a problem. She and Josh had discussed it, and just as he had to with his wife, from time to time, Calgary would have to endure Dom's advances to carry on the charade. When he touched her she flinched. Her body did not belong to him and it tore her apart to have to give it to him, even on loan.

On her wedding day, Calgary wore Joshua's pearls as a mark of defiance. Yes, she was marrying another man, but in her heart, and with every fibre of her being, she belonged to Josh. When she cried at the altar that day, her tears were not ones of joy. But marriage to Dom turned out to be no big deal. He was away a lot with work and so was she – except that when she travelled for business, Joshua came too! They muddled along for a few years and, other than his annoying dog and his irritating family and friends, life was almost palatable. There was no way Calgary would or could ever have children with Dominic though, and every time the subject loomed its ugly head she had to give him the silent treatment or instigate a fight.

Finally, the day approached when Josh could leave his wife. The divorce papers were ready and waiting for her on the day he told her they were through. And it didn't come a moment too soon for Calgary. Dominic had started laying it on thick about starting a family, and it was driving Calgary crazy. When, at last, she was able to tell him it was over, leave her wretched wedding band behind, and walk free from that restaurant, it was as if she was starting her life over. She caught a cab straight into Joshua's arms and she'd barely left them since. They were to be married next month and by the summer they would have a baby. If it was a girl, the couple had already decided that she would be called Patience.

Upper East Side, New York, 2012

Dominic's head was reeling as he tried to make sense of what he'd just heard. He leaned forward in the taxi, watching the road, willing the driver to make the short journey as quickly as possible. The address was only a few blocks away from Josh's place, but it was taking for ever. Dom considered calling Sophia, to tell her to turn round and come back right now, because everything had changed but, no, he mustn't. He had to keep his head right now. Common sense had to prevail. The woman sounded genuine. She sounded as if she was exactly who she said she was. But this was New York, a city full of crooks, cranks and extortionists. He had no proof that any of this was for real and until he did there was no point in raising Sophia's hopes. Finally the cab pulled up beside a grand, park-side apartment on the corner of Fifth Avenue and East 91st Street.

He recognised Aiko Watanabe as soon as she answered the door and the knot of anxiety in his stomach immediately dissolved into a warm, comforting glow. Perhaps the miracle they'd all been waiting for had happened. Mrs Watanabe was remarkably youthful, elegant and poised for a lady of her age. It was clear that she had been a great beauty in her time. When she smiled at him, and said a warm hello, Dominic saw a flash of fire in her amber eyes. Hell, she was a great beauty still, he decided, shaking her hand warmly and allowing her to usher him into her home.

He took the green tea she offered him, even though he hated the stuff (it reminded him of Calgary on a detox), and he listened intently to the story Aiko told him about her family. The pearls her mother and grandmother had collected from the bottom of the ocean had eventually been turned into Tilly Beaumont's eighteenth birthday present. Not that Aiko had known the connection to the actress until a few days earlier. All she had ever heard after she'd sold the pearls was a rumour about a US naval officer who had smuggled them out of Japan and sold them in

Singapore to an English gem dealer of dubious reputation, who had, finally, taken them back to London and sold them to a legitimate jeweller.

The money Aiko had received from the sale of the pearls had allowed her to move to the USA, where she had married her wartime sweetheart. Together the couple had built up a multinational computer company with Bo's technical expertise, Aiko's innate business sense and the funds from the pearls. The rest, as anyone who has ever read the *Wall Street Journal* will tell you, is history. But Aiko had never forgotten her legacy. She explained to Dom that the ghosts of her ancestors had been haunting her recently and that when she'd seen Tilly's necklace on television she had known what she needed to do.

She had had to email a man in London called Hugo in order to get Sophia's phone number but when she'd tried it, the girl's phone went straight to voicemail. Thankfully, Hugo had also forwarded Dominic's contact details to Aiko and so she'd tried him instead. Her timing couldn't have been better. If they hurried there might just be enough time to sort this whole business out before Sophia's flight left for London.

'And you're absolutely sure about this, Mrs Watanabe?' asked Dom, a little nervously. 'It's a lot of money.'

'Quite sure,' said Aiko, lightly, as if she was transferring a mere few dollars out of her bank account. She couldn't have been less ruffled if she'd been paying a ten-dollar grocery bill. 'I need to get my pearls back. I had not realised it was what I needed but now I do. It's the way things are supposed to be.'

She pressed a button on her laptop and then sat back and smiled at Dominic serenely.

'It is done,' she said, almost casually. 'Now you must go and get that necklace before it is too late. There is no hurry to get the pearls back to me. Have them for as long as you need. I have waited over sixty years to see them again. A few more weeks will not change anything now. Not for me, at least.'

She shrugged and smiled warmly.

'Don't you need some sort of deposit from me, or a legal document saying I have your necklace in my care?' asked Dominic, a little anxiously. This was a necklace worth twenty million dollars. How could Mrs Watanabe trust him, a virtual stranger, not to do a moonlight flit with it? It didn't make any sense.

'Dominic,' said the elderly lady, leaning forward and patting his knee. 'I have lived on my instincts for eighty years. They have always served me well. My instinct is to trust you and your Lady Beaumont Brown.'

'She's not my Lady Beaumont Brown,' Dom said sheepishly.

'Ah, but you would like her to be,' grinned Aiko, looking suddenly mischievous and very young. 'Every time you mention her name your eyes light up. 'Go now. Go get your pearls and then go get your girl!'

'Is there really an Arab prince who wants to buy my necklace?' asked Calgary.

Josh was trying to relax. He was reading the Sunday papers and drinking an espresso with his 'do not disturb' look on his face, but Calgary couldn't relax. She felt restless, unsettled, uneasy.

'Of course there's an Arab,' he muttered, sounding irritated. 'But he only offered fifteen.'

'Oh,' said Calgary, confused. 'I thought it was a bluff.'

'Nope,' said Josh, folding the paper loudly in protest at being disturbed.

Calgary stalked the room from the sofa to window.

'But we're not going to sell them, right?' she continued. 'I mean you said earlier there's no way I have to get rid of my pearls.'

Josh shrugged. 'If he ups his offer maybe we should. Once the old girl dies, they'll go up in value even more. We don't need them now, do we? I've bought you so many beautiful things, Calgary.'

'I know, but I wanted to wear them on our wedding day,' said Calgary.

She could hear the desperation in her voice and knew immediately that Josh would think she was whining.

'You've already worn them to one wedding, honey, and look how that marriage turned out. Maybe that necklace is a bad omen. I'm thinking maybe we wait for Tilly Beaumont to pass away and then we cash in.'

'I don't want to ...' said Calgary, feeling scared suddenly but not knowing why.

She leant her head against the window pane and stared out

at the street below. A taxi was pulling in and a familiar figure was getting out.

'Dominic's back!' she said, in surprise.

'Christ, don't sound so excited about it!' snapped Josh, throwing his paper onto the coffee table and standing up. 'What the hell does he want now? Doesn't that man take no for an answer?'

When the buzzer rang, Josh was waiting.

'What do you want, McGuire?' he barked. 'I told you, we're done. There's no deal to be had here.'

Calgary felt deflated. For some reason she couldn't put her finger on, she wanted Dominic to come back up into their apartment.

'Oh,' she heard Josh say. 'Right. Well, I guess that changes everything. Come on up, Dominic.'

'What?' asked Calgary excitedly. 'Why are you letting him in?'

'It's man's business, babe,' he replied dismissively. 'You're acting really jumpy and crazy today. I think you should leave this to me and Dominic. Wait in the bedroom. Have a lie down.'

'But I don't want to—' Calgary started.

'I said, wait in the bedroom,' roared Josh.

Calgary jumped. Josh very rarely shouted at her but when he did she knew not to argue. She swallowed her pride and headed for the bedroom.

'And Calgary,' added Josh, almost as an afterthought. 'Take the necklace off and leave it on the table there. You won't be needing it any more.'

With shaking hands, Calgary undid the clasp on her beloved necklace. Tears streamed down her cheeks as she placed the perfect pearls on the polished glass table top.

'You said they were priceless,' she reminded him, in a whisper.

'Everything has a price, baby,' Josh reminded her. 'I'd sell pretty much anything for twenty million. Surely you know me well enough to have figured that out by now.'

Calgary walked unsteadily towards the door. Twenty million dollars? How had Dominic managed to get his hands on that amount of money on a sleepy Sunday morning in Manhattan? And what did Josh mean he'd 'sell pretty much anything' for that price? She wondered, suddenly, what price she had on her own head. How much did Josh really value her? She lay down on her super-king bed and pulled the silk sheets over her body. Her hands stroked her rounded stomach and she closed her eyes. It was then she felt the first kick. And then another, and another. An unfamiliar sense of peace washed over her suddenly. Calgary no longer felt jittery or scared. Suddenly it all made sense.

Chapter Forty-Five

Dominic tripped out of the cab and ran into the departures lounge, straining to see if he could catch sight of Sophia. She'd left the Upper East Side almost two hours before he had but her flight wouldn't be leaving for a while yet. He hoped she'd taken her time, got herself a coffee maybe, anything but gone straight through to the gate. The airport was mobbed with people trying to catch flights to get away for their Christmas vacation. But Dom had something much more important than the holiday season on his mind. He scanned the departures board. Where was she flying to? London, but which airport had she said? In his panic he couldn't remember. There was a flight leaving for Heathrow in five minutes but that was too soon. It had to be the later Gatwick flight. Gate fifteen.

He barged past hordes of travellers, tripping over suitcases and small children as he went, shouting, 'Sorry! Sorry!' to everybody he banged into, getting lost, turning round, running in the opposite direction.

'I'm sorry, sir,' said the huge hulk of security guard on the desk. 'If you don't have a ticket to travel I have to ask you to step back.'

He was too late. Sophia's flight didn't leave for another hour, she was somewhere on the other side of this security desk, but he had no way of getting to her. He tried phoning again but it went straight to voicemail – again. He'd attempted countless calls to her since he'd left Aiko's apartment. Why had she turned her phone off already? This was infuriating.

'Hi, you've reached Sophia. I can't come to the phone right now but if you'd like to leave a message I'll get back to you as a soon as I can,' her voice purred again.

'Sophia, please, call me back,' he pleaded down the line. 'I'm in the airport. I've got a present for you!'

He queued for half an hour at the help desk, only to be told that no, they would not page his friend. Not unless she was a missing minor or a security threat.

'Think, Dominic,' he told himself sternly as he paced the aiport looking for a solution. 'Think.'

But however hard he thought, there was only ever one answer. He got in the long queue for ticket sales and waited impatiently as the line crawled slowly towards the sales desk. He kept trying to call Sophia but the hands on the clock on the wall told him that her flight had taken off by now. Then he called Dave and asked him to collect Blondie from the apartment and take her bck to Brooklyn. Finally, he got to the front of the queue.

'I want to buy a seat on the next available flight to London,' he told the girl at the ticket desk.

She looked at him as if he was mad.

'It's the twenty-third of December, sir,' she reminded him, as if he didn't know. He'd just waited two hours in a queue to buy tickets. 'There are no available seats to London until ... Let me see ... January the eighth,' she told him with a robotic smile.

'January the eighth!' he almost shouted back. 'That can't be right. What about if I change somewhere? Anywhere! It doesn't have to be a direct flight. Give me whatever you've got, any route, as long as it gets me there for Christmas Day.'

The woman's face softened. She smiled more genuinely this time.

'Are you trying to get to a loved one?' she asked.

'Yes!' he replied definitely. 'I need to get to my girl in time for Christmas. I have a very important present for her.'

'Well, let me see what we can do for you, sir. Let's see if we can get you there via Paris ... No ... Or Munich ... No ... Or Madrid ... No ... Or ...'

She stared at her computer for a few minutes longer. Dom watched her hopefully but finally she said, 'I'm very sorry, sir, but there are no indirect flights to London either. It's Chr—'

'I know, I know, it's Christmas,' he replied impatiently. 'I get it! Are there any flights, any time in the next twenty-four hours that will get me anywhere near London? Anywhere in the UK will do.'

'OK, let me have a look, sir ...' said the woman, going back to her screen. 'I have one cancellation on the Glasgow red-eye flight leaving tonight,' she said with a grin.

'Glasgow?' Dominic repeated, trying to picture a map of Great Britain. 'That's Scotland, right?'

'Correct, sir,' she replied.

'And how far is that from London?' he asked.

'Approximately four hundred miles,' she replied.

Dominic thought about it for a moment. Four hundred miles wasn't so far, right?

'Are there any connecting flights from Glasgow to London?' he asked, hopefully.

'No, sir, you would have to make your own way to London from there,' she replied. 'But it's not so far,' she added brightly. 'What's four hundred miles if you've already travelled across the Atlantic? And if you need to get that present to your girl ...'

She was either a very good salesperson or a huge romantic. Right at that moment, Dominic didn't really mind which it was. He was sold.

'Done,' he said. 'I'll take that flight to Glasgow. How much do I owe you?'

He threw his credit card onto the desk.

'That will be $6,328 dollars, sir. One way,' she replied. 'It is Christmas, after all.'

Gatwick Airport, West Sussex, 2012

Sophia rushed through customs and elbowed her way to the nearest payphone. She fed the payphone with as many loose coins as she could find. She'd been out of contact with the world for nearly an entire day and she had to speak to Hugo.

'Hugo, my phone's been dead since yesterday lunchtime so I didn't get my messages. I don't understand what you're saying. New York was a waste of time: I think I might have fallen in love with Dominic McGuire. And his ex won't give back the pearls, and now you tell me Granny is unconscious, and that my dad's kicking off. What's going on? Tell me what's happening.'

'I'm trying,' said Hugo. 'But you need to let me get a word in edgeways. Look, your dad called me last night in a terrible state, shouting and bawling, demanding to talk to you.'

'What?' demanded Sophia. 'My dad called you? But he hates you almost as much as he hates me!'

She heard Hugo take a deep breath on the other end of the line.

'He says your mum has thrown him out ... And it's all your fault.'

'That's ridiculous!' screeched Sophia, struggling to make sense of what Hugo was telling her. 'Mum would never have the balls to throw Dad out. Those two would never split up. What would the neighbours say? It was probably just a stupid row and Dad's taking it out on me. But why phone you? I don't understand.'

'I'm not sure,' said Hugo. ''He sounded really weird. And very, very drunk. I think he was telling the truth though, Sophes. He said your mum's changed the locks.'

Sophia's head felt like it might explode. This was madness! She couldn't even begin to comprehend the idea that her parents might have split up. But there were more important events unfolding. She didn't have time to think about her parents now.

'And Granny? How bad is it, Hugo?' she asked, her voice breaking now.

'I don't know, but she's hanging on in there,' he told her gently. 'I just spoke to the hospital. She had a comfortable night. Look, get yourself in a cab as quickly as possible and come home. Please. There's something I have to show you.'

'What?' asked Sophia, suddenly feeling very nervous.

There was a strange tone in Hugo's voice. He sounded scared, haunted.

'I can't show you it over the phone, can I?' he said quietly. 'Look, Sophia, just get yourself back here.'

'OK,' she whispered. 'I'm on my way.'

A wave of exhaustion washed over her as she hung up. She felt as if she was standing on a stormy beach and huge waves were crashing on her, and soon she wouldn't have the strength left to keep standing. One more piece of bad news and she would drown. She seemed glued to the spot as hundreds of people rushed past her in the arrivals hall. Everyone seemed to be smiling, as they juggled luggage with Christmas presents and excited children in their best winter clothes. Couples kissed, grown-up children embraced their parents, little kids threw themselves into their grandparents' arms. She stood there for ages, staring at life unfolding before her. Granny was lying unconscious in a hospital bed, her mum was alone, her dad was God knows where and Dominic was thousands of miles away. Nobody in her life was where they were supposed to be. Mustering the last of her strength, she dragged her suitcase slowly towards the taxi rank.

When she finally arrived back at her grandmother's house, Hugo was waiting for her at the window. He rushed out to greet her and hugged her so hard that she could barely breathe.

'What's up, Hugo?' she asked, handing him her suitcase. 'I know that look. You've done something you shouldn't have done, haven't you?'

'I've been snooping,' he admitted.

He took her into her grandfather's office and handed her a small, yellowing newspaper cutting.

'I found it in your grandpa's desk,' he said, sheepishly. 'I was being nosy, I'm sorry. I just thought I'd have a look to see what there was ...'

'What is it?' she asked, taking the scrap of newspaper.

'It's only short,' he said. 'And there's another one – a retraction a few days later.'

'I don't understand,' said Sophia.

'Read it,' urged Hugo.

Heiress in runaway mystery: Lady Alice Beaumont Perry, daughter of actors Tilly Beaumont and Frank Perry Junior, is reported to be missing in Italy. The teenager is suspected to have run away with a young Italian man ... Parents are beside themselves ... Italian police are searching Rome and the surrounding areas ... Anyone with any information ...

'What?' said Sophia, smiling for the first time that day. 'This is hilarious. My mum ran away in Italy and it made the national press?'

'Well, allegedly,' said Hugo, shrugging. 'I've gone through everything about her on the Internet and this is the only mention of her running away anywhere. One newspaper cutting. And then the retraction.'

'Shame. I kind of like the idea of my mum doing something

wild. It means she can stop being such a hypocrite and lecturing me about my "dubious lifestyle choices",' said Sophia, scratching her head and tutting. 'I suppose it has to be a mistake.'

Hugo shook his head. 'I don't think so. Why would your grandpa keep the cutting? And anyway, there's more. There's a letter here from the Italian police, dated three months later. I can just about follow what it says. It's talking about the successful operation, and saying they hope Alice is recovering well from her ordeal, and that the culprit has been dealt with.'

'The culprit?' asked Sophia, incredulously. 'But the newspaper article makes it sound as if she ran off with some bloke of her own free will. Oh God, it sounds like my mum got some poor Italian boy arrested! Just for having a fling with her! And she walks around like butter wouldn't melt ...'

She shook her head. 'This is all totally ridiculous. I can't even begin to get my head around what my mum got up to thirty-odd years ago. To be honest, it's the least of my worries. All I want is a short sleep followed by a long bath and then to go and visit Granny.'

'Um ...' Hugo jiggled from one leg to the other. 'There is just one more thing.'

'What?' she demanded. 'What can be so important that it can't wait for a couple of hours?'

'Sophia. I don't think your dad is actually your dad,' he blurted out. 'There. I've said it. Damon said it was best just to get it out.'

Sophia grappled for something to say but she could not find any words.

'What the hell are you talking about, Hugo?' she demanded, when her voice finally returned. 'Of course my dad's my dad. I mean he's a crap dad but he's definitely mine.'

Hugo shook his head. 'You were born in May 1982,' he told her as if she didn't know.

'Yes,' she said impatiently. 'I am aware of that.'

'And your parents didn't get married until December 1981,' he continued.

'I know,' she said. 'Mum was a tiny bit pregnant with me when they got married. I've always thought that was another reason that Dad treated me like spoilt goods. As if I had any choice in the matter.'

'But, Sophia,' said Hugo. 'You were conceived in August 1981. And your mum was in Italy in August 1981. Look at the letter from the Italian police. She wasn't found until the beginning of September.'

'Hugo, this is madness,' Sophia replied. Hugo had taken his Beaumont family obsession too far this time and worse, he had got it wrong. 'I was two months early. They didn't know if I was going to make it when I was born. My parents have told me that. I guessed that was part of the reason Mum and I never seemed to have bonded. There is no scandal,' she told him flatly, without even trying to keep the irritation out of her voice. She did not need any more drama. Couldn't he see that?

'No, you weren't premature,' said Hugo, shaking his head and handing her another document.

'What do you mean?' she almost begged. 'What is this?'

'It's your birth records. It says you were born by caesarean section at thirty-nine weeks and that you weighed eight pounds three ounces,' he told her.

Sophia stared at the document uncomprehendingly. How had Hugo managed to uncover all this so quickly when she'd been in the dark her entire life?

'But if you're right about Italy ...' whispered Sophia.

'It's all been a lie,' nodded Hugo, with a furrowed brow.

Sophia's heart froze. For a moment, she felt nothing. How could she grieve for the loss of Philip as a biological father? He'd been a terrible father. But the shock, the shock was paralysing. She could barely breathe. When she thought of the years she'd spent trying to please him, desperately grappling for even a hint of love from the man she called Dad, it was almost too much to compute. She thought of the little girl in the ballet dress, frantically pirouetting in front of her indifferent father. How could he have done that to her? How could her mother have stood back and watched when all the time she knew the truth? It explained so much, of course – the coldness she'd felt from him, the lack of love. But it also raised so many questions. She didn't even know who she was any more. Sophia felt like a mirror that had been smashed.

Finally she said, 'If Philip's not my father, then who is? I need to go to see my mum.'

'I know,' said Hugo, gently. 'I thought you would want to do that. Damon's waiting outside in the van. He's going to drive us to Virginia Water.'

Sophia paused for a moment. 'But what about Granny? Shouldn't I see her first? In case it's too late?'

'I think your granny would want you to see your mum, don't you?' said Hugo.

Sophia nodded, numbly. Perhaps this was what Granny had wanted all along – for Sophia to know the truth. Her head ached. She knew she must look a fright. She'd been wearing the same crumpled leggings and jumper for two days, yesterday's make-up had long since slid off her face, her hair was tangled and her eyes were bloodshot and crimson with exhaustion. She was overcome with a need to be held. Hugo's hugs were always lovely but that wasn't what she needed now.

'Does Damon have a phone charger in the van?' she asked, hopefully.

Surely Dom would have called by now. She couldn't miraculously bring him here but she could hear his voice at least. She could talk to him. It would help. The thought lifted her spirits slightly.

'Yes he does,' Hugo told her, ushering her out of the door. 'My Damon is fully tooled up in every way!'

'Too much information,' Sophia told him, kicking his bum lightly with her boot.

As she clambered into the van, Damon leaned over from the driver's seat and gave Sophia a hug (also nice, but not Dom-standard by any means). He obviously knew everything and didn't know what to say. She didn't blame him. What do you say to someone who's just found out they're illegitimate and their entire life has been a sham?

'She doesn't need a cuddle, darling,' Hugo scolded, climbing over Sophia to grab the seat next to his boyfriend. 'What she needs is your phone charger. The poor love has been without mobile contact for close to twenty-four hours and is quite rightly traumatised. Plus she had a whirlwind romance in the Big Apple so she needs to check her messages pronto!'

'Message received and understood,' said Damon, taking a phone charger out of the glove compartment and plugging it into the cigarette lighter.

'Come on, come on ...!' complained Sophia, shaking her

phone. 'Why does it always take so long to start up again once it's run out of juice?'

The first message was from Hugo asking her to call him immediately. But the next was from Dom. Sophia felt her heart lurch as the soothing sound of his deep, New York drawl flooded her ears.

'Hey, Sophia, baby, it's me, Dom,' he was saying. 'I'm at the airport! Where are you? I can't get through security to find you but I have a present for you. Please call me the minute you get this message. Please, Sophia. I need to see you before you go. It's important.'

She waited for ages before the phone connected. She held her breath and waited but it did not ring. As it went straight to voicemail her heart sank.

Glasgow Airport, Scotland, 2012

'London please,' said Dominic excitedly as he jumped in the back of the taxi.

The taxi driver turned round and looked at him as if he'd just asked to be driven to Timbuktu.

'London?' asked the guy with the broad Scottish accent, incredulously. 'Are you kidding me, pal? Have you got any idea how far London is from Glasgow?'

'About four hundred miles,' replied Dominic, still cheerful.

Nothing was going to ruin his good mood now. He was on British soil. He was almost there. And he had to deliver a very precious gift in time for Christmas. He felt like one of the Three Wise Men.

'I'm no' taking you to London,' said the taxi driver, shaking his head with certainty. 'It's Christmas Eve, for crying out loud. It takes eight hours each way. I won't be back until tomorrow morning. My missus will kill me. She'll have to wrap all the bairns' presents and do their Christmas stockings hersel'.'

'Whatever it costs,' said Dominic. 'I'll double it, OK?'

The driver was quiet for a moment. Dominic could see him doing his sums, weighing up the ear-bashing he would get from his wife against the money he would earn from the trip. Silently he willed the driver to say yes. A taxi was Dominic's only chance now. The last train before Christmas had already left from Glasgow to London, the overnight bus would take far too long, and none of the car rental companies in the airport had any vehicles left. It was the holiday season, everything was booked up – as everybody kept pointing out to him so helpfully.

'All right then, sonny,' said the driver eventually. 'It's a deal. I bloody hate wrapping presents anyway! But you'll have to put up with me smoking. I'm no' driving for eight hours without a fag.'

'Suits me just fine,' replied Dominic happily. 'I'll join you.'

Chapter Forty-Six

Virginia Water, Surrey, 2012

Alice saw the van arrive in the driveway and knew that the time had finally come to tell Sophia the truth. She'd called the hospital first thing, and they'd said there was no change in her mother's condition, that she was still 'hanging on in there', but Alice knew that time was not on their side. She swallowed and tried to centre herself. She couldn't allow herself to fall apart about Mummy now. One thing at a time, that was the only way she was going to be able to deal with the next few days. First she had to concentrate on her daughter, and then she would allow herself to think about her mother.

Philip had gone. It had been worse than she'd imagined when she'd finally told him their marriage was over. When she'd heard him banging on the door, unable to make his key work in the new lock she'd had fitted while he was out, she had expected shock, anger, violence even. She'd have forgiven him a slap to her face. She probably deserved it. She could have handled that. So she'd opened the door, just a little, scared, expecting an explosion. But instead she'd got tears. The big bully who had kept her prisoner for three decades had collapsed into a heap and cried on the doorstep. Worse, he had begged and pleaded for another chance, he'd promised to change, he'd even sworn he'd give Sophia another chance, but it was far too late for all that. Alice had had no idea that he still loved her, in his own way, and it had taken her by surprise. In all the months and years she'd imagined leaving him, she had never envisaged tears. She'd wondered if she should feel something for the man she'd shared her adult life with but she couldn't: there was nothing left except an empty, hollow indifference. Now all she wanted was for him to go. So she'd closed the door again and left him weeping on the doorstep.

It had been a hugely uncomfortable few days but surely even Philip would come to see that it was for the best. He had tried to save her in the beginning, and they'd almost been friends back in the early days, but their symbiotic relationship had become mutated and corrupted by resentment and lies. She didn't entirely blame Philip for the way things had turned out. It must have been hard to bring up another man's child, particularly when he knew who that other man was and what he had meant to Alice. Philip couldn't compete. How do you battle shadows? No, he could never have made her happy. Now, finally, they were both free to start living again. Philip would understand that in time. Beneath the pain of the last few weeks, Alice could feel a tiny seed of new life growing in her heart. But first she had a story to tell. She hoped Sophia would understand that it was a love story: a story of a girl's love for a boy and of a mother's love for her child.

Rome, Italy, 1981

Rome is the most romantic city in the world! Alice wrote on the postcard to her mother.

She was sitting at a café on the Palazzo della Consulta, milking the remnants of a cappuccino and wondering how much of the truth to share. She hadn't mentioned the fact that Claudia had long since disappeared to Monaco. Instead, when she called home once a week, or wrote the odd postcard, she carefully edited out anything that might scare them – like Claudia's departure or the fact that she had to wear little more than her underwear in the nightclub where she worked. So far it was working a treat. Her mum and dad appeared to be completely at ease with how well her year out was going and had somehow got the impression that the noisy, wild nightclub she worked in was more of an upmarket gentleman's club.

I have just thrown a coin in the Trevi Fountain, she continued writing truthfully. *Which means one day I know I'll be back in Rome!*

Did that sound too much as if she was leaving already? Her

parents absolutely mustn't know that she had just given up her job and spent the last of her wages on a train ticket to Genoa. They thought she was going to stay in Rome all summer but ... well, things happen, life moves on. Not that they would understand.

I've met a very nice boy ... she started, and then stopped, chewed the end of her pen, considered the facts.

Alice was so smitten with her new boyfriend Luca that she wanted to tell the whole world about him – particularly her mum, who she knew would adore him. But would they worry? Would her parents get suspicious if they didn't get any more postcards from Rome? No, she decided. It was fine. She wasn't a baby, she was allowed a boyfriend, surely, and how would they ever know that she and Luca were not where they were supposed to be?

His name is Luca, he's a very talented chef at the famous restaurant right next door to the nightclub where I work. He's smart, well-mannered, quite shy, but funny, and he is absolutely the most dishy boy I have ever seen. You would adore him, Mummy! And don't worry, Daddy, you'd love him too. He makes a mean rigatoni con la pajata and I know veal is your absolute favourite!

Hope you're both well. Love you loads! Alice (who is in Wonderland) xxxxxxxxxxx.

There. Done. She would post it at the station. Alice ran her finger underneath her pearl choker and felt droplets of sweat trickle down her collarbone and onto her breasts. Christ, it was hot today! Hopefully it would be a little cooler by the sea in Portofino. She knew that wearing her eighteenth birthday present for sightseeing and shopping around Rome probably wasn't what her parents had intended. Nor would her mother understand her need to team real pearls with denim cut-offs and a fluorescent pink vest top, but there was no way she could leave the necklace in the hostel with the bunch of reprobates she'd met there, so she'd taken to wearing it the entire time. She even had a tan line from the choker! Her rucksack was packed and waiting by her feet. Luca finished his last shift in half an hour and then they would go.

Once they were out of Rome, no one could tell them what to do. Luca had joked that they were like a modern-day Romeo and Juliet, being kept apart by their families, but she knew deep down he didn't find his situation funny. They'd only been together for a month but already Alice knew he loved her. Why else would he be doing this? Defying his family? Leaving his job? Running away from the only city he'd ever called home? It was his quiet, simmering passion that turned her on more than anything else.

Plus, she really needed to get him away from Anita, the girl his parents wanted him to marry. She knew Luca wasn't interested in Anita. He said he had never given her any sort of encouragement, but his mother had, and that was enough! Luca said he'd never been in love with anyone before, and that it wasn't until the moment he'd met Alice that he'd even understood what love was. But with his parents constantly on his case, and Anita being his boss's daughter, the pressure on him was huge. And Anita didn't appear to be the kind of girl who took no for an answer. She had already thrown a drink in Alice's face and a few days ago her brother had looked as if he was going to mow Alice and Luca down with his Vespa. Luca's parents were no longer speaking to him and Alice was not welcome in the family home. So Luca had decided this was the only way they could be together, and Alice couldn't think of anything more romantic than running away together and disappearing into the blue.

Alice wished she could tell Mummy everything about Luca. She wanted to tell her that his eyelashes were so impossibly long that when he kissed her they tickled her cheeks. She wanted to tell her mother that when Luca talked, all she could do was stare at his perfect, full lips and long for him to kiss her. She wanted to ask her mother if that was how she'd felt when she'd first met Daddy. She wanted to ask her mother if all this meant that Luca was 'the one'. Alice sighed deeply. When Luca finally turned the corner into the square and strolled towards her with his gorgeous lopsided smile, Alice's heart melted. She would have followed him to the ends of the earth at that moment.

The last of the afternoon light was fading as the train pulled into Genoa. Alice was tired but excited and she held Luca's hand tightly as he led her through the bustling crowd towards the bus station. Although he was tall and slightly built, he carried his own rucksack and hers with ease.

'It is not so far to Portofino,' he explained. 'I have been there for a holiday when I was a child. It is very pretty. We will be happy there.'

They waited for the bus for three hours, sitting on the dusty pavement, huddled together, sharing lingering kisses and making lifelong promises. They arrived in Portofino so late that they decided to sleep in the bus station. In the morning they found a cheap hostel close to the town centre and set about building a new life for themselves there. With his skills in the kitchen, Luca easily found a job at a restaurant on the harbour. With her pretty face and outrageous curves, Alice found a job as a hostess in a cocktail bar that catered for the wealthy yachting set. Once they'd both been paid a month's wages, they put down a deposit on a tiny one-roomed apartment that, if you leaned out of the window and strained your neck, actually had a sea view. Once the rent was paid, there wasn't much left, but Luca brought home leftovers from the restaurant and Alice brought home enough tips to keep the couple in wine. After her extravagantly lavish childhood, this new lifestyle was a huge change, but she had never felt so happy in her life.

At first, she continued to phone home every week, but after a while it became tiring to keep up the lies and she found herself making excuses not to make the calls. A week passed, then another, and another, until too much time had lapsed and it became impossible to explain her silence. Alice pushed home to the back of her mind, kidded herself that her parents wouldn't be worried, and concentrated entirely on the here and now. Nothing mattered but her and Luca and their passionate, all-consuming love.

One moonlit night he took her down to the beach and laid out a picnic blanket on the sand. The beach was deserted, the sky was black and clear and dotted with stars, the ocean lapped gently to shore. Luca lit candles, opened a bottle of Prosecco and laid out delicious dishes of *bruschetta alla romana*, *fritto di fiori di zucca*, *spaghetti all'Amatriciana* and *crostata di ricotta*. He handed her a plastic cup of sparkling wine.

'Will you marry me, Alice?' he asked, his enormous brown eyes pleading with her under the moonlight. 'I do not have any money, I do not even have a ring, but I have this heart and I have my future and it is all yours, for ever. Please will you marry me, Alice?'

'Of course I will, Luca!' she exclaimed, throwing her arms around his neck, spilling Prosecco all over the blanket and kissing him hard on his perfect, exquisite mouth.

The food did not get eaten that night. Most was knocked over into the sand and strewn around the beach to be enjoyed by the gulls later. Luca and Alice ripped at each other's clothes, far more hungry for each other than they were for pasta or seafood; they lost themselves in the heaven of youthful lust and love and the knowledge that nobody and nothing could ever tear them apart now. Luca held the back of Alice's neck and pulled her face towards his. He plunged his fingers into her thick, long hair and she gasped with pleasure as his tongue plunged into her mouth and ... *snap!*

'Shit!' she shouted, pushing him away suddenly.

Her hands flew to her throat in horror.

'What is it?' asked Luca, sitting up in the moonlight, confused.

'My pearls! My necklace just snapped. Shit! Shit, Luca! They've gone everywhere. We need to find them all. They're priceless! My mum will kill me!'

Luca's tanned face turned ashen.

'I am so sorry,' he said, immediately getting on to his hands and knees and grappling around in the sand. 'I am so stupid. I will find every single one. I promise. How many? How many pearls, Alice?'

'Sixty-seven,' she told him, stroking the sand carefully, picking up the clasp and a handful of pearls. 'I have eight already. And the clasp, thank God! You?'

'Twelve,' he said, and then he paused and plucked something gently from her cleavage. 'Thirteen. I have the big one at least!'

Alice smiled with relief and then she started to laugh.

'It doesn't matter if we don't find them all,' she told him. 'We're getting married – that's all that matters!'

'No. It does matter. I will find them all,' Luca repeated solemnly. 'I have made you a promise. I will give you back all sixty-seven of your pearls.'

They stayed on the beach, combing the sand for several hours until they had found more than forty pearls. But Alice was exhausted. Her eyelids were heavy and her head hurt. Eventually Luca carried her back to their tiny apartment and laid her on the bed. She was so tired that she didn't notice him leave. In the morning, Alice was awoken by bright sunlight hitting her face. She turned towards where Luca's naked body always was, wondering why she wasn't entwined in his limbs as usual, but the bed was empty, as was the rest of the apartment, and her fiancé was nowhere to be seen. For two hours she stood at the window, watching and waiting, already knowing where he was and what he was doing. She wanted to go and help him, but somewhere deep down she knew she must let Luca do this alone. He wanted to look after her. He wanted to be her hero. And Alice had no problem with that. When he finally appeared, carrying a shoebox, and wearing his lopsided smile, the sun suddenly shone brighter for Alice. He was her everything. Without Luca, there was no sunshine, no daylight, no life.

'I have sixty-six pearls,' he told her proudly. 'Only one is missing.'

'It doesn't matter,' Alice told him, meaning it.

Would her mother even notice one, tiny, missing pearl?

'No,' replied Luca, firmly. 'I will go to that beach every day until I find the last pearl.'

'I don't care,' Alice told him, truthfully. 'I have you. That's all I need.'

The Polizia di Stato came in the middle of the night. They broke the door down and found the young lovers naked and terrified in their bed. Despite Alice's screams and shouts that she loved him, that he was her fiancé, that he had done nothing wrong, the police handcuffed Luca and dragged him out of the door. She tried to run to him but a burly *poliziotto* held her back. She struggled and fought, screamed and cried, held her hands out towards her fiancé but it was no good, they would not let her reach him.

Luca kept shouting, 'I love you, Alice! I will keep my promise!' as he was manhandled out of the apartment.

'Don't worry, Luca, my dad will sort this out!' she shouted as they hauled him out. 'I'll keep my promise too. This is just a mistake. A stupid mistake. I'll see you soon. I love you!'

But she never saw him again. The *polizia* were kind to her but it only angered her more when they insisted on treating her like a victim. She kept telling them she was no victim, that Luca was no criminal and that she had gone to Portofino of her own free will. On the long journey south, she learned that her parents had contacted the authorities in Rome and reported her missing. It had taken them over a month to find her.

Alice's parents were waiting for her in Rome. They had been worried sick by her disappearance and had even feared that she'd been kidnapped. It didn't seem to matter how many times she told them that she had gone with Luca of her own free will, they just kept telling her that she had to go home and that everything would be better once they were back in London. Nothing felt better when Alice got back to London. She refused to eat. She couldn't sleep. She begged her father to tell the police in Italy that Luca was entirely innocent.

'How can they charge him with anything when he did nothing wrong, except to fall in love?' she demanded. 'And I did that too! So if he's guilty, so am I!'

'Alice, you are not a normal girl,' her father reminded her. 'Because of who we are' – he pointed to himself and her mother – 'you are at risk. You cannot go off to Italy and disappear and not expect us to contact the police. Anything could have happened to you.'

'All that happened was that I fell in love. I was happy, Daddy! Why did you have to spoil everything?'

'Alice, darling,' her mother said gently, stroking her hair. 'Luca is not in any trouble. He hasn't been charged or arrested. We just needed him out of the way while we got you home.'

'But I was home, Mummy,' sobbed Alice. 'Don't you understand? That apartment with Luca was my home. What have you done? Why have you done this?'

'You're only eighteen, Alice,' her father reminded her sternly. 'You had a holiday romance that got out of hand. Now you need to put it behind you and get on with your life. You have university to look forward to, new friends, new experiences. You have your whole life in front of you.'

'No,' Alice told him, her eyes narrowing. 'I have nothing to look forward to without Luca. You won't split us up. You'll see ...'

She must have called the restaurant in Portofino a hundred times if not more, but every time she called, they said that he had gone. So she started to call the restaurant in Rome, where he had worked before. It was owned by Anita's father, who was

349

a good friend of Luca's family. He would know whether Luca had returned to Rome. He would know where Luca was. He could get a message to Luca, at least, to tell him that she still loved him, that she wanted to come back, that it didn't have to be the end. But every time she opened her mouth to speak, the person who had answered hung up. She had no other number for Luca – his parents didn't have a phone – so she just kept trying and trying and trying. One day the person on the other end of the line did not hang up. She listened to what Alice had to say patiently and then she said in smug Italian, 'Alice, this is Anita. Luca and I were married on Saturday. You lost. I won. Have a nice life. *Ciao.*'

A part of Alice died that day. She guessed it must have been her heart. She already knew she was pregnant: eighteen, unmarried and pregnant. Hardly what her parents had in mind for their only child. Her father was furious at first. She heard the word 'adoption' mentioned more than once as she sat on the stairs and listened to her parents' hushed discussions about how to deal with the 'problem'.

'I'm not giving away my baby – Luca's baby!' she would scream from the bottom of the stairs, before fleeing back to her room and locking the door.

'He married someone else,' her mother would remind her through the closed door. 'You need to move on. You're so young ...'

'He had no choice but to marry Anita!' she shouted back, loyal to Luca to the end. 'You took me away from him. He'd defied his family to be with me. When he got back to Rome, he had no choice!'

Her parents could not persuade her to have the baby adopted. It was her mother who eventually thought of Philip as a solution to the 'problem'. Philip Brown was the son of Tilly and Frank's accountant. He had been in love with Alice since she was thirteen but he had always been far too pedestrian and safe for Alice's taste. Now, he was perfect. He was besotted with her, he was nice enough, he was older, he had already graduated from university and had good prospects in his father's accountancy firm in the City. He would give Alice and the baby a nice life. Alice no longer cared about her life. She was eighteen years old, pregnant, heartbroken and hopeless. She knew that the best time of her life was already over, the rest was just something to endure.

Alice loved Sophia from the moment she was born but motherhood didn't come naturally to the teenager. When Sophia opened her eyes and stared up at her mother with Luca's huge, brown eyes, Alice thought her heart would explode with love, yearning and pain. Alice had been depressed throughout her pregnancy but once the baby was born things got a whole lot worse. She found herself living in a house that would never feel like home, with a man she couldn't understand and a baby she couldn't soothe, no matter how hard she tried. Philip had a close friend at the golf club who was a doctor. By the time Sophia was four weeks old, Alice was being heavily medicated. She stayed on the tablets for thirty years.

When Sophia was a few months old she dropped her favourite pink bunny down the back of Alice's bed. Alice wearily crawled under the mahogany bedstead and there, beside the pink bunny, she found a dusty shoebox, containing sixty-six priceless Japanese pearls. Alice sat for hours, toying with the pearls, remembering the way Luca had sifted through the sand for hours, trying to find every last one. Her cheeks were soaked with tears as she counted and recounted them. The bottom of the box was covered in a thin layer of fine Portofino sand. She thought of Luca's promise to find every last pearl and she realised how hopeless it had all been, how fleeting and temporary her tiny speck of happiness had been in this endless, God-awful life. The baby wailed to be fed but Alice couldn't move. She was paralysed by her memories. It was all too much to bear.

The next day she drove to London. She did that often, when she couldn't think of anything better to do while Philip was at work. The baby slept best in the car and it gave her peace of mind. It also meant she could see bustling streets and interesting people leading busy lives and it reminded her that, even if her own life had been permanently paused, the rest of the world kept spinning. It made Alice feel relieved and envious in equal measure to see girls her own age working, chatting, laughing, drinking, smoking, flirting and teetering on stupidly high heels.

That day, she drove to Camden Town, for no better reason than she hadn't been there in ages. She pulled up on a double yellow line on Chalk Farm Road and left the baby in the car with the flashers on. What she had to do wouldn't take very long. The young girl with the tattoos sitting behind the desk at the charity shop didn't even look up from her magazine when Alice placed the shoebox on the counter. She had no idea how valuable the contents of the box were. But Alice knew. She knew, and yet she couldn't think of anything else to do with them but give them away. She wasn't strong enough to have the pearls anywhere near her any more. If she looked at them one more time she would break into so many little pieces that nobody would ever be able to put her back together again. She calmly got back into the car, replaced the dummy into the crying baby's mouth, and drove back to Surrey in time to make toad in the hole for her husband's dinner.

Virginia Water, Surrey, 2012

Sophia's legs had turned to jelly. It was ridiculous. This house had been her family home since the day she was born, the middle-aged woman, standing in the open doorway was her mother, and yet it all felt alien, disjointed, wrong. This house was not a haven, that woman was no one Sophia knew. The big, ugly, red-brick house swam before her eyes, and for a moment she thought she might faint, but then she remembered why she was here. She was exhausted with jet lag and ripped apart by grief but she would not let herself go now. This was her chance to find out who she really was.

She walked past her mother as calmly as she could and said, 'Shall we do this inside?'

Sophia sat on the blue velvet sofa in the drawing room and waited. She could see Hugo loitering at the door, peering in and then disappearing again. The Christmas tree loomed over the room, still crowned with the same gold angel that had adorned every tree for as long as Sophia could remember. Her mother had followed her into the room and was standing above her, staring down at her, and it was such a familiar face except ... except it looked different. A light appeared to have been switched back on in Alice. With a jolt of recognition, or a long-forgotten memory, Sophia realised that her mother no longer looked dead behind the eyes. Suddenly, she remembered the song her mum had sung that night in the car – 'Free Fallin'' by Tom Petty.

'I'm so sorry, Sophia,' her mother said.

She knelt down beside her daughter and tried to stroke her hair. Sophia flinched and pulled away.

'I'm so sorry,' repeated Alice.

'For what?' asked Sophia, the anger reigniting in the pit of her stomach. 'For lying to me my entire life? For letting that man, the one you made me call Dad, treat me like a piece of—'

'Shh,' her mum said, calmly, firmly. 'I made some terrible mistakes, sweetheart, but it's all over now. I can't change the past but I can do things differently from now on.'

'It's too late, Mum,' spat Sophia, trying to get up, to get away.

Her mother reached out and tried to stroke her hair again, and this time Sophia didn't stop her.

The truth was that, despite her protestations, it felt strangely comforting to be touched by her mum again. She remembered odd days off sick from school, before she was sent away. She remembered hours spent curled up on the sofa with her mum, watching daytime Australian soaps, eating Heinz tomato soup for lunch and drinking flat Lucozade. She remembered how much she loved those days, just the two of them, and how she dreaded the moment when her father's key would turn in the lock and the spell would be broken.

'I have so much I need to explain,' her mum started to say.

Sophia shook her aching head.

'Not now,' she said, more for her own sake than her mother's. 'You don't need to explain it all now, Mum. Right now we need to see Granny.'

'Thank you, sweetheart,' she said. 'You're right, it'll take a long time to explain it all but I know you deserve answers. Is there anything I can tell you right now?'

Sophia thought for a moment. A thousand questions spun through her head but there were only three she could pin down.

'Yes,' she said. 'But you can answer them while you get your coat. We need to go.'

Sophia followed her mother into the kitchen, where Alice's coat hung over the back of a chair and her handbag sat on the table. She watched her mother brush her hair in the mirror.

'Did you love him? My real father?' she asked, forcing herself to look into the mirror at her mother's tearful blue eyes.

She saw her mum's features soften and a wistful look cross her face and she knew the answer before the words escaped Alice's lips.

'Oh God, I loved him so much. He is the only man I have ever truly loved. Luca ...'

'Luca?' asked Sophia, tasting her father's name for the first time.

'Luca,' said her mum, smiling like a lovesick teenager.

Sophia's heart melted a little towards her mother.

'What happened? How did you end up married to Dad but pregnant with me?' she asked as her second question.

'I was eighteen years old, I met him in Italy. We were so in love, Sophia, you need to know that. We ran away together to Portifono. It was utterly blissful for a few weeks. We were so happy. We were going to get married. It all seemed so romantic at the time. But we were young and naive, and we didn't realise it was a fantasy. Of course, when I went off radar, your grandparents became worried, and the authorities got involved, and the next thing we knew the police were dragging Luca off like some sort of criminal and I was being bundled back home.'

Her mum took her lipstick from her bag and applied it almost defiantly, blinking back tears.

'And then what?' asked Sophia, her heart tearing at the thought of her mum and her real dad being in love, then ripped apart.

'And then I heard he'd married someone else,' her mother said quietly.

'What a bastard!' said Sophia. 'So my real dad is a total bastard too. Great!'

Her mum shook her head over and over again, the defiant look still in her eye.

'I don't think he had any choice. It was a different time. A different world. We were too young. We weren't free to love or to choose. That's why I married your dad ... I mean, Philip. It seemed like the sensible thing to do. I was determined to keep you but I couldn't face being a single mum or, worse still, people trying to take you from me. I was still a baby myself and I was in such a mess after Italy. And I suppose your grandparents thought it was for the best. I did what I was told. I don't know why. I was broken. Heartbroken ...'

Sophia's mouth tasted bitter. The thought of her beloved

grandparents, forcing her mum to part from her lover and marry Philip instead disgusted her. Why would they do that? She found it almost impossible to imagine her warm, loving grandparents making such a cold, pragmatic choice for their teenage daughter. And for their unborn granddaughter.

She tried to imagine being eighteen and pregnant. She hadn't had the commitment to own a goldfish at eighteen, let alone bring up a child. She almost understood why her mother had done what her parents suggested. But Philip?

'Why Philip?' asked Sophia. 'Why marry him? Of all people?'

Her mother put her hairbrush and make-up back in her handbag and picked up her coat. She was holding it together but her hands shook.

'My parents knew his parents. He'd always been around. He liked me. It was the simplest solution. Granny and Grandpa thought it was for the best, I suppose.'

Sophia tried to digest what she'd just heard.

'And no one thought this was a stupid idea?' Sophia said, angrily.

'Claudia,' replied her mum, nodding at the memory. 'When Claudia got back from Monaco and found out what I was doing she begged me to bring you up on my own. She said the world had changed and that I'd be OK. She thought I was throwing away all my dreams and she couldn't watch me ruin my life. Then she refused to come to the wedding and I never saw her again. I heard she moved back to France.'

'And you ignored her?' demanded Sophia. 'Your best friend.'

'No, I listened to my parents. I trusted them. I was scared,' said Alice.

'So Granny *made* you marry Philip?' Sophia asked.

'Not made me, exactly,' replied her mother, putting on her coat. 'But she definitely encouraged me. I'd done so many things of my own that had led to heartbreak, at the time it seemed like the only thing left to do – if I was going to be able to raise you. I knew marrying Philip would mean my parents would trust me to keep you. Come on darling, we have to go.'

Sophia almost laughed.

'And that's what this whole thing has been about?' she realised suddenly, stopping in her tracks. 'It isn't about the necklace. It's about her guilt. She didn't send me out to find the pearls, she sent me out to find the truth. Because she couldn't die without sorting out the mess she'd made. I thought Granny was the one person I could trust.'

'She made a mistake, Sophia,' said her mum, gently. 'Haven't we all made mistakes? And she put every last scrap of energy into fixing it before it was too late. Granny's no angel, darling. But she loves us very, very much and she did the right thing by us in the end. Don't you think?'

'I don't know what I think any more,' replied Sophia, clutching her sore head and collapsing onto a kitchen chair. 'All those years of lies. And Grandpa? What did he think about the whole thing? Did he feel guilty too?'

She watched her mother swallow hard.

'He thought it was for the best too. At the time, at least,' she said thoughtfully, sitting down opposite Sophia. 'But it ate him up in the end. We never spoke about it but he wore his guilt like a battle scar. He was such a jovial man by nature, and a brilliant actor, but that was the one thing he couldn't hide. Every time he looked at you, I saw it in his face. When your dad, I mean Philip, told you off or put you down, I saw it in his face: the pain, the remorse, the regret, the rage! He would whisk you off to safety, away from Philip. He'd take you to feed the ducks on the Heath and you'd come back covered in grass stains from rolling down Parliament Hill and sticky with strawberry ice cream from the Italian café in Highgate.'

'I don't remember ...' said Sophia sadly.

'He was never the same after the whole horrible business. He felt he'd let us down. I know he did. And although he and Granny still adored each other, they were both a little less ... Oh, I don't know what the right word is ... Frothy? Frivolous? Unscathed? I'm not quite sure. I suppose their life together had been so perfect and then they tarnished it with this terrible, terrible mistake which hurt the two people they loved the most: you and me. When he died, his heart attack, it came completely out of the blue. He was fit. Really fit. He rolled down Parliament Hill right beside you just the weekend before he died! Sometimes I think he died of a broken heart. I don't like to think about it too much. It's all just too sad.'

Sophia nodded. Perhaps her grandparents had more than paid their price.

'I know he'd be pleased that the truth's come out now,' her mum continued sadly. 'I'm sure your grandmother considered that before she decided to send you off looking for the pearls. She knew her beloved Frankie would approve. I think she did it to alleviate the sense of guilt they both felt. So she could die in peace. So they can both finally rest in peace.'

'Can you forgive them?' asked Sophia. 'Granny and Grandpa?'

'I can,' said her mother with certainty. 'I do.'

'Then I suppose I need to, as well,' said Sophia.

They sat there in silence for a moment and then Sophia realised she had one more question she had to ask.

'Did he want me? Luca?'

Her mum took her face gently in both hands and looked her straight in the eye.

'He didn't know about you, darling,' she said softly. 'If he'd known, he'd have walked all the way to London from Rome, I swear. If he'd known, he'd never have let you go.'

'But he let you go,' Sophia reminded her.

'We let each other go,' replied her mother, sadly. 'We weren't old enough to fight for what we knew was right.'

The phone rang in the hall, piercing the silence in the kitchen. It stopped ringing and then immediately started again. After several more times they heard Hugo answer it.

Sophia and Alice stared at each other, frozen with fear, both knowing what the phone call meant and neither of them wanting it to be true. Maybe, if they just sat there a moment longer, suspended in time, then none of this would be real. Hugo's words pierced the silence.

'We need to get to the hospital.' His voice sounded strained and anxious.

Sophia stood up. She knew there was no way of running from the truth this time.

Chapter Forty-Seven

Alice and Sophia travelled to north London in Alice's car, Hugo and Damon followed behind in the van. It already felt like a funeral procession, Sophia thought glumly as they crawled round the North Circular in the drizzle. The sky was heavy and an ominous grey colour but it wasn't cold enough for snow. There would be no white Christmas this year. Neither Sophia nor her mum could think of anything to say – there seemed no way to put the discoveries of the last few hours into words – and, glancing in the rear-view mirror, she could see that both Hugo and Damon were stony-faced and silent too. Sophia hated silence. It gave her too much time in her own head. Her view of her grandmother had just shifted to a strange and unfamiliar angle. She wasn't exactly the same granny any more. Sophia still loved her as much as ever, but she was no longer perfect. She was as flawed as the rest of them. Mortal. And she was dying.

'I wish I'd found the pearls,' she heard herself say out loud, just to break the painful silence, and then she immediately regretted it.

Tilly was her grandmother, but she was Alice's mother, and this must be even more difficult for her than it was for Sophia. And, of course, they both knew it was Alice's fault that the pearls were no longer in the family. Sophia had been livid with her mum about the pearls for weeks but now, suddenly, she felt guilty for bringing the subject up. Her mum must have had her reasons for getting rid of the necklace. There was no need to rub salt in the wound. She watched her mum's grip tighten on the steering wheel and the colour drain even more from her already pale complexion.

'I should never have got rid of them,' her mum said, staring at the road ahead. 'It was a dreadful thing to do. My grandfather gave those to Mummy, Mummy gave them to me, and I just threw them away.'

'To a charity shop in Camden?' asked Sophia, putting the jigsaw pieces together at last.

Her mum nodded.

'Why?' asked Sophia. 'Who in their right mind gives away a priceless family heirloom to a charity shop?'

Her mum laughed one of those sad, humourless laughs.

'Exactly,' she said. 'No one in their *right* mind does a thing like that. I wasn't well, Sophia. You were just a baby, I was so young, still pining for Luca, I'd married a virtual stranger and I was incredibly lonely and unhappy. I was depressed. For me, those pearls represented me and Luca. And you. The family I would never have. The necklace got broken and I couldn't put it back together again. I suppose I thought if I gave my memories away, then the pain would disappear too. I burned all my photos of him, you know? At about the same time. But I couldn't destroy what was inside my head. And every time you looked at me with those big brown eyes ...'

'Do I look like him?' asked Sophia.

Her mum glanced at her quickly and smiled sadly.

'You're a fifty-fifty mix of Luca and Granny, I've always thought,' she said. 'You don't seem to have anything of me in you at all.'

Sophia stared at her mother closely, as if seeing her as a real, living, loving, breathing, vulnerable, flawed human being for the first time. She was not so different from Sophia.

'Oh, I don't know,' she replied, patting her mum on the knee briefly. 'Running off to the Italian Riviera with your lover as a teenager and having to be rescued by the police? That sounds like something I would have done, doesn't it?'

Her mum smiled weakly. 'I suppose so,' she conceded. 'Maybe the apple doesn't fall far from the tree after all.'

'Mum?'

'Yes, darling?'

'I remember one night when I was little,' Sophia began. 'We were in the car. That yellow Mini you had. You were happy and you were singing "Free Fallin'" really loudly and I thought we were going somewhere but in the morning I woke up back in my own bed ...'

Her mum nodded and half smiled at the memory.

'Where were we going?' asked Sophia.

'I don't know really. I headed for Dover. I think probably I was going to drive us all the way to Rome.'

Sophia nodded. It's what she'd hoped her mother would say.

'Why didn't you?' she asked.

'I stopped at some services somewhere near Canterbury and that's when I realised I didn't have our passports. I mean, I had had them, earlier in the day. They were in my handbag. I know they were! But Philip must have been watching me. He always kept them locked in his desk drawer after that.'

'And the pills?' Sophia continued, feeling brave. 'I found them in your purse once.'

Alice glanced at her daughter, obviously shocked.

'You knew about that?' she asked. 'Oh my God, Sophia. And you said nothing to your dad? I mean Philip. Even when you were a teenager and you hated me, you kept my secret?'

'I never hated you,' replied Sophia. 'I tried! God, I tried, Mum! But I would always have protected you against him. I understood what the pills meant. I knew you didn't want another child. I just didn't know why. I thought maybe it was because I was such a pain, you didn't want to risk having another one like me. But now I get it. You just didn't want to have a child with him.'

'Philip has been a victim in all this too,' said her mother.

'He deserves everything he gets,' muttered Sophia.

Her mother didn't argue. Finally, they pulled into the hospital car park.

The two women looked at each other for a moment and then they threw their arms around each other and hugged silently for what felt to Sophia like hours. She realised, with surprise, that when her mum held her, she felt safer than she had done for a long, long time – even after the years of distance, disagreements, resentments and tears, her mother was still her mother. Still the one who could kiss it all better when Sophia's life fell apart.

'Ready?' asked her mum, finally, when they untangled their arms.

'Ready,' nodded Sophia, although she felt anything but.

360

'So she hasn't come round at all?' asked Sophia as they walked reluctantly along the deserted corridor towards Granny's room. Hugo and Damon were waiting in the café.

'No, darling,' replied her mum. 'She went into a coma just after you left for New York. She hasn't eaten or drunk anything for days. It's probably for the best. For her, if not for us. She was in so much pain, darling.'

'I wish I could have said goodbye,' said Sophia, struggling to swallow the lump in her throat.

'That's what we're here for,' replied Alice, squeezing Sophia's hand. 'She knows you love her, Sophia. You were always the apple of her eye.'

'I know,' admitted Sophia. 'But I've never understood why. I was a pain in the arse!'

'A perfect mistake,' said Alice quietly. 'That's what she called you when you were born. I'll never forget her saying that. She picked you up out of the crib in the hospital ward, kissed your tiny face and said, "What a perfect mistake."'

And it was then that Sophia finally understood why her grandmother had always loved her so fiercely: it was her way of atoning for the wrong she'd done her own daughter. She could never fix her mistake, but she could lavish all her love on the 'perfect mistake'. She had tried to protect Sophia because she had failed to protect Alice. In that moment, Sophia forgave her grandmother. She forgave her, because finally she understood.

The door to Granny's room was closed. Sophia held back and let her mum open the door. She was being a coward, she knew that, but she dreaded seeing her grandmother unconscious, barely clinging on to life. She wanted to turn on her heels and run straight back down the corridor, out of the hospital, back into the grey London streets where the rest of the world was looking forward to Christmas, oblivious.

'Come on, darling,' said her mum, grabbing her hand and pulling her through the door. 'We need to be brave.'

Sophia took a deep breath and stepped into the dimly lit room. It took a few moments for her eyes to acclimatise to the half-light. Granny was no longer wired up to endless machines and feeding drips. There was no need for all that now. Only the heart monitor now beeped, slowly but reassuringly, by her bed. They weren't too late, at least. Sophia and Alice stepped gingerly towards the bed and then they both stopped dead in their tracks. Alice clutched Sophia's arm and made a strange strangled noise. She looked as if she'd seen a ghost.

Sophia stared open-mouthed at her grandmother. The old lady was nothing but skin and bone. Her eyes were shut tight and her face was a terrifying shade of ghostly grey. The covers were pulled up to her bony chest. Above the covers, her skeletal body was covered in a white cotton nightgown with a lace trim. And above the lace trim, around Tilly's slender throat, glistening in the half-light, was a choker of perfect, iridescent pearls.

'The necklace,' said Sophia, in disbelief. 'It's the necklace! I don't understand.'

'The handsome young man gave it to me,' said a weak voice that was barely more than a whisper.

'Mum!' 'Granny!' shouted Sophia and Alice in unison.

'They said you were in a coma,' said Alice, kneeling beside her mother's bed and holding her hand. 'They said you'd gone.'

'What do they know?' whispered Tilly, opening her eyes.

Sophia felt a strange sense of peace descend upon the room. There was very little time left, that was clear. But she was conscious, talking – just! – and she was wearing the pearls. Something amazing had happened here. Out of the corner of her eye, Sophia sensed movement through the window to the corridor outside. She turned her head to see and there, smiling broadly, with his forehead resting on the glass, was Dominic McGuire. Sophia felt her mouth drop open.

'Hi,' he mouthed through the glass.

'Hi,' mouthed Sophia back, her head spinning. How? Why? What the ...? Dom was here. And he'd brought the pearls.

She grinned at him broadly, dragged her fingers through her tangled hair, and then she realised that this man had somehow got his hands on her grandmother's necklace and flown across the Atlantic to get it to her. Dominic would not care how dishevelled Sophia looked right now. He smiled back warmly and whispered, 'Go see your grandmother. I'm not going anywhere.'

Sophia knelt down beside her mum at her granny's bedside. Granny was struggling to say something.

'Sorry, for L ...' she was whispering.

'L?' asked Sophia, stroking her grandmother's papery cheek gently. 'Shh, Granny, you don't have to speak.'

Tilly narrowed her pale blue eyes and frowned with concentration.

'Luca,' she managed to say eventually.

Every word was evidently an enormous struggle for her now and it pained Sophia to watch her try to spit her sentence out.

'I'm so sorry. For Luca. Alice and Sophia. My darlings. I took him away from you both. I'm so sorry. So very sorry,' she eventually said and then she closed her eyes again, as if the effort of saying the words had taken the last of her energy.

'You and Daddy did what you thought was best at the time,' said Alice, kissing her mother's hand. 'I understand, Mummy. I'm not angry with you. I never was. It was my mess and it was all very difficult. And look how much you've fixed! You knew what you were doing and it worked. You got me and Sophia back together again, I've left Philip, and Sophia found your necklace. She found your necklace, Mummy.'

Sophia stared at the pearls, glistening around her grandmother's neck, and she could barely let herself believe they were really there.

'Papa,' whispered her granny weakly. 'Darling Papa gave me my necklace. My pearls. It feels heavenly, darlings. Heaven ...'

Upper East Side, New York, 2013

The actress Lady Matilda Beaumont, known simply as Tilly Beaumont to her fans, died peacefully in her sleep on 25th December 2012, one week before her 83rd birthday. Her daughter Alice and granddaughter Sophia were by her side. When she died she was wearing the now infamous Beaumont pearl necklace: a gift from her father, the Marquess of Beaumont. Sophia Beaumont Brown's search for the necklace hit the headlines recently and it is believed that the pearls (worth an estimated $20 million) were bought by a kind beneficiary and lent to the family for the actress's final hours. The identity of the beneficiary remains a mystery. Lady Matilda will be buried in Highgate Cemetery, London, beside her late husband, the actor Frank Perry Junior.

Aiko read the obituary with a mixture of interest and sadness. She wished she had met Tilly Beaumont. It felt as if they had somehow shared more than a necklace over the years. Their lives had been entwined, on different sides of the world, over oceans and decades, and neither of them had known. And yet, now, with Tilly's death, Aiko knew she would finally be re-united with her mother's legacy. Soon she would hold in her hands the pearls she had traded for her freedom more than sixty years ago. She hoped Tilly would have approved of the way things had turned out.

New York felt quiet and peaceful today. It was as if the fine blanket of snow had muted and muffled the city's roar. Aiko sighed happily. She was eighty-seven years old now, and her bones were getting creaky, but in her heart she was the same girl who had arrived in Tokyo barefoot all those years ago.

She would fly back to Japan in the morning. She was to open the new Pearl International Communications and Conference Centre – yet another branch of the family business – on the first day of the new year. Another year, another challenge: it was the way Aiko liked to live. Pearl computers were everywhere, of course, and had been since the 1980s when Bo and Aiko first launched them. But this was a new venture and change kept Aiko young. She was looking forward to returning to Tokyo this time. She would see in 2013 with Kenny and his family. The ghosts would not disturb her in Japan any more. Aiko was no longer frightened of them. All they had done was try to help her – to guide her back to the pearls.

She had led a long and fruitful life. She had four children, thirteen grandchildren and even two great-grandchildren. Her darling Bo had died fifteen years ago, and although she missed him every day, she was happy, healthy and surrounded by a loving family. Plus she had the business to occupy her. Pearl had made Aiko an extremely wealthy and important woman. As its name suggested, from tiny seeds great things can grow.

Most of her children and grandchildren worked for Pearl – either in Silicon Valley or in Tokyo.

But while most of her family were high-flyers – MDs, law-yers, marketing gurus and technical wizards – there was one grandchild Aiko was particularly proud of. Aiko's youngest granddaughter, Manami, had not done well at school. She had always been too free-spirited to conform and would run away from Beverly Hills High School to go to the beach.

Manami didn't wear business suits and her name never appeared in any Rich List. She shared a one-bed apartment with her surfer boyfriend and worked shifts in local cafés to support her dreams. But six months ago Aiko had flown to the Bahamas to watch Manami in the world free-diving championships. Manami was Ama through and through. It would be Manami who would one day inherit the pearl necklace. It would give her the financial freedom to dive to her heart's content. Aiko smiled to herself. She felt a hand touch her cheek briefly. It did not make her shiver. It made her feel safe and loved, and she knew her mother was proud.

Epilogue

The sound of the key in the door made Sophia jump. She'd completely lost herself in her grandmother's letters and had no idea what time it was. Had she made them late?

'Hey, baby!' shouted Dom cheerfully. 'You ready to roll?'

Sophia felt her face break into an involuntary smile, as it always did when Dominic re-entered her world. He'd only left the apartment earlier that morning but it didn't matter how briefly he'd been gone, Sophia missed him like crazy.

'Almost ready,' she called back, folding up the last of the letters, neatly replacing the red elastic band back around the bundle, and placing it carefully into the trunk with the rest of her treasured possessions and important documents. 'I'm just putting away the last few things. Then I'm done.'

Dom sauntered into the empty room, carrying two cardboard takeout cups and wearing a particularly sexy smile. He leant down and kissed Sophia full on the mouth, his lips lingering just long enough on hers for the familiar butterflies to start fluttering around her stomach. God, she loved him!

'The last two lattes from Gerry's diner we'll have for a while,' he said, handing her one of the coffee cups.

'We're going to Italy, darling,' she reminded him, grinning. 'I believe their coffee is just as good as Gerry's!'

'Yeah, sure, I know,' he replied, good-humouredly. 'But we needed something to toast our success and I thought it was a bit early for champagne. That can wait until we get on the plane.'

'Success? What success?' she asked, allowing Dominic to pull her up to her feet.

He lifted his coffee cup high up into the air and encouraged her to do the same with hers.

'To Team McBeaumont!' he said, knocking her paper cup with his own. 'And our first commission.'

'Oh my God, no way!' grinned Sophia excitedly. 'You finally heard from the TV company?'

Dominic nodded and pulled her towards him. He kissed her again and then said, 'Felicity called about an hour ago. She loves the idea for a documentary about your grandmother and your search for her pearls. She's so scared we're going to take the idea to the competition that she emailed a contract over straight away.'

'Dominic McGuire, you are a genius,' grinned Sophia, proudly.

She was going to help Dominic make a documentary. She was going to tell the whole world how amazing her grandmother had been. She was going to have a proper, paid job for the first time in her adult life. And best of all, she was going to do it all with the man she loved. When did it all start going so right?

'Felicity says our pitch was perfect. She loves every single idea, all the detail, but she especially wants one scene,' said Dominic, his eyes twinkling.

'What?' asked Sophia.

'Footage of you with your dad,' he smiled, squeezing her to him. 'So, my gorgeous girl, we'd better drink up, get your precious trunk put in storage, and catch that plane.'

Sophia allowed her body to melt into Dominic's broad chest. He kissed the top of her head lightly. She shut her eyes and breathed in his familiar, heady smell. Sophia loved and was loved. She knew where she came from and she knew where she was going. Tomorrow she would see her mum. Better still, tomorrow she would meet her dad.

Portofino, Italy, 2013

'Luca, darling,' Alice said. 'Come back to bed. The flight doesn't arrive for six hours yet. They'll barely have taken off from New York. Come.'

She patted the space beside her in the wrought iron bed.

When he turned and smiled at her, Alice felt her stomach lurch, just as it always did when Luca's brown eyes met her gaze. How could she ever have let him out of her grasp all those years ago? If she thought about the thirty years they'd wasted, it almost drove her insane. She knew Luca felt the same way. They had made a pact not to dwell on the past, to concentrate on living and loving and enjoying the here and now, but it was difficult sometimes not to think, 'What if ...?' especially when the boy she'd fallen in love with was still so evident in the man she loved today.

Luca had not changed over the years. He'd made a great success of his life, restaurants in Rome, Genoa and Portofino itself. It turned out he had not gone back to Rome after Alice left Italy. Not for many years, at least. Nor had he married Anita. That had been a lie: a cruel trick for one young girl to play on another through jealousy and a desire for revenge. Alice felt sure Anita had no idea the damage she had done with her lie. What if she had been honest? What if Alice had known that Luca had waited for her?' But no, as Luca said, it was a waste of time to constantly wonder about things in the past they could never change.

In fact, Luca had settled in Portofino, because it was where he had been happiest, and he had never married. Unlike Alice, who had settled for a loveless marriage, Luca had chosen to be alone, rather than put up with second best.

'We were still engaged,' he reminded her, only half joking. 'I was waiting for my bride to return. It was a long wait but you came. Eventually!'

He had never stopped hoping she would come back one day. When he finally received her letter – just a short note, wondering if he remembered her and containing her email address and phone number, just in case he wanted to get back in touch – he said he had wept with joy. And then he'd drunk a bottle of Chianti to celebrate, called every single one of his friends to tell them the good news and then spent three whole days coming up with a suitable response.

'I wait thirty years and then it takes me three days to think of what to say!' he'd laughed at himself. 'What a stupid old fool. As if we could afford to lose one more precious minute, let alone three whole days!'

He told her he'd looked for her for years. He'd trawled the Internet too. But he'd been looking for Lady Alice Beaumont

Perry. He didn't know she had become Alice Brown. It had taken years before he'd made the link: a newspaper article about Alice's daughter, Lady Sophia Beaumont Brown, and a wild party she'd had at her parents' house. There had been photographs of the gorgeous but wayward Sophia, but also one of Alice Brown, with her husband Philip. She had looked, to Luca, as breathtakingly beautiful as she had a eighteen, but the couple in the photograph had appeared to be the epitome of English middle-class respectability. The article stated they had been married for almost three decades. They had a daughter and a life in another country, another world. Luca had known he had no right to disturb this woman's life and so, with a heavy heart, he had decided to leave Alice Brown alone. He had never searched for her online again; although he had continued to think about Alice Beaumont every single day.

But Alice Brown was gone. She had changed her name back to Beaumont Perry as soon as the divorce was finalised (although she no longer felt at home being a lady). Alice and Luca had emailed each other at first. Then there was a very nerve-wracking Skype call. Soon, they were talking twice, three, four times a day.

But she waited until she met Luca face to face, at Genoa airport six months after she'd sent the letter, to tell him about Sophia. How do you tell a childless bachelor, who has always dreamed of being a father, that he's had a daughter for more than thirty years? Alice had been terrified of telling him. Not because she thought he would reject Sophia – she already knew he would embrace his daughter with open arms – but because she thought he might reject her, Alice, for stealing his only child. Thankfully, Luca didn't see things that way.

In fact, he admitted that when he'd first seen the newspaper article, three years earlier, and read about Alice's daughter, he had wondered – hoped even – for the briefest moment that she might, perhaps, be his. But Sophia, being Sophia, had never been exactly straight with the press about her age and the journalist had accidentally shaved off two years. Luca, like the rest of the world, had assumed that Sophia was Philip's daughter and had felt like a silly, old fool for allowing himself to have such a ridiculous fantasy.

And now? Now he thought that Alice had finally given him

the greatest gift of his life – a little late maybe, but still the most miraculous gift a woman could ever give a man. All Luca saw was what she had given him, not what she had taken away. Alice knew how lucky she was to have found such a man. Twice. There was no way she was letting him go this time.

'Come,' she told him again. 'Come back to bed, Luca.'

'I have something to show you,' he said suddenly. 'I was going to wait until ... I don't know. Until after we have seen Sophia and Dominic but ...'

'What are you going on about?' asked Alice, bemused.

Luca got down on his hands and knees and started scrabbling around under the high antique bed.

'What are you doing?' she asked.

Finally, he emerged. His greying hair flopped over his handsome face as he grinned up at her.

'Here,' he said, clutching a small red box, and climbing into bed beside her. 'I can't wait another minute.'

'What?' she asked again.

'Alice,' said Luca, brushing his hair off his face. 'I have asked you this once before. I do not want to have to ask you again. Will you marry me?'

He handed her the small red box.

'Open it,' he urged. 'Then give me your answer.'

Alice's heart thumped in her chest. After all these years, she had lost nothing, except precious time.

With shaking hands, Alice opened the red box. What she saw there, nestled in white satin, took her breath away. There, set on a delicate band, was one perfect, iridescent pearl. One perfect, unique engagement ring.

'The missing pearl,' she whispered, breathless, staring up at Luca in awe. 'You found it.'

'Eventually,' he said. 'Just as I promised I would. I found every single pearl. But by the time I found this one, you had gone.'

Alice nodded. She stared at the ring for the longest time, taking in its beauty. What had she done to deserve this second chance at happiness? It was too much. It was heaven ...

'Alice,' Luca interrupted her thoughts.

'Yes?' she asked, smiling at the man she adored.

'You did not answer my question,' he grinned.

'Yes, of course,' she said, leaning in to kiss her fiancé. 'I said yes thirty years ago and I say yes now.'

It had taken decades, but the time was right. Today, Alice would introduce Luca to Sophia. Their perfect mistake.

Acknowledgements

The writing of this book has been a long (and sometimes painful!) process, and it would never have happened without a great deal of help. First, I'd like to thank everyone at Orion, David Higham Associates and all my family and friends for standing by me throughout. Specifically, I'd like to thank my fantastic agent and good friend, Lizzy Kremer from David Higham Associates, for her unflinching support, encouragement, loyalty, and the odd much-needed kick up the backside. To be honest, Lizzy, you deserve a medal, not just an acknowledgement! I must also thank my brilliant editor, Genevieve Pegg at Orion, for her vision, dedication, kindness and, of course, her amazing editing skills. Whenever I (literally) lost my plot, you were there for me, Gen. Thank you! A huge thank you also goes out to the lovely Laura Gerrard at Orion for taking over the reins so expertly and enthusiastically.

I can never properly repay my devoted (and long-suffering!) parents, Anne and Bob Agnew, for the decades of love, help and support they've lavished on me. Nothing I've achieved in my life, this novel included, could ever have happened without you, and I hope you both know how much I appreciate and love you. I would also like to send the biggest thank you and all my love to my gorgeous children, Olivia and Charlie, for being such a constant source of pride, joy, love, fun and inspiration to me. None of this would be worth anything without you to share it with, kids. You're my stars. To my wonderful partner, Matt Stone, I'd like to say a massive thank you for all your practical and emotional support and help, your advice, opinions and inside knowledge of Japan, and also for sharing the highs, the lows, the excitement, the stress, the laughter and the tears. I know it can be a bit of a roller-coaster ride for my nearest and dearest, sharing their lives with a 'difficult' creative type, but I hope that reading this book will show you all just how important love and family are to me. You really are my world.

And finally, I'd like to thank my fabulous friends for listening to me waffle on endlessly about my book, for cheering me up when things got tough and for entertaining my children, walking my dog, feeding me, cleaning my kitchen and sharing rum in our pyjamas (a special thank you to the Lovely Emma Reynolds here). I'd like to say a particular thank you to my dear friend Pegeen Rowley, for being my 'Executive Research Assistant' in Italy and for always being there to help me work out my complicated plots (usually aided by a bottle of Prosecco). I'd also like to take this opportunity to thank one of my oldest and best friends in the world, Nancy Hillenbrand, whose intelligence and opinions I admire greatly and who has always encouraged my writing – even when we were students and I was making up quizzes for teen magazines! You're a long way away, and I don't get to see you nearly as often as I'd like to, Nancy, but you've always been one of my biggest supporters in both life and my career, and you're never out of my thoughts.

To all of you, thank you from the bottom of my heart. I guess, now it's finally done, the drinks are on me!